LOVE IN A TIME OF MONSTERS

A GOLDEN AGE OF MONSTERS STORY

BY TERESA YEA

ISBN (ebook) 978-1-943087-00-6

Cover Design by Jenny Zemanek at Seedlings Design Studio

Visit me at http://teresayea.com
Sign up for my newsletter: http://eepurl.com/bftvYP

PART I
INFERNO

CHAPTER 1
THE SPACE BETWEEN THE TREES

Scotland, 1867

That blasted dog was at it again.

Sniffing the soil.

Snarling at the air.

Howling loud enough to wake the dead.

"Virgil!" Rob sprinted after his brother's Border Collie. The pup had been dodgy all morning. "Virgil, get back here!"

Rob started off strong and fast, but he was no match for Virgil's agility. By the time he crested the last hill, Rob doubled over, palms against knees, wheezing. "Bad dog," he reprimanded the thatch of thistle sprouting between his boots. "I'll flay you alive! See if I won't!"

Massaging the stitch in his side, Rob squinted through the haze. Virgil had receded into a black and white dot on a field of green.

The drizzle stung his cheeks and seeped through his hunting jacket. Rob was used to the foul Highland weather, but he didn't want to spend his birthday catching pneumonia and smelling like wet tweed. He stifled a cough, longing for the warmth of his father's library and the shelves of leather-bound books. He would've been content turning seventeen while reading about shooting if it weren't for Alec dragging him outside and shoving a rifle into his scrawny arms.

Kill something.

Be a man.

These were his brother's orders—the laird's orders. How could he possibly disobey?

He lurched down the hill and into a glen.

Whipping off his cap, Rob collapsed against a spire of rock protruding from the valley like a towering monolith. The rock dug into his backside, a small discomfort when his entire body hummed with pain. He wiped cold drizzle from his brow and glanced up. A fortress of intimidating black brier and evergreens loomed before him, barring entrance to the dark woods where the fae, gremlins, and evil spirits walked in the spaces between the trees.

In the distance, Virgil scouted the forest line, ears perked and fur standing on end. Rob stripped off his rifle as Virgil snarled at the moss-covered trunks.

"Slacking, are we?" Alec's voice boomed in his ear. A hand with big blunt fingers descended upon his shoulder. His brother's smile was a white crescent against a swarthy face. Rob shrugged the hand away, feeling pale and insignificant so close to Alec—a rabbit next to a bear.

Rob nodded to Virgil. "What the devil is wrong with him?"

"He's just primed and ready to take down a stag."

"He's a Border Collie," Rob muttered. "They herd sheep."

"I ought to have Virgil herd you." Alec ruffled Rob's helmet of carefully pomaded hair. "England has made you soft."

Rob slicked his hair back, making sure each white-blond strand was in place. He got the same treatment at Eton, except the chaps there did more than muss up his hair. They dribbled ink on his dress shirts, pissed on his pillow, made him lick the horseshit off their boots. Boarding school life descended into a special circle of Hell when they discovered the sonnet penned on the edge of his Latin conjugations. They wrote a poem about him that day. It was called "Faggy Rob" and spawned a nickname he'd rather forget. Though it should be noted their poem was horrendously spelled and blatantly disregarded iambic pentameter.

Dashing the unpleasant memory away, Rob nodded to the string of dead grouse pinned to Alec's side. "I think we've shot enough poultry to feed the entire estate."

"No, brother. *I* shot the poultry. *You've* yet to shoot a thing. We're not turning back until you've hit something." Alec scrubbed his jaw, fingers scraping thick black stubble. Another week or two and Alec would look like Blackbeard.

9

Rob palmed his own smooth cheeks. He'd tried growing a mustache once. A year later, he was still trying. "I did hit something."

"Empty air." Splotches of sunlight glinted off the sapphire ring on Alec's pinky. Rob shuddered at the unimaginable horrors "Faggy Rob" would've endured if he wore a ring like that to Eton—a treatment his big brother would never know.

He remembered hiding in the shadows outside his father's bedroom as the laird lectured Alec about his birthright. The sapphire, along with their land, was a gift from Bonnie Prince Charlie to the first Earl of Balfour, their great-great-grandfather. Father wore it until the crofters dragged his body from the loch. Now it was Alec's turn, and the ring fit as if the gold had been forged for his finger. No surprise. Alec was born to lead, while Rob, born last, born sickly, was destined for smaller things.

"Up!" Alec looped a hand under his elbow and yanked him to his feet. "We've got to shape you up before you set foot on that ship, and you haven't given me much time." His bushy brows furrowed as he scrutinized Rob's slender frame. "Five years is a long time to be away from home. Who will look after you if you have a relapse?"

"I haven't been ill in years and well you know it." Rob brushed the wrinkles left by Alec's hand. He'd only just returned from England and was already suffocating beneath his brother's fretting. With both parents dead, Alec was mother and father to Rob and their sister Waverley, but sometimes Alec could be a right tyrant. Rob's commission from the Royal Geographical Society, finalized right after graduation, couldn't come as a more welcomed escape.

The West Indies.

His mind swirled with accounts of the old captains' logs. Of white sand beaches and palm fronds swaying on a distant shore. Rob's heart drummed with excitement. In a week's time, he'd leave his brother's shadow and finally be able to walk in the sun.

"I don't see why I need to learn how to shoot." Rob propped his rifle—a hand-me-down from Alec's enormous collection—against the boulder. "Collecting and cataloging insects is hardly a treacherous activity."

"Not treacherous?" Alec shouted above the incessant barking of his Border Collie. Virgil scrambled back to his master and nudged Alec's thigh with his snout. "Tell that to Hugh Mornay. He sailed to Africa collecting beetles and butterflies, just like you. Where is he now?"

Rob stiffened at the mention of the infamous scientist. "Mornay *used* to study insects."

But in Mornay's final days, his interests had changed to creatures of a different nature. Rob was still in school when he read the headlines of the ill-fated Mornay expedition and the ghost ship docking in Liverpool with only one survivor.

11

"We're living in a time of monsters." Alec picked up the rifle and shoved it into Rob's unwilling hands. "Take care of yourself. I won't always be there to protect you."

"'A time of monsters' is actually a falsity," Rob hitched the gun over his shoulder, "a bastardization of Mornay's lecture at the Society of Unnatural Creatures." He recited the transcript by heart. "Monsters have lived in the shadow of man since the dawn of creation. Now their numbers are multiplying. The height of our empire is also the golden age of monsters."

"How stimulating." Alec rolled his eyes. "Race you to the woods?"

"What race? You always win." Shoving his hands in his pockets, Rob attempted to kick a pebble and missed. Coordination was not his forte. "This better not take all day."

"It's only as long as you make it." Alec slapped his thigh and whistled for Virgil. "Come on, boy!"

Virgil circled his master's legs. With a low-throated growl, the Border Collie darted into the brambles.

"Virgil!" Alec jogged after his dog and halted in front of the tree line. "What do you suppose has gotten into him?"

"That's what I've been trying to tell you all morning." Rob stared past his brother's broad back to the briers straining to reach the sky. Even in daylight, the forest was suffused in darkness.

Rob listened for rustling, heard nothing. The villagers called the divide between forest and glen "The Gates of Hell." Cheery lot, the local folk. He'd never been one to believe in superstitious rot. Now, he couldn't help but wonder if Virgil had stumbled into another realm.

Good riddance. He and the dog never got on anyway. "It's a sign we should go home."

"What's that?" Alec whistled. "Virgil! Stop playing games!"

"I said, maybe we should call it a day."

Fingers drumming against his leg, Alec hollered into the dark woods, "Virgil! Come back, boy! Virgil!" His voice bounced off the neighboring crags. He turned around, forehead wrinkled in worry. "He's never like this, Rob. Never…"

"He may be sick. Rabid. You might have to consider the possibility of…well," Rob paused, nodding to his brother's rifle, "putting him down."

His words hung in the air with the drizzle—cold, wet, and portentous. Alec blanched and Rob wished his physician, Dr. Jekyll's, bedside manners had rubbed off on him.

Alec's jaw tensed. "I'm going after him."

"Shall I go with you?" Rob offered, even though the prospect of wandering the forest in the damp was not exactly inviting. *Please say no. Please say no.* He coughed into his fist, drawing a hacking fit out of a tickle.

Alec swatted him on the back until Rob cleared his throat. "I won't be about a minute. Just…" He seized the loose ends of Rob's wool scarf and knotted it. "Take care of yourself."

Rob chewed on his inner cheek to keep from grinning. Being the family invalid had its advantages. "I'll just wait here."

With a nod, Alec whirled on his heels and slipped inside the forest.

"That was easy." Rob found a comfortable spot in the grass.

Plucking a leather journal from his breast pocket, Rob turned to the page he'd been working on before Alec dragged him outside. He tapped the pencil's tip on his tongue, tasting lead, as he tried to recall the song he'd invented to accompany the fireside story he'd made up for Waverley. His sister had requested a tale about buccaneers and buried gold.

He scribbled a few lines, scratched them out, then wrote: *Fifteen men on a dead man's chest.*

Rob leaned against the boulder and stared at the sky. The sun peeked through shifting grey clouds, casting a radiant light on his pages. As Rob set to work, his chills and aches seeped away. It no longer mattered that he was fragile, thin, prone to coughs and fevers. In letters he was a titan. A king confined to a pointy line of scrawl.

Rob burned through ten pages when the *boom* of a gunshot snapped the lead off his pencil. Birds exploded from the canopy, cawing, screeching, flapping in chaotic zigzags.

BOOM!

Rob flinched, shoulders bucking against the boulder.

A second shot?

Seafaring dreams of schooners and maroons quite dashed, Rob scrambled to his feet. His notebook tumbled to the grass. The first serpent of trepidation slithered inside his stomach.

Knees knocking together like a newborn calf's, he stumbled to the fae woods and halted at the line where the green grass ceased growing. Rob glanced over his shoulder. Should he run back for help? Would he have enough time?

BOOM!

Three shots?

Christ, Alec. How many times are you going to shoot the poor mutt?

He got his answer when the third shot gave way to screams.

◆

His rifle landed in the soft peat bed. Rob knelt and scooped up the gun with trembling hands.

The screams, cut short long before he summoned the courage to venture into the woods, echoed in his head. Never before had he heard a man—or another human being for that matter—make such a desperate sound. It reminded him of the same high-pitched shrieks the piglets made when the farmers took them to slaughter.

Rob forced himself to move.

Kill something.

Be a man.

His boots trampled across mushy leaves. A droplet splashed on the back of his hand. Rob glanced at the sky. Scant light diffused through the canopy, turning early morning into darkest night. The forest creaked and groaned like a set of moldering bones.

"What am I doing here?"

He was no man. No brave hunter. Alec was all of those things and more. Alec was trying to teach him how to hunt and he'd refused to listen.

He wished he had. Oh God, he wished he had. Now Alec had ceased to scream.

A twig snapped.

Whirling around, Rob aimed his rifle at a wild hare. The hare glared across the barrel, whiskers twitching.

Rob lowered his rifle and the hare darted through the underbrush. If he couldn't scare a rabbit, what made him think he could take down a—

These are glorious times, gentlemen...

As Hugh Mornay's words rang in his ears, Rob willed himself not to jump to conclusions.

A golden age of monsters.

Every phenomenon under the sun could be explained coolly, logically, with the aid of reason.

My blood is singing.

Rob trekked on. Alec was laird. The best shot. Never sick a day in his life.

He was going to bring Alec home.

The forest hushed to an unnatural quiet save for his harsh breathing and the crunch of leaves beneath his boots.

His lips moved soundlessly, "Fifteen men on a dead man's chest..."

Fifteen dead.

The newsprint of that year-old article swirled before him. Cold statistics drummed up by reporters who had never been there.

15 May 1866.

Fifteen lost to the jungle, including Hugh Mornay, never to see the light of day.

The rest slaughtered on board ship. The deck stained with blood. The bodies in the hull, ripped to pieces. One survivor. A girl gone mad.

As he entered a clearing, Rob wrinkled his nose. The reek of carrion pervaded the air. Flies swarmed and buzzed in a black cloud.

Covering his nose, Rob peered around a fallen trunk and recoiled at the sight of a dead ewe, her fleece stained with blood and dirt. The carcass was missing several crucial parts, notably her head and foreleg.

She had been ripped apart.

He stumbled to the nearest tree and retched. This was not how he'd expected to spend his birthday, hacking up this morning's porridge. Wiping his mouth, Rob stared at the maggots squirming inside the ewe's decapitated stump. He recalled the hushed conversations between Alec and his housekeeper in the days after Rob's return. The tenants were complaining about wolves making off with their livestock. The McBains' rooster. The Abernathys' heifer. Two or three sheep from the Callahans' flock.

Click.

Rob surveyed the gaps between the trees.

Click.

He thought he heard a faint rasp and rustle of leaves. Except there was no wind. The air was heavy with the stench of death. The calm before the storm.

Then the storm struck.

Saplings snapped and bent like an archer's bow.

A shadow yawned across the clearing.

Rob raised his rifle. The barrel bobbed in the air. As his index finger grasped for the trigger, the rifle tumbled to the ground.

"Useless. So bloody useless." His hand hovered above the rifle, slender and white, no calluses except for the writer's bump on his index finger. These were not the hands of a hunter. As this morning's lesson sadly demonstrated, he couldn't hit the hide of a cow.

Rob grabbed the gun. A newspaper article flashed through his mind and the most inopportune questions bombarded him. The sole survivor. Hugh Mornay's daughter.

Catriona.

Gone mad after months on board with a monster. How did she manage to live when the others perished?

The blurry newsprint came into focus: *Found under a pile of corpses.*

The last of the branches snapped and a swarming blackness encroached upon the clearing. In a blind panic, he forgot about the gun and leaped over the trunk.

Landing next to the sheep carcass, he wiggled as close to the dirty fleece as he could stand. Broken branches snagged his shirt and scraped his stomach. Bile rose in his throat. If he lived through this, he was going to scrub his skin with lye.

Catriona. He'd thought of her often. In the dark of his dormitory at Eton and under crisp sheets. He fantasized about meeting her one day. What would she look like? A Greek goddess, obviously.

Catriona.

Rob recited her name like an incantation; he'd never dreamed the day would come when he would call upon this goddess for guidance. Seizing the ewe by a leg, he crawled under it and gagged soundlessly in the dirt.

Something pounced in the air and landed at the exact spot where he'd stood seconds before. Its shadow stretched and slithered over him. It sniffed the air like a wolf, but when he expected it to growl, it made a *clicking* sound much like the transmission of Morse Code.

Click. Click. Click.

With a final sniff, the creature began to move.

The crush of leaves echoed through his ear. It crawled with remarkable stealth and perched upon the log. Rob squeezed his eyes shut. A maggot plopped on his wrist and wriggled on his skin. He sensed the creature's eyes boring down on the top of his head, felt a blast of hot air as it opened its mouth. A foulness beyond measure sliced through the stench of the sheep.

Click. Click. Click.

Another nasty little worm tumbled down the back of his neck and squirmed along the base of his spine. He clawed the dirt, grounded his cheek more firmly against the forest floor.

An eternity passed.

The creature waited and it occurred to Rob this entity, this *monster* was a devious thing.

It was studying him, trying to determine if he was indeed dead.

It waited for him to slip up.

A plump maggot writhed between his fingers. He formed a fist, squishing the maggot into pulp. The creature crouched forward and sniffed the carcass.

Rob stifled a scream. If he moved or breathed, he was as good as dead. Just like Catriona Mornay, Rob felt his mind disintegrating, descending into madness—mathematical equations, sonnets, sonatas unraveling like a spool of yarn.

The air pressure shifted again. The ground trembled. The creature sprang off the log.

Rob dared to crack open an eye. The *thing* scrambled up a trunk like a lizard and leaped.

Tree after tree bowed under its weight. Shielding his eyes from the shower of debris, Rob caught the sunlight glimmering off the creature's armored back.

Black plating.

A foreleg three times the size of a horse's.

Talons.

The creature disappeared into the leaves, absorbed into the pores of the forest.

Stiff and dazed, Rob crawled from under the carcass.

A whimper greeted him. He lifted his head. "Virgil!"

Breaking into a smile of sheer relief, he flung his arms around that blasted pup. If Virgil was unharmed, surely Alec must not be far behind.

"Where's Alec, boy?" He scratched the dog behind the ear. The fur was slick and sticky. He glanced down at his blood-smeared palms. Rob scanned the forest, searching for his brother. "Where—"

Virgil held something in his mouth: a hand with big blunt fingers.

Rob's smile vanished. His bottom smacked the earth with a *thud.* Virgil dropped the severed hand and whimpered. Trotting toward Rob, the pup buried his blood-smeared muzzle in his new master's side.

A gust of wind stirred the canopy, casting dapples of daylight over his brother's sapphire ring. Rob tilted his head at the section of sky. The clouds dispersed and the sun blazed, glorious and bright, the beginning of a new day.

And somewhere in the distant treetops, the creature lifted its head to the sun and screeched.

CHAPTER 2
A WORLD WITHOUT MONSTERS

Scrambling to a river ditch, Cat clamped her hands over her ears and surrendered to the nightmare. Her screams slashed across the moors, igniting a chorus of caws from the ravens on the bridge. Black birds circled the sky and for a moment, Cat wished she could shed her body and join the flock.

Just fly away.

Far, far away from this waking hell.

Cat hugged her knees and rocked. Even with a year and an ocean between them, she could still hear the crew of the *Hispaniola*. They were sea dogs cured by the sun into jerky. Hulking men who could swing two barrels of molasses over their shoulders without breaking a sweat. But in the face of the creature, they wept for their mothers and screeched for God.

Poor fools. There was no God in the jungle where blood orchids bloomed and insects walked like men.

With a growl, Cat stripped off her leather knapsack.

Her crossbow landed in the mud with a *thud*. Daggers clinked against the ivory handle of her pistol. She found the parcel beneath a hunk of stale bannock her sister Vivian packed for the journey. As the shrieking in her head reached a crescendo, she unrolled the parcel and took out a vial of Hyde's

Elixir. Her hands trembled as she filled a glass syringe with the emerald-colored drug.

Cat rolled up her sleeve and tapped her forearm. She located a vein beneath the mass of purple bruises and jammed the needle into her skin.

The drug was quick—as she knew it would be.

Although she'd never met him face to face, Cat trusted Mr. Hyde to take the edge off her nightmares, and he'd never let her down. For the exorbitant price the elusive dealer charged, there'd better be absolution in every drop. Lolling her head against the stone pilings, Cat gazed at the wide expanse of sky. A sea of wild heather stretched before her. The moors had never seemed so infinite or sublime.

She sank her fingers in the mud and sighed in ecstasy.

It was a new world.

Glorious.

Muted.

A world without monsters.

◆

The sun disappeared behind the roof of the Hawkins' pisshole shack and the world, once so glorious, was a dark and unfriendly place.

Cat held her breath against the stink.

24

Her latest client, Widow Hawkins, didn't believe in bathing. Nor did the brood of children swarming behind her like lice. Cat counted ten filthy faces. The eldest, a girl of no more than fourteen, cradled a wailing infant in her arms. Cat's gaze lingered on the girl's hangdog expression before focusing on the brown smears on the infant's legs. The babe had soiled himself and no one had bothered to change his diaper. Cat wrinkled her nose. *Country folk.*

The old woman held Cat's calling card up to her nose and squinted at the block letters. Greasy strands of grey clung to a face with the complexion of rancid gravy. Shaking her head, the woman handed the card back to Cat. "I can't read."

"It says *I kill monsters.*" Underneath her cloak, Cat scratched and clawed at her arms. When Elixir wore off—and it wore off faster these days—Cat itched all over. There were worms under her skin, and she'd like nothing more than to take a knife and cut them out.

"You're *the* Cat Mornay?" Widow Hawkins' lazy-eyed gaze lingered on Cat's trousers and boots. "You're a skinny slip of a thing. How old are you?"

"Old enough." She was only nineteen, but no one need know that. She looked old for her age and Liam Barclay, her sometimes mentor, was fifteen when he slew his first monster.

"Is it true, then? That you lost your mind in Africa?"

I lost more than my mind. Cat yanked her hat brim over her eyes. Eager to start back to Edinburgh with her earnings, she cut to the chase. "You've a creature in need of killing. In your letter, you wrote"—*paid someone to write*—"that you already have the creature in captivity." Strange request. Normally, she'd have to catch her quarry, but after a long day's travel, Cat couldn't be more grateful for the easy job.

Widow Hawkins barked at her daughter to mind the children and shut the door. She stepped outside, barefoot. Cat couldn't tear her eyes away from the woman's feet. They were truly ugly specimens of weeping sores and crusty talons.

"Were I not a God-fearing woman," the widow said, "I'd have burnt the demon the moment they'd taken my Jim."

Cat frowned. "They?"

"The wee folk."

The fae. "And Jim, I gather, is your son?"

"My *real* son is dead." She handed Cat the agreed upon fifty shillings. "I'll show you where I keep *it*."

Infants switched at birth. A fairy child sent to foster and feed off the human world. A changeling. A parasite.

"How old is Jim?" Cat asked.

"Ten."

She harbored a moment's misgiving. To all outward appearances, the monster would look like a boy. Whenever Cat felt herself growing soft, she remembered Africa and what the creature did to her friends, her father, and her heart filled with hate. It could look like a bleeding archangel for all she cared.

Cat pocketed the money. "I'll wipe it off the face of the earth."

As Cat followed the crone through a weed-choked turnip garden, she fumbled inside her cloak for her trusty dagger. The blade was long and curved, made from rare dragon's bone. Her thumb glided over the jade carving of a Siamese cat's head on the pommel. The dagger, along with a vial of Elixir, came as a package straight to her home after her first assignment. A note accompanied it:

To my little kitten, who caught her first fish.

Cordially,

Mr. Hyde

When her sister demanded to know what the note meant, she'd been too ashamed to tell Vivian about the nature of her new job. Whenever she unsheathed the dagger, she was instantly transported back to the Isle of May, where the sea ran red with mermaids' blood.

Cat and the widow plowed through a peat bog before hiking to a windowless shed. The door was barricaded from the outside with a chain and lock.

Cat tugged on the chain. She remembered her father's lectures at the Society of Unnatural Creatures. Iron weakened the fae. She glanced at the mother. The woman watched her while picking at a boil on her neck.

"How long have you been keeping him locked up?" Cat yanked the chain. Sturdy. Unyielding. Must be one dangerous ten-year-old.

Widow Hawkins reached into her apron for a skeleton key and fiddled with the lock. The chain clinked and coiled at her feet like a snake.

"Since he grew old enough to bite." She held out her grizzled hand and rolled up her sleeve.

Cat examined the scars on her wrist.

Teeth marks. Tiny teeth. *Baby* teeth.

Her stomach roiled. Nevertheless, she readied her dagger. She'd been paid to do a job and always delivered.

She pushed the door open.

The stink hit her like a punch to the face. Cat covered her nose with the back of her hand. As her eyes adjusted to the dark, she saw the source of the stench: a wooden bucket filled with shit.

Dagger at her side, Cat looked to the pathetic sack of rags in the corner. She took a cautious step toward the boy, who hadn't acknowledged her presence. His eyes were fixed on the slats in the ceiling. Cat tipped her head, following the direction of his gaze: a section of night sky filled with stars. Da had a wild theory about monsters. All creatures of darkness crave the light. The changeling was no exception.

"Don't bother trying to speak to it." Widow Hawkins leaned against the doorway. "He's never spoken. Can't even get him to scream. I give him a poke once in a while to keep him in his place."

Cat's grip on the dagger slackened and she knelt in front of the changeling. She studied the boy's lice-ridden hair. He shifted and the starlight bounced off the wounds on his arms. Taking him gently by the hand, Cat examined the burn marks—the old ones were black welts, the fresh ones bleeding pus. She set his arm down and tugged at his collar. More burns. On his chest. Raised scars on his back.

"Good work, that," Widow Hawkins boasted. "As good as any professional hunter."

The prison cell closed in around her. A memory stirred from her childhood. She and Da were playing at King Arthur and the Knights of the Round Table. As Sir Gawain, Cat proclaimed that she would grow up to be a knight, slay dragons, and save the world.

The changeling boy's big black eyes flickered over the curved blade of her dagger, fearless and ready in the face of imminent death.

Da used to say "man was the only creature with a choice." Choose to live in harmony with our unnatural brethren or choose to become their overlords. He believed the monster hunter, who preyed on and exploited these beautiful creatures, was the lowest form of vermin.

Standing up, Cat backed away. In many ways, she was glad her father was dead so he'd never see what his knight had become.

Widow Hawkins seized her arm. "Where are you going?"

"I won't do it."

"What do you mean 'you won't do it'? I'm paying you, ain't I?"

Cat looked to the hand detaining her arm. This "madness" the papers spoke of, well, it was a dormant beast about to wake up. It took all her self-control to keep from seizing this bitch by the throat and snapping her neck. Cat reached inside her cloak and chucked the money at the hag's feet.

"Shove it up your arse." She walked away.

"Coward!"

Cat's shoulders tensed. Halting at the door, she turned around.

Widow Hawkins approached until they were nose to wart-covered nose. "I thought you 'killed monsters.'" The crone's foul breath blasted Cat in the face, triggering the stench associated with the jungle.

Of men ripped to pieces and left to ripen under the sun.

And the creature's maw, dripping Da's blood over her cheeks.

"I do…" Cat watched Widow Hawkin's rubbery lips contort into a sneer. She bet this woman liked to laugh. Bet this witch just laughed and laughed while she gave Jim his dose of hot poker. The Great Mother played with her food, too. The youngest of the sailors had only been thirteen. The creature kept him alive while she peeled the meat from his bones…

Widow Hawkins spoke, though Cat couldn't hear a word over the sailor's screams. She stared inside the woman's maw and found a black hole through which she could see orchids blooming.

"I do…" With a flick of her wrist, hot blood splayed across Cat's face, her clothes, her skin. "I do kill monsters."

The widow collapsed against Cat and the madness, born in Africa, flowed and overflowed in wave after glorious wave.

◆

Huddled beneath an archway of the old Roman aqueduct, Cat scrubbed the blood from her hands.

It was a ritual she performed after every kill, checking under the fingernails, making sure her palms were clean and saintly white. It kept her mind from running through facts and figures.

Three days wasted.

Fifty shillings forfeited.

Debts, debts everywhere.

With her sister growing thinner by the day and Mr. Hyde hounding her to pay her debt, Cat wondered if refusing to kill the changeling boy was the biggest mistake of her life. She should've, at the very least, nicked the money from Widow Hawkins' corpse, but even now, her wispy dreams of knighthood and honor lingered.

Cat leaned against the crumbling arch and watched the lightning fork the sky. Rain pounded the lonely moors, turning the foot roads and horse trails into mud.

Drawing her cloak against her body, Cat shivered. Black hair snarled around her cheeks and dribbled icy water down her neck. Distant screams echoed in her ear. The sailors again, crying for mercy. And the screech of the Great Mother as it tore them limb from limb.

Mercy.

Ha.

She'd seen the monster's eyes loll to the back of its head as it gorged itself with blood. The creature knew nothing of love or hate. It killed to feed and the only thing it answered to was the omnipotent eye of the sun.

Cat dug her fingernails into her scalp and moaned. She rooted in her knapsack and found an empty vial. Without Elixir, she was in for a long night. Cat banged her head against the damp stone, hoping the pain would drive away the screams, but only succeeded in giving herself a headache. She chucked the empty vial; it sailed through a curtain of water and landed at the bare feet of the changeling boy.

"You again!" Cat sighed. "Stop following me!"

The boy stared at her with eerie black button eyes. He'd been trailing her from farm to farm, across rocky ravines and steep crags. Never once tiring or making a sound. And all in his bare feet.

Cat grabbed a handful of pebbles and hurled them at the boy. "Sod off!"

The rocks pelted the boy's narrow chest. Instead of scaring him off, the boy crept closer.

More annoyed than frightened, Cat unsheathed her dagger and slashed the air. "You want me to kill you like I killed your mother? I will! I'll cut off your head and feed it to the wolves!"

The boy cocked his head to the side.

"All right." Cat's shoulders slumped. "Climb in. Climb in."

Cat scooted back as the boy climbed into the archway. Hugging her knees, she studied the changeling's sticklike arms and legs, his dirty feet and tiny hands. Brown hair, washed clean from the rain, was plastered to his forehead. His ears were pointy like an elf's.

"Jim Hawkins," she said.

The boy's eyes lighted at the sound of his name. He had a long nose and a high regal brow. In the fae world, he could be royalty—a prince who'd grow up to rule empires, but here on earth, he would've died in a shed.

Fumbling with the clasp of her cloak, Cat draped it around Jim's skinny shoulders. Then she fished the bread from her knapsack. She sat back and watched Jim wolf down her supper. Licking the last crumb from his fingertips, he looked to her.

"Do you expect me to entertain you, too?"

Jim stared at her, unblinking. Did his eyelids even work?

"Stop staring at me."

The boy continued.

Cat chewed on her inner cheek. "You trouble me, demon child," she said, rooting in her knapsack for a necessary distraction. She fished out her most prized possession.

"Do you know what this is?" She shook a glass vial filled with tiny silver pills. "There's no other of its kind in Scotland."

A pang ripped through her heart as she recalled the market stall in Beijing and the shelves stocked with sun-dried scorpions and jars of pickled ginseng. The shopkeeper's face crumpled like rice paper as he handed her father the vial.

Da knelt down to show her his purchase. His face was ruddy underneath his pith helmet and his khaki shirt was damp from the stifling heat. She remembered the way his eyes crinkled when he smiled and his dark mustache, always meticulously waxed, twitched as he placed a silver pill into her palm. The pill was round and lumpy, the size of a musket ball.

What's that, Da?

I'll show you, my brave knight. The Chinese call these...

"The Chinese call these 'Dragon's Breath.'" Uncorking the vial, Cat dumped a silver pill onto her palm. "Want to know why?"

Jim nodded, watching her every movement with wonder.

Ducking her head outside, Cat collected rainwater on her tongue. She popped the pill into her mouth and blew a plume of fire into the night.

CHAPTER 3
NO MAN OR ANIMAL

Rob twirled his brother's ring around his pinky.

It was too big.

The fire crackled in the hearth, casting sinister shadows on the stone wall of the caretaker's cottage. Rob ran a thumb over the polished facets of the sapphire, replaying the morning of his birthday. Had he known it would be Alec's last moment on earth, he wouldn't have acted like such a prig. Alec was going to teach him how to be a man. Now he'd have to learn alone.

"Lord Robert?" Brandon, the caretaker's son, stood behind a concrete slab on which Alec's remains rested. He wielded a pair of shears.

Rob blinked and wiped his eyes. "Call me Rob. Just Rob."

He noticed a scuff on the toe of his boot. Normally, he made it a habit to keep his boots polished and pristine, but he hadn't time to think about his appearance during the past two days.

When he was certain his voice wouldn't crack, Rob asked, "Did you cut the shroud?"

Brandon shook his head. He was a brawny chap about Rob's age with guileless green eyes and a big moon face studded with freckles. "It's a most unusual request, Lord Robert, er, Rob. I warrant you leave this alone and wait for the funeral."

Rob slid the ring on his thumb and strolled over to the hut's one window. Tugging his wool scarf loose, he peered out the frosted glass. In the tiny cemetery, two girls flitted like sprites amongst the weeds and headstones. He spotted Waverley, dressed in knee-length britches, mousy brown hair woven in a sloppy braid. For the thousandth time, he reminded himself to force his sister to dress like a girl. She was eight now. In a few years, she'd be a proper lady. He looked to Brandon's sister, Jenny, primly gathering dandelions while Waverley whacked a wooden sword against a headstone.

Rob sighed. In the last two days, he'd aged fifty years. Childhood for him was long over. Time enough for Waverley to grow up. Let her have one more night of peace. Let her believe—as their servants and the village believed—that wolves had mauled Alec.

His attention swerved to the woods, dark and menacing even at high noon. Ground mist swirled around the tree trunks as Rob shivered and rubbed his chest through the layers of wool and tweed. Covering his mouth with a fist, he coughed—a nasty, wet cough.

Brandon said, "You're ill."

"I've been sitting too close to the fire." Rob cleared his throat, but a strongman had his lungs in a mighty grip. He was probably catching a summer cold, a likely explanation since he hadn't slept in forty-eight hours. He'd never sleep again until he got some answers. "Let me see my brother."

"Now, Lord Robert." Brandon planted his feet apart. "You really should get to bed and take care of that cough. The wolves weren't kind to your brother."

Rob shook his head. There had been a hunt in the aftermath of Alec's death. Eight bloody wolf pelts now hung in the village square and yet, the slaughter of the entire pack did nothing to erase the fear in his heart.

He'd seen the bloody thing, heard it bray in ecstasy after it tore his brother apart. The creature was both beautiful and grotesque. The curves of its body: almost feminine. Her movements: human and insect.

Rob had no idea what manner of evil haunted the woods by his home or how the village men managed to slip in and come out alive. Perhaps the creature had been too full after feasting on Alec to eat again.

But of this he was certain: she was no wolf.

Rob coughed again. "No man or animal."

"What's that?"

Prying himself away from the window, Rob stumbled toward the slab. He reached into his breast pocket and handed Brandon a tooth three times the size of his forefinger.

"Do wolves have jaws that big?" Rob watched Brandon turn the tooth, round face growing paler with each rotation. Finally, Brandon shook his head.

"Let me see my brother."

As Brandon picked up the sheers and snipped away the shroud, Rob listened to the screaming match outside. He hoped Waverley refrained from shoving Jenny's face in the dirt like last time.

Brandon pried the linen apart.

Rob diverted his eyes to the soot-stained ceiling. How many times had his father slapped him for crying? *A real man never cried. Look at Alec. Why can't you be like Alec?*

Yes. *Look* at Alec.

Neither breathing nor moving, Rob stared down at the gruesome collection of parts.

A leg. Severed from the knee down.

The hand brought to him courtesy of Virgil.

A naked torso torn at the waist.

A bloody stump where the head had been lobbed off.

No head. Where was the head?

Brandon crossed himself. "Ungodly."

The tears flowed hard and fast. Brandon swatted him on the back. What did it matter if it was unmanly to cry? His brother was dead. Butchered.

Alec...

Alec, who always made sure he had the choice slab of mutton for supper. Alec, who wrote him poorly spelled, grammatically horrendous letters every week when he was away at school. Alec, who fussed with his scarf and made sure Rob wore three layers of sweaters so as not to catch a chill.

For this gentle soul to meet with such a violent end and be denied a proper burial...

Sniffing, Rob wiped his nose. He didn't hold much with ghosts. He thought Mrs. Nix, his housekeeper's, monthly séance gatherings to speak to her dead husband an unnecessary—and ridiculous—hobby. But he couldn't help imagining Alec's spirit barred from Heaven, wandering the woods in search of his head all because this creature, this monster...

"Rob!"

He flinched, startled by the pounding on the door.

"Rob!" Waverley sounded close to tears. "Let me in!"

Rob locked eyes with Brandon. They both stared at the corpse. The doorknob rattled, then creaked open. In three quick strides, Rob slammed the door on his sister. "Stay outside!"

41

"But Rob, I'm done playing with this stupid, stuck-up slag. I hate her. Let me in. I wanna go home!"

"Do as I say! We'll go home in a moment."

The rattling ceased, followed by a defiant kick. "I hate you, too!"

Rob crept toward the window and watched his sister swing her sword at a Celtic cross marker.

He glanced over his shoulder.

Brandon pulled the shroud over the body. He stood motionless beside the slab, taking it all in. "A monster, then?"

Rob nodded.

"What kind?"

"What species, you mean?" Rob fell into a pensive silence. He'd only seen flashes of the creature. And while he harbored a suspicion, he prayed it went unfounded. This species was not native to the Highlands. Or the British Empire for that matter. But if he was right, they were in a lot of trouble. "I know a thing or two about insects. Monstrumology is not my forte."

For all his bulk, Brandon trembled, knocking the tooth to the dusty ground. "What do we do? Do we warn the village?"

Rob fiddled with the laird's ring. A wasted face stared back at him from the many prisms. He rubbed the spot between his eyes. His brow was hot to the touch; he might be running a slight fever. Explained the congestion in his chest.

"See to your family first. Leave the others to me." He strolled to the door. "I'll see you at the funeral."

When Rob stepped into the cemetery, Waverley was decapitating dandelions with her sword. He tapped her on the shoulder. "Come on, Duck…" He called her "Duck" because she was a filthy thing, prone to dirty feet and sticky fingertips, ugly as a duckling. "Time to go home."

Waverley shrugged his hand away. "To hell with you."

Sighing, Rob casually scanned the crooked grave markers and spotted a mangled wreath strung atop a tomb. The kirkyard was empty. His heart skipped a beat. "Where's Jenny?"

"Jenny!" Wiping his hands on a rag, Brandon shut the door and called, "Jenny? Come on now. Stop hiding. Jenny?" His voice escalated into panic.

As Rob watched Brandon scout the graves and jog into the clearing, fear trickled down his spine. He seized Waverley's shoulders and whirled the girl around. "Where did Jenny go?"

Waverley rolled her eyes. "Don't know."

Rob gritted his teeth. "Yes you do. You were fighting. What about?"

Waverley chewed on her inner cheek, brown eyes flashing with a defiant light. She turned around and swung her sword.

Rob caught her by the wrist and pried the toy from her hand, flinging it away. It clattered in the weeds. He shook her by the shoulders until her teeth chattered. "Tell me!"

43

"You!" Suddenly her eyes brimmed with tears. "That daft cow said you were jealous of Alec. That you fed him to the wolves so you could become laird. I told her she could rot in Hell and she ran away."

"Ran away where?" He drew her into his arms as she descended into uncontrollable sobbing. "Ran away where?"

Burying her face in the crook of his shoulder, Waverley pointed to the woods.

CHAPTER 4
AND DARKNESS SWALLOWED THEM WHOLE

The moment Cat walked through the door, her sister drew her into a crushing embrace.

Nestling her face in Vivian's hair, Cat caught a trace of their mother's honeysuckle soap. She shut her eyes and pretended she was in the warm circle of her mother's arms.

"You're unusually pleasant." Cat felt her shoulder dampen with tears. Her fingers glided over skin and bones. "I hardly know you."

Pulling away, Vivian pinched her arm. "Selfish git!"

"That's the sister I remember."

"You were gone so long I thought you were dead." Vivian's grey homespun made her look like a dove covered in grime, but even the most unflattering dresses couldn't disguise her sister's exquisite beauty. Vivian was a rose while Cat, with her gangly height and unruly hair, was a weed. At least there was one good thing about being a weed.

"I'm indestructible." With a sad smile, Cat tucked a golden curl behind her sister's ear. Their mother had plans for Vivian: finishing school, a parade of balls and soirées, and marriage to a handsome duke. Mama would've been so disappointed.

Under Cat's care, Vivian had begun to wilt. "Unfortunately."

Vivian frowned. "Is there something wrong?"

Cat nudged the front door with her toe. With his back turned, Jim Hawkins gawked at the gas lamps and rows of redbrick town houses.

Vivian's eyes widened. "Who's this?"

"The monster I was hired to kill." Cat stripped off her hat and propped it on the stand. Snarls of damp black hair clung to her cheek. She brushed them off and motioned the boy inside. "Meet Jim Hawkins. He's a changeling prince from a fae kingdom. I don't care for children, but this one is mute and quite tiny. I can rest my elbow on his head if I tire."

"Oh Cat." Vivian rubbed her brow.

"In any event, I've decided to keep him as a pet."

A whistle shrilled through the smoggy darkness. Jim raced to her side and seized her hand.

"It's all right." She nodded to the cluster of smokestacks in the distance. "It's just the factories signaling the end of the workday."

Jim's brows pleated into a frown.

"You probably don't know what factories are, do you?" A horse-drawn hansom clattered by, wheels churning on cobblestone. Cat knelt down and gripped him by the shoulder. Another whistle sounded. The street reeked of steaming horseshit, and the blue hydrangeas on the neighboring sill were covered in soot. Cat looked to the polluted sky and couldn't spot a single star. "Jim Hawkins, welcome to Edinburgh. Welcome to the fastness."

As Cat led Jim inside the townhouse, Vivian touched her arm. "You don't have the fifty shillings then?"

She shook her head. Anger flashed in Vivian's green eyes before dissolving to tears. Cat stared at her muddy shoes. She hated making her sister cry, but there was no help for it. Her existence was a disappointment.

With a defeated nod, Vivian knelt in front of the boy and forced an inviting smile. "Let's have a look at you."

Cat nudged Jim on the back. "Don't be shy. She'll nag but she won't bite."

"My, but you are a handsome lad," Vivian said.

The boy stepped forward, took Vivian's hand and gave it a peck. "I do believe, Cat," Vivian sniffled, "that you brought home a charmer."

While Vivian got acquainted with the new addition to their family, Cat slinked down the hall. She stood in the center of the parlor, staring at the bare walls, which, only a month ago, had been covered in paintings. The rug was missing, as were several pieces of furniture.

Cat sat in front of the pianoforte and lifted the lid. She tapped a clumsy rendition of Mama's favorite composition, *The Last Rose of Summer*.

She could see her mother so clearly. Golden ringlets against green brocade. The graceful tilt of her head. Slender hands fluttering across the ivory keys like doves' wings.

Cat's hand hovered over the piano.

This was where all their troubles began. Had it only been two years ago? When her mother, playing and singing after supper, descended into a coughing fit and splayed the keys with blood.

Standing up, Cat circled the empty parlor. She pressed a palm, then her nose to the damask curtains. The faint scent of tobacco still lingered in the fibers, conjuring up memories of Da in his favorite armchair, puffing on his pipe and reading the paper. That was how Cat wanted to remember him. Dignified. At home. Instead of in the clutches of the creature.

"Cat?" Leading Jim by the hand, Vivian tapped Cat on the shoulder. "Jim is absolutely filthy. While I give him a bath, will you add more water to the stew?"

Cat quickly rubbed her eyes. "Give him my share." She strolled to the door, propped her hat back on her head. "I won't be staying for supper."

"Where are you going?"

"Out." The cloak came next.

"I can see that. *Where* are you going?"

She slipped out the door. "To catch up with old mates."

Vivian chased her down the steps and onto the sidewalk. "Mates? I know about your *mates*. I know where you're headed. You're off to buy more Elixir."

"I don't know what you're talking about." Cat hurried her pace.

Her sister caught her arm. "Stay. Please, Cat? Come back inside."

And spend an evening amongst ghosts?

"Indestructible." Cat pecked Vivian on the cheek and yanked her arm free. "Remember that."

With a swirl of her cloak, Cat ran into the city and the darkness swallowed her whole.

◆

Rob shielded his match against the wind. The rain stung his cheeks and chilled him to the bone. Lighting the kerosene lamp, he ascended the crag and joined the search party. The men and boys from the village parted for him.

"Where did you find her?" he asked Hamish Abernathy, the blacksmith's youngest.

"Outside there." The boy pointed to the forest. "Slung across the branches of a tree."

Just like Alec. Or the parts of Alec the men were able to recover.

With a heavy heart, Rob knelt beside Brandon and placed a hand on his broad shoulders.

"What am I going to tell her?" Brandon's sobbing echoed across the rain and wind—a low, desperate sound Rob would remember for the rest of his days. "What am I going to tell Mother?"

Rob looked to the turret and stone ramparts of Balfour Manor, longing for hearth and home. He wanted to clamp his hands over his ears and run. Board a ship and leave this wretched place behind.

But a laird couldn't run away.

He glanced down at the tartan-covered body. Already the wool and the grass beneath the corpse were soaked with blood.

Rob peeled away the blanket. Half-expecting a bloody neck stump, he was pleased to find Jenny Coyle's head firmly on her shoulders. With her blonde hair curling lightly around her face, she was a sleeping angel.

He pulled back the rest of the blanket. One of the boys broke away from the circle, dipped his head between his legs, and retched.

From the waist up, the girl was intact. From the waist down...

Fighting back nausea, Rob shut his eyes. When he was ten, he'd gone to Glasgow to watch a traveling caravan of gypsies. There were striped tents and spiced wines, fortune-tellers and acrobats. In the magic show, Rob witnessed a lady being sawed in half. While he realized now that her screams were merely for show, he'd been terrified then. Tugging on Alec's sleeve, he'd begged his brother to stop the evil mustached man from torturing his assistant. But Alec hushed him. "Just watch."

The lady vanished in a puff of smoke. Or at least part of her did. Her sequined top half remained on stage, giggling and waving, but her bottom half was conspicuously missing.

"Where's the rest of her?" A scream echoed from the audience. He whipped his head around. The lady's stocking-clad legs had materialized on an empty seat in the back row.

Rob drew the blanket over Jenny Coyle. Would her legs magically appear somewhere in the village? He had a good idea where her bottom half might be. Rising on shaky feet, Rob stared at the fortress of trees.

"Boy!" Mr. Abernathy approached him. "The thing that killed your brother, it's the same creature what did this to young Jenny?"

Abernathy was a big man with a face like granite and ropey veins running through his forearms.

Rob objected to being called "boy" but decided to drop the matter. "Aye."

51

"What's that, boy?" Abernathy cupped his ear. "I can't hear you."

"I-it..." His tongue twisted into a knot. Rob glanced around the crowd. All eyes were on him. Their bumbling laird. Times like these he wished he could carry a chalkboard and write his thoughts instead of having to speak. He was much more eloquent on paper. Seeing Abernathy grow impatient, Rob nodded in defeat.

"Tomorrow at dawn." The villagers gathered behind Abernathy. "We're going inside the Gates of Hell and not coming back till we have the creature's head."

"Or the...the cre...creature has yours."

The blacksmith raised a bushy eyebrow and stepped forward. Rob had to peer around his shoulder to see the others. Seizing Rob by the elbow, Abernathy steered him away for a private talk. "Don't you care nothing about Alec?"

"Of course I care about Alec."

"Then join us."

"I've seen..." He swallowed, forcing the words out his mouth. "Seen the bloody thing." At least part of it. He'd seen what the creature could do. Rob lowered his voice. "Alec was the best shot and it tore him apart. This is fool..." He shut his eyes. "Foolishness."

"Alec was one man," Abernathy said. "There are six of us."

"I wooo...won't do it." Rob shook his head. "A-and n-n-either will...will you. Let me hire a professional."

The older man snorted and shouldered Rob aside. "No *boy* is going to tell me what to do. Come on, lads, we best get ready for tomorrow while wee Robbie sits back with the women."

Rob pleaded with the other boys. They were farmers. Bakers. Butchers. They may be able to kill a pack of wolves, but none of them knew the first thing about hunting a monster. One by one, they shoved past him. Rob raked a hand through his damp hair. In a matter of seconds, an invisible line had been drawn between the living and the soon-to-be dead.

Brandon stood up. In a panic, Rob caught his arm. "No! Not you."

The larger boy shook Rob's hand aside. Soon Brandon had crossed the line.

Rob watched the search party march into slaughter under the leadership of Abernathy. Their lives slipped through his fingers like water. He saw these misguided souls in the clutches of the creature and called in desperation, "I am your laird!"

Abernathy turned around, arms held wide in challenge. "Our laird is dead."

CHAPTER 5
THE BARCLAY BOYS

Cat's mates threw her the warmest of homecomings.

Liam Barclay, Mr. Hyde's right-hand man, jammed his knee into her spine and twisted her arm behind her back. "Here Charlie," he beckoned to his brother, "cut off her ear."

Charlie stepped forward with a fourteen-year-old's hesitation. He was a pretty lad with rosy cheeks, which Cat would've pinched if he hadn't been holding a nasty-looking knife.

Pinned to a stone sarcophagus, Cat caught the moonlight gleaming off the sickle-shaped Bedouin blade. Her eyes flickered over the statues of saints and angels. The courtyard of Tron Kirk cathedral was deserted. A horse whinnied in the distance. The squeak of wagon wheels on the cobblestone streets told her help was just a scream away.

She sucked in her breath, ready to roar, but Liam—always one step ahead—clasped a hand over her mouth.

"Shhh." His speech was hypnotic, never rising above a whisper. "Quiet or I shall become very angry." His lips pressed against her temple. "Do you want to make me angry, Miss Mornay?"

She shook her head. No, she did not want to anger Mr. Hyde's Avenging Angel.

A year ago, Cat witnessed Liam slit the throat of a man twice his size. He'd made it look as graceful as a waltz. After wiping the blood from his blade on his victim's shirt, he'd apologized to the barkeep, paid for the dead man's tab, and left the seedy pub whistling a hymn. At only twenty-two, Barclay was a true artist with a knife.

Cat's eyes watered. "Mmmph."

Liam removed his hand and patted her on the head. "Good Kitty."

Cat pressed her cheek against the slab. Since returning from Africa, her life had been a series of cock-ups. She could be safe at home slurping watery stew in front of the fire instead of bent over a tomb in this cold and dismal place.

A boot splashed into a puddle. Cat smelled Charlie behind her. He reeked of coal and kippers, not at all like Liam, who always carried lavender and cloves in his handkerchief.

"Charlie, please," she said, mindful to keep her voice calm. "This is all rather unnecessary. It's just a misunderstanding."

It occurred to her that she hadn't met Charlie before. All Liam's "brothers" blended together: blond-haired, blue-eyed angels who came and went by the season. Last spring, it had been Henry. The winter before: Thomas, or something.

Once she was brave enough to ask Liam why all his "brothers" looked alike. In a much friendlier mood, Liam had answered, "Copies of an original," then added, "Because I can't own the sun." Suffice to say, he'd left her more confused than ever.

When Charlie pressed the cold blade behind her ear, Cat saw the sailors again.

Torn to pieces.

No arms or legs.

A severed torso crawling along the orchid grotto.

She didn't fear death. In fact, in her darkest hours, she welcomed it with open arms. But in her nightmares, she was in pieces and alive—a human being no longer. There was a fate worse than death: dismemberment. If they were going to kill her, then do it already. Just please don't reap a body part.

A ribbon of blood trickled down her cheek. "I can pay! I can pay!"

The knife halted. "C-can't we just tell Mr. Hyde we couldn't find her?"

"Shame on you, Charlie," Liam said. "What've I always taught you about lying?"

"Gentlemen never lie?"

"Aye." He patted Charlie on the cheek and straightened his collar. "And we're going to learn to be toffs like Hyde, ain't we? All posh and proper-like." Yanking Cat by the hair, he flipped her on her back and slammed her head against the tomb. Cat yelped as the hard edge dug into her spine. Liam tipped back his bowler hat. His features were angelic and androgynous. When she'd first met him, Cat thought Liam the most exquisite man she'd ever seen. She'd even fancied herself in love with him—another mistake she'd like to forget. Liam knew nothing of love or hate. The only god this monster served was Mr. Hyde, whom, after a year in his employ, Cat had yet to meet. Was this drug lord and father of the monster hunters more myth than man?

She lolled her head against the stone slab. Hyde's wrath was real enough.

As the courtyard spun, Liam's face blended with the statues, right down to the soulless stone eyes. The tip of his long nose bumped against Cat's temple. He sniffed and grimaced. Plucking a handkerchief from his breast pocket, he wiped the soot from her cheeks. "Mr. Hyde has been very lenient, but all good things must come to an end. We're only going to collect your ears."

"Liam, please. I thought we were friends."

"If we *weren't* such good friends…" He held out his hand and Charlie placed the knife called Culler in his palm. Liam positioned the tip dangerously close to her eyeball. "I'd have cut out your eyes already. Now don't make this any more difficult than it has to be."

Liam tugged on her earlobe.

As he began to saw through her flesh, Cat lost all sense of dignity. "Not my ear. Please not my ear. I'll do anything. Anything…" Tonight's shot of Elixir had been especially potent. The drug, combined with fear and desperation, loosened her tongue; she listed all the things she'd allow Liam and Charlie to do to her. But Liam wasn't interested.

"You disgust me, Miss Mornay." He yanked up her sleeve and studied the needle marks. "Some people are content with one shot of Elixir and they play by the rules. They pay for their vials like good, law-abiding citizens. Not you. You seem to think you're special. You don't want to play by the rules. You are a *bad kitty*."

"I can pay." Fear made her into a blubbering fool. "I'll be good. I'll be a good kitty. "

"So you've been saying." The crack of his vertebrae sounded distinctly insect-like. It seemed to Cat that Liam was made of exoskeleton instead of skin. Liam's hair swished against the shoulder of his black coat as he gave Charlie a long-suffering stare. Having no stomach for this line of work, Charlie collapsed against the foot of a saint and clasped his hands over his ears. "You know better than to lie to me. You have no money."

"I have something better than money. Check my pockets."
She probed the cut behind her ear and winced. "Something better than money."

Liam sighed. "If this is a trick, I think I might just visit you at home. If I'm not mistaken, you live with your pretty sister. *Vivian*, is it?" His blade tickled her jugular. "A delectable strawberry just ripe for the plucking."

Cat gritted her teeth. The urge to kill him sifted through her body, exploding like a thousand angry suns. If she attacked, he'd probably carve up her face and give her the Glasgow grin. She swallowed her fury as he patted her down. His hands roamed lewdly over her body, slipping over her thighs and between her legs.

Cat squirmed. "I'm not hiding anything there!"

"I know," he said. "I just want to touch it. For old time's sake."

She blinked away her tears. If she got out of this alive, she'd cut off his fingers one by one.

Liam unearthed the vial from Cat's breast pocket and shook it. Tiny silver balls clinked against the glass. "What's this?"

"Something Mr. Hyde has never seen." She caught a gleam of interest flickering across his icy blue eyes. A drop of rain pelted her forehead. Cat glanced at the sky. A storm cloud blotted the moon. "It's a pill. Why don't you give it a try?"

"And give you the satisfaction of poisoning me?" Liam uncorked the vial and poured one of the silver pills onto his palm. "Let's see that pretty pink tongue."

Cat turned to Charlie. Humming a merry tune, the lad cleaned his nails with a dagger. She wondered if he was a tad touched in the head.

She opened wide.

"Good Kitty." Liam placed the pill on the tip of her tongue. She gathered rainwater into her mouth.

"Well?" Liam sneered. "I'm waiting to be amazed."

Cat crooked her finger and he humored her by climbing on top of her. Propping himself up on his elbow, Liam whispered, "Show me what I've never seen."

He asked.

She delivered.

Swishing the water from cheek to cheek, Cat blew a ball of fire into his face.

His hair ignited like dry hay. A high-pitched scream sliced through the cathedral quiet. Liam stumbled around the courtyard, a human torch splaying the night in a blaze of orange. His entire head was aflame, his skin melting like candle wax.

He dove for the fountain, ducked his head beneath the murky water, and collapsed in a lifeless heap.

Cat sat up, basking in a stolen moment of triumph.

"I'll kill you!" Charlie rammed her from the side, sending them both sprawling to the ground.

She scrambled to her feet. Dagger at the ready, the lad slashed at her stomach.

Cat leaped back. "Walk away, Charlie."

Charlie's hand shook and tears streamed down his tender cheeks.

"Charlie..." She circled him, studying his weak grip on the dagger, and held out her hand. "Be a good lad and give me the knife."

He lunged.

"Give me the sodding knife!" Cat seized his wrist, but Charlie was stronger than she gave him credit for. Their shadows splayed across the cathedral walls, merging into a beast with four arms and two heads.

The blade vanished between their bodies.

Charlie gulped. His eyes bulged like marbles and locked on his murderer. A shaky hand fumbled with the dagger's hilt. Cat could almost read his thoughts. *What's this knife doing in my throat?*

"I'm sorry..." She backed away.

Charlie shambled toward her, his mouth soundlessly opening and closing. Blood bubbled over his chin. As if to tell her he did *not* accept her apology, he collapsed, whip-thin body bucking until the lad stilled.

Cat studied her blood-smeared palms. The sky rumbled and fat raindrops pelted the cobblestones like marbles. She whirled around. Stone saints flocked her, watching and judging. "I'm sorry…"

A moan floated from the ground. Liam crawled toward the dead boy and raised himself on wobbly elbows. His face, once angelic, had transformed into a demonic mask of blisters and blood. Runny red eyes locked on her until his arms gave out and he collapsed next to his "brother."

Backing away, Cat fled the courtyard and took a staircase down…

Where the peaked roofs blotted out the moon.

Down.

Into the deserted streets.

Down.

Into the jungle.

◆

Light from the hallway wall sconces spilled into Da's study. Huddled in the darkest corner, Cat shielded her eyes.

Vivian materialized in the doorway carrying a candle. Her body appeared backlit, her limbs soft and willowy beneath her muslin nightgown. Jim Hawkins, his hair now trimmed and scrubbed to a shine, trailed in, circling the map-covered walls in awe. His new haircut revealed pointy pink ears.

A draft whipped the candle's flame back and forth. Vivian hurried across the room to shut the window. Her pale feet glowed in the darkness, leaving toe-prints on the Turkish rug.

"Where have you been all night?" Vivian knelt in front of Cat. "You had us worried sick!"

Cat opened and closed her hands. The blood had dried into the lines of her palms. Dried blood was darker than fresh, a black spot upon her soul. For the rest of her life—what was left of it anyway—she'd never forget the look in Charlie's eyes.

What's this knife doing in my throat?

It was the same with the crew after the creature attacked. Surprise trickling into terror. Terror to grim acceptance.

Where's my arm? What's it doing all the way over there?

Charlie was only fourteen, rosy cheeks, squeaky voice and all. Such a pretty corpse.

Vivian brushed the tangles from Cat's forehead "You're soaking wet. What—" She gasped and stared at her slippery fingertips. As she pushed the rest of Cat's hair back, Vivian's sobs filled the quiet study like a sad symphony. "Oh God. Oh God. What's become of you? Who did this to you?"

In a daze, Cat caressed Vivian's cheek. Rosy cheeks. Just like Charlie.

"Cat?"

64

She buried her face in Vivian's hair. A hint of honeysuckle still clung to the tendrils. "I've done a bad, bad thing…"

"It's all right." Vivian patted Cat on the back. "Whatever it is, it can't be the end of the world."

She had Liam at her mercy. But she was a monster hunter, not a cold-blooded murderer. Or maybe she was and didn't know it yet? First the old hag, now Charlie. Without really meaning to, she'd taken two lives and committed the mother of all cock-ups: failed to kill Liam. But would she have stabbed him in the back when he was helpless to defend himself?

After her return from the jungle, she'd wandered the streets, chased by shadowy creatures, consumed by hate. If it hadn't been for Liam, she would've tipped slowly, irrevocably, into madness. He had funneled her insanity into monster hunting, harnessed her hate on behalf of Mr. Hyde. He taught her how to trap, torture, and harvest the aberrations of the world. When she was lost and unformed, Liam shaped her identity and gave her a purpose. More than just her mentor, he was her creator. Once upon a time, she'd considered him a friend and yet, after all they'd been through, she'd never stopped being afraid of him. That was part of his appeal. The promise of danger, the thrill of death.

Now he knew where she lived. When he found them, he'd probably set her on fire, "pluck" her sister, and bugger young Jim. It *was* the end of their world.

Her eyes flickered to Jim Hawkins, who didn't seem the least bit afraid for his life. Holding the candlestick, the lad browsed Da's cabinet of relics from his days as a naturalist. Jars of jellyfish and octopi shared the shelf with cases of Monarch butterflies and shimmery green beetles. Jim gazed up at a fossil of a Galapagos lizard.

The lad came upon a collection of Da's more *unnatural* interests and halted in front of a jar housing a baby sandworm from the Gobi Desert. Its ugly beige body swam in slimy purple gel. Curled into a spiral, the creature's sucker revealed three rows of razor-sharp teeth. The adult, Da was fond of boasting, spanned the length of the Royal Mile.

Standing on his tiptoes, Jim reached for the sandworm. The jar tipped over the edge and shattered. Jim stepped back from the shards of broken glass and cocked his head.

"Pack your things." Cat watched Jim pick up the worm and unravel it like a roll of measuring tape. "Only the essentials. We're leaving tonight."

Vivian wiped her runny nose. "What? Tonight? But—"

Jim, alarmed by Cat's tone, returned the worm to the shelf and whirled around.

"Listen to me very carefully." Cat cupped Vivian's face. Her fingers left bloody prints on alabaster skin. "We're in a lot of trouble…"

66

♦

Rob was in a lot of trouble.

He'd been digging all morning and only managed a pitiful mound of dirt. His palms smarted with blisters, but he soldiered on and wrapped his hands around the shovel. The backbreaking work was a welcome distraction from his fear. Someone had to bury young Jenny. Someone had to recover the vanished hunters.

Three days had come and gone. Abernathy and his followers had yet to return. This was confirmation of what Rob knew all along. They were dead.

"Fools." His breath twined in the morning air like ribbons. "Stupid fools."

Normally Rob enjoyed being right. Not today.

A bark echoed at the far side of the kirkyard. Rob spied Virgil chasing a squirrel between the headstones.

"Virgil! Come here!" Leaning against the shovel, Rob rubbed his breastbone and grimaced. There was a firestorm in his lungs, a burning that hadn't fully gone away since the day of Alec's death. "Virgil!"

Virgil's ears perked at the sound of his new master's voice; the dog padded toward Rob.

Rob scratched Virgil's muzzle. "Wanna dig a hole, boy?"

Virgil barked, tongue lolling.

"Wanna dig a hole? Come on, come on!" Rob drove his shovel into the earth, stomped on the spade. Taking a hint, Virgil pawed the dirt and Rob's pathetic mound grew into a respectable one.

"Good boy." Rob could get used to owning a dog. As the pain in his lungs intensified, Rob reached into his breast pocket and extracted a small glass vial filled with emerald liquid, thumbing the elaborate script of his childhood physician. He wrinkled his nose at the memory of the briny sea taste. His entire boyhood revolved around guzzling vials and vials of Dr. Jekyll's serum.

He hadn't touched the serum in years, never thought he'd need it again, if not for the pain.

He glanced over his shoulder. In the family mausoleum, there was a tiny grave. The headstone had his name on it. Father had it carved after his baptism. Weak lungs, the midwife called it, and a paper-thin heart never expected to beat past infancy.

"Rob!" Waverley jogged through the weeds. The squirrel saw her coming and scurried up the nearest tree. His sister liked squirrels. The feeling was not reciprocated.

He tucked the vial back into his pocket and resumed shoveling. He cleared his throat, but couldn't clear the fire in his lungs. "What are you doing here?"

"Mrs. Nix sent me to fetch you back." Waverley fiddled with her white dress, rolling and unrolling the sleevess. Rob had never seen his sister look so uncomfortable. "She thinks you've gone mad."

"Aye, well," Rob grunted, driving his shovel into the ground. "I've always thought she was batty, so there we are. Run along home now. I'll be back before supper. What happened to your ugly culottes? Finally tired of being mistaken for a peasant boy?"

"Mrs. Nix burnt my trousers and threatened to paddle me if she caught me in pants again."

Rob hid a smile. This was the first time he'd had occasion to smile in a week.

Waverley folded her arms. He sensed her creepy eyes watching his every clumsy move.

Finally, he stopped and wiped his brow. *"What?"*

"That's not how you dig a hole."

For such a little girl, her voice boomed through the kirkyard. Rob liked to hear his sister's advice as much as he liked a paddling from Nix. Were he as nimble as the squirrel, he'd be in the branches, too. "It's my first time."

"It shows." She marched to the discarded tools and plucked a spare shovel from the pile. *"This* is how you dig a hole."

Not one to argue an extra set of hands, Rob followed his sister's lead.

"It's like we're digging for buried treasure," she said after a while. "Not burying Jenny."

Her blue ribbon came undone from her braid and flapped in the breeze. Rob plucked it off and stuffed it in his pocket.

"Rob?" Waverley scratched her nappy hair. Lice, he was sure of it.

"Hmm?"

"Brandon and the others…" Waverley stopped shoveling. She swallowed, fighting back tears. "They're all dead, aren't they?"

Rob fixed his sights on Virgil, blissfully digging. To be a dog with no sense of responsibility. What a creature to be.

"Rob?"

"Uh-huh?"

His silence seemed to satisfy her curiosity. She nodded. "How will we recover their bodies?"

"I don't know." That was a good question. These were the same men who killed the wolves and recovered Alec's remains. With the strongest hunters gone, the village was now short of able-bodied men. Unless, of course, the women wanted to try their luck. All of a sudden, Rob wanted to run back home and hide under his covers. He coughed into his fist.

"Rob? What did the monster look like?"

"Large."

"As a man?"

70

He tapped her on the scalp. "As your head," he said and received a kick to the shin. Rob nodded to the mausoleum. "Large as that and agile as a cat."

Waverley jumped into the grave. "Did it have fur? Fangs? Claws?"

"I didn't get *that* good a look." *I was hiding like a coward, one step away from pissing myself.* "Talons. And something else…"

Her eyes widened. "What?"

"Exoskeleton." Rob sighed, relieved to finally be able to tell someone.

A frown pleated her brow. "What's that?"

"Like the armor on a mantis or an American scorpion."

She turned to the fae woods. "Suppose it came out one day and came after us—"

"Hey, hey." Hopping into the grave, Rob grasped Waverley by the shoulders. "Stop that. It won't come out. It's quite comfy in the woods. It would never leave."

"Are you certain?"

No, he wasn't certain about anything. "Sure!" He puffed out his chest. "Fortunately for us, I happen to be an expert on insects."

She snorted. "Says who?"

"Says the Royal Geographical Society." He attempted a confident smile, but she wasn't buying it.

"Rob? What are we going to do?"

He wrapped his arms around her. His head hurt almost as much as his lungs. "Can't think of anything, but I'll think of something."

"That makes me feel so much better." Waverley picked up her shovel. "In the meantime, I'll dig your grave, you dig mine."

♦

Rob came home coughing.

"Robbie?" Gathering her shawl around her grey homespun dress, Mrs. Nix wobbled to greet him. His housekeeper cupped his face in her plump hands and felt his forehead. Kind brown eyes, framed by crow's feet, widened in alarm. "You're burning up! Why didn't you tell me you were running a fever?"

"Mrs. Nix, please…" Rob turned to Waverley for help. She held her palms up and ducked past him. Little feet pattered off to the kitchens. *Traitor!*

Mrs. Nix smacked the dirt off his blazer. "You're absolutely filthy! What do you think you're doing? Digging graves. You're laird now."

"I know." He stared at the top of her head. Her black hair was streaked with grey and done up in ringlets like a little girl. "Stop reminding me."

72

"You're not wearing nearly enough clothes."

As she unlooped the scarf, Rob eyed the mole on her double chin and wondered if it had spouted a third hair. He sighed. "I'm wearing three layers of sweaters already. I could hardly move as it is." He tried to hold in the cough, but failed.

"Your bronchitis is acting up again."

"Rubbish, Mrs. Nix, it's just a cold! Nothing to throw a wobbly about." Her smothering was sucking the life out of him.

"Snap to, Finley," she ordered their butler, a relic with eyebrows Alec used to say resembled "buggering caterpillars" as they tugged apart when he grinned and merged when he frowned. "See to the fire and fetch my Robbie a cup of tea and his medicine."

Finley nodded. His forehead was a collection of deep lines. He claimed to wear a white wig for tradition's sake, but Rob knew baldness had a lot to do with it. "Very good, ma'am." He began to shuffle toward the kitchen. With each step, his knees creaked like rusty door hinges.

"Ugh, I don't need to take my med—" Rob waved off Mrs. Nix's fussy hands. "No, Finley, come back."

The butler halted and shuffled back. "Very good, sir," he said in a voice as coarse as gravel. When Finley bowed, Rob could hear the old man's spine realigning. Yellow lace dangled from his collar and sleeves. His brocade jacket and knee breeches always reminded Rob of a matador. Alec and

73

Waverley used to have great fun waving a red blanket and shouting "Toro! Toro!" at Finley's expense. Compared to his siblings, Rob was the nice one.

A sniffling made Rob glance down. Mrs. Nix's eyes brimmed with tears. "What is it now?"

"Baby boy." Without warning, she flung her arms around his waist and wept into his chest. "I can't lose you, too."

Even though he was practically an orphan, he was in no short supply of people who wanted to coddle him. His mother, when alive, was much too interested in her letters and reading Lord Byron to fret about him as much as his housekeeper did.

"I'm not going anywhere," Rob said, patting her on the back. "A cold is hardly something to cry over. Now, please, I've some important business to attend to." He pried himself out of her arms and raced from the room. Then, forgetting his manners, Rob whirled around and pecked Mrs. Nix on the cheek.

She turned scarlet. Not to play favorites, he swatted Finley between the shoulder blades and received a grunt. "Lordship."

"Robbie!" Mrs. Nix hollered as he climbed the curving staircase. "I'm going to order an extra crate of serum from Dr. Jekyll anyway!"

At the sound of her shrill voice, Rob quickened his pace. His destination: the third floor, where his blissfully *silent* solarium served as a welcomed respite from Mrs. Nix's never-ending chatter.

On the second-floor staircase, he lost momentum on the sixth step. By the seventh and eighth, his breathing thinned into shallow gasps.

Why did his ancestors build. *Pant.* Such. *Pant.* Steep. *Pant.* Steps?

Clutching the banister, Rob climbed the rest of the way, determined not to make a sound and alarm Mrs. Nix.

He stumbled into his room and collapsed against his desk. Wheezing, he tugged at his collar. The fire in his lungs ignited into an explosion.

Rob doubled over and gave in to the coughs he'd been trying to hold back all morning. His arm swept over the clutter.

Papers cascaded over the side.

Glass shattered to the ground.

The hacking fit lasted a long time—the longest attack since he was ten. In pain and exhausted, Rob hoisted himself up. He felt like he'd swallowed a vat of acid and it was disintegrating him from the inside out.

He knelt to pick up the papers and gather the shards of a shattered ship in a bottle.

Slumped in his chair, Rob began the slow and painful process of tidying up his papers, reorganizing them by page number. He located the title page and noticed something amiss.

There was a drop of blood clinging to the "A" of *The Black Arrow*. Rob rifled through the manuscript. Some pages were clean, covered only by his spiky cursive. Others were speckled with blood.

He glanced at the broken glass. He turned his hands over. Clean palms. No cuts.

He reached into his breast pocket and withdrew a handkerchief. With a shaky hand, he dabbed it against his mouth.

A spot of dark blood, no bigger than a tick, stained the pristine linen. Rob licked his lips, checking for a wound. None.

Crumpling the handkerchief, Rob returned his attention to that droplet on the manuscript. He pressed his index finger to the drop, leaving a smudge between the title and his name.

For a long time, Rob stared at his fingerprint. The maroon whorl stared right back at him. It seemed to scream: "Rob was here."

But he won't be here for long.

In the meantime, he had a monster to kill.

The only way he knew how.

Rob reached for a fountain pen and a sheet of blank paper. He cracked his knuckles and wrote the three most important words he'd ever written.

Wanted: Monster Hunter.

CHAPTER 6
TICKET TO PARADISE

"Wanted: Monster Hunter." Scooting under the halo of the gas lamp, Vivian squinted at the newspaper. "Are you listening, Cat?"

"You have my undivided attention." Cat's eyes darted around the crowded platform. Beneath her cloak, she gripped a loaded pistol. Jim Hawkins, dressed in new tweed knee-breeches, mimicked her nervous movements.

The steam engine hissed a plume of smoke. She scanned the disembarking passengers. Footmen carrying luggage. Ladies in bell-shaped dresses linked arm-in-arm with gentlemen in black dusters. A slender man in a bowler hat materialized through a billow of coal smoke. Cat cocked her pistol, pressed her finger to the trigger.

The man passed by, checking his pocket watch.

Cat exhaled a whoosh of breath. A feather tickled her cheek. She slapped the purple ostrich plume away and glanced at the monstrosity atop Vivian's head.

Vivian stifled a sneeze and read, "Creature is large, fast, and dangerous…"

Cat snatched the hat. A cascade of pins pelted the platform. "Take off this ridiculous thing. I told you to put on something inconspicuous, not wear a dead parrot on your head."

"This is the latest Parisian fashion." Vivian snatched the hat back and propped it at a rakish angle. "Just because we're on the 'run' doesn't mean I have to look as bad as you." She nodded to Cat's trousers. "You're calling more attention to yourself by dressing like a boy."

Cat looked to Jim. The lad rolled his eyes. She still didn't care for short people, or "children," as they preferred to be called, but Jim was growing on her.

Vivian repinned her hat. "Maybe if you tell me where we're going."

No time for explanations, Cat grabbed Jim's hand and steered him around the piles of steamer trunks and carpetbags toward the ticket window. "We're leaving Scotland," she barked over her shoulder.

"To where?"

"Leith." Squeezing past a woman in a black crepe dress, she said, "Then a ship. Across the Atlantic if we can afford it. Across the channel if we can't. Far away from here."

Vivian brightened at the prospect of a journey. "I'd like to see Paris and the lavender fields in Provence. We can make perfume."

"The Mornay perfumers." Cat smiled and ruffled Jim's hair. "What about you, Jim Hawkins? Where would you like to go after Paris? The Swiss Alps, perhaps? Or India?"

Jim shrugged with stoic indifference and smoothed down his hair.

"I know where you'd like to go." She reached into her pocket and handed him a shard of sun-bleached coral. The trio joined the line at the ticket counter. "Once Da took us to Antigua to collect a rare species of beetle…"

Jim turned the coral between his tiny fingers.

"It's always summer there and the flowers bloom year round. The air is so sweet and syrupy you can taste it on your tongue like toffee." They advanced one person. "And the sea is so translucent you feel as if you're sailing on glass. Da called the West Indies 'Heaven on Earth.'"

"Oh Cat." There was a hitch in Vivian's voice. "That's all past…"

She took the coral back from Jim. "The past is all I have," she said, and hoped no one heard. When she glanced down, Jim was staring at her and she wondered if he could read lips.

It was her turn at the ticket counter. She slid a wad of crumpled banknotes under the window. "Three tickets," she mumbled, keeping her eyes trained on the curl of the clerk's waxed mustache.

The clerk flattened the bills and counted the notes. "That would do for one. Passage for three is five pounds sterling."

"Five pounds! The sign said three."

"Rates changed last week."

Vivian tugged on her sleeve. "Please, Cat, you're causing a scene."

She jerked her arm away and pointed at the clerk. "He's trying to cheat us—"

"No one is trying to cheat you, miss. Now please step aside. You're holding up the line." The clerk's mouth moved on hinges. He resembled an automaton, dead eyes and all.

Cat wanted to break him. "The sign says three pounds. In writing. Plain as day. You expect us to pay five, you put up a new sign."

Vivian seized her arm. "Look behind you."

She checked over her shoulder. A copper with a bushy walrus mustache lumbered toward the ticket booth—baton in hand. Cat rubbed her brow. She was sick of dead ends. Sick of being down on her luck. Sick of this piss-hole city and its filthy, thieving, murdering denizens.

"Come on," Vivian tugged her elbow, "let it go. Just let it go…"

Cat slammed her fist against the window. The clerk shielded his face. Guess he was human after all. "Change your bloody sign," she said, allowing Vivian to drag her away.

Vivian marched her to a secluded awning and smacked Cat on the forehead with a rolled-up newspaper. "Have you gone absolutely bonkers? What is wrong with you?"

"What's wrong with me?" She snatched the paper away. "What is wrong with *you*?"

"Why are you acting like this? You've been like this since Da—" She sat down on a damp bench and buried her face in her hands.

"Cry then." Cat kicked the brick pillar. "*Wah. Wah. Waahhhh.* That's all you're good for, isn't it?"

"You disappear at all hours of the night. You scream in your sleep. You scream when you're awake. You spend all our money on drugs and you spend more time passed out on the floor than hunting monsters."

"Whine and nag. That's all you do. Who do you think puts food on the table? Who do you think paid for that pug-ugly hat?" She poked herself in the chest. "That's who. I'd like a bit more appreciation."

"You're an abomination!" Vivian's face was puffy from crying. Jim patted her on the head.

"To hell with you! The lot of you!" Tossing her hands in the air, Cat stomped off and halted at the edge of the platform. She stared down at the tracks and contemplated throwing herself under the train. Ever since her return from Africa, the idea of suicide was more and more seductive. There was always a moment, during the harvest of a new monster, when she'd loosen her grip on her dragonbone dagger to give the wendigo or manticore the advantage. Or during a heavy injection of Elixir when she hoped she'd never wake up. She supposed she could've avoided Liam Barclay if she wanted, but maybe that night, she craved the cold kiss of his Culler.

The conductor whistled for the last passengers to board. The train rumbled away in a cloud of black smoke. Cat rubbed her arms. Three days without Elixir and she'd never felt so hopeless or unpredictable. The drug divided her into two people. Calm, rational Cat on good days, a monster on the bad. Liam once said all monster hunters had a history of violence and it only took a catalyst to help them realize their killer instinct. Africa was her tipping point, Elixir her catalyst of choice. But lately her dark side seemed to consume her better self so much so that Cat didn't know where the girl ended and the killer began.

She eyed Vivian, sobbing into a handkerchief, and shame brought her back under the awning.

Cat sat down next to her sister. Jim clambered onto the bench. His legs dangled in the air and his shoe knocked against her shin.

"The fellas who sold you the Elixir," Vivian wiped her red nose, "they're the ones who tried to cut off your ear? They're the ones after us, aren't they?"

She rolled and re-rolled the newspaper. Her silence was as good as a confirmation.

"Will you tell me what you've done?"

Cat shook her head. Vivian would never know of her sordid world, not if she could help it. "You're my princess and I'm your knight, remember? They'll never touch you."

Vivian turned away. Finally, she muttered, "My hat isn't pug-ugly."

With a sigh, Cat unfolded the newspaper. "Creature is large, fast, and dangerous." Seven men, including the former laird, one girl. The advertisement made no mention of the species but went on to underline the creature's deadliness. Weren't all monsters deadly by nature? "£500 to anyone who can bring me its head. Signed, Robert Stevenson, Earl of Balfour."

"Five hundred pounds." She whistled. Three days ago, she'd considered herself retired. No more drugs. No more kills. From here on out, she was going to clean up her act, wash the blood off her hands and return to that white sand beach in Antigua where violets bloomed year round.

Heaven on Earth was just an ocean away and the price of entry: the head of a monster.

For five hundred pounds, Cat could afford to come out of retirement.

"We go north," Cat said to Vivian. "To Balfour Castle."
She handed the paper to Jim. "Well, demon boy. You might see
Paradise yet."

CHAPTER 7
CATRIONA MORNAY, MONSTER HUNTER

Rob studied the monster hunters from afar.

There were six in all, and a more scraggly band of riffraff he'd never seen.

"See that giant over there?" Rob squinted against the stinging rain. "The man with the great black beard? I swear I saw him at the circus."

"Look at that one!" Waverley pointed to a bald man with a tattooed face. "He looks like one of the pirates in your bedtime stories."

"And the tattoos are actually a treasure map..." Rob leaned against the moss-covered leg of a Titan from the old Greek myths.

Across from the Titan, there was a goddess with branches for arms and a serpent weaving in and out of the earth. The statue garden was Rob's favorite place on earth. He used to haunt these ruins as a boy, looping around stone heroes and monsters, mesmerized by the beautiful and the macabre.

He'd hiked up the same hill countless times; now he was winded to the point of collapse. Rob drew his jacket closer and willed himself not to cough in front of his sister. Thankfully, she was too preoccupied with the spectacle to notice his strained face.

Waverley drove her wooden sword in the mud. "Don't you think you ought to be down there?"

He glanced at the hunters. The prospect of meeting a swiftly growing crowd of strangers made him sick. "No."

"But you placed the advertisement. You're laird."

"Facts I already know, Duck."

"You're just going to mill around? You have to choose a hunter, *Lord* Robert."

There was no getting out of it. One way or another, he was going to have to socialize. Perhaps make a speech of some kind.

Rob let the mist settle on his palm. Under the garish light of day, his hand was startlingly pale and thin, his thumb and forefinger ink-stained from long evenings writing. His hand was shaking. "You go."

"What?"

"Take my place." What a coward he must seem to her. No help for it. He knew what would happen the moment he opened his mouth around strangers. He'd bumble and stutter like a village idiot and they would all laugh at him, fancy title or no. "You pick the hunter. One look at your dirty face," he added, "and they'll run for the hills."

A pebble bounced off his shoulder. "Hey!" He picked up the pebble and flicked it at her.

Waverley dodged and giggled. "Have it your way, laddie. Good practice for me anyway. I'll be laird when you're gone."

Rob frowned. "Gone?" She couldn't have known about the blood—it only happened that once and he was damn sure— okay, *somewhat* sure—he'd bitten his tongue. In any event, his coughs had been spotless ever since.

"On your grand world tour." Waverley tossed another pebble in the air, caught it. "You still plan to go, don't you? When this is over?"

He turned to the goddess with branches for arms and an insurmountable sadness seeped into his heart. The statues were here long before he was born—and they'd stand long after he's dead. "Aye."

"So when you're sailing around the world having all your adventures, I'm you. I should learn now."

Rob rubbed his palms together. This blasted rain was stinging his eyes. "Off with you now. Pick a man with brains. Brute strength isn't going to matter against the creature and I can't handle another death."

"Rob?" Waverley's forehead rippled in concern. He sensed her keen eyes studying him. "Why do you look so sad?"

"I'm not sad."

"You're doing this…" She tugged the corner of her lips and cheeks down. "Your face is all strange."

"That's just my face."

"No, you usually look like this…" To demonstrate, Waverley tipped her chin up and marched around.

Rob massaged the spot between his eyes. "And what is that?"

"All snooty like you've got the largest stick shoved up your bunghole and rather like it."

"Waverley!"

"Well, you do."

"You're an annoying little girl and you'll grow up into an annoying woman. Get out of here!" he ordered with a playful kick to her rump.

Waverley broke into a run, then jogged back to Rob and threw her arms across his midriff. Rob hugged her tight and pecked her on the top of her head. His lips grazed a twig. "What do you have growing in there?" he asked, riffling through the greasy tangles.

"Wisdom. Want some?" Just as suddenly, Waverley released him and sprinted down the hill. He watched her lithe figure marching toward the men, hollering, "All right you lot, gather 'round!"

Rob smiled as Waverley pushed a man the size of a mountain out of her way. All the hunters glared down at her with a mixture of curiosity and trepidation. That was usually how he felt around Waverley. Queasy. Irritated. Consumed with the urge to flee. She ought to whittle down the brave ones from the cowards.

Alone at last, he dug inside his pocket and uncorked a fresh bottle of Dr. Jekyll's serum. True to her word, Mrs. Nix had ordered a lifetime supply. Rob stared down at the emerald liquid with a heavy heart. He loathed drinking his medicine, and not just because of the dead-fish taste. While the drug brought swift relief from the pain, it dulled his wits and transformed the world into a glittery illusion.

A life of smoke and mirrors.

What kind of life was that?

Once, when he was thirteen and rebellious, he'd dumped the contents of all his vials into an Erlenmeyer flask and carried the brew to the courtyard outside his dormitory. Striking a match, he flicked it inside and watched the flames lap against the flask's lip until the concoction exploded in a mushroom cloud of green fire. He still had a puckered scar on his shin from an imbedded glass shard and memories of the hiding the housemaster gave him afterward. An important lesson was beaten into him that day: fire and serum *don't* mix.

With a flick of his hand, Rob poured his medicine in the grass. The mud fizzled. How liberating it must feel to take a match to the rest of Mrs. Nix's pantry stock.

Dr. Jekyll had deemed him cured. What he suffered from now was summertime cold, exacerbated by stress and grief, nothing more. "I bit my tongue," he whispered.

Feeling healthier already, Rob corked the vial and turned around. "Blast!"

A boy of ten or eleven stared up at him with sinister black eyes.

Rob clutched his chest and glared at the strange boy. His heart galloped like a team of wild horses. "I didn't hear you there, lad. Where'd you come from?"

Not even a blink. The boy was dressed in a neat, albeit travel-weary, outfit of tweed jacket and knee-britches.

Rob cleared his throat. "You're not from around here, are you? What's your name?"

Silence.

A raven landed on the goddess's stone head and cawed. Rob shifted from foot to foot, shrinking under the boy's unrelenting stare. The boy must've come from somewhere. "Where's your mother?"

He braced himself for another awkward bout of silence when a gravelly voice called, "I killed his mother."

Rob looked up. A lithe silhouette strolled toward him. He assumed the stranger was the boy's older brother, but as the cloaked figure stepped out of a veil of mist, Rob realized his mistake.

"You're a girl." He stared incredulously at her ghastly trousers—they were as filthy and mud-splattered as her boots.

His eyes traveled to her face, or what he could see of it beneath her wide-brim hat. Pointy chin. Full lips twisted at the corners. Rob had a feeling she was smirking at an inside joke and the joke was on him.

"You are correct," she said finally. "And they say you Highland boys are no smarter than the cattle you herd."

Rob stiffened. "I beg your pardon?"

Ignoring him, the girl rested her hands on the little boy's shoulders. "I see you've met my ward. His name's Jim Hawkins and you're wasting your breath: he doesn't speak." The girl plucked a strand of hair off Jim's head and blew it in his direction. "Do you, Jim?"

The boy cocked his head to the side.

"See? No answer. But I've come to learn when his head slants to the left, it usually means 'yes.'"

Leaving Jim behind, she stepped toward Rob. She was tall for a girl and they stood shoulder to shoulder. Peering down the ledge, she stripped off her hat. Her black hair was gathered in a braid as thick as a man's hand. Rob immediately noticed the ghastly bruised-plum color of her ear. He knew it was rude to stare, but good god! Were those…stitches?

"All these men are going to die," she said.

"I'm sorry, but *who* are you?"

She held out a calloused hand with fingernails gnawed to nubs. "Catriona Mornay," she said, then added, "I kill monsters."

"*The* Cat Mornay?" Absently, Rob took her hand but the second their fingers touched, a spark zipped up his arm. He snatched his hand back. He felt like he was falling through space alongside the girl, trying to reach her before a black hole sucked her into oblivion. When the vision cleared, Rob was seized with an eerie sensation that spoke of the merging of two lives.

The girl must've felt the shock, too. She flexed her fingers, wiped them on her coat. Her voice lost some of its bravado. "I-I take it you're a fan?"

Rob arched a brow.

She grimaced. "Don't look so disappointed."

"I don't believe it."

Frankly, he didn't *want* to believe it. Cat Mornay was a goddess. Perfection made flesh. Rob's eyes flickered over the girl's flat chest. *His* Cat Mornay had a bosom—an ample one. Somehow this seemed important. She needed big breasts to help her stay afloat when she wrestled krakens and other creatures of the deep. Buoyancy: this girl didn't have it.

This girl was rude and uncouth —as far removed from a goddess as a guttersnipe, which she kind of smelled like. Her eyes, however, were beautiful: deep blue, almost violet, melancholy and haunted. They were the only features about Cat Mornay that hadn't died in the face of reality.

"I don't care what you believe. I am who I say I am." She wandered to the edge of the hill, yet her last words danced in the air. *I am. I am. I am.* "But you, Lord Robert, are making a terrible mistake if you hire one of these amateurs over me."

He took a step toward her. "How did you know—"

"Know who you are?" A strand of hair flapped across her face like a black ribbon. She tilted her head to the side, sizing up her competition. She moved like a cat, not so much watching as sensing. "Servants talk. Especially the kitchen maids. Nine deaths, one week. Seven men, one little girl, and..." She glanced over her shoulder. "Your brother."

"I'd thank you not to speak of my brother, Miss Mornay." Rob turned away and bumped into Jim. Where did the boy come from? He obviously didn't believe in personal space.

"I'm here to avenge your brother."

"Are you now?"

"I'll expect payment in half before the kill," she said. "The other half when I deliver the monster's head. Now if we're agreed—"

This girl was a bleeding loon. "What makes you think I'll hire you?"

Cat shrugged and smiled. Her whole resume was reflected in the smug curl of her lips. The sirens she slaughtered at the

Isle of May. The harpy beheaded in Aberdeen. There were even rumors of a Sphinx which she single-handedly dismembered in Egypt. But nothing compared to her first, the creature that made her famous.

Rob found himself staring into those blue eyes again. He saw the jungle in her irises, a claw-shaped demon darting between the figs and lianas, and he began to believe she really was Cat Mornay. No imposter could fake this type of naked tragedy.

"See that lass down there?" Cat pointed to the clearing.

Rob was still studying Cat. While no goddess, she was actually quite fetching. He sighed. He really wished she had more of a bosom. They'd felt so nice in his dreams.

He felt a smack to the thigh. Jim, seeming to spawn out of the grass because *he wasn't standing there before*, urged Rob to pay attention.

Down the hill, the hunters parted for a wispy slip of a girl in a striped purple dress. She glided amongst the crowd like a swan. Now *there* was a goddess.

"My sister Vivian." Sidling behind him, Cat whispered in his ear. "Exquisite, no? But her hat…" She stuck a finger down her throat.

Her breath warmed his neck. Her proximity made him nervous, so Rob stepped away and collided with Jim again.

The hat in question was also purple and covered in fluffy ostrich plumes. He shrugged. "I don't think it's half bad. It's the latest Parisian fashion."

Cat turned to him as if *he* were the daft one. "It's like a bird sat on her head and died." A melodramatic sigh. "So many times I've told her to get rid of it, but how she loves the thing!"

With a wink, Cat brushed past him and leaped on the Titan's muscular thigh.

"Stop that! You can't do that! These ruins are sacred!"

"Oh lighten up!" Cat scaled the Titan's spine, planting one foot in front of the other, arms held wide like a tightrope walker.

"I demand you climb down from there at once!"

Planting one booted foot on the statue's shoulder, Cat flipped aside her black overcoat, withdrew a long-barreled pistol, and aimed it at the crowd.

Rob shielded his eyes and watched, with a mixture of horror and fascination, as the barrel shifted from the tattooed man to Waverley to the mountain-sized hunter.

Until she settled on her target: Vivian.

Spurred into action, Rob grabbed onto the giant's thigh and hoisted himself up. He slipped and cursed under his breath. "I'll have you hanged!"

Cat squinted and adjusted her mark.

Vivian's head.

"If I were you, Lord Robert—" Cocking the pistol, she braced the barrel on her forearm. "I wouldn't want to distract me."

"God help you if you fire!" Rob gritted his teeth and heaved. He dangled off the knee, determined to climb up the torso and tackle this insane sniper to the ground. To Rob's horror, he slid off the slick stone and landed on his bum. He smacked the Titan's thigh. "Mornay! Stop! Mornay!"

She pulled the trigger.

♦

Rob scrambled to his feet.

His ears rang from the shot. The reek of gunpowder pervaded the air.

A hand tugged on his sleeve. Jim again, materializing out of nowhere, pointed over the ledge.

Holding his breath, Rob summoned the courage to look down. All eyes fixed on the hilltop garden. To his surprise, Vivian's head was still in one piece. Her hat, however…

"I don't believe it," he said.

Waverley stared up at them, her mouth a perfect O. Tilting her head, she blinked at the purple blizzard and, laughing, plucked the feathers from the air.

Vivian fumed. Folding her arms, she glared at Cat with pure loathing.

"What say you, Lord Robert?" Cat pounced off the Titan's shoulder and landed on the balls of her feet. She strutted to him until they were face to face. "Do I have the job?"

Rob shoved past her and stomped down the hill. "Oh, believe me. I know exactly what to do with you."

♦

"Get your hands off me!" Cat dug her heels in the ground, but a strong pair of hands hooked into her armpits and tossed her like a sack of flour.

She sailed through the air and landed in a mud puddle.

A swine nuzzled her cheek with its slimy snout. Two piglets rooted at her side.

Raking her fingers through the muck, Cat glared at her assailants. A big dumb oaf and the bald pirate with the tattooed face. They were part of the application pool, hired on as temporary goons.

"If Lord Robert ever catches you lurking around his lands again," the oaf slapped his meaty paws together, "he'll have you shot."

The tattooed one was a man of few words. He pointed to his lazy eye, then at her, and growled.

97

When the thugs were gone, Vivian loomed before her. Her pointy-toed boot tapped in the puddle. "This is what you get for ruining my hat."

Cat planted her face in the mud. She was really starting to hate this Lord Robert.

♦

Rob paid his new monster hunter half the reward money and an extra quid for tossing the lunatic and her entourage off his estate.

"You'll get the other half after the job's done." He tried not to stare at the dotted lines spiraling the man's face or the boar tusk pierced through his nose. "And please try not to get eaten."

The hunter sneered, revealing stained teeth filed to points. "I ate a monster once."

"That's nice." Rob studied the monster hunter's eccentric outfit. Instead of a shirt, two leather straps crisscrossed the man's muscular chest, also covered with tribal tattoos. Two gold hoops dangled from his nipples. Rob rubbed his own tweed-covered chest; his nipples ached in sympathy.

Monster hunters were a strange lot. His thoughts returned to Cat Mornay and his decision was suddenly weighted with regret. What if she was right and he'd made a big mistake?

He forced these doubts out of his head. Cat was a good markswoman, he'd grant her that, but reckless and unbalanced. If she could use her own sister for target practice, what else might she be capable of? *His* Cat Mornay wasn't real, and this saddened him most of all.

"Good luck." He offered the hunter his hand.

The man stared down at Rob's hand and growled.

"Right-o." Rob tucked his hands under his armpits in case the new hire decided to bite him. "Well, off to work with you then. If you need help I'll just...I'll just wait right here."

Slinging his machete over his shoulder, the hunter marched toward the forest.

By nightfall, the monster would be dead, Alec's death avenged, his village safe. The pain in his lungs subsided to a dull ache, a sign, surely, that his health was on the mend.

Rob rocked back on his heels, confident he'd hired the right man for the job.

◆

Wind lashed against a three-sided hunter's shed and rain dribbled through the holes in the roof. Cat cupped her hand around the wavering candle flame and held it above the newspaper on her lap.

Huddling next to her for warmth, Jim rooted through her knapsack, then tapped her on the shoulder. He pointed to the pathetic flame and puffed up his cheeks to blow into the air.

"I don't have the Dragon's Breath."

Jim arched an eyebrow. *Why?*

Cat sighed. "I lost it." In her retreat from Tron Kirk, she'd forgotten the vial of silver pills: the last keepsake she had from Da.

She grew silent and turned the page. A fat drop of rain plopped on the paper, streaking the ink. Dragon's Breath would come in handy now.

Across the shed, Vivian drew the ends of a ratty blanket over her shoulder and sneezed into her finger. One. Two. Three quiet "lady" sneezes.

"Come join us." Cat patted the dirt next to her. "It's warmer over here."

Vivian blew her nose like a trumpet. Well, not everything could be ladylike. "It's warmer at home. Nice fire. Warm bed." She gestured to the howling night. "Four walls instead of three. If we start back tomorrow—"

"We can never go home," Cat said softly. "We wait here. He'll change his mind."

"After the stunt you pulled?" Vivian snorted. "Not likely. I've never been so embarrassed in all my life!"

Cat's lips twitched. "Oh come now. That hat was doing you no favors. Patience, sweetling. By tomorrow evening, our fortunes will change."

"Our fortunes? Our fortunes! Lord Robert has already hired someone else. His new hunter has a machete."

"Anyone could use a machete," Cat said. "I know the fella. He's a drunk and a fraud. Aye, he's killed all right—helpless lasses like you, wee lads like Jim—but never a monster. That bloke is dead. In the meantime, we wait."

"You sound so sure of yourself. You're not the only monster hunter in Scotland."

Cat turned the page. "I'm the best." Second best, actually, after Liam Barclay. But after Africa, Cat decided she deserved a promotion.

"That's what you always say." Another sneeze. Vivian rubbed her raw nose with the back of her hand. "What makes you the best?"

She pondered her sister's question for a long time. She was no faster or stronger than the men in the clearing. Probably not half as smart or pretty as Liam—well, pre-Dragon's Breath Liam anyway. "The others do it for money."

"As do you," Vivian said.

"No."

"No?" Vivian raised a blonde eyebrow. "That explains why you never make any."

Cat exchanged glances with Jim. "She's only a shrew when it rains," Cat whispered, and the lad's shoulders shook.

Vivian scowled. "Pray tell, Cat. What is your noble reason?"

"*Hate*." Cat cracked her knuckles, one finger at a time. "Sometimes I feel my whole soul grow black with it. Hate for all the mermaids and sphinxes and serpents and aves that infest the land, the sea, the air. Hate, and the belief that all unnatural creatures deserve to die. In a time of monsters, hate is all you need."

Cat guessed that was a good enough answer. For a few precious minutes, Vivian ceased whining. Even Jim had grown silent, if it was possible for a mute boy to become muter.

"Sorry, changeling," she amended, "you're the only exception."

Narrowing his eyes, Jim pinched her knee.

"Ow!"

Apology not accepted.

Bother him. She flipped another page in the paper.

A moment later, Vivian sighed.

Cat glanced up. "What is it now?"

Vivian lolled her head against the wall. A dreamy haze clouded her eyes. "Did you see the size of the sapphire on Lord Robert's ring? With a stone like that, we could live like gods."

Cat barely glanced up from her reading. "I don't fancy lads with jewelry."

"Lord Robert is very handsome, isn't he?"

Cat thought about the slender laird with the meticulously combed white-blond hair and pretentious airs. His face was perfectly symmetrical. His boots polished to a shine. His coat and trousers tailored and pressed. She'd like to mess up his hair, step on his boots, and push the toff in the mud.

In fact, Rob actually looked like an older, more refined, more attractive version of Charlie. Liam would eat him up, and the thought made Cat glad Rob existed in a snootier-than-thou circle far removed from her Edinburgh cage. As much as she disliked this snob, she'd never wish Liam Barclay on anyone.

"He's as pretty as you, sweetling," Cat said. "Naturally you would be drawn to yourself."

"Why do you have to ruin everything?"

Cat flexed her fingers, recalling the shock he gave her when they shook hands. She'd felt like she was flying through space, plunging into a black hole while he was dragged toward the sun.

Shaking her head, she returned to her reading. "Listen to this," she said, "*Here he lies where he longs to be. Home is the sailor, home from the sea. And the hunter home from the hill.*"

"Who's the author?" Vivian asked.

"R.L.S." Cat tore her eyes away from the paper. The words carved a hole in the dismal hut through which Cat could see palm fronds swaying on a distant shore. "I should like to meet this man."

♦

"He's not coming back, is he?" Waverley asked.

Brother and sister stood in the clearing, watching the towering briars sway against the dusky sky. The storm had cleared; dark clouds remained, rolling and regrouping for another go.

Rob popped the lid of his gold pocket watch. A droplet splattered on the glass face. He swiped it with his thumb. The *tick tick tock* of time mirrored his nerves. His new hire had been gone more than twenty-four hours. "We don't know that."

"He's dead."

He turned to his sister. "He's probably setting up a trap. Waiting."

"Hunter makes ten."

"How easily you can reduce a man's life to a number, Duck," he said.

"Twenty-four hours without a word. I think we can stop being optimistic."

Deep down Rob knew Waverley was right. Wisdom. She had it. He could use some. The next drop on the watch face belonged to him. "I sent a man to his death," he admitted. "Th-this is all m-my fault…"

Seizing him by the forearm, Waverley shook him and shouted, "Don't start weeping now! Are you a man?"

"*Noooo.*" Rob hid his tears in the crook of his elbow.

"You're laird."

"I hate being laird. I'm going to sail away, write my novel, and research the mating cycle of the West Indian beetle. To hell with this!"

"For the love of… I should've been born a man," she muttered. "Rob, bend down. I need to tell you something very important."

He followed her instructions and she slapped him dead across the face.

"Duck!" He rubbed his cheek, stunned.

"Pull yourself together!" Waverley ground her boots in the mud, her mouth puckered into a resentful line. "If you'd let me choose—as you'd promised—I would've chosen the tall girl. At least we know she can shoot."

Standing up, Rob glared at the top of Waverley's head. He could read her thoughts and did not like the direction this train was heading. Tucking his pocket watch inside his waistcoat, he stomped back to the manor. "No!"

"Why not?" Waverley ran after him.

"She's probably long gone by now."

"You know of the shed by the creek? The one old man McCord used to hang the stag hides? I have it on good authority that it's now occupied." Waverley tugged on his sleeve. "She's got to be famous for a reason."

Rob marched on. He could see the purple feathers floating through the darkness and Cat Mornay astride the shoulders of the Titan. As much as he loathed to admit it, in that moment, she looked every bit the legend.

"Devil take her." Out of the corner of his eye, he caught Waverley smiling. "And *you!*" What did he have to lose beside his pride, and perhaps Cat Mornay's life? "Hunter makes eleven."

♦

Cat rolled her trousers to her knees and stepped into the stream. The water chilled her bare feet, but the noonday sun warmed her back. She waddled into the speckled pond, stepping over a bed of pebbles and waterweed, and slipped her fingers beneath the surface.

She spied a gleam of scales.

A flash of fin.

"Cat!" Vivian slid off her rocky perch and gestured to the path beyond the foothill. "There's a rider ahead!"

She pressed a finger to her lips. "Shhh…" The unmistakable thunder of hooves told her they'd soon have company. Hunched over the stream, Cat listened for the gentle stirring of the trout.

The rider dismounted.

"Lord Robert!" Vivian sounded out of breath.

"Miss Mornay." For a boy so slight, his footsteps were clunky. Cat grinned. Lead-footed laird, a rhino trotter.

Behind her, Rob gasped and said, "Oh, I didn't see you there, Jim."

"To what do we owe the pleasure of his Lordship's visit?" Vivian asked.

"Rob. Please, just Rob."

His snooty accent was ingrained in Cat's memory. There was nothing more pathetic than a Highlander who longed to be an outlander, a Scotsman who spoke like an Englishman.

Rolling her eyes, Cat curled her fingers toward the palms and swayed her hands gently to and fro.

"I'd like to speak to your sister. What…" He cleared his throat. "What, may I ask, is she doing?"

Spotting a groping mouth, Cat motioned for silence. The trout swam toward her, hypnotized by the swaying of her hand.

"Fishing."

"Why are we whispering?"

The scales tickled her palm and Cat dove in. There was a sudden explosion of water. When she emerged, Cat was soaked from head to toe. She grappled with the slippery trout, holding it at arm's length to avoid the slap of its tail, and shuffled to the pebbled bank.

With a grunt, she smacked the trout against a rock, killing it instantly. Only then did Cat meet Rob's eye. She flashed him her sweetest smile. "What happened to your new hire?"

He squared his shoulders. His hair was slicked back into a shiny blond helmet. His posture could shame a ruler. Rob flicked his riding crop against his thigh. He looked as though he'd like to slap her with it. "Still in the woods."

"Did he…" Cat petted the grey trout belly. "Did he catch your monster?"

Silence, followed by a barely imperceptible shake of his head.

"So you've need of another hunter? A *good* one?"

Rob glared down the length of his long, aristocratic nose.

"I had a feeling you'd join us today, so I caught this… "
She strolled toward him and dumped the dead fish in his arms. "For you, Your Highness."

CHAPTER 8
BOY PROBLEMS

Rob nudged his horse up the rise and drew an arm around Vivian's slender waist.

With a gasp, she settled against him. Her booted heels and yards of rustling petticoats dangled over the side of his mare. Wisps of gossamer hair tickled Rob's jaw.

He leaned forward, just enough to inhale her scent. Wildflowers after the rain. Heavenly.

Rob tilted his head and let the sunbeams warm his face. He felt lighter already. No more nasty coughs. Clear blue skies after the storm. A fair maiden in his arms. Rob drew her closer, feeling like Sir Lancelot. Hold on. Dash that. King Arthur. He was laird after all.

Vivian Mornay was everything a well-bred girl should be. Fashionable. Demure. Sane. "Miss?" he began, "You and your sister are as diff—"

"Different as night and day?"

That was one way of putting it. "You grew up together?"

Vivian nodded. "Unfortunately."

"Forgive my impertinence..." Rob tightened his grip on the reins. "But how is that *possible?*"

"Cat was our father's favorite," she explained. "He always wanted a boy, which worked out perfectly because Cat is… Well, you know how Cat is."

He snorted. "How can I forget?"

"Da took her everywhere. Dragged her all over the world while I stayed behind with Mother, not that I wanted to go to those dirty, uncivilized places anyway. Our mother used to say he was turning her into a heathen."

"Where is your mother now?"

She ducked her head. "Passed."

"Oh, I-I'm so sorry…"

"Quite all right," she said. "She'd been very ill for a long time."

"You are very brave, miss. If I may be so bold, a true saint."

Vivian's profile was the picture of loveliness. "I'm not half as brave as you. Or as noble. Why, your quest to avenge your brother's death…" A sigh. "How romantic!"

A clucking to his right drew Rob's attention away. He scowled.

Leading the second horse by the reins, Cat hiked down the hillock. Jim Hawkins, perched atop the speckled mare, waved to him as they passed. He wore Cat's rakish hat, which was too big for his head. Three dead trout, strung with fishing wire, dangled at the mare's side.

"Oh Lord Robert, you are so perfect," Cat said. "No, Miss Mornay, *you* are…" She glanced over her shoulder and a teasing light flickered though her eyes. "Chivvy along, you lazy sods. We've still got a ways to go and three more hours of light."

Vivian gave him a long-suffering look. "See what I have to put up with?"

"I feel sorry for you."

Ahead, Cat drew Jim's attention to a lone bird soaring in the sky. She cupped a hand to her mouth and a high-pitched call breached the quiet. The bird cawed in reply.

"Oh dear," Vivian muttered, "She's making those savage noises again."

"Red bill diver," Rob said.

"Lord Robert?"

"The bird. A red bill diver."

"How fascinating…" Vivian changed the subject. "How'd you like Eton, Lord Robert?"

"Glad to be done with all of that." He glanced down at her with some surprise. "How'd you know I went to Eton? Been studying up on me?"

Vivian blushed. "I read the society pages."

"Of course."

She lowered her head, long lashes fanning her fair cheek. "And England?"

"Much better than here."

"You sound like an Englishman."

Rob grinned. "That's not a compliment around these parts."

"Oh but it is! I've only been to London once, but I found it infinitely more civilized than Edinburgh. In fact, I…"

Rob nodded politely, his attention drifting back to Cat. She wore no petticoat, no corset, and her damp linen shirt clung to her small, pert breasts, which, Rob was relieved to see, existed after all.

He shifted in his saddle. Although he knew it wasn't gentlemanly, he couldn't help staring. His eyes traveled over the long, sleek line of her legs and the apple curve of her bottom. Not realizing it, he clutched Vivian tighter.

Vivian ceased prattling and stiffened in surprise. "Oh."

Rob glanced down and scooted as far back as the saddle would allow. "I'm sorry, I… Oh God."

"It's all right." Vivian stared straight ahead like a frightened rabbit. "I understand."

Rob no longer felt like King Arthur. At least Arthur had the "I'm carrying Excalibur" excuse at his disposal. He wanted to die. Crawl into a hole and die.

"Ya!" He cracked his riding crop and his mare sprinted past Cat and Jim. The cold wind seared his flushed cheeks, but Rob kept his eyes fixed on the stone ramparts of Balfour Manor.

"Lord Robert!" Vivian wrapped her arms around his neck in a death grip. "Slow down!"

They plowed through a ravine and thundered over an obstacle course of hills and valleys before racing across the manicured lawn of his estate.

Rob rode his horse to the ground, yanking on the reins before they collided with the groom. He dismounted and tossed the reins to the lad. Without meeting her eye, Rob offered Vivian his hand and helped her down.

She gazed up at him, eyes bright with exhilaration. "That was so fast!"

"Finley will see to your needs," he said, "Again, I am mortified." Although it was the height of ill manners, Rob whirled on his heels and left her to the perplexed groom.

Finley and Mrs. Nix greeted him at the grand entrance. Waverley, thank God, was nowhere in sight, or she'd be the first one to point out his "problem."

Mrs. Nix rushed to hug him, but Rob sidestepped her. "Don't touch me!"

"Robbie?" She frowned. "What's wrong?"

"I'm all dusty. Just…" He stepped behind Finley, using the butler as a shield. "No hugs."

"You're acting rather strange." Mrs. Nix peered behind the old man's shoulder. "Did you hire someone else?"

"Aye." Rob stripped off his riding gloves just as Cat galloped toward them and dismounted. Tilting her head, she gawked at the castle in awe. The sunlight streamed through her transparent blouse, yet the nippy spring air made her...

"Oh dear," Mrs. Nix muttered, "I see you've brought home a lady of the night."

"She's not a prostitute," Rob said, feeling a need to defend Cat's virtue, "she's my new monster hunter."

Finley followed his master's gaze and nodded in understanding. "I'll have a bath prepared for you, sir." He lowered his voice. "A *cold* one. In the meantime, where should we put her?"

Rob watched Cat pace with her hands clasped behind her back. She was studying the turret and the hundred windows, oblivious to their attention. Then, without warning, she ceased pacing and her eyes flicked toward him.

He turned away. "Servants' quarters." *As far away from me as possible.*

Mrs. Nix folded her hands across her round belly. "Mark my words: that lass is trouble."

"Miss Mornay goes into the woods tomorrow. She won't be here for long." But as he raced up the stairs, he was inclined to agree.

♦

"I don't see why *I* have to wear a dress to supper." Cat gritted her teeth as Vivian dragged a tortoise comb through her damp hair. "In fact, I don't see why I need to dine with that snob at all. I'm perfectly happy eating in the kitchen with the cook. *Ouch!*"

"Speak for yourself. We've lived like paupers for so long you've forgotten what it was like before Da died. Well, I remember." Vivian, a vision in a cream tea gown, tackled another knot. "Hold still. This wouldn't be so hard if you'd combed your hair once in a while."

"Charity." Cat wrapped her towel more securely around her bosom. "He's only doing it out of charity. The gentry do it all the time. Makes them feel better about being rich."

Vivian shrugged. "I think it's a jolly kind gesture."

Cat caught Vivian's wistful expression in the vanity mirror. "By the way, what on earth is the matter with Lord Robert? I'd never seen anyone ride so hard." In the mirror, she witnessed Vivian blush and walk away. "Viv?"

"You can wear the blue brocade. It brings out the color of your eyes." Vivian busied herself digging through her trunk. "It's my favorite, so you better not spill or tear—"

"Viv!" Swiveling around, Cat clutched the wooden back of the chair. "Since when are you keeping secrets from me? I demand to know what happened!"

115

Vivian looked to Cat, then glanced at the shut door. "All right," she whispered, "But you are *not* to say anything to him, understand?"

Cat crossed her heart. "Unless it has to do with my fee, I don't see why I need speak to him at all. Come on, out with it."

Vivian took a deep breath. "Lord Robert and I were riding. I don't know if it was the jostling or something I did or said but I…" She squinted at her satin evening slippers. "*Felt* something."

Cat frowned. "You felt what?"

"You know…" Vivian waved a hand in the air. "*Something.*"

"Oh." Cat was so confused. Then her eyes widened. "*Ohhhhhhhh!*"

A peal of giggles filled the tiny room.

All sorts of lurid images now crowded Cat's mind. "Bloody hell, Viv, now I wish I hadn't asked." She coiled a damp tendril around her finger. "How did you even feel it through your petticoats?"

Vivian thought for a minute before collapsing face-first onto her bed. "Oh believe me, there was no avoiding it. Even through all my layers."

"Really? *Rob?* But he's so scrawny!" Cat laughed in disbelief. She recalled Rob slumped against the Titan's thigh, looking so exhausted she'd thought he'd tip over. It was a wonder he stood upright at all, what with all that extra weight he carried beneath the belt. She narrowed her eyes at her sixteen-year-old sister. "How do you even know about these things?"

"I read." Vivian snatched a book out of her carpetbag and flipped to a marked page. She handed the book to Cat. "Sir Burton's latest translation from the Arabic. *The Perfumed Garden*."

Cat glanced at the illustrations. "This is obscene! I don't want you reading this."

"Fine. I already have the good bits memorized."

Cat waited until her sister's back was turned before tucking *The Perfumed Garden* in her personal belongings for later.

The grandfather clock chimed six. "We've got to get you ready!" Vivian said.

As Vivian scrambled around the room in search of chemise, corset, and stockings—all the bothersome items it took to look presentable—Cat stood up and peeled off her towel.

Glancing over her shoulder, she examined the claw marks on her back. Four diagonal slashes running from shoulder to hip. She turned to the side. One of the slashes stretched as far as her abdomen.

Cat shut her eyes. The screams trickled in. This time, it was *her* screams. Loud. Shrill. Desperate.

A hand traced one of her scars, snapping her back to reality. In the mirror, Vivian frowned. "I'm glad you made it out, even if Da didn't." Her finger grazed the needle marks on Cat's inner arm. "But you've never really left, did you?"

◆

An hour later, bathed and dressed in a tuxedo, Rob followed the gentle drift of music to the parlor. He stood outside the door, adjusting his ivory cuff links and fiddling with his stiff collar and white bow tie. Waverley was playing the first movement of Mozart's Piano Concerto No. 9—over and over again.

Rob arched a brow, surprised to hear his sister so persistently practice the notes. It was good to see Waverley devote her time to something other than swordplay. But when he stepped inside the parlor, a vase crashed to the floor.

His sister was poised over what used to be a priceless Ming vase, wooden sword in mid-swing.

Rob massaged his brow. "I knew it was too good to be true."

Waverley shifted from foot to foot. "It was like that when I got there."

"I suppose it was a ghost, then?" His attention drifted to Jim Hawkins behind the baby grand, legs barely touching the floor.

Rob strolled to the piano in a daze.

Jim's tiny fingers danced across the keys. The boy repeated the same movement.

Rob looked to the book of sheet music; the book was closed. "Why is he doing that?"

"Because that's all I taught him."

Frowning, Rob glanced over his shoulder. His sister was squatting in a most unladylike manner and brushing the ceramic shards under the sofa.

"Smashing, isn't he?" she asked.

"You mean to tell me..." The movement repeated. Rob's eyes widened. "He *just* learned this afternoon?"

"He watched from over my shoulder." Waverley stood up and brushed her bare knees. There was already a smudge on the hem of her blue dress. "Then he plopped down and began playing." She lowered her voice to a whisper. "I'd keep an eye on him if I were you. He's tricky."

Flipping his tuxedo tails over the bench, Rob took a seat and watched Jim play. The boy reminded him of an automaton he'd fashioned out of spare clock parts at Eton. He'd been bored to death after blazing through that week's Latin conjugations and needed something to occupy his wandering mind. The model was crude, not nearly as intricate as the automatons he crafted now, but beautiful in its simplicity: a windup man with a keyboard. The man played four notes. C, D, E, F.

"Stop," Rob said softly. "Stop."

The music ceased. Jim's fingers hovered over the ivory keys. The boy glanced at him expectantly.

Rob scooted closer and cracked his knuckles. He played the second movement in C-minor, straight from memory. Rob finished with a flourish then raised an eyebrow at Jim.

Jim Hawkins cracked his knuckles and repeated the same notes. Not a perfect imitation, but eerily close.

"You rushed this part," Rob said, playing in demonstration. "It's a hard piece to learn. When I was your age, it took me about three tries to master."

Behind him, Waverley muttered, "Show-off."

"It might take you longer," Rob continued. "Don't feel bad, you've already surpassed Waverley in both skill and dedication, but I've many years on you and you can't expect—"

Flawless music drowned out the rest of his sentence. Rob's jaw dropped as he watched Jim repeat the piece.

Waverley nested her chin on his shoulder. "Told you he was tricky."

Not one to be bested by a child, Rob removed his cuff links and rolled up his sleeves. He took off the sapphire laird's ring and set it beside the cuff links.

"*Oh*," Waverley whispered in Jim's ear. "The ring is coming off."

120

"Try this one." He selected a frenetic composition he'd heard in London, at the newly constructed Albert Hall. The score reminded him of a hive of bees.

When he finished, Rob slumped against the piano bench, smug. Jim watched him with a cock of his head before rolling his sleeves up to the elbows.

Before Jim's fingers touched the piano keys, Rob took the lad by the wrist. "Wait!" He studied the undersides of Jim's arms.

As he ran a thumb over the grotesque burn marks, his eyes brimmed with rage-filled tears. "Who did this to you?"

Jim just blinked at him.

"His mum," Waverley said. "His foster mum anyway. Burned him with a poker and locked him in a shed until your hunter set him free."

Rob had difficulty speaking. He recalled Cat's strange words when they first met: *I killed his mother.* Apparently, this Catriona Mornay was a monster hunter in more ways than one. A new respect replaced some of the annoyance he felt for her.

He released Jim's wrist and the boy set to work, playing the composition until the parlor buzzed. "How do you know all this?" he asked over the music.

"Jim told me."

He turned to his sister. "He *speaks* to you?"

"Sort of. It's like I hear a voice in my head. The voice sounds like Jim, so I assume it's Jim." Waverley shrugged. "When he reclaims his throne, he says he plans to take Cat home and make her his queen. Since he likes me, he'll make me his Minister of War. He says I'm very wise."

"Right." Rob blinked. "His throne? So he's royalty, then?" This was directed at Jim, who sat up straight, just like a little prince.

Waverley nodded with a solemn air. "The heir to a very old fae dynasty. But there was a revolution when he was a babe and his mother sent him to our realm to keep him safe."

Rob sighed and reached for his ring and cuff links. "I envy your imagination, Duck." He received a punch to the arm. *"Ouch!"*

Waverley smacked him again. "I'm not making this up! Jim's got his return sorted out and everything."

"Oh, aye?" Rob arched an eyebrow. "When would that be?"

"Winter solstice. Every ten years," Waverley eyed Jim for confirmation, "there's a tear between the worlds. Come December, the gates to his kingdom open again."

Rob rubbed his arm. It was late June. "Where is his kingdom?"

"In the space between the trees," a voice answered from behind.

Rob jumped to his feet, knocking the back of his knees painfully against the bench.

Cat was the picture of awkwardness in an ill-fitting brocade gown the color of the deep blue sea. She scooted aside to let her sister into the parlor.

The sisters exchanged a knowing smile that made Rob burn with a new wave of mortification. Had Vivian told Cat about the ride?

Vivian, radiant in cream chiffon, floated in like a dream. She offered him a delicate, white-gloved hand, which he took absently. "Lord Robert, oh your house is simply divine…"

Rob nodded, eyes shifting to the monster hunter. Cat teetered into the parlor on unstable heels and spun around like a dog chasing her own tail.

"Lord Robert? Are you listening?" Vivian followed the direction of his gaze, sighing. "Cat, stop that! You're making a spectacle of yourself."

"I look like a camel and feel like a stuffed sausage." Cat swatted the crinoline frame beneath her gown and stared straight at him. "Well, Lord Robert. Now that you have us trussed up like peacocks, where shall we dine?"

Her eyes were melancholy even when mischievous, and despite his resolve to stay afloat, Rob found himself drowning in their blue depths—five fathoms deep.

♦

The monster huntress ate little and hardly spoke at all. From his place at the head of the table, Rob watched her peck at her veal like a bird.

During the salad course, she'd been her usual unpleasant self, pestering him about why Jim and Waverley weren't allowed to sit at the table.

"Because they're children," he said.

"Then why are you here?" Her eyes gleamed with a wicked light, but as the night wore on, the light went out.

"Is the meal not to your liking?" he asked out of politeness.

Cat peeked up from her untouched plate. Her complexion was bleached white, her lips drawn in a thin line of pain. A sheen of sweat beaded her forehead. "I'm not very hungry." She scooted her veal across the plate, soaking the roasted potatoes in blood. "Thank you."

Thank you? This was the first time he'd recalled her being nice. Rob turned to her sister for answers. Vivian watched Cat, brows knitted in worry.

"Is she ill?" he whispered.

She took a sip of her water. "You've read about my sister in the papers? About what happened to her…in the jungle?"

Rob nodded. He knew a thing or two about being haunted. At night, he'd watch the shadows claw along the wall and he was transported back to the woods. The monster pounced on his chest, dug its talons into his lung, and when he woke, choking and hacking, he tasted blood and knew the monster had won.

Rob looked to Cat once more. She scratched her inner arms, fingernails frantically clawing at silk brocade, and he wondered what unimaginable horrors lurked inside her head.

Setting his fork on the table, Rob folded his napkin into a meticulous triangle. He had also lost his appetite. "Might we have a word in private?" he asked Cat.

Sweat slid down her temple. She nodded. Her chair creaked as she stood up.

"Please excuse us," he said to Vivian. "The business of monsters."

After bidding goodnight to Vivian, Rob and Cat retreated to the parlor. A silver tray containing a single vial of medicine waited for him atop his piano. The serum glowed an unearthly green next to the kerosene lantern.

"Unbelievable," he muttered under his breath. After he'd expressly ordered Mrs. Nix not to badger him with the serum again, she was still force-feeding him like a babe. Wasn't he laird? Shouldn't his orders carry weight?

"What's that?" Cat stumbled toward the silver tray.

"A tonic for aches and pains and ailments of the lungs," he said, then added, "I don't need it anymore."

She picked up the vial, studied it in the golden lantern light. "Where did you get it?"

"It's my physician Dr. Jekyll's special concoction. Strange color, isn't it?"

"Splendid." Her tone was a caress reserved for a lover. The light returned, flickering in her irises, a gleam that reminded Rob of a maroon discovering a drinking hole. "Absolutely lovely...."

Rob cast an uneasy glance over his shoulder and gestured for the lingering footman to take the serum away.

The footman swept in. "Beg pardon, miss." He pointed to the vial. "May I?"

A dark squall clouded Cat's face. Her fingers closed around the vial. With great reluctance, she handed the serum over, eyes trailing after the silver tray until the footman disappeared from the parlor.

Back still turned, Cat cracked her neck and shook the tension from her shoulders. "Now that you have me alone, let us speak of tomorrow's hunt. 'Creature is large, fast, and dangerous,'" she quoted his advertisement. "Were you purposefully trying for vague?" She tapped a key on the piano. "What manner of monster are you hiring me to kill?"

"I've been thinking about this creature for some time." Rob took a deep breath. "What it is. How it got here."

Another discordant note. "You've seen it?"

"Only quick flashes, hence the 'fast.'"

"And? How large?"

"Eight feet at least."

She tilted her head. "Identifying characteristics?"

He'd harbored his suspicions, but given her history, Rob was afraid he'd scare her off and he couldn't lose another hunter. "My brother was going to teach me how to hunt," he said, easing her in. "It was supposed to be my birthday present. He was set on making a man of me, though I don't know why he bothered. After Alec... After he... I can still hear him scream. Even now—like an echo when I close my eyes. He appears in my dreams, always sad. He can't enter heaven until I find his head."

Cat shut the lid over the keys, but she didn't turn around.

"I've sent for transcripts of Hugh Mornay's lectures at the Society of Unnatural Creatures," he continued. "He spoke of a creature in the Congo so feared the local tribes worshipped her as a goddess. They called her 'The Great Mother' or *Banyale*, 'Eater of Men.' To appease her appetite, they'd send their *male* virgins into the jungle. It was considered a great honor to serve the Mother..."

Rob drew closer. Cat's hair was gathered in a chignon and his breath stirred the stray wisps on the back of her neck. "Miss, I read about the expedition. I read about you."

As she cringed, Rob forgot all about their petty squabbles. His heart contracted in sympathy for this lost and tormented girl. "When I went in search of Alec, I was so frightened, but I thought of what Cat Mornay went through and it kept me strong. And when the monster came for me, you kept me alive. I believe, Miss Mornay, that you've faced this creature before."

She whirled around. Her face drained of all color as if she'd just received her death sentence.

Rob fumbled in his pocket and pressed the monster's tooth in the palm of her hand. "Your father called the monster 'The Hand of the Devil.' In Latin, you know it as…"

Cat ran the flat of her thumb against the tooth's sharp edge. "Manu Diaboli."

CHAPTER 9
MANU DIABOLI

The tooth slipped from her hand and fell between the golden tulips on the Turkish rug.

Cat could see the same tooth ripping into the belly of a man and yanking out his intestines. Her back bumped painfully into the piano.

"Are you all right?" Rob stepped toward her, handsome features dissolving into a swiftly growing darkness. His hand stopped just short of her elbow. "Shall I call for smelling salts?"

"No smelling salts." Her nails worried at silk brocade. "I-I need…"

What did she need? The grandfather clock chimed eight. A black hole materialized in the corner, waiting to suck her in. There was a jungle in the nightmarish landscape of her mind where monsters and men were the same species. A scream echoed in her ear—a solitary drop in a well—soon to grow into a flood.

"Take me somewhere quiet," she pleaded. "Take me somewhere bright."

After a worried pause, Rob nodded. "Follow me."

He led her from the parlor. Cat shuffled close behind him. When he halted, she nearly collided with his back.

"Up," he gestured and they climbed the serpentine stairs in silence.

Cat's gaze shifted from each shut door and alcove. The shadows morphed into primal shapes, clawing across the portrait-lined walls, ready to slash into her.

On the third floor, Rob led her to a door at the end of the hallway. With a sweep of his hand, Rob ushered her inside. "Somewhere quiet, somewhere…"

In a daze, she strolled past him into a grand room with floor-to-ceiling windows. The stars blazed blue and bright, flooding the solarium with peace and light. Hitching in her breath, Cat exhaled as all her nightmares disintegrated into stardust.

She looked at Rob as if she'd never seen him before. He stood at the window, gazing down at the jagged crags and the swath of forest cloaked in night.

"I used to come here when I was a boy." With the stars at his disposal and the green world beneath his feet, Rob could be a prince in the kingdom of heaven. "I was never allowed to play outside with Alec. But here, I could be left alone to watch and dream."

His reflection in the glass pane smiled at her.

She smiled back.

A weighted silence passed between them; in it, bits and bobs of Cat's old life resurfaced through the Elixir haze. The sound of her mother's laugher. Her Da's tobacco-stained fingers. Her mother spoke eloquently, enunciating every syllable, but her Da's brogue was thicker than gooseberry jam. Cat shut her eyes. In the blessed quiet, she could see her parents in the solarium with her, their faces graced by bars of starlight, and for first time since her return to Scotland, Cat felt safe.

"Thank you," she whispered and meant it with all her heart.

Rob's lips twitched in surprise. "For what?"

As her father vanished, her mother lingered beside Rob. He was just the type of lad her mother nagged Cat and Vivian to marry. Handsome. Titled. Normal. A scholarly gent who didn't know how to wield a knife, let alone try to carve up her face. Maybe she should've taken Mother's advice to heart instead of running around with pirates and monster hunters. Cat fingered the stitching behind her ear. Too little, too late.

"For being a nice bloke," Cat said, watching Mother peck Rob on the cheek before fading away.

He stuck his hands in his trouser pockets and kicked a scuff on the hardwood. "I wasn't such a nice bloke before. Tossing you in the mud…" A swath of blond hair fell over his eyes. He brushed it back and glanced at her shyly. "I daresay it was ungentlemanly and unforgivable of me."

"Now that you've mentioned it," she said. "You were a bit of a wanker, weren't you?"

Rob flushed.

Seeing him looking absolutely gutted, Cat added, "Don't get your knickers in a knot, mate. I'm just taking a piss at you. Hope you can handle it."

"I could handle being…ha ha…pissed on," he paused, loosening his collar and standing up taller, "mate."

Fighting the urge to laugh, Cat circled a table crowded with ink-splattered papers. "What's this, then?"

Pages of what appeared to be a half-finished story overlaid elaborate architectural blueprints of ships and lighthouses. She passed her hand over a bell jar containing two wires bound by a copper hook and gasped as electricity crackled beneath her fingertips.

"Did you make this?" She touched the bell jar again, squealing with delight as the voltage caused her hair to stand on end.

Rob nodded. "It was a project for school. Father wanted me to become an engineer. We own a fairly profitable lighthouse company."

Tipping her head to the side, Cat smoothed out the blueprint. "Designed by you?"

A humble shrug. "I try to be useful."

His eyes followed her as she wandered to a cabinet of miniature windup figurines and automatons. Cat made her way down the line, marveling at the craftsmanship and attention to detail. A boy in a powdered wig at a piano. A magician sawing a lady in half.

Stars. Automatons. Electricity. Genius. Cat felt like she'd been whisked away—not to a solarium—but to a sublime region of the young laird's mind.

"Don't tell me you made these, too," she said.

"I won't tell you."

These infernal devices were just as intricate as the clockwork beetle Liam showed her during her training as a monster hunter. The beetle fitted in her palm and there was a glass chamber in the abdomen which could hold a thimbleful of Elixir. A thimbleful, Liam instructed, was all they needed for the task at hand. Cat searched the shelves for the same beetle. She found a colony of windup spiders and bees. Unable to locate this particular automaton, Cat breathed a sigh of relief.

"They teach you this in school?" she asked.

"I taught myself, actually," he said, rubbing the back of his neck. "Building an automaton is not so different from playing a sonata or fashioning the perfect sentence. Each is about trying to capture truth and beauty— to wind it in your hand or hear it float in a melody or watch an entire world take shape one word at a time."

Cat watched his face light up. "How young you are."

He frowned. "But I'm seventeen," he said as if that were some great accomplishment.

She shook her head. "I suppose you believe in a silly thing called love."

"Love's the only thing worth believing in," he said with a lift of his chin. "In this time of monsters."

"Not you, too." People were always misquoting her father. It annoyed her to no end. "*Golden Age* of Monsters."

"I know," Rob said. "But my brother was always saying 'Love in a Time of Monsters' and there's a poetic ring to that. I didn't hear it then, but I can hear it now." Sadness eclipsed his features, tucking down the corners of his mouth. "Too little, too late."

"Like I said, how young you are." A lump materialized in her throat. *Too little, too late.* She turned to the shelf. "Is there anything you're not ace at?"

"No."

Cat grinned over her shoulder. "You taking a piss at me?"

He rocked back on his heels but didn't say anything.

"Well, cheeky monkey, is there a hobby you don't have?" She couldn't drum up the slightest memory of her old hobbies and wondered if she had any ambitions outside of monster hunting. It seemed she dwelled in a vacuum before Africa, existing yet not really living, waiting to be born in blood.

134

"Hunting," he said softly.

"Aye. Leave the killing to me." Suddenly snatches of her younger self studying sheafs of hand-painted maps and old admirals' logs crystallized before her eyes. She turned to Rob in surprise. Somehow being around this boy and his marvelous inventions reminded her that before she was Mr. Hyde's mercenary, she was a girl with grand dreams of captaining her own ship and sailing the seven seas.

"A knight on water," she whispered. "Can you resurrect a dead dream?"

"I'm sorry?"

"Never mind." Cat picked up a man in a ruffled collar, doublet, and balloon-shaped britches. An Elizabethan gentleman by way of dress, the man fitted neatly in the palm of her hand. On his back, Rob had soldered a pair of wings.

"You've heard of the Aventine ballads?" Rob leaned against the edge of his worktable, so exhausted and wispy she could probably tip him over with her index finger.

Cat fingered the wings' filigree gold. "Da knew the old tales by heart. He used to recite them on the ship. 'In Aventine, sandstorms reign in place of men...'"

Aventine. A criminal colony turned empire, lost and buried under the red sands of modern-day Brisbane. Its name came from the "species of inauspicious aves" the first settlers encountered upon setting foot on shore.

Humans with wings.

The origin of the first monsters.

"But you're not in Aventine, are you?" Rob coughed into his fist. "You're in the jungle. I can see it in your eyes."

Cat dropped her attention to the figurine; the gentleman's copper features blurred in a watery haze.

"Miss Mornay..." Rob's gentle eyes pleaded with her. "Won't you tell me how it was?"

She'd never talked about Africa. Not to a living soul. But in this corner of Rob's universe, nothing could harm her.

"My mother was sick," she began, winding up the birdman. "Da was looking for a cure. He'd discovered a new species of monster, which he called *Manu Diaboli*. Shaped like Lucifer's Claw, though no one, with the exception of the natives, had ever seen her. Da was going to bring her back to Scotland and her arrival..."

Cat unfurled her palm and the birdman took flight, flapping around the solarium with a mechanical *buzz*. "...would be a wonder."

♦

Cat listened for the *buzzzzzz*.

Wiping the sweat from her forehead, she swatted the back of her neck.

Buzz.

Loud and clear in her left ear. Wings grazed her cheek. Cat waited for the daring little bugger to try its luck.

"You can't kill all the mosquitoes in the world, darling."

Her smile broadened at the sight of her father. Da, his khaki shirt soaked through, sloughed past her, hacking at the lianas with a battered umbrella.

Her palm came down on her forearm with a resounding *slap.*

"No." She lifted her hand. "But I can try."

"Cheeky miss." Lips twitching under his bushy black mustache, Da smacked her on the back with a rolled-up map. "Pick up the pace. We're almost there."

She peeled the mangled mosquito from her forearm. Her skin was a mass of red bumps and welts. "That's what you've been saying for the past two days."

"This time I mean it. We're nearly at the heart." Da whipped off his pith helmet and fanned himself. His cheeks were ruddy from the heat and his bushy sideburns glistened with perspiration.

Cat made sure the others weren't looking before brushing his sweat-matted hair back into neat lines, just as she'd seen her mother do.

Da's forehead crinkled; he was probably thinking about Mother, too. "I will make her well again."

"I know you will," she said, taking his hand.

The *clashing* of metal bars caused them both to jump. Cat squinted at the commotion ahead. The two men charged with hauling the collapsible cage had dropped it. Once the cage was assembled, it'd stand eight feet tall and serve as home for Manu Diaboli.

"Dolts." Propping his helmet back on, Da marched ahead to oversee the crew. "Treat it like a teacup."

Cat trailed behind the sailors, the runt of the litter behind fourteen of the *Hispaniola*'s strongest.

She made the fifteenth.

Cat scrubbed her shorn hair. When they'd boarded three months ago, her father introduced her to the captain as his son. Cat was as tall as most men, thin as a whip with no curves to speak of. She was blessed—or cursed, according to Mother— with breasts so nonexistent she never had to bind them. She ate little of the hardtack and pea mush to halt her monthlies, smoked cheroot until her voice grew raspy.

After three months at sea, her identity was neither boy nor girl. She was an ape climbing the rigging. A lizard crawling along the bowsprit. Da let her run wild. To practice her marksmanship, Cat shot the gulls from the sky and the fish from the sea. At night, Da taught her how to navigate the stars so as to always find her way home.

Then there were his stories, told as the ship rocked and the shadows yawned over bow and stern.

The blood of Manu Diaboli, brewed with belladonna, served as a stronger drug than mermaids' scales. The heart of the adult Manu Diaboli, when consumed, cured the sick and dying.

They'd barely made it to Africa. To fund the expedition, Da had curried all his favors with the Society of Unnatural Creatures, the Royal Geographical Society, and any Society worth their salt—and all their income.

A welcome breeze stirred the ferns. Cat clutched her pistol in one hand, dagger in the other. In the thick of the jungle, she remembered a trip to old Tron Kirk. She'd gone to light a candle and pray for a cure for her mother.

You look like you could use a friend.

A bowler hat on his head. A curved Bedouin blade at his hip. Liam Barclay's face was as flawless as the flock of cathedral saints. At the time, she thought she'd been visited by an angel—one with powerful friends.

Mr. Hyde would like to be your friend.

All of Edinburgh knew of Mr. Hyde, a drug lord never seen or heard, as ephemeral as fog.

Mr. Hyde has taken a special interest in you, your father, and Manu Diaboli.

Cat stepped under a colony of dangling orchids. Leathery petals, reminiscent of dead flesh, caressed her cheek and neck. She recoiled at the touch and fell in step beside the boatswain,

Bones, who was as ugly as Liam was beautiful. His squished face and bulging eyes reminded Cat of a toad.

One egg.

Cat brushed past Bones and slipped two silver doubloons into his grubby palm. A necklace of human fingers *clinked* as he pocketed the money.

Bring back one tiny egg.

They spoke nary a word, but she knew she would not be alone in this mission.

And you shall find Mr. Hyde can be very generous to his friends.

Bones was Mr. Hyde's friend, too.

The crew sloughed on, tramping through an alien world teeming with exotic flora and fauna. Despite the ache in her travel-weary joints and the damnable humidity, Cat's soul lighted with joy. She watched a yellow caterpillar with bright pink bristles crawl across a rotted log.

The canopy rustled.

A chorus of caws echoed across the cathedral of the jungle.

The men shuffled on booted feet, some reaching for their rifles. Even Bones tightened his grip on his machete. Her father pressed a finger to his lips. Da hadn't reached for his gun—in fact, he didn't carry one, trusting his life to the belief that monsters were God's creatures meant to live peacefully with man.

Cocking her pistol, Cat scanned the treetops.

The foliage exploded in a flurry of blue and gold feathers. Cat held her fire. Along with the others, she marveled at the swoop and grandeur of the macaws. She met Da's eye and smiled.

"I've never seen grown men get so worked up over a few birds." With a wink, he shooed the crew along. "Nothing to be afraid of, lads. This isn't Aventine. No aves here. Nothing to fear."

They entered a grotto surrounded by orchids of the deepest indigo.

Cat sniffed, detecting a dank stench that reminded her of fruit rotting in the cellar. She turned to the crew, but each man's attention was fixed on the nest. Da stumbled toward the nest on wobbly legs and knelt in front of the eggs.

Three massive eggs. Each the size of a man's head and as green as the Elixir sold in the alleyways back home. Da picked up one of the specimens, holding it up like an idol for the crew to see.

Sunlight streamed through a near-transparent shell. The embryo was curled up like a human fetus, except its back was hunched into an unnatural arch. Its face, pink and gilled around the ears, reminded Cat of a salamander's.

The egg pulsed and thrummed like a heart.

"Marvelous." Da's throat trembled with reverence. "Ten fingers. Ten toes. Just like us."

Despite the heat, Cat shivered.

"It's the wrong color," she said, recalling Da's etchings and the tribe's carvings. Manu Diaboli was supposed to have an exoskeleton as black as onyx.

"Its armor forms when the hatchling is one week grown…"

One week? Cat allowed this new fact to sink in. That fast? She checked the grotto once more.

"For now," Da smiled, "she's as vulnerable as a peeled grape. A true beauty…"

Cat differed from her father in her definition of beauty. All she could see was a repulsive fetus she wanted to squash beneath her boot.

Squatting on her haunches, Cat pried off a piece of the nest and rubbed the black pulp between her fingertips. She wiped the slime on her shirt and checked behind her shoulder. "Is there a father…a male Manu Diaboli?"

"Like the praying mantis, the Great Mother bites off the male's head after copulation. There's even one report, brought to my attention by the High Priest, that she has no need of a male at all, but lops off the bangers and beans of the tribes' sacrifices, inseminating herself with their semen." He turned the egg for better view. "Hence the humanoid characteristics of the embryo."

A collective gasp emanated from the crew. One man cupped his privates. The coxswain, Israel Hands, a man of few words until now, muttered, "Blimey," which summed up the feelings of the sailors. As the only girl in the crowd, Cat was only partially disturbed.

"In a world with no shortage of men, Manu Diaboli can breed anywhere. This creature," Da told his audience, "is a marvel of evolution."

Silence descended upon the jungle. One man crossed himself, but Cat paid him no mind. For all their boast and brawn, the sailors were a lot of superstitious ninnies.

Something of greater import gnawed at her.

Why was the creature's nest in plain view?

No camouflage. No cover of mud or leaves. Easily—almost insolently—accessible to any predator. *Like a spider luring flies into its web.*

Cat licked a sun sore on her bottom lip, eager to get out of here.

Da tucked an egg into his knapsack. When she reached for the other, he slapped her hand. Cat dropped the egg and glared at her father.

"Only what we need," he said. "One specimen and the mother."

"Why take the mother when you already have the egg?"

"We need the adult heart. The hatchling's heart will only buy her time, but the Great Mother's will cure her."

Da snapped his fingers and the crew hoisted the collapsible cage, filing out of the grotto like ducklings in a row. Bones folded his brawny arms and leaned against the trunk of a fig tree.

Meeting his eye, Cat snatched up the second egg and tossed it to him. The egg disappeared inside his leather knapsack. She stuffed the third egg in her own knapsack.

As she raced to join the men, the first screams began.

♦

The birdman glided toward Rob in a haze of gold. He plucked it from the air and set it next to his other creations. He'd designed the birdman of Aventine to fly home.

Cat was thousands of leagues from home. Her tale chilled him, particularly the genital-reaping part, which caused his own privates to roll up like a pair of socks.

"She slid from the tree—" Cat's story dissolved into a desperate whine. "She was magnificent. Tall and sleek. Her armor glinting in the sun like black diamonds. Manu Diaboli. Goddess. Mother. Idol…"

144

Hunched on the settee, she rocked back and forth. Rob's hand hovered over her knee. He doubted if his touch would calm her.

"The first man, Flint, was a hulking fellow with a face full of tattoos. She knocked his head clean off." Her fingers twined around her skirt, twisting and picking the blue brocade. "Flint stumbled against all of us until Da caught him in his arms. He sprayed Da's face with blood, showered the lot of us in a red rain. After that, the men screamed and hollered. Some tried to run. Some pissed and shite themselves. The braver blokes tried to fight back with pistols, machetes—" Cat clamped her hands over her ears. "She picked them off one by one."

"Cat. Stop." Gently, he pulled her hand away from her ears. "Come back. Come back to me."

"Da was one of the brave ones," she continued. "He tried to save the others. He never screamed when it happened. Perhaps he'd seen the victims and knew screaming was useless. S-s-s-s-s-she ripped out his throat…" She buried her face in the crook of her elbow. Acting on instinct, Rob gathered her into his arms. Cat dug her fingers into his back. Haunted sobs echoed in his ear.

"After Da," she pulled away, hiccupping, "Bones had his turn. He was not so brave. He tried to make a run for it. In the end, she tore him in half. Fourteen. She killed fourteen. Stamped them out like ants. Then she came after me."

145

Teetering between horror and curiosity, Rob asked, "What did you do?"

"I was not as brave as Da. I was faster than Bones, not as fast as Manu Diaboli. I ran and she jumped me from behind." Cat ripped at her collar, popping the silk buttons. Twisting around, she bared the puckered and pink skin on the back of her neck. "I like to say I faced death with dignity. In the end, I *begged*. But the Great Mother knew nothing of mercy. Every time I screamed, her eyes lolled back in ecstasy."

"Yet you escaped." Rob swept a strand of hair from her brow. He brushed a tear from her cheek with his thumb. "Your first monster."

She met his eyes. "My first kill."

"How?"

"She was so full by the time she got to me. Bloated like a leech gorged with blood. Da had a theory about monsters. He used to say 'All creatures of darkness crave the light and in their desire for what they could never have lies their weakness.' The Hand of the Devil was no exception. When she pinned me beneath her talons, Manu Diaboli could not help but look up."

"Up?" Rob asked. "Up to what?"

"To the sky. To pay homage to her god: the sun. That's when I saw the chink in her armor. A spot, right here…" Forming a fist, she thumped her beaded bodice so hard Rob winced. "As transparent as rice paper. And underneath, a

146

beauty pulsing and glowing like the rubies of forever in the Aventine ballads. I suppose no man or animal ever got as close as me. Lucky me. There it was—" Her hand grasped empty air. "—her heart right before my eyes. I struck with my dagger and ripped out her sodding heart."

Rob took it all in. Every gruesome detail. She'd overlooked one crucial piece of information. "What happened to the egg you nicked?"

Cat wiped the snot from her nose. Her face was puffy and red. Her skirt had ridden up past her stocking-clad knee. "It was in my knapsack," she answered in a dead voice. "I'd like to say I forgot to dump it out, but I wasn't in my right mind when I boarded the ship. The rest you've read. The second terror. A girl found beneath a pile of corpses." Her head drooped with shame. "The egg hatched."

Knees knocking together, Rob crossed to the window and braced himself against the pane. The briars of the Gates of Hell loomed like black pitchforks. Alec. Jenny and Brandon. Abernathy and the men.

All lost in the space between the trees.

All because of an egg.

An egg lifted out of greed.

By purpose. By accident.

By Cat Mornay.

Now Cat Mornay stood behind him. "You have every right to despise me," she said. "Your brother. Your friends. Their deaths are on my hands." A pause. "Do you…do you hate me?"

He studied her sad and broken eyes in the glass. Finally, he turned around. "We can't afford to hate each other."

Her face crumpled into a fresh wave of tears.

"But we're in a bit of a tight spot." He held out his hand.

Cat sniffled. "That we are."

As their fingers touched, Rob felt the spark again. He embraced the shock. After a while, he wondered how he'd ever lived without it. He gave her a soft smile, which she returned with a shy curl of her lips. Another moment of silence passed, but it was not at all awkward; in it, they'd become friends.

"It's a good thing I've hired a damn fine hunter," he whispered.

"As your hunter…" She clasped his hand tight, almost like she was afraid to let go. "I promise you this: I will bring back your brother's head. I will tear our monster limb from limb as her mother did my father and friends. Manu Diaboli will suffer, and I think I shall enjoy that very much…"

♦

"As far as The Hand of the Devil is concerned—"
Rob coughed.

"I am—"

Cough.

"—the Hand—"

Cough.

"—of God." Cat frowned as Rob stumbled away. "I say, you all right?"

He nodded before doubling over and hacking uncontrollably into his fist. *Cough. Cough. Cough.*

Trying to be helpful, Cat swatted Rob on the back. Her hand slammed between his shoulder blades. There was so little of him, this boy she thought a prince, that he could be made of starlight. Physically, he felt like he was made of sticks. One powerful swat and he could break in two.

The door opened without a knock. Finley creaked toward Rob with a green vial on a silver tray.

"Drink." Rubbing calming circles onto his master's back, Finley tipped the vial to Rob's lips. "Drink."

Cat peered over the old man's bony shoulders and spied Rob's scarlet face. "Is there anything I can do?"

"The laird needs his rest."

Forgotten in the chaos, Cat slinked out of the solarium and shut the door behind her. In the dark, she listened to the hollow and dirty echoes of Rob's coughing fit.

So much like Mother's.

Too much like Mother's.

The comparison saddened her. Why should she care? She hardly knew him.

And yet, he'd helped her surface from her nightmare. His kindness was a rare sun in this dark and unfriendly world. Pressing her back against the wall, Cat watched the shadows crawl across the ceiling.

"Nothing lasts." Hot tears dribbled down her cheek. "Nothing lasts but I'm indestructible." She slid to the ground, drew her knees to her chin, and wept as quietly as a mouse.

After a time, Rob's coughing ceased. Cat lifted her head. The door opened and Finley shuffled past her with the silver tray.

Rubbing her eyes, Cat fixed her attention on the half-empty vial.

Slowly she slipped off her shoes and followed Finley.

He led her down the stairs, knees groaning with each step. Cat glided behind him, drawn by the bobbing orb of Elixir. The sight made her body ache with longing. Elixir never failed to erase the pain from her heart and exorcise the demons from her head.

In the kitchen, her bare feet scuffed across the straw-covered floor. She darted in the nook behind the great stove and watched the old man fiddle with the pantry door. He disappeared inside, leaving Cat holding her shoes and staring morosely at the hanging shadows of pots and pans. There was a stray goose feather caught between her toes. She kicked it away; it floated through a hollow square in a floor grate. Cat watched the feather drift under the bowels of the castle.

At long last, the old man emerged from the pantry and lumbered up the stairs. She crossed the kitchen in two strides and unclasped the hook.

When she yanked open the door, an incandescent glow bathed the stone floor, the walls, her face...in green.

She'd found a treasure trove: row upon glorious row of Elixir.

Cat lunged forward, then halted in a spurt of shame. *What am I doing here?*

Was this a proper way to repay Rob's kindness? By plundering his medicine supply?

She recalled his coughs, so like her mother's, and the ceremonial grave dug for her father even though his remains rotted away in the jungle.

Cat scratched her arms.

Nothing lasts.

Everyone dies and turns to dust.

She was here to feel nothing.

Her question answered, Cat stepped inside.

CHAPTER 10
ELIXIR KISSES

The next morning, Rob discovered a curious assembly of weapons on the lawn.

Crossbow. Broadsword. Dagger. Rapier. Rifle. Pistol.

The rifle belonged to Alec. The broadsword, too, a Stevenson family relic from the days of William Wallace. Rob didn't recall giving Cat permission to raid his armory; then again, it wasn't as if he was putting the weapons to much use.

Rob surveyed the clearing. Sunlight streamed through the early mist, drawing halos in the air and casting a golden blanket over his estate.

He strained to see around the castle's corner for signs of Cat, but a secret part of him cringed at facing her after last night. Dr. Jekyll's serum quelled the burning inside his lungs, culled the congestion and coughs, and while he felt leagues healthier, Rob still wanted to crawl into a hole and die. When your butler spoon-feeds you in front of the girl of your dreams, well, there was no recovery from that. He'd seen himself reflected in her eyes: a poor sick boy, someone to be pitied, someone broken.

Pacing from one end of the weapon row to the next, Rob flipped open the cover of his hunter-case pocket watch. "Damn."

Snapped it shut. "Damn. Damn."

He kicked the rusty hilt of a broadsword. "Damn, damn, damn."

Where was Cat? They'd agreed her hunt commenced at dawn. The sun crept above the cloud bank; Cat was officially one hour late. He'd heard of monster hunters being prima donnas, but this was ridiculous.

Rob whirled around, nearly clocking Jim Hawkins with his elbow. "Bloody hell, Jim! Where'd you come from?"

The boy canted his head.

Rob shivered. He was bundled in wool and tweed, but the chill had a way of seeping under the layers. "How would you like it if I snuck up on *you*?"

Jim glared at him in challenge. *You can try.*

"You trouble me, Jim Hawkins." Rob studied the lad's shoes. Leather soles, cheaply shod, yet no more different than his immaculately polished riding boots.

Why didn't the boy make a sound?

Did he glide above the ground?

Did the blades of grass part for him?

"You wouldn't happen to be a ghost?"

Jim was silent.

154

Rob sighed. Of course. "Where's Cat?"

Jim motioned him aside and marched toward the weapons.

"So *you* raided my armory!" Rob followed him.

Sitting cross-legged on the lawn, the lad unearthed a stone from his pocket and a pair of scaly gloves. The gloves were forest green and about three sizes too big, but Jim took extra precaution slipping them on.

Once all five fingers were inside, the gloves shrank to fit his hand. With his hands protected, Jim picked up a rapier and began to polish the blade.

Iron. He's afraid iron.

Rob knelt beside Cat's quartermaster. He recalled Waverley's ludicrous story the night before. Jim Hawkins, changeling prince. Now the tale took on a weird sort of validity.

"Are those made out of real hydra-skin?"

Jim nodded.

"I read about them once in Mornay's *Book of Unnatural Harvests and Remedies.* They're only sold on the black market. Where'd you get them?"

Jim cocked his head toward the castle.

"Right. Cat. Do they really work?"

Jim paused, considering. He slid the top of his index finger along the blade, slicing through glove and skin. The lad held up his bleeding finger; both hydra-skin and human skin melded back together.

"Brilliant!"

Jim returned to his work.

"Is it true if you cut off a finger, another will regenerate? Or two will grow in its place?"

Stone grinded against steel. Jim was too busy to chat it up. Rob picked up the broadsword; a scaly hand slapped him on the wrist. He dropped the sword.

Jim bared his teeth in a snarl.

Savage little beast. Hands held high in surrender, Rob said, "Aye. Don't touch. I get it," then added, "Can I help?"

Jim's eyes narrowed into slits. Finally, the lad handed over the polishing stone as if bestowing a great favor.

Rob plucked the stone gingerly from Jim's fingers. "I'm very honored, Your Majesty," he muttered, garnering a disapproving shake of the head.

Giving the blade a few absent strokes, Rob peeked over his shoulder. Where in blazes was Cat? Was she not up to the task? Maybe she was afraid and decided not to face Manu Diaboli after all.

He wouldn't blame her. He was afraid.

Jim grasped his wrist, yanking Rob out of his reverie.

"What?"

Jim snatched the stone from his fingers and demonstrated the "correct" way to polish a blade.

"I think I know what I'm doing. I bet I could polish all these swords better and faster than you."

Jim delivered a hand gesture, which reminded Rob of Henri, son of a French diplomat come to board at Eton for a term. Henri smelled of cheese and was fond of such gestures. Suffice to say, Rob was quite offended.

"Is that the way of it?" Rob snatched the sword back. "A challenge!"

Jim produced another stone and readied a rapier.

"On your mark…" Stone poised over blade, Rob gave the castle a second glance.

Where the devil is Cat Mornay?

◆

"I'll tell Lord Robert you're unwell."

Cat shielded her eyes against the ungodly brightness. "Shut the curtains."

Her sister's bell-shaped silhouette darted toward the window and darkness descended upon the room.

A cool hand clamped her brow. "No fever," Vivian said, a deep frown materializing between her eyes. "Where do you hurt?"

Sprawled on her back, Cat threw an arm over her forehead and groaned.

"You've rings around your eyes as black as spades," Vivian said. "I'll tell him to postpone the hunt."

"No, no. I can do it."

"You're not even dressed."

Cat rolled to her side. Her clothes were draped across a chair, muddy boots scattered about the floor. Vivian was dressed in head-to-toe black, her hair pinned in a neat coiffure with a veil, also black.

"How very encouraging," Cat said. "You look like you're dressed for my funeral."

Vivian fiddled with her hairpins. "Once again, you are drunk on your own levity." She stripped off her veil. "Are you afraid?"

Easing herself up, Cat smiled. "Not a bit." In her lap, her hands twisted the sheets into knots. It would not do for Vivian to see her terrified. Let ordinary people be afraid. Monster hunters were beyond fear. "Indestructible, remember?"

"But Cat! Even after what Lord Robert told us over supper. All those deaths. His brother and the village men. That poor Coyle girl. The last hunter." Vivian gnawed on her bottom lip. "What if you... What if?"

Cat cupped her sister's face. "I kill monsters. That's what I do." She swiped an eyelash from Vivian's cheek with the callused pad of her thumb. "I'm good at what I do."

Vivian smoothed the wrinkles from her skirt and lingered by the bedside.

Cat leaned against the headboard. Despite the morning chill, her chemise clung to her chest in a film of sweat. "Go on now. I'll meet you down on the lawn."

At the last moment, her sister paused at the doorway. "Even you are not invincible, dummy. If you were smart, you'd be afraid."

Cat chucked a pillow at Vivian. "Piss off!"

In a flounce of black taffeta, Vivian slammed the door. Her sister's warning wormed its way into her head and left a painful nick on her heart. Cat stripped the blanket from her legs and dropped to the floor.

She unearthed a bundle from under the bed. Unrolling her stash, she studied the contraband: three vials of precious Elixir.

Rob's so-called "Dr. Jekyll's cough serum" *was* Mr. Hyde's Elixir. She recognized the color at first sight, an incandescent green that could only belong to one creature. Before her first harvest, Liam had revealed some of their employer's trade secrets. Crushed mermaid scales, consumed in moderation, brought temporary relief from aches and pains; in concentration, it was a hallucinogen.

Cat filled the syringe to the top mark, but paused with the needle midway to her arm. Her skin was so bruised she couldn't spot a vein. A green droplet gathered on the needle's head and plopped on her lap.

At the station, she'd promised Vivian she'd never touch Elixir again.

She'd sworn on their parents' souls.

At the time, she'd been full of good intentions.

At the time, she wasn't about to face Manu Diaboli. Surely if Vivian knew what they were up against, she wouldn't deny Cat one last shot.

"This is the last time," she whispered.

With trembling hands, Cat jammed the needle into the big blue vein of her inner thigh. As the Elixir coursed through her bloodstream, Cat shut her eyes. When she opened them again she'd ceased to be afraid.

♦

Rob was making small talk with Vivian when he heard the hunter.

The sound of her laughter mingled with the drizzle. Rob turned his head to find Cat approaching them with a bounce in her step.

Her trousers hugged long, shapely legs. Her flimsy blouse left nothing to the imagination.

Rain aggregated on his lashes; Rob blinked the droplets away for a better view.

Here was Cat Mornay strolling out of his dreams. Brave. Cocksure. Huntress. Killer. Legend.

Cat halted by the armory. She lifted the hilt of a rapier with her toe and caught it one-handed. Slashing the air, she tossed the rapier to Jim. "No."

Only after he exhaled did Rob realize he'd been holding his breath.

As Cat picked up another rapier and began to teach Waverley how to fence, Vivian whispered in his ear, "It's all a game to her."

Rob gave Vivian's mourning gown a once-over. He didn't have the heart to tell her that black wasn't doing her complexion any favors. Vivian was undoubtedly the bonnier one, but this morning, she seemed colorless and ordinary compared to Cat.

"What was that?" Rob asked, unable to tear his eyes from Cat as she advanced and parried with one hand tucked behind her back. She was an artist with a blade, painting the air with poetry.

"… easy for her to go off on her hunts," Vivian sniffled, "but it's hardest for the ones left behind." That said, Vivian burst into tears.

"Oh. Oh no. Oh miss, don't cry."

Vivian only sobbed harder. "One day she will die! I know it!"

Rob fumbled for a handkerchief. Christ, this girl cried more than anyone he'd ever seen. He shifted from foot to foot, watching her dab at her runny nose, though she sounded so nasally he couldn't hold his tongue any longer. "It's all right to blow your nose in front of me."

She shook her head. "No, I can't."

"Please do." If one sister can parade her breasts in broad daylight, why can't this one blow her bleeding nose? "I won't judge."

"Lord Robert!" Vivian's red-rimmed eyes widened. "How can you ask this of me?"

Oh for the love of God! "It's Rob. I told you to call me 'Rob.' Indulge me. Blow. Your. Nose."

Casting him a sidelong glance, Vivian moved from earshot, turned her back, and quietly blew her nose.

Rob rolled his eyes. When she returned, she appeared thoroughly debased and had nothing to say to him, which was a fine thing since everything that came out her mouth ended in tears anyway.

Eager to escape the weeper, Rob joined the action just as Cat whacked Waverley's sword to the ground. "No, not this one either."

"But you were so good with it," Waverley insisted.

"Doesn't feel right."

"What about this one?" Waverley handed her a broadsword.

Cat patted Waverley on the head.

"Don't stroke my head," Waverley said.

"Short people, stand back!"

Rob realized she liked to call the children "short people." He thought it was funny and true, but Jim and Waverley were not amused. The short people scurried out of the way as Cat hacked at invisible monsters.

"Too heavy." She handed the sword back to Waverley, who gazed upon the weapon in wonder.

Making her way through the armory, Cat pointed at her long-barrel pistol and green dragonbone dagger. "These are all I need." Slapping her hands together, she held her arms wide. "Suit me up, Jim, I'm ready."

As Jim strapped a holster around Cat's shoulders, Rob strained to see her eyes beneath the shadow of her wide hat. What happened to the sad and broken creature who confided her darkest secrets to him? He missed that girl. As alluring as Cat the legend may be, she hardly spared him a passing glance.

When he recalled how he embarrassed himself hacking in front of her, he felt the tips of his ears burn like fiery coals.

Darting back and forth, Jim jammed an extra pistol in her holster. He knelt down, raised the hem of her trousers and bound the curved dagger to her ankle with a leather strap.

With the arming finished, Jim stepped back and Cat hoisted a knapsack over her shoulder.

Her hat-obscured gaze fell on Rob and Vivian. "What's this? Who's this silly girl crying on my behalf?" Strolling right past Rob, Cat headed straight for her sister. "Dry up those tears, sweetling, I'll be back before the midday meal." She wiped Vivian's tears on her sleeve. "We're all right?"

Vivian nodded.

"Good." She pointed at her cheek. "Give us a kiss."

Afterward, Cat knelt before Jim. The two stared at each other and something of great importance passed between them. "Well, demon child, what do you have to say for yourself?"

Jim, as usual, said nothing.

"That's what I thought." Cat brushed the droplets from Jim's shoulder. "Give us a kiss."

Jim pecked her on the forehead.

Cat turned to Waverley.

"Don't expect me to kiss you," Waverley said.

"I wasn't going to ask."

"Then why look at me?"

"Because I'm down here. At your level." Cat stood up. Her hand descended upon Waverley's head.

"And don't stroke my head!"

At last came Rob's turn. His stomach twisted into knots as he waited for her to ask for a kiss. She could also stroke his head if she wanted.

Instead, she brushed past him. "Walk me to the woods. We've the matter of my fee to discuss."

"Right." At least with her back turned, she couldn't see his disappointment. Un-kissed. Un-stroked. What a blue morning this was shaping up to be.

He trailed behind her like a lovesick puppy, waiting for a word, a friendly glance, but the legend gave him nothing. While she treated him like he was invisible, Rob was intensely aware of her every movement.

The swish of her trousers between her thighs.

The scuff of her heels against the rocky hillside.

The brush of her sleeve against his arm.

Rob led her to the same jutting rock where he'd stopped to rest the morning of Alec's death. He even spotted the pencil he'd dropped when Alec screamed. As he bent to pick it up, Cat whirled around.

"I guess this is it," she said.

"Guess it is." His words were weighted with regret. He didn't want her to go into the woods, which was ridiculous since he was paying her to do exactly that.

"Well…" Cat rocked on her heels.

"Well?"

"About my fee."

"Oh yes." Rob dug into his breast pocket for the notes.

Her hand wrapped around his wrist. "Give the money to my sister," she said as she considered the foreboding fortress of trees. Sadness bent her mouth into a frown. "Right." She swatted him on the arm. "Farewell, then."

Rob swallowed, but he swatted her back. "Take care."

Nodding, Cat walked exactly three steps, and halted. "Sod it," she muttered and stomped back toward him.

"I beg your par—" Her lips mashed against his and the last part of his sentence sounded like "Mmmmph!"

Locking her arms around his neck, Cat slammed him against the rock. A jagged edge jammed against his lower spine. She pressed her body tight and—

Dear God was this happening?

Rob kept his eyes wide open. Cat's sooty lashes fanned her cheek. His hand hovered over her back but he couldn't bring himself to touch her, much as he wanted to. His lips were frozen and Cat was…Cat was… Cat was…

Cat pulled away, breathless. Her lips were pink and swollen. "Kiss me," she whispered in his ear, "stop being so stiff and have a little fun."

When her tongue slipped between his lips, a switch went on. He wrapped his arms around her and dissolved into sublime happiness.

The kiss was short. But if he were to die tomorrow, he'd have no regrets. Most people took a lifetime to realize the desires of their hearts, but Rob didn't have a lifetime.

A moment was all he had.

He grasped it and gave everything of himself.

A moment was all it took to fall in love.

"Open your eyes."

Rob shook his head. His entire body glowed as if he'd swallowed the sun. "I don't want to."

Her lips brushed the underside of his jaw, papery soft as butterflies' wings.

Cat's wild laughter echoed across the glen.

Rob blinked the drizzle from his lashes. The kiss had knocked her hat off. At last, he looked into her eyes and his spirit, which had been soaring so high, plummeted back to earth.

Her pupils were dilated.

She was high.

And the kiss?

An illusion.

Meaningless to her, but so real to him.

Cat retrieved her hat. Noticing nothing amiss, she propped it atop her head. "To be continued," she said, inching in for another kiss.

Rob jerked his head away. She seemed unfazed by his coldness. He doubted if she'd remember any of this later and the thought, quite simply, broke his heart.

With a confident smile, she turned to go.

Rob slowly slipped back to his senses and a more pressing danger eclipsed his wounded ego. In a half-panic, Rob caught her by the elbow.

She glanced at his hand. "What's this?"

"Don't go."

"Why ever not?"

"You're not fit to hunt."

She freed herself. "A little faith…" Whirling on her heels, she broke into a run.

"Cat!" Rob jogged after her, but he was no match for her speed. Bracing his hands on his knees, he watched her slip inside the silvery fringe of trees and wondered if he'd ever see her again.

CHAPTER 11
IN THE HAND OF THE DEVIL

Midway into the woods, the drug receded from Cat's bloodstream. These low tide moments were the worst.

Under the spell of Elixir, she could slay dragons and harness the ephemeral starlight of the universe. When the drug wore off, she was small, afraid, and the universe, of which she was so recently the master, became a vast and crushing weight.

Her body was one raw nerve, yet she trekked deeper into the forest.

The more she trekked, the darker the sky became.

The darker the sky became, the more she hurt.

The more she hurt, the more she longed for Elixir.

The more she longed for Elixir, the more she forgot where and who she was. Cat walked in circles, a lost soul spiraling through Hell.

A pheasant squawked in the nearby bramble. Her boots squished black peat and her cheeks froze in the chill.

A cluster of elms paved way to a clearing. Cat sniffed the air, recoiled. The stench earned top marks in her book, far more repugnant than her memory of the jungle.

Cat clutched the ivory handle of her pistol tight. "Once more into the breach, dear friend," she muttered, and stepped between the trees.

Da's words rang in her ears.

In a world with no shortage of men, Manu Diaboli can breed anywhere. This creature was a marvel of evolution.

Cat stripped off her hat and stared at the nest. "Bugger me."

♦

"Bugger her." Rob had better things to do than mull over Cat. Or her kisses. Or the troubling fact that she'd dashed off to hunt a monster—*the* monster—under the influence of a powerful hallucinogen.

In an attempt to keep his mind occupied, Rob spent the morning composing an extensive letter to the one friend he made at Eton, who, strangely enough, didn't actually attend Eton.

He'd blazed through five pages detailing every unfortunate thing that had happened—which mostly consisted of meeting Catriona Mornay—when he set down his fountain pen. What was he doing? His friend never replied to a single one of Rob's letters.

Besides, the conversation felt one-sided whenever the topic of girls arose. He was always the one who rambled on about a fleeting crush, but for as long as he remembered, his friend never volunteered any information about the girls he fancied. In fact, whenever he mentioned a girl, his friend became curt and evasive.

Frustrated, Rob set the letter aside and stepped to the floor-to-ceiling window of his solarium. He observed the fae woods, but the thought of Cat broke his heart all over again.

He considered himself cautious in most things. His world was governed by the immutable laws of reason. The shortest route between two points was a straight line. Cat kissed him, ergo, she must've fallen for him as hard as he fell for her. He'd taken a leap in logic and fallen flat on his face.

Rob sighed. When it came to people, he was horribly blind.

Down below, Jim and Waverley darted between the herb garden and the octagonal glasshouse. As Rob watched the sneaky lad disappear behind a hedge, a spark of inspiration struck. He dashed for his supply drawer, rummaging for the materials he'd need to keep his mind occupied.

A length of wire as fine as mermaid's hair.

Tiny copper bells.

Pliers. Tweezers.

Rolling up his sleeves, Rob dove into his new project. A distraction was just the cure from her…

Her eyes.

Her lips.

Her phantom kisses.

And the loss of something that never really existed in the first place.

♦

Cat cocked her pistol and approached the nest as if it were a cobra.

The nest was grounded, plainly—almost arrogantly—left in the open for a lynx or boar to feast upon the eggs.

Three was the magic number.

Three eggs. Emerald green and resplendent. A translucent shell hugged the black blob of the embryo. In a certain slant of light, the eggs pulsed like a heart and as Cat drew closer, she saw the embryo looked even more human than in the jungle.

The nest, too, had been improved upon. Instead of twigs, mulched grass, mud, and brambles, this Manu Diaboli employed a different building material.

Cat gritted her teeth. Monster hunters do not retch and she prided herself on a cast-iron stomach, but at the moment, she was about to reel and spill.

A finger poked out of the peat.

Next to it, a leather boot with soles flopping like a rubbery lip.

A child's bare foot.

A man's forearm.

An entire torso, still clothed in bloody grey wool, and several heads in various stages of decay. She recognized the former hunter by his tattooed face.

Cat circled the human nest with equal parts repulsion, terror, and awe.

"Oh Da," she whispered, "If only you were alive to see this…"

Her father was right. Manu Diaboli was adapting and breeding. This was evolution in the making.

As Cat drew closer, one head in particular caught her attention.

His skin had softened to pulp, his lips twisted back to reveal his molars. A maggot wiggled through his eye socket and the cadaver was coated in slime. Despite the state of decay, she could see the family resemblance in the straight nose and noble brow.

"Alec."

♦

After completing his project, Rob set out to find Jim. He jogged downstairs to the parlor, poked his head in the great library, and startled the maids in the kitchen.

"Don't mind me," he said after the chorus of "milords." "Have you seen the monster hunter's ward? Creepy, toe-walking lad about—" He placed a hand around hip level. "—yea high?"

"No, milord."

Rob ventured inside the herb garden and checked behind the lavender bushes. He ducked inside the greenhouse, where orchids and mangos thrived in the artificial humidity. No Jim. Or Waverley, for that matter, who tagged after the lad as if the two were joined at the hip.

Back in the cold, Rob was just about to head home when he spotted a stoic lad about "yea-high" toe-walking about the lawn.

A devious idea took root. He plastered himself against the castle corner and waited. As Jim glided by, Rob jumped out and yelled, "Ah ha!"

His "Ah ha!" was aimed at nothing.

Rob blinked, confused. So much for sneaking up on Jim. He could've sworn he saw...

He felt a tug on his jacket. Rob whirled around. "AHHHH!"

Jim stared up at him and shook his head. *Amateur.*

Something smacked him between the shoulder blades. This other one was not so quiet and twice as annoying. "*What were you trying to do to Jim?*"

Waverley crept up to his other side. While Jim looked as normal as a demonic changeling boy could look, Waverley had painted half her face blue.

"Duck!" There were actual duck feathers in her hair, along with pheasant, goose, and rooster. "What did you do to yourself? Wait till Mrs. Nix sees you, poor lady will have conniptions."

Jim and Waverley backed him against the wall.

Dear God, I've angered the short people.

His sister poked him in the chest with the tip of her wooden sword. "Declare your intentions and we shall decide if your pathetic life is worth sparing."

Rob squinted at her face. "You got into my art supplies, didn't you?"

The sword was at his throat. "Confess, infidel! You were trying to assassinate Prince Jim." Waverley stepped on his foot.

"Stop that, you'll scuff up the polish on my boots!"

"Know what we do to royal assassins? We feed them to the beast!"

"Who's the beast?"

"BEAST!"

A bark answered her call. Virgil romped up to Rob and nuzzled his shin. He stuck out his hand and received a sloppy lick to the palm. "I'm really scared."

"Beast is a turncoat," Waverley whispered in Jim's ear. Jim seemed more disappointed than shocked.

175

"Spare my life, Your Majesty." Rob fell to his knees before Jim. "I come bearing gifts. I made this for you."

Jim pointed at himself. *Me?*

"Aye, you," he said, fastening a bracelet of dangling copper bells onto the lad's wrist.

"What about me?" Waverley asked.

"You're not royalty."

"Hmph!"

Jim studied the gift, then him. He shook the bracelets and the bells chimed. Finally, Jim patted him on the head.

Waverley said, "His Majesty approves. You may keep your life…for now."

Pardoned, Rob rose to his feet. He'd charmed a prince, thwarted a ferocious beast, and now there was a much less pleasant task to attend to. "I've a civil dispute to settle in the village. Chicken theft, messy business. Join me? I'll need your sage advice."

Jim nodded.

Rob glanced in the direction of the woods. Two hours and counting. "After you…"

Head held high, Jim took the lead and a jingle heralded his every step. Rob hid a smile, for the sound of bells was the sweetest music of all.

◆

Cat grabbed a handful of Alec Stevenson's hair and yanked.

The head loosened from the nest with a suction and film of slime. Fighting the urge to gag, she shoved Alec in her knapsack. Out of sight. Out of mind.

Slinging the knapsack over her shoulder, Cat doubled back and scanned the canopy.

Working quickly, she looped a leather belt around the trunk of the tallest elm and climbed up as nimbly as a monkey.

At the top, Cat made a comfortable perch in the branches and surveyed the entirety of the clearing. No squirrel, woodcock, or hare could dash in or out without her notice.

Cat drew her pistol, cocked it. "This time, you scurvy bitch," she aimed for the nest, "this time you come to me."

◆

Seated upon a knee-high stone wall, Rob folded his arms and tried to look serious. Per Waverley's advice, this was accomplished by frowning. His face hurt from frowning. He liked to smile, but it often made him look all of twelve years old.

"Shake your head," Waverley whispered in his ear. "Try to appear annoyed. Old people always look like they're in a nark."

So Rob relived his fake kiss with Cat and his face became the picture of solemnity. "Mrs. Andrews…" He gestured to a beak-nosed woman who reminded him of the Aves in Aventine. "You accuse the Muir brothers of stealing your prized cock."

At the mention of "cock," the two brawny twins snickered until their grandfather, an old man as gnarled as petrified wood, slapped them both upside the head. They hushed up.

"The lads," their grandfather stepped forward, "had no part in the strangling of this old harpy's cock."

"No part, my arse!" Mrs. Andrews pointed a bony finger at the old man. "And that's not all. Maybe you should ask this old coot where his thieving hell spawns hid my newborn calf."

"What a load of codswallop!"

"Shut up, the lot of you." Waverley axed the air with her wooden sword. "Let the laird speak."

"Now, madam," Rob massaged the spot between his eyes, "Alec already sorted out the heifer heist last month. Let us speak of the chickens. Jim! Bring the evidence."

With one of Cat's rifles slung across his back, Jim resembled a toy soldier. At Rob's command, Jim held the dead rooster up by the feet.

"I've witnesses who say they spotted two redheaded lads carrying a squawking burlap sack."

"Shame," Waverley piped in. "For shame!"

Jim shook the evidence, rattling the cock's wattle and jiggling the bells on his royal bracelet.

The Muir twins dropped their heads, stout legs kicking pebbles.

"The two suspects stopped by the bakers and stuffed their freckled faces with Dundee cake and spiced plums, burlap sack clucking..."

"Confess," Waverley said. "Save yourselves."

Jim sighed and shook his head in disgust. Rob could learn a lot from Jim.

Twisting the sapphire ring on his thumb, Rob peeked over his shoulder at the woods. Three hours and counting.

Rob righted the ring and set about his duties. "I've made my decision..."

♦

There was a cramp in her leg.

If she didn't move soon, she was in for a bout of pain. Cat kicked the kink from her calf. She carried no watch, but used the splotches of light to measure the time. High noon and the only creature to come within range of her pistol had been a hare.

The stench from Alec's head made her own head ache. Flashes of this morning leaked in with the pain.

179

His lips were soft, eager, and tasted faintly of Earl Grey and lemon. His body had felt so fragile in her arms, yet she had felt…against her leg…and *that* hadn't been fragile in the least. Vivian hadn't been exaggerating; her sister would kill her.

Cat groaned and banged her head against the trunk. She didn't think it was possible to die of mortification until now.

"Why did I do that? Why? Why? Why?"

Elixir was to blame. But if she had to be honest with herself, it hadn't all been the drug's fault. She'd never met such a soul completely devoid of deception. And when she saw herself through his eyes, she was a knight. She'd *wanted* to kiss him, to taste, if only for a moment, some of that goodness.

All creatures of darkness crave the light.

She was no exception.

A rustling in the neighboring foliage diverted her attention. She lifted her head. The chaos came from ahead.

Cat braced her pistol on her forearm and aimed.

"Come on, you ugly…" A bead of sweat dribbled down her lip. She licked it away, tasting salt and panic and fear. The branches rattled and snapped; the leaves rasped and whispered. "Come on. I got you."

The shaking ceased, sealing the forest into a vacuum of silence.

A lynx scampered out on a limb, leaped onto a lower branch, and vanished from sight.

Letting out her breath, Cat slumped her shoulders. She removed her finger from the trigger; her thumb slid off the hammer with a *click*.

Which was followed—

By a different *CLICK*.

Click.

To her right.

Click. Click.

Every muscle in her body froze. She saw the forest in micro detail.

An ant crawling across the back of her hand.

The dirt beneath her bitten fingernails.

Every sound was magnified.

Click. Click. Click.

A puff of rancid breath stirred her hair.

Slowly, Cat turned. What she saw was her own skinny face—seven faces, in fact—reflected in the prism-eye of death. Seven mouths gaped in an O of horror.

Her gaze traveled to the monster's scissor pinchers. "Oh…"

The creature's maw opened; dagger-like teeth dripped with slime.

She swung her pistol around and Manu Diaboli pounced. Cat's screams cleaved through the forest as hunter and monster tumbled to the ground.

♦

The rooster tumbled to the grass, dead eyes staring at the sky.

"Lord Robert?" Mrs. Andrews poked her beak nose into Rob's face. "You've decided...?"

"I've dec—" Rob studied Jim's tense profile, turned toward the Gates of Hell. "Jim? What is it? Waverley, what's wrong with him?"

"I don't know. I can't hear him." Waverley passed a hand over Jim's face. "Jim? Jim?"

Jim barely blinked.

"When I speak to him," she said, "it's like I'm yelling into a seashell and he always answers back. All I hear now is my own echo."

In the grips of some hypnotic trance, Jim hopped over the fence and marched toward the woods.

"Odd little creature," said Mrs. Andrews. "Where'd he come from?"

"Shhh!" Rob frowned at the eerie cant of the boy's head. "What's he up to?"

Following Jim's lead, Rob clambered over the wall and stood in the clearing beside the lad. Something was stirring in the air, a subtle shift in pressure that no one saw or heard, but everyone felt like the passing of a ghost.

This is the prologue to a bad, bad thing.

As if reading his thoughts, Jim lifted his rifle and aimed at the fae woods.

Rob watched the lad's pointy ears twitch and turned to his shivering sister. He motioned her over and she ran into his arms.

A wail echoed from the canopy. Waverley jumped an inch off the ground.

A second shriek trailed in wake of the first.

BOOM. Gunshots. BOOM. BOOM.

The foliage rumbled. Saplings snapped and bent like bows. BOOM.

One final shot.

"RAWWWWRRRRR!" The nails-on-chalkboard screech belonged to Manu Diaboli.

Rob squinted through the mist. The trees ceased rustling and someone or *something* lurched toward them.

"Rob?" Waverley whimpered.

Rob's stomach twisted and twined. He wanted to run, but his legs were frozen to the spot. He looked to Jim, who readied his rifle, finger on the trigger.

As the thing lumbered closer, Waverley clutched his blazer. "Rob!"

At last the mist dispersed and Cat limped right out of Hell. Her face was white as winter, her blouse and trousers dirty and slashed, but what did it matter? Cat Mornay, hunter, legend, was alive.

The trio's shoulders sagged in relief. Rob pressed a hand over his hammering heart, legs bucking as he fought the urge to sink to the ground.

She halted in front of him, her eyes unblinking silver pieces. Like a sleepwalker, she tossed the slimy knapsack to her quartermaster.

Jim caught it, reached inside, and pulled Alec's head out by the hair.

"I brought him back." Her lips curled into a strained yet triumphant smile. "As promised."

"Did you kill her?" Rob asked.

"After the thrashing I gave her? I should say so."

"But are you sure she's dead?"

Her smile wavered. The fingers on her right hand twitched.

He nodded. *She didn't know.* "At least you're all right," he said, looking her over. She was a sight to behold, but didn't appear mortally wounded. "Are you hurt?"

"It wasn't all Elixir." She limped toward him, dragging her left leg. Lines of pain bracketed her mouth.

They both glanced down as a ribbon of blood seeped through her trousers.

"It was because I wanted to…I wanted…wanted you." Her knee snapped in two, bone through skin, and Cat Mornay collapsed into his arms.

CHAPTER 12
BIRDS OF PREY

Rob tapped Vivian on the shoulder. "How is she?"

He saw the answer in Cat's face. Her skin was drawn like a mummy's, chapped lips twisted in a rictus of agony. Sweat-matted hair tangled around the pillow like black adders. Even so, she glowed with the kind of tragic beauty which only surrounded heroes.

Cat Mornay was a hero.

He'd been a fool to think otherwise.

After the hunt, Rob had her moved upstairs to a palatial bedroom with a grand four-poster bed and a roaring fireplace. If Queen Victoria came to call at Balfour Manor, this would be the bedroom he'd put her in.

In the days since Cat's hunt, there had been no more deaths or unearthly screeches and the only animals that disappeared could eventually be found in the Muir twin's barn. For killing Manu Diaboli and bringing Alec back home, Cat deserved to be treated like royalty.

"You've telegraphed your doctor?" Vivian's golden hair had come loose from her braids and her eyes were puffy from tears.

"He's boarded a train. He   says three days…"

"Three days is too long." Vivian's lips trembled. "She used to say she was indestructible."

"She still is." His eyes traveled to Cat's splinted left leg. He'd seen the damage firsthand; beneath the bandages her kneecap was ground meat. When Mrs. Nix changed the linens, the wound stank of festering death. "Any one of us would be dead already."

Gathering her shawl around her shoulders, Vivian soaked a washcloth in a basin of cool water and dabbed her sister's forehead. She swayed and stifled a yawn.

He took the cloth from Vivian. "Go to bed. If her condition worsens, I'll send Jim to wake you."

Left alone, he pulled up a chair and felt Cat's brow. He could fry an egg on her head. She wore a thin chemise and her bare arms were a mass of purple bruises. His hand hovered over the needle marks. Not for the first time, Rob wished people were as easy to fix as his automatons. He would like nothing better than to erase the track marks from her arms and exorcise the demons from her mind.

"Be indestructible." He raked a hand through his hair. "Stay alive for three more days."

"Should we kill it now?" Her eyes flickered beneath her lids.

Rob poked his head up. "Who are you talking to?"

Her hands clawed the sheets. "Let me. I'll…"

"Where are you?" Rob brushed the matted hair from her temples. "Where are you?"

"I'll make her suffer." Cat whimpered. "I'll kill them all…"

♦

"I'll make her suffer…"

Dragonbone dagger at the ready, Cat peered past the brim of Liam Barclay's bowler hat. A leathery wing slapped against her shin. The harpy, pinned beneath Liam, uttered a shriek that bounced off the slate mountainside. A chorus of screeches answered her distress call.

Cat tilted her head to the sky.

Two sleek silhouettes swooped through the cloudbank, their wings eclipsing the sun. The harpies circled the summit of Ben Nevis and perched on the highest ledge.

Moments before, she'd surveyed the nest through a spyglass. Five adults. Three babes. Four speckled eggs. A colony constructed from rocks and twigs.

Recalling Africa, Cat curled her fingers into fists. "I'll kill them all."

With a grunt, Liam slammed the butt of his pistol against the harpy's skull. "Mr. Hyde told me you were an eager learner," he said, studying her over his shoulder. A smile played across his lips. His profile was chiseled perfection against the misty glen and slate mountain range. Hopping to his feet, Liam slapped his hands together.

The harpy, a wee one, was still, but her tawny-feathered chest rose and fell. Her skin and features were disturbingly humanlike, but her magnificent beak glimmered like black diamonds in the drizzle.

Cat's attention rested on the creature's talons, which they'd been sent to harvest.

Harpy talons, crushed into a fine powder and combined in a poultice with white bryony, cured syphilis and other ailments of the down unders. Rightly so, Elixir was not Mr. Hyde's bread and butter. There was no shortage of fine ladies and gents who would pay a pretty pound to slather Hyde's Pox Potion on their speckled privates.

Cat looked to Liam for instruction. "Shall I do the honors?"

This was her second hunt. On their first mission, they'd been ordered to slaughter a colony of mermaids and she'd impressed Liam with her talent for killing. She'd hacked and slashed until the mermaids' screams drowned out the roar of the surf, yet in her mind, Cat tried to silence the sailors and the eternal wails of the jungle. At the end of the bloody day, Liam had to haul her off the last mermaid.

"There's nothing left." Liam's hands detained her like shackles and true enough, when Cat glanced down at the carved-up carcass, she knew her humanity to be lost forever…

"Tell me how you'd do it." Liam propped his bowler on her head. "And spare the butchery. You ruined my best shirt last time. Bloodstains—"

"—are the hardest to remove. Aye, stop reminding me of the shirt. I'll buy you a new one." Cat licked her lips, eager to impress. "I'll start with this slag here," she nodded toward the unconscious creature, "slit her throat. Then I'll climb the lee side," she pointed at the mountain, "take the others by surprise. Knock off the weaker ones first, then…" Raising her dagger, Cat slashed the air.

"You're going to fight the adults?" Liam winged his brows. "All by yourself?"

"I won't be by myself." Cat shrugged. "You'll be with me."

Jamming his hands in his trousers, her mentor whistled. "Not me, Kitty. I'm afraid of heights. You're going to be knackered once you reach the peak, and one feathered beauty is stronger than three men," he said, tracing a line from her brow to the tip of her nose. "A shame, too. I've grown quite fond of you." His voice was a velvety caress, irresistible. Cat stood on tiptoes and molded her lips against his. But when she slipped her tongue inside his mouth, Liam pulled away. For a moment, his face was naked with disappointment.

Liam loved someone else.

She sensed it by the way he held back and how, in the second their lips touched, it felt like he was molding her into his mysterious beloved.

But what kind of girl did Hyde's Avenging Angel love?

Indeed, what kind of girl would love a killer?

"I-I suppose you have a better way," she said, trying to break the tension.

Liam turned his back on her. She watched him square his shoulder. "Always." His hand disappeared in his breast pocket, reappearing again with a strange device held between thumb and forefinger.

She frowned. "A beetle?"

"An automaton," Liam said, lifting the wings to display the clogs and wheels underneath. "Please hold, but don't turn the key until I say."

The beetle's gold filigree legs tickled her knuckles. Upon closer inspection, each leg had a joint held together by a pin no bigger than the period at the end of a sentence. "Extraordinary," she whispered. "Who made this?"

Liam dug out a vial of Elixir and a syringe from his pocket. "Mr. Hyde has an inventor." His face softened. "A genius, actually."

If Cat wasn't mistaken, she detected a tender catch in his voice at the mention of the inventor.

He plucked the automaton from her palm and injected the beetle with the syringe. "A thimbleful of Elixir," Liam showed her the now-emerald belly, "is all we need."

"Need for what?"

Holding the beetle like a treasure, he wound the key. "Man is the only creature with a choice. Your Da's words. Hyde made me memorize it. 'Choose to live in harmony with our unnatural brethren.'" A second turn of the key; the gears clicked into place. Liam tilted his head in consideration. "*Live* in harmony? That doesn't sound right, does it? Your Da isn't exactly *living*."

"No." Forever and always, she would associate her father's words with the jungle and seethe with bitterness over what could've been.

"Mornay hated the hunters."

Cat nodded, her eyes brimming with tears. "My father had been horribly misled."

"Well, Hyde is a friend to the hunter. To kill a monster is not a sin." Liam knelt beside the harpy. "If God didn't intend man to kill, why then give him a choice?"

"When will I meet Hyde?" she interrupted.

"When he wants to meet you."

"He really is God, isn't he?"

"You don't know the half of it…"

He released the key.

Six mechanical legs clicked into motion. The beetle sprang off his palm and scuttled across the grass. It latched onto the underside of the harpy's wing, legs drilling into the membranous tissue.

"Rouse her," Liam ordered. "But don't hurt her."

With a hesitant glance at her mentor, Cat nudged the harpy with the toe of her boot. "Wake up." She kicked the creature in the ribs. "Wake up, you piece of sh—"

The monster's eyes snapped open. In one swift motion, the harpy leapt to her feet. Yellow eyes with slit pupils darted from one hunter to the next. It puffed out its chest and spread its wings. A series of caws spilled from the harpy's beak.

Cat gripped her dagger, but it didn't seem like she needed it. The harpy stepped back, its wings furled around its body like a blanket. It seemed more afraid of them than the other way around.

Dragging Cat to the nearest boulder, Liam shooed the harpy away. "Off with you, wee one. We've no fight with you."

"This is your plan?" Cat muttered, and received an elbow to the ribs.

"Be free!" Liam waved.

"Have you gone absolutely bonkers?" she asked, watching their quarry take flight.

Liam tilted his head to the sky. "Look at her wingspan. Makes your blood sing to be alive in this glorious time, doesn't it?"

Cat checked her pistols, dagger, and crossbow. She'd be damned if she was coming back to Edinburgh empty-handed. "If we start climbing now, we'll infiltrate the colony before sundown—"

"Shhh." Pressing a finger to her lips, Liam nodded to the harpy's flapping wings. "Let me tell you about the beetle. When you shake it up, a spark ignites in its belly, melting the cogs inside. Our inventor friend labeled the prototype as defective, but Hyde snatched the beetle from the trash and ordered a dozen more. He requested just one improvement: a glass compartment to trap the flame." When the harpy receded into a brown dot, Liam whispered in her ear, "Ever wonder what happens when you mix Elixir with fire?"

Cat watched the harpy swoop toward the colony. And when it landed—

"*Kaboom*," Liam mouthed.

A puff of fire mushroomed from the colony. Rocks cascaded to the ground. The body of an adult harpy, wings aflame, plummeted with the debris. Wails of agony filled the glen like a symphony. They sounded disturbingly humanlike for a pack of monsters. Cat covered her ears. She wished she could cover her eyes, but Liam grabbed her wrist and ordered her to watch.

"Do you want to be a great hunter?" he asked.

A tear slid down her cheek. Slowly Cat turned to her mentor. In the face of mass destruction, she expected sadistic glee, but there was weariness in his eyes as he watched the rain of blood and body parts.

"Rip out your heart. And remember this: killing monsters is the divine right of man." The words weren't his own, but of Hyde, their god and prophet. Clearing his throat, Liam thumped her on the back. "Ready your dagger, Kitty. We've talons to harvest."

♦

Less than three nights later, a coach drawn by a black stallion clattered toward Balfour Manor.

Rob squinted past the drawn curtains for a glimpse of the occupants. Rain stung his cheeks and soaked through the broadcloth of his coat, but he hardly felt the cold. He rocked on his heels, bouncing with anticipation.

"Lordship." Finley held an umbrella over his head.

"You ought to be inside." Mrs. Nix huffed in his ear.

Rob waved off the umbrella. "Really, Mrs. Nix, I can handle a little rain."

Finley, dressed in a nightshirt and red cap, rubbed the sleep from his eyes.

Rob poked him in the arm. "Look alive, Finley."

The butler grunted.

"Calling in the middle of the night," Mrs. Nix muttered, "I never heard of such ill manners."

"I telegraphed 'Post Haste,'" Rob said. "He's never let me down yet."

The carriage pulled into the turnaround and the driver dismounted to open the door. A polished shoe appeared, followed by the familiar sight of a top hat.

"Doctor!" Rob raced into the rain amid Mrs. Nix's protests.

The man peeked over his shoulder, lips curling into a charismatic smile. His eyes were a piercing grey, crinkled and deep set in a lined yet handsome face.

"My dear lad!" With a swirl of his black cape, Dr. Jekyll gathered Rob into a hug. They embraced for a long time before the doctor held Rob at arm's length. "Let's have a look at you. How much you've grown! Last I saw you, you came up to my shoulder. This is rather unfair. How am I supposed to pat you on the head now?"

Rob was having trouble speaking. "You can still pat my head. Just ah…in private."

"Too much stretching." Dr. Jekyll frowned. "Who gave you permission to grow?"

"Robbie!" Mrs. Nix waved him back.

Taking him by the elbow, the doctor ushered Rob out of the rain.

Mrs. Nix gathered her shawl over her massive bosom. Instead of withering under her glare, Jekyll seized her by the shoulders and smothered her plump face with kisses.

"Get off me! You want a clip about the ears, you old coot!"

As his red-faced housekeeper swatted off the doctor's advances, Rob watched the footman unload Jekyll's trunks. One set of luggage. It didn't seem anyone else was getting out. "Did you travel alone?"

His disappointment must've been plain. Jekyll clasped him on the shoulder and steered him inside. "Time enough to catch up later. Tell me about this girl, your hunter."

On the way up the stairs, Rob described Cat. Her wit and beauty. The details of her heroic hunt.

Jekyll's lips twitched.

"What?" Rob asked.

"Are you describing a real person or a goddess?" The doctor's face was cloaked in shadows. "I suppose you fancy her already."

Sensing his ears burn, Rob munched on his bottom lip.

A hand descended out of the darkness and ruffled his hair. "You are too precious."

"Don't stroke my head." Rob jogged three steps ahead. "What if I did fancy her? Is that so wrong?"

"If I were you, I'd tiptoe instead of run."

"It's not like I'm going to declare my everlasting love anytime soon. I hardly know her." But what he felt during that kiss was damn near identical to the writings of Tennyson and Keats: poetry immortalized by the joining of lips and the merging of souls. He grinned, recalling how Cat had admitted to wanting him before slipping out of consciousness, but the image of her lying in a bloody heap erased the smile from his lips. One glance at the doctor's shrewd eyes told him Jekyll had read his mind. Rob tucked his hands in his pockets, wishing his face wasn't always such an open book. He didn't understand any of it. If you liked someone, why not just say it? Life was too short. "Love at first sight is not such an odious thing."

The doctor shook his head. "So hopeless."

"Have you read 'Annabel Lee' by Poe?"

"God no, I try not to touch anything by an American."

"*Neither the angels of Heaven above nor the demons down under the sea,*" Rob recited.

"Monstrumology in rhyme," the doctor interrupted.

"*Can ever dissever my soul from the soul of my Annabel Lee.*" Rob wiped his eyes. "To die for love—"

"Is no way to die at all." Jekyll chuckled. "I'd rather live a hundred years and never love. Upon my deathbed, they will say, 'He survived.'"

"*Who* will say?" Rob arched a skeptical brow. "You'll be all alone."

The doctor's lips twitched. "Touché."

"But not to worry," Rob added, "you've still got me."

Jekyll's smile vanished. The wavering wall sconces deepened the lines of his face into runnels.

Rob slowed down. "Did I say something wrong?"

"Some people..." Jekyll stumbled into a patch of shadow and for a second, he appeared cleaved in two: one half in darkness, the other in light. "*Most* people spend their entire lives building walls around their hearts. You, lad, have no walls. I just don't want to see you get hurt. Let me..." Sighing, the doctor brushed the rain from Rob's black coat. "Let me be your wall."

They trekked the rest of the way in silence. As they neared Cat's room, Rob asked, "Do you promise to save her?"

The doctor paused for a long while. "For you, I'll move heaven and earth."

Cat would live; Jekyll swore it. Ever since Rob was seven, he believed Jekyll's promises held more weight than God's. Rob flung his arms around the older man.

The doctor hugged him back. "To be loved by you," he shook his head, "this Cat Mornay doesn't know how lucky she is."

♦

The room pitched back and forth like a ship in a gale. Cat tried to lift herself from the bed, but a new stab of pain zipped up her leg.

"Easy, easy…" Gentle hands pressed her back on the mattress and slipped a fresh goose down pillow beneath her head. "Don't tax yourself, lass. How do you feel?"

Cat squinted at the source of the disembodied voice. All she could make out was a silhouette of a small man with a squarish-shaped head and big ears. His calming voice made her let down her guard. "Hot. I feel…so hot."

His hand descended upon her forehead. Slender fingers massaging her temples. His skin felt so cool that she whimpered when he took his hand away.

"Where are my manners? Allow me to introduce myself." There was movement in the dark. Seconds later, a fire sparked. A gold watch chain gleamed off a black velvet waistcoat. The gentleman lit a lantern and the flames cast a warm glow on a handsome, albeit tired, face.

Cat's heart fluttered for just a second, soaring to unimaginable heights of happiness before plummeting back into her usual state of despair. She fought to stem the tide of tears.

"Henry Jekyll." He poured water from a pitcher into a glass. "Lord Robert's private physician at your disposal." He frowned. "Why Miss Mornay, what's wrong?"

Cat shook her head. "I thought…" A tear dribbled like quicksilver down her cheek. "Never mind."

Jekyll caught the tear on the tip of his finger. "You thought what, lass?"

"F-f-for a moment, I thought you were my father," she said. "You look just like him. I'd thought I'd died and we were together again."

"You will, but not today. Our mutual friend forbids it."

"Rob." Despite her pain, a smile flickered across her cracked lips. "Where is he?"

"Right outside your door." Jekyll rubbed cold water across her lips. "The lad cares about you very much."

"I don't know what I've done to deserve it." She turned away, ashamed to look the doctor in the face. *I can't remember killing Manu Diaboli. I arsed around with Elixir and botched the hunt.* "Anyone else would've tossed me out on the street."

"Rob is not anyone else. When he was a boy…" Jekyll backed away to a worktable where he'd set up a pristine linen cloth. "He'd often stay at my home in Edinburgh for treatment."

He reached into his medical bag and laid out his surgical tools one by one. Scissors. Scalpel. A bone saw.

Cat tensed at the sight of the saw. "Treatment?"

"Weak lungs." Jekyll caught her reaction and said, "Not to worry. It's a ritual of mine. I like to clean all my instruments before we begin, though I rarely use them all."

She let out a breath. Her father had the same reassuring quality to his voice, as calming as a cup of chamomile tea. At least she wouldn't have to worry about infection with this doctor. Her shoulders relaxed and she fell back into listening to his story.

Stripping off his coat and draping it over the back of a chair, he continued, "One spring we were taking a turn around my rose garden when Rob found a sparrow hobbling behind the hedgerow." He rolled his sleeve up to the elbow. Soon the smell of carbolic acid pervaded the room. "Poor thing's wings had been torn off and Rob wanted to take it home…"

Jekyll fiddled with the cuff of his other sleeve. "But I advised him to leave the dying thing be. 'Even if you saved it,' I'd said, 'It would only have one wing. What good is a bird that cannot fly? The other sparrows would scold and peck at it, the alley cats would tear it to pieces. Let it die. This, lad, is

Nature's way of sorting out the strong from the weak.' To which Rob replied, 'Am I not weak? Why not let me die?'"

He poured warm water into a basin and washed his hands with lye. "Rob came home that night and drew a blueprint and spent all spring fiddling with his project. I got him all the materials he needed. Pliers. Copper wires. Tiny springs made of finest Italian gold. I treated him, he treated the sparrow, fitting it with these strange contraptions. He was so obsessed with undermining Nature that one couldn't help but wish him success."

"Did he succeed?" Cat asked, thinking of the birdmen of Aventine.

Jekyll dried his hands on a towel. "One day I stopped outside his door. I could hear the gentle flapping of wings. When I opened the door, the sparrow had taken flight."

She sensed him reaching for his black medicine bag. A green glow bathed the room. Cat watched the doctor's reedy shadow ready a syringe, filling it to top mark.

"There were other strays after that," he said, approaching her with the syringe. "Poor broken things he patched up and brought back to life." He took her arm and studied the bruises. "I trust you're not afraid of needles?"

"No, Dr. Jekyll," she said with a wry smile, "I think I can handle it. Am I his sparrow, then?"

"I think so." The needle breached her skin. His thumb pressed the plunger. "Let me help you take flight."

As the drug coursed through her bloodstream, Cat shut her eyes and exhaled a deep sigh of relief. When she opened her eyes, she caught him watching her with the most curious expression.

"How do you feel, Miss Mornay?"

"Heavenly. Is that—"

"Hyde's Elixir. Made from crushed mermaid scales. I shouldn't be telling you this. In Edinburgh, it's quite illegal."

Cat sunk into the pillow, a dreamy smile playing across her lips. The pain, along with her inhibitions, was no more. "How did a respectable physician like you acquire a bad, bad thing like Hyde's Elixir?"

His fingers brushed her temples like flower petals. "I'll let you in on a secret."

"Hmmm?" She was soaring and floating.

Jekyll leaned down and whispered in her ear, "It's my own concoction…"

Cat's eyes snapped open. She tried to lift herself up, but a firm hand pressed her down. "Mr. Hyde?"

"Shhhh, my little kitty." The doctor glanced over his shoulder. The door clicked open and a shadow yawned across the room. Whoever it was leaned against the doorway, neither moving nor speaking. Just staring, staring at her.

"I would like you to meet my apprentice," the doctor said, beckoning the intruder closer.

And when the man came into the light, Cat squirmed and whimpered.

His skin was melted wax, his lips pulled back into a grotesque snarl. A truly hideous face; the face of all the monsters she'd ever tortured and killed.

"Do not be frightened, little kitty. Would you believe our friend used to be the prettiest young man in the city?" Dr. Jekyll stroked her hair as Liam strolled by the table of surgical instruments. "That is, until his run-in with a fire-breathing hellion."

"Noooo...." She couldn't move her arms or legs. Her eyelids were granite weights. Darkness edged in and the birds of prey swarmed around her.

The doctor patted her gently on the head. "Rest assured, Miss Mornay, we shall take good care of you, won't we, Liam?"

Liam picked up the bone saw. "Absolutely."

CHAPTER 13
THE WINTER ANGEL

Somewhere in the castle, something was burning.

Rob tore his attention away from his writing and sniffed. Smoke clung to the air, making his eyes water. He debated investigating the source and dashed the notion away as a side effect of too much anxiety. The cook had probably scorched a side of lamb, no more no less. Most of the meals that came out of the kitchen tasted burnt anyway.

He returned to his current project: an adventure novel about shipwrecks and buried treasure. He scribbled a few lines and immediately crossed them out. Icy fingers of misgiving gripped his heart. *She's been in surgery too long.*

As much as he tried to slip back to his private island, the words, which had flowed effortlessly, now read like a clunky, jumbled mess. In a fit of frustration, Rob crumpled the top page and chucked it against the wall. He steepled his fingers and took a gulp of smoke-tainted air, coughed.

Too long.

The grandfather clock chimed midnight.

Rob lifted his head and stood up.

He decided to investigate.

The smoke was thickest on the second floor, seeming to emanate from under Cat's bedroom door.

"What are you doing, Doctor?" he muttered. "I hired you to save the girl, not burn down my house."

The doctor was renowned for his "unusual methods," and Rob would be the first to admit that he would not be alive today if he hadn't spent his childhood drinking funny-tasting concoctions and lying in lead-lined coffins. Doubting Jekyll now seemed like blasphemy.

Holding his kerosene lamp at eye level, Rob strained to see through the smoky haze. As he neared Cat's bedroom, the hackles rose on the back of his neck.

A sixth sense told him he wasn't alone.

Rob whirled around.

Down the seemingly infinite stretch of hallway, he spotted a slender figure dressed head to toe in black. At first, he assumed the intruder was a footman, but his servants usually addressed him when passing. The man's head was insolently cocked, watching him.

"Who's there?"

The maids spoke of sightings in the turret where his great uncle had his throat slit from ear to ear and of evil shades flitting through the hundred rooms and passageways. Rob never heeded these superstitions, preferring logic to nonsense. Perhaps he might need to revise his creed.

Although his heart thrummed in fear, he shouted, "Who are you? What are you doing in my house?"

In reply, the stranger slinked toward him with a lithe, almost feline gait. Brown hair swished against the shoulders of his coat.

Rob took an involuntary step back. "You will declare yourself to me!"

There was something familiar about him but Rob couldn't place his finger on where or when, if ever, they had met before. The shadows cloaked the stranger's face like a mask.

The intruder halted a yard away from Rob, just shy of the lantern's glow.

Rob shifted from foot to foot, feeling the man's eyes rove over him, drinking in every nervous tick. "W-why don't you show your face?"

"Because you may not like what you see, mate."

The silvery voice struck him like a blast of winter wind. When he'd heard it for the first time, he'd been much younger, alone, and so cold he couldn't feel his toes.

Rob raised the lantern. "Come closer..."

The intruder stepped forward and the lamp's light bathed a face so deformed that Rob turned away.

His skin was a mass of blotchy scar tissue, his features more monster than man.

It was a face that haunted the nightmares of children.

But Rob remembered a different face, one with no earthly equal…

◆

In the evening, the first snowfall dusted Eton's dormitory rooftops and yew hedges like powdered sugar. Rob looked to the sky. The stars shone brightly. Snowflakes drifted against his cheeks and lashes; one fell into his eye and for a moment, he marveled at its six-sided symmetry before the crystal dissolved into his tears.

Rob yanked at the bindings on his wrists.

The more he struggled, the more the twine cut into his skin. He tried to kick himself free, but the ropes around his ankles were even tighter, cutting off the blood flow to his toes. He twisted around. The stone angel, below where he was bound, stared down at him with lifeless eyes and he knew there would be no mercy.

Exhausted and defeated, he bowed his head in shame.

"Stupid."

He'd been making his way from the library to the dormitory when Philip Cowen and his three mouth-breathing minions descended upon him like vultures. If his head hadn't been in the clouds, he would've heard them coming. Philip made his first term at Eton a living hell. Now Philip was no longer satisfied with Indian burns and pissing on his clothes. It wasn't enough to humiliate him; apparently Philip wanted him dead.

Rob coughed, wincing as a fresh stab of pain pierced his side. Certain they'd broken a rib, he tried to cull the coughs, but he'd have more success holding back a gale.

Cough. Cough. Cough.

Drops of blood stained the new snow; red on white like a Tudor rose.

Sapped of strength, Rob yanked feebly at the ropes. Philip's father was a lieutenant in Her Majesty's Navy and while Philip was the dunce in school, he'd certainly paid attention during his father's demonstration on how to tie a bowline.

The snow fell fast, sinking beneath his starched collar. Shivers wracked his scrawny body. His morning coat and trousers were soaked through.

"Help!"

The winter wind drowned his pleas.

There was no help to be had in the courtyard, no soul to come to his rescue. Up high, the glow of the dormitory windows dimmed one by one. Lights out for the lucky ones who got to spend the first snowfall between warm sheets. "Help." His voice was as weak as the mewing of a kitten. "Help me…"

Cough. Cough. Cough.

His lids felt like ice blocks. He jerked awake. If he fell asleep, he might never wake up. Would that be so bad? Sleep lulled him in her warm embrace. His lids drooped shut and Rob drifted with the snow.

He didn't hear the footsteps at first. The caress of a cold hand on his cheek roused him.

"Open your eyes, mate," a silvery voice commanded. A thumb cleared the frost from his lashes, brushed away the frozen tears. "Wake up. Wake up."

Rob opened his eyes. A face swirled into focus, a face of such exquisite beauty that Rob thought the stone angel had come to courier him to heaven. Rob frowned, unable to decide if the angel was a he or she. It was dressed in trousers and black coat, but its hair was tied back in a ponytail and its face was prettier than any girl Rob had ever seen.

Mentally flipping a coin, Rob decided on "male" and estimated him to be about sixteen or seventeen. "Have you come to save me?"

"That depends on who you are." The angel reached into his breast pocket. An exotic knife with a crescent blade flashed silver against the blue twilight. "I'm looking for a boy of eleven in need of a friend. You are Robert Stevenson, I presume?"

Rob nodded vigorously, never wanting so much to claim his name. "I am. I am. I am."

His boy smiled and reached for the binds. "Then I'm a friend." He cut the twine.

"Are you an angel?" Rob smiled back in spite of the pain.

The older boy studied him for a moment. "I've been called many things in my life, but never an 'angel.'" He sliced the binds on Rob's ankles. "I've been sent to help you."

"Help me?" Rubbing his raw wrists, Rob asked, "Sent by who?"

"Dr. Jekyll. He received your letters and thought you could use someone on your side. Throw your arm around my shoulder. Lean on me."

Rob groaned as his rescuer hoisted him to his feet. White lights exploded before his eyes as a bolt of pain blazed through his side. No more wondering about his ribs being broken. They *were* broken.

His rescuer's deft fingers probed his side. He muttered a curse and Rob felt himself scooped off his feet and carried back inside.

"When you're better," his rescuer whispered in his ear, "perhaps you can give me the names of those who did this to you."

"Please don't tell the headmaster. They'll call me a snitch. They'll make me pay…"

"Who said anything about telling anyone? Me and those bad dogs, we're gonna have ourselves a chat."

Rob nestled his cheek against the boy's shoulder. "You *are* an angel..."

"Don't call me that."

"...sent to watch over me, and I don't even know your name."

"Liam." His rescuer climbed the stairs. "Liam Barclay." There was a long pause and then Liam sighed. "I guess I can be your angel."

◆

"I warned you." Liam backed into the shadows like a dog that had been beaten too often. "You won't like what you see."

"Wait!" Rob grabbed Liam's arm and dragged him into the light. He forced himself to look again. As his hand hovered over the burns, Rob's eyes brimmed with tears. "Your face." His *beautiful* face. "What happened?"

"Never play with fire." Ashamed of his deformity, Liam ducked his head. "And never cross people who like to play with fire." His attempt at a smile made him look all the more hideous and sad. "I told you I was much changed."

"Aye," Rob said, "I'm afraid you don't look like an angel anymore."

Liam nodded in defeat.

"But the eyes," Rob added with a shrug, "The eyes are still the same."

Liam glanced up in surprise.

And when his best friend began to weep, Rob folded Liam into his arms.

CHAPTER 14
BODY COUNT

Cat opened her eyes to the canopy. Silver moons and stars threaded the purple velvet, an entire constellation watching over her as she slept. She blinked and studied the embroidered universe in a state of perfect serenity.

Mr. Hyde. Liam. Even Manu Diaboli.

All a dream.

As the bubble burst, Cat licked her lips with a tongue as scaly as a lizard's back. Her dirty hair crunched against a pillowcase stiff with sweat and tears. She turned her head and found Rob hunched in a chair by her bedside. His collar hung askew and his white shirt and black trousers were wrinkled in several places.

"You look like hell." Her voice sounded as raspy as a wasps' hive.

Rob lifted his head, eyes widening in astonishment. "You're awake."

A smile of sheer relief ghosted his lips. Just as suddenly, the smile vanished and his face became strained with dread.

With a groan, she probed her forehead and found a bandage. Her head swam in an emerald green cloud. "How long have I been sleeping?"

"Three..." He scrubbed his hair, making the already disheveled blond strands stand on end. She'd never seen him with such messy hair. "No, three nights and four, yes, four days. You were running a high fever." Rob twisted the oversized ring on his pinky. He looked like he'd been awake for as long as she'd been sleeping. "But it's over now. The worst is over."

"My sister? Jim?" Cat suddenly felt cold. Why was he so nervous?

He held up a hand. "Fine. Worried about you, but fine."

"Manu Diaboli?"

"The Gates of Hell have been quiet since you came out. No deaths, not a peep," Rob said, silencing her fears. "I believe you killed it."

"Did we recover her remains?"

"No one's exactly volunteered to look."

"I misjudged." She shook her head. "Stupid. I've been so stupid. I should've— There's a nest."

Rob paled. "She's breeding?"

"Three eggs."

She saw how much the revelation worried him. After a long pause, he changed the subject and took her hand. His fingers were thin and ink-stained, but warm. "You've brought my brother back. You've done more than enough. I'll see you're paid in full and you can rest here until you've recovered."

"I should've been more alert." *I had Elixir flowing through my veins. Elixir I lifted from your pantry. Maybe you wouldn't be so forgiving if you knew.*

Cat tried to sit up, but Rob placed a gentle yet firm hand on her shoulder. He tugged her goose down comforter to her chin. "You ought to go back to sleep."

She'd been sleeping enough. Reality, complete with the aches and pains of a failed hunt, struck her hard. Her head, which she vaguely recalled hitting when she and Manu Diaboli tumbled from the tree, felt like it'd been split open with a rock. Perhaps it had.

"She came at me from the side and we had ourselves a proper fight. I almost had her, nearly shot her bloody arm clean off. I had the dagger in my hand, the same one I used to cut out her mother's heart. I was so close. So close..."

Cat brought a shaky hand to her face. Her fingers were a bloody mess. Two of her nails had peeled clean off. There was also an itch below her left knee. "But the thing with Manu Diaboli: she's always one step ahead, always faster."

"Nonsense."

"She caught me by the leg. Drove her talon into my knee and when I screamed, she twisted and twisted. I looked into her eyes and she seemed to say to me, 'I remember you.'"

219

Rob chewed his thumbnail. She'd only known him a few days, been unconscious for a majority of that time, but even she'd picked up on his meticulous grooming. Something was wrong. Very wrong. For the first time since waking up, she noticed he was staring intently at her legs.

Cat tried to wiggle her toes. The right foot rippled the covers, but when she tried to move her left foot, the blanket didn't move at all.

"Rob?"

Without warning, Rob stood up and pulled back the curtains. Sunlight streamed past his lanky body and stirred the dust motes into a haze. "You have to remember: Dr. Jekyll did all he could."

"Jekyll?" Everything after her fight with Manu Diaboli had become a blur. Cat eased herself up and watched Rob pace back and forth. "Now you're making me nervous."

Taking a deep breath, he stepped toward her and took her hand again. "I don't know how to tell you…" Rob's eyes brimmed with tears; he wiped them on his shoulder. "So I'm just going to say it."

"You sound like I'm about to die. I'm a little beaten up, but I'm perfectly…"

And then she noticed a black spot on the canopy—a burn mark.

Cat reached for the drapes and fingered the singed velvet. The Elixir cloud parted and her memory resurfaced. She felt both fire and ice. The bite of cold steel teeth and the kiss of Dragon's Breath. She smelled her own flesh roasting…

Two men loomed over her bedside.

One wore the identity of Dr. Jekyll like a mask.

The other one's face was monstrous; a face born in fire.

"You see, Cat. You were gravely injured." Rob knelt before her, flushed from temple to neck. "Dr. Jekyll worked through the night."

Her shin itched.

She wiggled the toes on her left foot. To her relief, she felt the toes move.

Yet.

There was no ripple beneath the blanket. No indentation of a foot. Dread gathered in her heart, dripping into her veins like poison.

"He had to do it," he said.

Meeting Rob's eye, Cat gathered the hem of the blanket and peeled it away. She began a careful inventory of herself. A body count.

Two arms. Two hands. A total of ten fingers.

"… the wound had turned gangrenous long before he arrived. I can vouch for that."

One bruised and battered torso.

"You would've died otherwise."

One right leg. She never appreciated the simple yet intricate mechanism of a human leg until now. Knee. Shin. Foot. Five toes. Each part working in perfect harmony.

On to the left…

One left knee. One bandaged knee. But where…? Oh God *where*…?

Where was her shin?

Her foot?

The five toes she could still wiggle even now?

Her breath transmuted into pants.

"He had to do it." Rob wrapped his arms around her and held her tight. "He had to take your leg…"

Cradled in Rob's arms, Cat screamed.

And screamed.

And screamed.

PART II
PURGATORIO

CHAPTER 15
SUICIDE AND SWORDPLAY

Rob flinched as the cold ear of a stethoscope pressed between his naked shoulder blades.

"Inhale." Dr. Jekyll tapped him on the back. "Hold."

Taking in a deep gulp of air, his cheeks inflated like a puffer fish. A chuckle drifted from the darkest corner of his solarium. He shot his friend a dirty look, but Liam turned his back and played with Rob's automaton collection. Plucking the Aventine birdman from the shelf, Liam wound the key. Gold wings flapped against his hand, but he kept the automaton grounded.

The stethoscope migrated to his lower back. If one could *hear* a frown, Rob heard Jekyll's brows knit together. "Exhale."

Rob expelled a pathetic *whoosh* of breath. The doctor remained silent, but it was a heavy silence that said "you failed."

Fortunately, Liam provided a welcome distraction from Jekyll and his insistence on another physical. Liam liked to touch everything, and he rarely put anything back in their proper place. After leaving the automaton collection in shambles, Liam sat on the edge of Rob's worktable and dipped his fingers into a square bin of pins, cylinders, and copper springs.

Rob arched a brow as Liam plucked a spring from the pile and began to stretch it out of shape. "Do you mind?"

"What's that?" Liam glanced down at the mangled spring. "Sorry," he said, sheepishly putting it back with the others. "Guess some things are not meant to be straight."

"Truer words have never been said," Jekyll muttered, then tapped Rob once more. "Inhale, lad...good job."

Liam nodded to the rosewood box in front of Rob. "What's that you're working on?"

Rob snatched the box away before Liam could ruin that too.

"Someone's miffed," Liam said. "Not at me, I hope."

"Of course at you." Rob folded his arms across his naked chest. "Did you get my letters?"

Liam turned away. "Aye."

"Did you read them?"

"Sure."

"Why didn't you write back?"

Liam dismissed his question with a casual wave of his hand. "I'm not much for letter writing, mate."

Six years of posting letters to Liam. Six years without a reply. Rob bowed his head. "Would it have killed you to write back?" he asked, unable to conceal the hurt from his voice. "Just once?"

Liam had no comeback.

"Lads! Sorry to cut this—" Jekyll swished a finger between Rob and Liam. "—whatever *this* is—short." Tapping Rob on the back, he said, "Would you kindly *inhale.*"

Eyes locked on Liam, Rob took a deep breath.

"Good." Jekyll glanced at his pocket watch. "Exhale."

This last breath sounded worse than the first.

With Rob caught off guard, Liam dove for the box.

"I'll show you, just don't touch." Rob unhooked the golden clasp and a lady in a mourning gown rose from a secret compartment. As she twirled, three ravens suspended on invisible wires flocked around her. A lullaby wafted through the solarium. "It's a music box."

"Lovely." Jekyll ruffled his hair. "Did you compose the tune, too?"

"It's called *The Last Rose of Summer*. The Etonian choir used to sing it all the time." Rob caught Liam eyeing the music box like he wanted to smash it to smithereens. "What's wrong?"

"Make it for *her?*"

"Her? You mean Cat? No, it's for a friend of my father's who is now my friend. He's shipped off to California now, but still writes me now and then. This is a gift for his new bride. She's been melancholy lately and he thought this would cheer her up."

"Sad song like that isn't going to cheer her up, is it?" Noticeably cheered up himself, Liam fingered one of the ravens. The wire snapped and the bird dropped to the table.

Rob's eyes widened in exasperation. "Kill my bird, why don't you?"

"Barclay," Jekyll snapped, "Must you destroy everything you touch?"

Liam shrugged and studied his slender fingers. "I have the touch of death."

"It's all right." Rob found a new wire and began to mend the damage. "I don't suppose a sweet song would dry Miss Mornay's tears. I'll have to build her a leg."

Rob shut the music box and Liam checked under his fingernails. Cat's amputation was a sore topic for everyone involved. Well, maybe with the exception of Manu Diaboli.

Whipping off his spectacles, Jekyll polished the lenses with a handkerchief. "How is our fallen hero?"

"Mending." Cat's bruises were fading, her cracked ribs healing, the wound on her forehead closing. True to her claim, Cat was indestructible. Rob sighed. "But…"

"But?" Jekyll pressed.

"Broken." Yesterday, he met up with Vivian pushing Cat through the herb garden. When he said hello, her head lolled against the wicker backing of her wheelchair and she made no sound. Her eyes were leeched of life, empty and sad. Where was the goddess who stood upon the shoulders of a titan? This girl was a husk of a human being.

"I wish I could see to her injuries. Every time I knock on her door, her mute guard hisses at me. Why, just this morning, blasted lad tried to bite me." Jekyll checked his lenses for scratches. "Will today be the day Her Majesty lets me in?"

Rob shook his head.

"Still afraid of doctors?" Jekyll asked.

"Deathly."

"Odd Cat." Liam grabbed a handful of the invisible wires and began curling them with his Bedouin blade. "I don't care for the deaf mute either."

"Please don't call him that," Rob said, feeling a need to come to Jim's defense. "He's mute, but I don't think he's deaf."

"I think I may spank him," Liam said.

Rob's lips twitched. "While you're a guest in my home, I ask that you refrain from spanking the short people."

"Listen to the laird, Barclay, and control yourself." Jekyll wrapped the spectacles' wire temples around his ears. "Has our hero been putting the balm on?"

"She has," Rob said, "Every day." Thanks to Jekyll's Tiger Balm, an import from the Orient, Cat's leg stump had already completely healed. "Is it made from real tigers?"

"Just their nuts," Liam said. "Gives the balm that extra *bite*. Doctor rubbed it all over my face after I was kissed by fire. I rather liked it."

"I'm sorry, Barclay," Jekyll cocked an eyebrow, "are you implying that you like balls...rubbed all over your face?"

"Just tiger balls."

Jekyll shook his head before returning to Rob and the topic of Cat. "What's done cannot be undone. But enough about her. It's you I'm concerned about. You've lost quite a bit of weight."

Rob shifted in his seat. "So has she." There were even fresh needle marks on her arms.

"I can count every one of your ribs. Don't you ever eat?"

"Polished off an entire steak and kidney pie for breakfast."

Laughing, Jekyll motioned with his stethoscope for them to resume the physical. "I see you are still a consummate liar. How do you sleep at night?"

"Like the dead."

The cold ear migrated over his heart. There was a long, extended pause. "I don't like the sound of your ticker."

"I told you I'm fine. I *feel* fine!"

"Now be a good boy and you shall have a sweetie."

"I'm seventeen, laird, and the youngest member inducted into the Royal Geographical Society. You cannot offer me candy like I'm seven."

Jekyll, listening to his heartbeat, whispered, "I should've sprinkled anti-growth serum on you when you were seven because you were *sooo adorable.* Now one more time, inhale or I'll be forced to pinch your cheeks."

"I'll pinch your cheeks, laddie." On the table, Liam crossed his long legs. "My pleasure."

"I'm clenching them already," Rob said, garnering a laugh from both his friends. Defeated, he inhaled, but the same inferno rekindled in his lungs. He fired three ugly coughs which sounded worse than they really were.

Jekyll swatted him on the back. "Now that this monster mess is behind you, get yourself to a warmer climate. Then again," he considered, scratching his sideburns, "the passage alone would likely kill you."

Rob reached behind his chair for his shirt.

Liam hopped off the table and snatched it up. "Let your valet do the honors," he said, holding the shirt out.

Rob slipped his arms inside the sleeves. "I'm not as fragile as all that. In fact, I've written to the Society and they said I could board the next ship." He began to button, but Liam turned him around. Rob watched his friend's deft fingers slip the whalebone buttons inside the slits.

"Brilliant, I'll go with you." Liam brushed the wrinkles from Rob's shoulder, down his arm and back up again. Liam was always rubbing him like that, but Rob figured his friend had a vendetta against wrinkles.

When it came to tucking his shirt into his trousers, Liam was about to do that too, but Rob caught his hand. "I can take it from there, friend."

Beside them, Dr. Jekyll gnawed on his inner cheek. "Hmmm." It was a disapproving "hmmm" and Rob stepped back, flushed with guilt. Guilt for what? Damned if he knew. He and Liam were just joking.

Liam snatched a brass spyglass from one of the shelves and twirled it around like a sword. "To the West Indies. To the Americas. We'll have ourselves a time."

Tossing his stethoscope inside a black medical bag, Jekyll coughed.

"What?" Liam stopped twirling.

The doctor shrugged. "Just thinking about you on shipboard. Skipping the meal and going straight for dessert, are we?"

"Wanker." Liam strolled toward the window.

Rob looked from doctor to apprentice. "I'm so confused. I thought we were talking about me?"

"In a way, we kind of are." Jekyll straightened his collar. "In any event, I must be on my way."

"You just got here. Surely you're not leaving us so soon?"

"By the end of the week. In the meantime, that blasted Mrs. Nix is making me earn my keep. I best treat her first or her nagging will haunt my dreams."

Rob raised his brow. "I trust she's not ill? She hadn't mentioned anything to me."

"Oh, she's healthy as a horse. Voice like a bag of cats, but aye, strong enough to make us all wish we were deaf." Jekyll lowered his voice to a whisper. "But I'd stay downwind of her after supper if I were you." With a wink, Jekyll bid him farewell.

Rob joined Liam at the window.

Liam was looking through the spyglass. "Seems like our alley cat found herself another leg."

"That's a bit cruel, isn't it?"

"Don't believe me?" Liam passed him the spyglass.

"Sometimes you have a very queer sense of humor," Rob said, raising the spyglass. He paused and turned to Liam.

In the lawn below, Cat Mornay was *walking*. Of course, she leaned on crutches and her shoulders dragged grotesquely as she tackled the hill, but she was out of her wheelchair. Rob zoomed in. "I'll be—"

"A peg leg." Liam sneered.

Midway up the incline, Cat's peg jammed between a cluster of rocks. Losing her balance, she pitched face-first into the grass and slammed her hand on the ground. "Shit!"

A murder of crows loitering about the statue garden took flight.

Rob sucked in his breath. Next to him, Liam made a sound that could either be a chuckle or a clearing of the throat. Rob hoped it was the latter because laughing at Cat would be mean.

Cat was sprawled on the ground long enough for Rob's optimism to take a dive. Then Jim materialized in his viewfinder, offering her his hand.

With Jim's help, Cat stood up. Jim dusted off her hat and handed it back to her.

Still holding on to Jim's hand, Cat climbed step by arduous step until she crested the top and stood amongst the stone statues.

Rob set down the spyglass and exhaled, only now realizing he'd been holding his breath. When he shut his eyes, their silhouettes were seared into his retinas. The fog and dismal Highland skies gave way to another setting: Cat and Jim were walking in the sand and surf, their skins kissed brown by the sun. They were searching, ceaselessly searching for gold doubloons.

"Now the leg would be cut off at the knee, now the hip." Rob ran a hand over a forearm covered in goose bumps. A wild sea-song echoed in his ear and his sickly body hummed with joy. "Be on the lookout for a seafaring man with one leg."

"What?" Liam stared at him as if he were off his rocker.

Perhaps he was. "Nothing…" Rob raised the spyglass. Liam said something else, but Rob heard none of it. In the landscape of his mind, he'd already joined the hunter and changeling on their treasure island. "Nothing and everything."

♦

Three days after trying out her new peg, Cat hobbled up the stairs to the roof.

With each step, her sadness festered and grew like a tumor. Every time she glanced at her stump, misery devoured her from the inside out.

Cat Mornay, the monster hunter, was no more.

She was a one-legged girl. A cripple. A freak. She could no longer stand without tipping over or walk without leaning on Jim's scrawny shoulders. She could no longer do any of the things that made her feel most alive. And if she could not run, jump, fight, climb, or slay the monsters of the world, she no longer wanted to live.

Cat had a plan.

She would to climb to the roof of Balfour Manor's highest turret and step right into the green void below. With her streak of invincibility, perhaps she'd sprout wings and soar instead of plummet. Wings would almost make up for her missing leg.

Midway up the crumbling steps, Cat halted and stared at her new peg. She could never tell Jim that she hated the blasted thing. The lad had taken great pains to carve her new limb from the trunk of the finest weirwood and even fashioned a velvet cushion she could rest her stump on. The straps were purchased from the tannery's best hides, the buckles melted gold, and the etchings on the peg resembled hieroglyphs. Cat suspected the markings were an ancient fae language; a spell weaved in the wood to keep her safe.

Despite Jim's good intentions, the peg could not replace her leg. It sunk in the mud and clattered upon the stones. The straps bit into her thigh and left ugly red welts upon her skin.

She came to despise the peg and the cumbersome crutches she must always lean upon to move about. She loathed the audible scrape of wood against the manor's stone floors, a sound that proclaimed the death of the silent and stealthy mercenary she'd trained to be.

Most of all, she hated the sight of her feeble shadow, gnarled and mutated to the shape of a devil's claw. When she limped around the halls, the gaggle of maids scattered out of her way.

Rob treated her cordially, of course, but she'd catch him studying her awkward gait. Sometimes he'd even scribble observations in a pocket-sized leather journal. She was a subject of morbid fascination for him, like that nice gentleman

Da took her to meet when she was six. She knew him as Mr. Merrick, but everybody else called him "The Elephant Man."

Then there was Vivian, who expected beauty and perfection in everything and everybody. Cat knew her stump was troubling to her sister, though Vivian was too polite to admit it. But last night, while Vivian was helping her into the tub, Cat caught disgust ripple across her sister's face. As quickly as it appeared, the moment was gone and Vivian was all smiles and chatter. The water had been scalding hot, but Cat had never felt so cold.

Only that ugly tosser Liam gloated every time she crossed his path, which wasn't often. While they never exchanged words, she got the message. *Now you appear as you really are: a monster like me.*

Cat lurched up the steps.

The mornings were the hardest. In her dreams, she was a whole person and there was a slip of time upon waking when she could wiggle her toes. Then reality would set in like a blade sinking between her ribs and she'd curl onto her side, weeping for what was lost.

There was a war in her mind by the time she reached the roof. Casting aside her crutch, Cat hoisted herself onto the ledge and clung to the ramparts by her fingernails. She cautioned a glance down. The lawn whirled before her in a dizzying arc of green.

Cat stood up and turned her palms to the sky. A weak ray of sunlight kissed her cheeks and out of all the horrible memories of her eighteen years on earth, only one overpowered the rest. This memory was as far removed from the jungle as Heaven was from Hell: it hinged on the moment Rob opened the door to his solarium and showed her the stars. She'd felt so safe and peaceful in his presence.

Suddenly her decision was weighted with regret. She wished she could've known him for just a bit longer. They existed in different circles, she in the dark, Rob in the light, but they'd collided for a stolen moment here on earth. It almost seemed a shame to end it; once she leapt off the ledge, she might never see him on the other side.

Losing some of her resolve, Cat took a wobbly step backward when a hand clamped around the back of her neck. "Bad Kitty…"

♦

The hand snaked around her hair. Starbursts of pain exploded across her scalp. Liam dragged her off the ledge and bent her over his knee.

A hand descended upon her bottom.

She yelped.

238

"Bad Kitty." The second smack was harder than the first and twice as humiliating. "After all the trouble—" The third smack brought tears to her eyes. "—we went through trying to save your bloody life! Ungrateful. Stupid. Bad—" The fourth came down like the golden hand of God, bringing the pain, bringing the apocalypse. "Bad, bad Kitty."

Liam pushed her off his lap.

Cat scampered away, scooting backward until her back bumped against the rampart. Liam loomed over her. Sweat beaded down the scar tissue of his face. On one slender hip was a needle-thin rapier with an elaborate hilt. On the other hip bounced the curved blade of Culler. With a silent groan, she snatched up her crutch, ready to strike should the snake bite.

He glanced over the ledge and whistled. "Long way to fall." *Tsk. Tsk. Tsk.* "I'll never understand what's going through that tiny pea you call a brain."

Cat spat at his polished boots.

His hand fluttered to his heart in effrontery. "Is that any way to treat he who saved your life, not once but..." He pounced and squatted over her until they were face to face. His eyes gleamed like cruel sapphires as he studied her every tick. Her fear brought a smile to his peeling lips. "Why Kitty, you're upset..."

"You cut off my leg!"

239

"We merely clipped your wings is all. And look," he swatted her on the shoulder, "we patched you up and this is the thanks we get: you trying to do yourself in. We can't have that."

"Why should you care if I live or die?"

"Who am I going to play with if you're dead?" He patted her on the peg. "May I be the first to carve my name on this beauty?"

At least one good thing came out of this ambush: Cat no longer wanted to kill herself. She wanted to live so she could gut this piece of shite and lynch him with his intestines. She swung her crutch at his skull.

Liam dodged out of the way.

"Ho ho!" He leaped to his feet, swayed back arched like a bow. His agility was salt to her wounds. "This cat still has claws!"

Cat scrambled to her *foot*. The cumbersome peg nearly tipped her over.

Liam swept a bow. "Does Miss Mornay fancy a dance?" He unsheathed his rapier and, to Cat's disbelief, tossed it to her. She caught the hilt one-handed. At least her upper body reflexes still worked. A flash of silver sliced her thoughts short. If she hadn't dodged to the left, she'd be missing a nose.

"A duel then!" Liam tossed Culler from hand to hand. He lunged, slashing at her jugular. "Doesn't a proper fight make your blood sing?"

Cat weaved, parried, then pressed for attack. "What are you doing here if not to"—she jabbed at his heart, but Liam leapt onto the ledge—"kill me?"

"Mr. Hyde wants to offer you"—Liam skirted the rampart like a tightrope walker—"a reprieve from your debts." He brought his blade down in a deadly downcut. Sparks flew as steel kissed steel. "It ought to be like old times. Remember the Isle of May? All those lovely sea slags for his Elixir?" He advanced, faster and faster, slashing, hacking, jabbing, stabbing...never tiring, slowing or stopping.

Cat blocked him blow for blow. Sweat poured down her temples and dribbled beneath her blouse. "Your point?"

"Mr. Hyde has a more powerful formula in mind. Shall I tell you the ingredient?" Liam hopped off the ledge, driving her backward. "Manu Diaboli."

Her shoulders ached, her stump screamed with pain. "Another egg? You wankers really are persistent. If you think I'll go back into the woods to steal—"

"Once again, there is nothing you can do I can't do better." He raised Culler. "We've already got the egg."

"What?" That she was not expecting.

His blade raked her shoulder; warm blood oozed down her sleeve. Her peg jammed into a crack and Cat went down. The rapier flew out of her hand, skidding out of reach. She broke the fall with her sword arm. A boot slammed into her stomach. Cat doubled over, hacking up bloody spittle. Liam kicked her onto her back and planted his boot on her chest.

Propping his elbow on his knee, he smiled down at her. "But I give credit where credit is due. I didn't run into the mother, so..." He grounded his boot against her sternum. "Thank you."

"What do you want from me? You have everything you want."

"Lucky you." The sole of his boot eclipsed the sun. "You get to be there when it hatches," he said, and slammed his foot down on her face.

CHAPTER 16
LIFE EVERLASTING

Rob pushed the laird's ring over his knuckle and swiped his thumb over the sapphire. The silver band was slick with perspiration. "I don't believe it!"

Dr. Jekyll, sleeves rolled up to the elbow, shoved clay pots aside to make room. His arms were scrawny and covered with a fine sprinkling of blond hair. "Believe it," he called over his shoulder, "then help me move these blasted flowers aside."

The sight of another lumpy sheet transported Rob back to the smoky caretaker's cottage where his brother remained in pieces. "How could you force Liam inside the Gates of Hell?"

"He volunteered, lad." Jekyll glanced carefully away. "I never *forced* him into anything."

"When did he go?"

"This morning." Jekyll rooted in his medical bag. "After breakfast, in fact."

As Rob resumed his frantic pacing, Jekyll clasped him on the shoulder. "Not to worry. Liam procures rare ingredients for me all the time. You know that."

"Like herbs, but *monster eggs*?"

"Nothing is rarer than the egg of Manu Diaboli."

Rob snatched a handkerchief from his pocket and mopped his brow. The glass ceiling dripped with condensation. Even the walls were sweating.

When he was nine, Dr. Jekyll asked him where in the world he'd most wished to go. Even though he'd been too sick to get out of bed that day, he'd named the West Indies and gone off on some boy's fancy about marauders and maroons. The next time he returned home, the estate was swarming with builders. They were constructing an octagonal glasshouse especially for him. For years, every time he strolled amongst the rows of banana orchids and African violets or felt the warm mist from the elaborate network of copper pipes, he thought of how blessed he was to have such a dear friend.

"Doctor?"

Preoccupied with setting out his surgical instruments, Jekyll's eyes gleamed with a fanatical light and Rob gleaned a darkness he never knew existed. Suddenly Rob felt like he didn't know his friend at all.

"Where is Liam?" He had a horrible vision of Liam splattered across the forest floor. But Cat had killed the Great Mother, so… "Is he injured?"

"This may come as a surprise to you, but Barclay is more resourceful and resilient than you give him credit for."

Jekyll poked his head up, but the eerie light hadn't abated. Rob followed the direction of the doctor's gaze.

244

"As you can see," Jekyll said, nodding to the lanky figure ambling over rocks and witch grass toward the glasshouse. Ground fog snaked about his legs like ribbons. He appeared to be carrying a dead body in his arms. "Barclay is very much alive."

With a fresh jolt of alarm, Rob realized that Liam was carrying Cat and dashed to the door.

Jekyll shook his head. "What'd that hellcat do now?"

Rob flung the door open and chilly air blasted him in the face. "What happened to her?"

Liam slipped inside, angling past Rob to get to the table. "Found this one on the roof," he said, setting Cat down next to the lumpy sheet. Her head lolled against a pot of baby Venus flytraps. Her peg clattered against the table edge. "She was trying to fly."

Rushing to Cat's side, Rob brushed the hair and mud from her face. The arm of her blouse was soaked in sweat and blood. He inspected the wound on her shoulder. "Did you cut her?"

"I had to, mate." Liam held up his hands in self-defense. "She tried to pink me with her dagger."

Rob nodded in understanding. "Then I'm glad you were around…" He paused, noticing a smudge on Cat's forehead. Was that a *boot print*? "Did you step on her face?"

"Did I step on her face!" Liam's eyes shifted to Jekyll.

The doctor rubbed his brow.

Heart thrumming with panic, Rob tapped Cat gently on the cheek. Her lids fluttered, revealing the whites of her eyes. He felt her wrist. He'd only known her for a short time, but something special was stirring; he sensed it like a kiss from a ghost.

The sweet perfume of mangos wafted through artificially heated air. As a steady pulse thumped beneath his fingertips, Rob sighed in relief and pressed her hand over his heart. He didn't know why he did it; it just seemed like the thing to do.

Cat opened her eyes.

"Why did you try to kill yourself?" he asked. "Is it because you lost your leg?"

A tear rolled down her cheek.

Rob swiped the tear away with his thumb and whispered, "I'll make a new one for you. A better one."

The offer, once uttered, solidified into a promise. The gears inside his head switched on and his mind turned like clockwork. As when he embarked on an engineering project, the numbers materialized before him. Angles and calculations dancing in the air, so tangible he could reach out and rework them as if on a chalkboard.

"Dreamer." Cat surveyed him beneath wet lashes. "Am I one of your broken birds?"

"You, Miss Mornay," Rob said, "need mending most of all."

A hand clapped him on the back and tugged him away from Cat. "Keep this up and I may leap off the roof, too."

Liam's words were light enough, but his tone sounded jagged, wrong. Rob let go of his tenuous grasp on Cat's hand and turned to his friend. A shadow of jealousy eclipsed Liam's face.

But why?

Rob turned to the fallen huntress, who had raised herself on her elbows. Cat's gaze shifted from Liam to Dr. Jekyll with a look much like...hate.

Why?

He glanced over his shoulder. Jekyll, stroking his manicured goatee, didn't look too friendly either. The three of them were having a conversation conducted entirely in stares, and damned if he knew what was being said.

"Is there something going on that I don't know about? Do you..." He wagged a finger between the doctor, Liam, and Cat, drawing an invisible triangle. "Do you three know each other?"

"No," Liam said.

Cat shook her head. "Never met."

The doctor had a more philosophical answer. "Do any of us really *know* each other?"

Rob frowned. He was so confused.

Jekyll stepped toward his tools and picked up the scalpel. "Let's attend to the business at hand, shall we?"

The blade glinted under the morning sun.

Cat flinched. Rob saw her hands ball up into fists. Was she afraid? Of Jekyll?

"Miss Mornay…" Jekyll grabbed a stone and sharpened his scalpel. "Would you kindly remove the sheet beside you?"

Cat turned to her right and Rob noticed a tremble appeared in the thumb-shaped divot between her collarbones.

The egg thumped beneath the sheet.

Rob stepped back. Liam's hands snaked inside his coat pockets. Only Cat remained still. With a sharp intake of breath, she snatched off the sheet and scooted off the table. Her peg struck the ground with a *clunk* as she stumbled behind a row of orchids, which was a rather poor choice of hiding place if that was her intention.

The egg was exactly as she'd described: a green jewel pulsing with life.

Jekyll crooked a finger. "Gather round, chickens. Nothing to be afraid of."

Liam took his place by the doctor's right hand.

Rob stepped forward, but Cat seized his elbow. "Don't go near it."

"I believe he intends to dissect it," Rob said, mesmerized by the pink fetus curled up like a seashell. "Aren't you the least bit curious?"

Fear clouded her eyes and transformed her complexion into ash. "I'd rather stay alive."

Rob gently pried his arm out of her grasp and joined the others.

Liam draped an arm over his shoulder. "She's a right ball 'n' chain, mate," he whispered. "I'd cut that bitch loose if I were you."

"Don't be cruel."

Behind them, Cat backed against the network of copper pipes. The fact that she hadn't run screaming from the glasshouse told him she shared his curiosity.

Under the sunlight, the egg emitted the same fluorescence as the beetles in the summer garden. Waverley called them glow flies, but he was fond of correcting her with the proper nomenclature, *Lampryis noctiluca*.

No one had ever attempted to dissect a Manu Diaboli egg. This was scientific history in the making and Rob was going to be part of it.

Jekyll pushed up his spectacles. "How long have I known you, lad?"

"Ten years," Rob said.

"You were seven and on the brink of death when your father brought you to my doorstep."

"Aye." A lump formed in his throat. His father was hardest on him, probably because he was a sickly runt compared to

249

Alec and a disappointment in all things. Yet here was a memory that had nearly slipped his mind. His father had been the one to seek out treatment after treatment for his illness before finding Jekyll.

"He was scared out of his wits, but you weren't the least bit afraid. Even at seven, you'd already made your peace with death, which is something my grown-up patients never learned, not even at the end."

Around him, Rob sensed the others straining to hear.

"Do you remember what I said the night you became my patient?" Jekyll smiled and a crop of wrinkles creased his eyes.

"You told me," Rob said, recalling a younger doctor with no wrinkles or graying sideburns, "that my heart was greater than my body and you promised to help my body catch up."

"I always keep my promises." Jekyll tapped the scalpel's blade to the apex of the egg. "Manu Diaboli: the deadliest predator ever to walk the earth. So feared that the tribesmen swear she is the living embodiment of the Devil's right hand. Hence the name, The Hand of the Devil." He peeked over his shoulder at Cat. "I hope I'm doing your father's research justice."

"Actually..." Huddled at the far end of the glasshouse, Cat probed a bruise on her forehead and winced. "My father named her The Hand of the Devil because she's shaped like a giant claw. He's rolling over in his grave."

"Dear me, so young and yet so devoid of poetry. A shame." Jekyll shook his head. "Let's carry on."

"Oh *let's*!" Cat echoed.

Ignoring her, Jekyll turned the egg so the embryo was on full display. Was this the creature that would grow into the world's deadliest predator? The hatchling was nothing more than a squished-faced lizard with gills. Rob scooted closer and studied the monster's hand. Five humanoid fingers.

"Manu Diaboli: a creature of contradiction," Jekyll continued. "A second in the presence of the adult spells certain death to all, with the exception of our charmed Miss Mornay."

"What of your *kept boy*?" Cat pointed her dragonbone dagger at Liam. "He snuck into the woods, same as me. Is he not charmed, too?"

"You forget," Liam said, "I met no monster."

"Maybe you did." The green blade rapped against her peg. "I warrant she took one look at you and thought you one of her spawns."

Liam bared his teeth and chomped down. His canines were sharp, like a wolf's.

"Children!" Jekyll gave Rob a long-suffering glance. "I ought to bash their skulls together. Thank goodness you operate on a higher intellectual plane… A deadly creature," Jekyll raised his voice, "but like you, lad, Manu Diaboli has a heart greater than the sum of her parts. A heart which, Hugh Mornay believed, would cure his dying wife." He poised his scalpel over the egg and the bickering ceased. "What? No protest, Miss Mornay?"

Cat stared at the ground. Her lashes glistened with unshed tears. "Everything you say is true."

"And your poor mother. She never got to consume the heart which was meant for her, did she?"

No answer.

Rob sensed Cat studying him. She left her place in the shadows and hobbled over to the table.

Jekyll waited for her to join the fold before continuing, "Life everlasting, lad. My gift to you…" Meeting Cat's eye, Jekyll brought the scalpel down on the egg.

A shriek echoed through the glasshouse. Rob clamped his hands over his ears. His gaze darted around, afraid the walls and ceiling would shatter and slice them into ribbons. But when his attention returned to the egg, Rob gave a start.

The egg was still intact. The doctor's scalpel, on the other hand, was bent at an angle. Liam and Cat stared at the phenomenon in open-mouthed shock, but Jekyll studied the useless blade and set it aside. "A shame."

Liam stepped forward, Bedouin knife in hand. "Let me."

"No." Jekyll touched his elbow. "Save Culler for later. You'll be needing it, boy."

"Culler?" Rob watched Liam tuck the blade back inside his coat. "You named your knife 'Culler'?"

"All blades should have a name," Liam said. "What do you call yours?"

"I don't have a blade."

Cat braced her palms on the table. "Viv and I call it Excalibur," she muttered.

Liam's eyes lighted with interest. "Is it really?"

"The mightiest sword in all the land."

This time, Jekyll did bash their skulls together. Liam and Cat spewed Shakespearian noises like ZOUNDS! and more colloquial ones like KRAKEN'S COCK!

"I'm still really confused." Rob frowned. "Excalibur isn't even real."

"So sheltered." Jekyll patted him on the head. "So blond..."

Massaging her forehead, Cat stepped up with her dagger. "Dragonbone trumps steel. I suppose it's my turn. Someone gave me this dagger a long time ago, and though his name escapes me, I have a feeling he'd want me to use it."

The doctor swept a hand toward the table and stepped aside. Rolling up her sleeves, Cat tackled the egg. The noise was no better.

Afterward, Rob wiggled a finger in his ear. "I think I've ruptured an eardrum."

In the end, dragonbone did trump steel. Cat's dagger retained its former shape, but the shell, despite a hairline scratch, was still intact.

Rob tapped the shell. Solid as marble. Invincible.

"What to do?" Jekyll looked to him. "What to do?"

Like any star pupil, Rob felt obliged to answer. The scientific portion of his brain began churning and the answer he arrived at was ridiculously simple or simply ridiculous. "Shells dissolve in vinegar."

Cat tapped the egg with the tip of her dagger. "We're going to need something stronger than vinegar."

"A corrosive, then?" Liam asked. "Acid?"

The doctor beamed proudly. "Tell them, Rob."

"My family owns a lighthouse in Orkney," Rob began, standing a little taller. "It's in horrible disrepair, practically disintegrating into rust. Alec used to post money every winter for its upkeep, but upon mid-summer *Scoliophis atlanticus* returns to nest."

Liam frowned. "*Scolio* what?"

"A sea snake, you snake," Cat said.

"The salivary gland of *Scoliophis atlanticus* contains the most powerful corrosive on earth," Rob said. "One blast can burn the blubber off a whale and turn a kelpie into mush. The venom will dissolve iron and steel, monster eggs, the hatching, and the exoskeleton of the adult…"

His impromptu lesson was met by silence. Finally, Jekyll slapped his hands together. "A monster to hatch a monster. Even you, Miss Mornay, cannot deny the poetry in that. Now it's a question of how badly we want this dark treasure." He draped an arm over Rob's shoulder. "Who will help me fulfill my promise to Lord Robert?"

"Me." Liam stepped forward without a second's hesitation. Rob smiled. "Thank you, mate."

Jekyll's eyes flickered to Cat. "And what says the huntress?"

Cat began scratching her inner arms.

Taking her silence as a sign that she was planning to pack off and leave monster hunting—and him—behind, Rob thought it only gentlemanly to step in and help the poor girl save face. "She's in no condition or obligation to—"

"Me too," she said, so softly the three of them had to strain to hear. "Count me in."

"Well, King Arthur," the doctor whispered in his ear, "I believe you have your knights now."

CHAPTER 17
INTERVENTION

Rob inventoried the materials he'd need over a steaming bowl of turnip stew.

He performed the heavy calculations while absently turning over a slice of veal braised in red wine. By the time the footman marched in with lavender sorbets on silver trays, Rob had a complete blueprint. If he worked throughout the night, he'd have most of the project assembled before morning. Before Cat left the safety of Balfour Manor to kill another monster for his sake.

"You're not eating," the doctor whispered in his ear. "What did I tell you about finishing your plate?"

"What was that?" Rob gazed down at the cut-glass bowl. A mint leaf floated on purple slush. Spooning the melted sorbet into his mouth, Rob admired the intricate contraption of steel springs and leverages meant to replicate tendons, joints, and toes. He felt proud at solving yet another feat of engineering and wondered if this was how God felt when he made Eve out of Adam's rib.

A hand passed in front of his face.

"When dining with dreamers," Jekyll snapped his fingers, "I might as well be talking to myself."

Rob set down his spoon and surveyed his surroundings through the filter of a swiftly vanishing haze. He blinked away the numbers, but the blueprint left a ghostly imprint in the air.

As far as farewell suppers went, this one lacked flair. There were just the three of them at the lonely table. As laird, Rob sat at the head, flanked by the doctor on his right, Cat on his left. Liam had declined his invitation, preferring to take supper in his room away from the thinly veiled disgust of the servants. Vivian was in her room too, probably weeping over Cat's next hunt.

Embers crackled in the fireplace, casting shadowy fingers across portraits of Rob's ancestors. They were a fierce lot, bearded and kilted, posing with broadswords or hunting rifles.

Rob pawed his cheek—baby smooth with no hint of fuzz— and sighed. "Sorry, I had something on my mind." Virgil's wet snout nuzzled against his palm. He plucked a boiled potato from the table and fed the dog. Virgil licked his hand.

"Whatever is on your mind," Jekyll said, swirling his whiskey around, "I hope it's more pleasant than what's on Miss Mornay's."

Turning to his left, Rob noticed Cat's head was bowed. Black hair shrouded her face. She was rocking.

The doctor leaned forward and cupped her by the chin. Her hair parted, revealing glassy, drugged-over eyes.

Rob folded his napkin, the euphoria of creation quite dashed. "Oh Cat, tell me you didn't..."

"When was the last time you checked your pantry?" Jekyll released Cat and wiped his fingers on his napkin. "It looks like a mouse has been at your serum supply."

"If I'm a mouse, you, sir, are a *rat*." Lolling her head against her chair, Cat gazed at the doctor with a dreamy smile. "A giant rodent with beady eyes and a greedy black heart. I had a vision about you, Jekyll, if that is in fact your real name." She giggled and covered her mouth.

Jekyll arched a brow. "If by 'vision' you mean 'drug binge,' then by all means, entertain us with your hallucinations."

"Well, all right." Cat sat up straighter and her nails worried at her arms.

Did she have no sense of self-control? Rob rested his elbows on the table and massaged his temples. To get this high on the eve before another monster hunt? Did she learn nothing from the last one?

"I was dressed in the strangest clothes," she began.

Rob lifted his head. "I don't want to hear it. Doctor, don't encourage her. Here, Cat, I'll have Mrs. Nix show you to bed."

"...the strangest clothes and carrying this odd lantern that required no kerosene or fire," she repeated. "And wandering through a labyrinth of hallways. There were doors of all shapes and sizes. I opened them one by one, searching and searching. The hours ticked away, but I couldn't leave until I'd found it. I think I would've searched for all eternity."

"What were you searching for?" Rob asked. Even sour spirits could not dampen his curiosity or hunger for a good story. What were these strange clothes she spoke of? And what was this lantern that required no kerosene to light?

Cat swiped at a strand of hair snagged in her mouth. "I could very well be searching for life everlasting, but *she* was there. Lurking in the shadows. Always one step behind me. Always with me."

Rob leaned toward her. "She?"

"The Great Mother, Manu Diaboli." Cat's face turned the palest white. "We are linked, she and I. Even when we're both dead, we'll find each other across space and time. I could *not* let her touch me and then I fell. Right through the floor and straight into Hell. That's where I met you, Doctor..." She picked up her knife, ran her thumb across the dull blade. "You, Barclay, and all the rats of the city who call you king."

Rob frowned. It was obvious Cat and Jekyll—and Liam for that matter—didn't get on. For the life of him, he couldn't figure out why. All three of them were flawed, sure, but good at heart. He wished they could see what he saw.

"What's she talking about?" he asked.

Jekyll downed the last of his whiskey. "Damned if I know. My dear, put down the knife. We wouldn't want you to hurt yourself."

"…you tried to eat my leg, Doctor. I couldn't have that—" Her hand came down with a *crash*. Rob leaped to his feet. The knife was impaled in her uneaten steak. "I stabbed you through the gut and you squealed and *squealed.*" Snatching up the knife, Cat tossed the rare steak at Jekyll. It fell just short of his plate and landed on the tablecloth with a *plop*. "A rat like you…"

As her hysterical laughter bounced off the walls, Jekyll folded his napkin. "Well, lad, we have seen true madness now, haven't we?"

♦

A dreamer he may be.

Blind and stupid he was not.

Rob led Liam to the scullery.

They stopped at the door. Rob peeked inside. The kitchen was deserted. He felt foolish sneaking around in the wee hours, but the silly maids would have a screaming fit at the sight of his disfigured friend. He motioned for Liam to follow. It couldn't be easy to fall from exquisite beauty to extreme monstrosity. Ever since his accident, Liam had become a creature of darkness, embracing night, chasing shadows, shunning daylight.

Liam lifted the padlock on the pantry door. "Key?"

Rob shrugged. "Mrs. Nix has it and she isn't going to give it to me."

"It's your house, mate." His hand disappeared inside his broadcloth coat.

"'Young masters,'" Rob quoted Mrs. Nix, "'have no business in the kitchens.'" He glanced uneasily behind his shoulder. The bulky outline of the gas stove loomed like a hungry beast. "She invented the rule because of Alec. We had to send a few maids home because of him. They were in the family way. Quite the scandal."

"And you?" The curved blade flashed and the lock popped. "Have you developed your brother's fondness for pretty maids?" Liam dropped the padlock into Rob's palms. Slender fingers wrapped around the door handle. "Or are your tastes only specific to one-legged drug fiends?"

"She won't be a drug fiend much longer." His voice grated in the dark, steely and determined.

"But she'll still only have one leg." Liam tugged Rob's earlobe. "I thought you fancied her, but you're really a sadistic little shite. Your hunter is going to hurt and hurt bad."

262

Recalling the morning of the hunt, Rob rubbed his bottom lip. If Cat hadn't gone in the woods with a bloodstream full of Jekyll's serum, she'd still have her leg. Rob blamed himself. He should've tried harder to keep her from the hunt, but he'd been fixated on his own heartbreak and overly confident in Cat's invincibility. He couldn't take back that day, but he could prevent history from repeating itself.

"That's a risk I'll have to take," Rob said. "Cat Mornay will never see a drop of green again."

"Heartless." A slow smile spread across Liam's lips. "I love it."

Liam returned to the pantry, but Rob touched his elbow. "Wait, I have something for you." Rob fished out a small velvet-wrapped bundle from inside his breast pocket and shoved it unceremoniously into Liam's hands. "I know you and Cat don't get on, so this is a token of my appreciation for helping me do this."

Arching a singed off-eyebrow, Liam fumbled with the wrapping.

He uncovered a silver mask and frowned.

"I made it from memory. Now people can see you as I've always seen you: an angel in winter." Rob shifted from foot to foot, waiting for his friend to say something. "But you don't have to wear it," he amended, taking Liam's silence for offense, "I'll take it back—"

263

Liam surprised him by swooping in and pecking him on the cheek. It was an innocent kiss, brotherly, but close enough to his mouth that he could feel the warm imprint of Liam's lips. It was not an unpleasant feeling—not unlike Cat's soft kiss.

"I'll never take it off." Liam's voice was unsteady. A wet cheek grazed his temple; a teardrop dampened Rob's collar. Rob didn't know whether to wrap his arms around his friend or push him away. He cleared his throat and swatted Liam on the arm. "We better get to work before Mrs. Nix finds us, and I've got a lot of explaining to do if the old bat finds us like this...I mean, if she finds us breaking into her pantry."

"Right." Sniffling, Liam turned around. He tucked the mask's leather strap behind his ears and smoothed down his hair. When he turned around, Liam was an angel in winter once again, beauty and dignity restored.

Liam yanked open the wooden door and a green glow glinted off his silver mask. Rob stepped inside and picked up the first vial. He nodded to Liam and together they gathered a total of fifty vials.

At the sink, Rob held one of Jekyll's serums at eye level. Recalling the madness lurking behind Cat's dilated pupils, he uncorked the stopper. "This is for your own good," he said, and poured the medicine down the drain.

◆

After tossing fifty empty vials in the garbage, Rob retreated to his solarium and unfurled the blueprint of the leg from his mind.

He was a poor excuse for a laird. In life, he was merely a "boy" amongst men and the grand world dwarfed him. But in the arena of his imagination, he could spin kingdoms and forge empires.

Rob cracked his knuckles. The calculations danced in the air. He reached out and grasped the numbers, tackling the plans and molding them into reality.

He had no need of candle or lantern, but harnessed the light from the stars. There would be no sleep for him tonight.

There was a darkness in the corner of the room, and in the coughs he stifled in the folds of his handkerchief, but his love for Cat kept the darkness and the illness at bay.

◆

Cat slammed the pantry door and stared at the monstrous outline of the great stove. The steel grid seemed to be grinning at her.

In the window above the sink, a pink streak blazed the sky. A rooster crowed in the distance. Her head lolled against the door, listening to the scuffing of worn soles on stone. Soon the kitchen would swarm with servants and she hadn't gotten what she came for.

Cat shut her eyes.

Gone. All gone.

The pantry, which once glowed like an emerald beacon, was suffused in darkness. The shelves were mysteriously barren. Some rat had snuck in during the night and stolen all her treasure.

"Mr. Hyde." She tightened her grip on her crutch. If Mr. Hyde and Liam thought they could get the best of her by cutting off her supply, they'd better think again. Cat remembered the stash under her bed and scratched her arms. She'd nothing to worry about. There was enough to last her for the journey.

The sunlight crept across the floor. Instead of stray straw and chicken feathers, she saw lianas and towering fig trees. The voices in the hallway were drowned out by the first of the sailor's screams.

As the nightmare won over, Cat banged her head against the door.

♦

Her stash was gone.

The ten vials.

Her glass syringe.

Even the leather strap she used to tie around her arms.

With her cheek pressed to the floor, Cat slid her hand underneath the mattress. Her hand grazed splintered wood. She searched again, hoping for a different result. A bead of sweat dribbled into her eye. Panic hammered against her temple, obscuring the creak of the door.

"Cat?" Dainty footsteps drew closer. "They're waiting for you," Vivian said. "What...what are you doing?"

"Where is it?" She eased herself up and caught Vivian staring in disgust at the bunch of her trousers around her stump. Cat reached for her peg, which she'd been forced to take off as the blasted thing made bending and crouching next to impossible.

"I don't know what you're talking about." Vivian averted her eyes as Cat rolled up her trousers.

"I believe you do." After strapping on her peg, Cat scavenged the floor for her scattered crutch. "Don't play stupid with me. You're the only one who knows where I keep it."

Sunlight turned Vivian's curls into spun gold and streamed through her white muslin gown. "All I know is you're not even packed and it's nearly time to go."

"You have a tremble, just here," Cat pointed to her own throat, "like you swallowed a bird. That's the truth, sweetling, pecking its way out. You're bloody lying and yet you stare at me with such guileless eyes!"

"He told me that stuff was killing you…" The tears fell, one after the other.

"He?" Hoisting herself up, Cat lurched toward her sister. "Who's 'he'? Dr. Jekyll? Or that faceless maggot?"

Shaking her head, Vivian took a step back. "He made me promise not to tell."

"It was Jekyll, wasn't it? You touched my things. Gave it to that rat!" Cat caught Vivian by the shoulders. Her sister felt so fragile, bones like a bird's. "Tell me!"

Crying was an art Vivian knew well, and she managed to look tragic and lovely while doing it. The more her sister wept, the angrier Cat became.

"He cares about you, too. Please, Cat, don't be angry." Vivian's hands fluttered about Cat, trying to cup her face.

Cat shook her off.

"I was only trying to help," her sister said.

Cat seized Vivian by the arm and twisted. "What did you do with my Elixir?"

"I was…. *Ahhhhhh.*"

"What did you do with my Elixir?" Cat repeated, twisting harder.

But all she got for an answer were incoherent pleas for mercy.

She had no mercy. Did Manu Diaboli ever show mercy to her?

With another twist, her sister's pathetic mewing turned to screams.

No Elixir.

No mercy.

♦

While Cat was spending quality time with her sister, Rob searched for his.

Upstairs: Waverley's room was empty.

Downstairs: she wasn't in the kitchen badgering the cook for an extra morsel of lemon tart.

He tried the stables where she liked to loiter and bicker with the lads. The groom jumped and cast nervous glances around as if the very mention of her name would spook the horses. "Not here," he said, and crossed himself in relief.

He made a round of the herb garden where she liked to speak to the squirrels and commune with nature. The squirrels seemed happy without Waverley there.

Rob slapped his riding glove against his palm and stomped by an ivy-covered section of the castle. She had to be somewhere. Bothering somebody.

Just as he was about to head inside the glasshouse where he'd expressly forbidden her to go, Waverley jumped out of the hedges.

"Waverley!"

Uttering a war cry, she swung her wooden sword at his shin.

Rob fell to his knees. "Bloody hell!"

"This is for leaving to Orkney without me!"

The flat of her sword struck him in the back. "Argh, little savage! Who told you?"

"Jim! Jim, who by the way, is going instead of me!" She raised the sword executioner style.

"Mercy!" Rob shielded his face. Girls liked his face, and he wouldn't want anything to happen to it. "Mercy!"

Rob cringed, expecting another bludgeoning, but Waverley tapped him on the shoulder. "All right," she said. "Don't piss yourself."

He cracked open an eye. His sister loomed over him, feet planted apart in a warrior stance.

"Is it safe to get up?" he asked.

"Depends." Waverley shrugged. There was a smear of blackberry jam on her chin and her hands were grubby and peasantlike. "Why Jim and not me?"

Because he isn't an abusive little scrub. "Not like I invited him along." Rob got to his feet and rubbed his sore shins. "I don't even really like him. He has no regard for personal space and he never blinks or eats. You ever notice he walks on his toes? Toe walkers are never to be trusted."

Waverley's teeth clamped down on his wagging finger.

"You bit me!"

"Don't you dare insult Jim!" She poked him in the chest. "He's my best friend."

"You never used to bite." Rob studied the teeth marks on his skin. "You learned this from Jim, didn't you?"

Another poke. "—and when we grow up we're going to be married!"

"*Married?* I don't think so. You'll marry who I tell you to marry!"

"La la la." Clamping her hands over her ears, Waverley circled him like Virgil.

"Stop running!" Rob swiped at her collar and was rewarded with an obscene hand gesture. His eyes widened. "Where'd you learn a nasty thing like that? Jim, isn't it? He's a bad influence!"

"I love him!"

"You're eight!"

"LA LA LA." Ducking beneath his arms, Waverley ran right into the castle. For a moment, Rob thought she was going to ram the wall and wail about a broken nose, but she disappeared as if absorbed into the hedge.

Rob blinked. "Waverley?"

When she didn't answer, Rob rolled up his sleeves and stomped toward the bush. Prickly leaves and branches swatted him in the face until he found a hip-high slit in the stone—a secret doorway he never knew existed. With an uneasy glance around the lawn, Rob crouched down and slipped inside.

She was huddled at the entrance of what looked to be the beginning of a tunnel. The inside was dank and reeked of rat droppings.

"Where are we?"

Waverley hugged her knees to her chest. "My dark place."

"It isn't very clean, is it?" Tugging a handkerchief from his pocket, Rob swiped a spot opposite his sister and sat down. The pristine linen came away black. "How come I never knew about it?"

"Maybe because you were in England with all your posh friends?"

Once his eyes adjusted to the darkness, he spotted a Catholic cross nailed in the corner and it occurred to him that Waverley's "dark place" was a priest hole from the Reformation. "Where do the tunnels lead to?"

"To the kitchens." A spider crawled across the back of her hand. She let it trickle over her knuckles and bridged its progress with her other hand. "Then to secret chambers all over the castle. One even leads to the Mornays' room. I saw your

272

hunter naked. She's got bruises all over her arms and big ugly scars on her back."

"Stop it, I don't want to know what she looks like naked!" He ducked his head. Even in the darkness, he was sure she could see him blush. "Hey," he nudged her foot with his shoe. "Still cross at me?"

"I will hate you until I die." She plucked the spider off her hand and dumped it on the floor. Rob cringed and scooted away. "Unless you let me come along."

"Now Duck—"

"You're going and you're as sissy as they come. I'm a better monster hunter than you. I've already thrashed you."

"Which is precisely why I need you to stay home."

"But Rob!" Her voice bounced across the walls of her subterranean hiding place. For a girl so small, she sure was loud.

"I'll need a true warrior to look after the clan when I'm gone," he said, tugging the sapphire ring from his finger. Digging in his pocket, he located the silver chain he had bought especially for his sister and looped it through the ring. He scooted toward her and draped the necklace around her. "Can you do that for me? Watch out for Finley and Mrs. Nix? Keep an eye on the fae woods?"

Waverley played with the sapphire. A sniffle echoed in the dark. "Alec's ring."

"*Your* ring. You're laird while I'm away."

"Will you be wanting it back?"

"Keep it. It fits you better." He tugged on her earlobe. "Still cross at me, Duck?"

Waverley flung her arms around him and planted a sloppy kiss on his cheek. Back in her good graces, Rob decided to press his luck. "Now about this marrying Jim business…"

◆

Cat sent for Jekyll.

Much as she loathed the man, she needed a doctor and this bloke asked no questions. She huddled in the corner as Jekyll popped Vivian's shoulder back into place. When it was over, Jekyll guided a nearly catatonic Vivian to bed.

"There, now." The doctor tightened Vivian's linen brace. "Just like new."

Cat scrubbed a hand over her face. "Will she be okay?"

"Your sister's a lucky one. A nasty fall like that would've snapped her arm like a flower stem but she got off with only a minor dislocated shoulder." He tweaked Vivian on the nose. "Watch your step, pretty one. Next time you might not be so lucky."

Taking Vivian gently by the wrist, Jekyll pulled up her sleeve and brushed his thumb over the hand-shaped bruises. Cat met the doctor's stare straight on. Jekyll's lips twitched as he covered the evidence. "It's a good thing," he said to Vivian, "you have a sister such as Cat to look out for you."

Cat felt Vivian's eyes shift to her.

"I'm truly blessed," Vivian said.

There was a crack in her corner of the room. Cat wished she could crawl into it.

"You've a late start, lass." Jekyll draped a wool blanket around Vivian's shoulders and tucked her injured arm inside. "I trust you're packed?"

What else did she require on a kill besides her dagger, sword, and pistol?

Cat limped toward the bed. "I'll be back in no time. We'll talk then." She spoke to the top of Vivian's head. Her pathetic attempt at reconciliation was met by silence. "I love you, my darling." She bent down to peck her sister on the cheek, but Vivian turned her head away.

Picking up her knapsack of weapons, Jekyll touched her elbow and accompanied her to the door. In the hallway, he extended a hand. "May I have the honor?"

She stared at his manicured fingers, but didn't take it.

"Come now, Miss Mornay, forgive and forget. I'll forget what you did to that poor girl and perhaps you can find it in your heart to forgive the very negligible fact that I amputated your leg to save your life. Come, come," he wiggled his fingers, "shake shake."

"For what you did for Vivian, I thank you. But I know…" Her teeth clenched. "I know you took it."

"Took what?" Jekyll frowned. His confession seemed about as genuine as his nice doctor act.

Cat clasped his hand between both of hers. "Know something funny? I always wondered what our prophet would look like." Her eyes flickered over his wrinkled face. "Hyde would have kind eyes, like my father…"

His eyes were indeed kind. Even Cat had to concede that was not something one could fake. But Jekyll's irises were two black windows through which evil crawled and slithered. And that was not something one could fake either. Good and evil resided in the house of one man.

And that man cooed, "Wayward angel, are you so in need of guidance? If you let me, I shall lead you, as I've led Barclay, into the path of light…"

She tightened her grip. His hands were surprisingly brittle; if she squeezed harder, she'd crush every bone. Let's see him try to perform surgeries now.

The doctor grimaced, yet managed to uphold his calm demeanor. "Dear me. We *are* in an arm-breaking mood today, aren't we?" The grimace morphed into a strained smile. *"Bad Kitty."*

Cat leaned in and whispered in his ear, "Die screaming, you two-faced rat fink."

◆

After bidding Dr. Jekyll a fond farewell, Cat hitched her knapsack across her shoulder and limped away. The drag of her peg echoed down the hallway, a broken and lonely sound.

Midway down the stairs, Cat sensed she wasn't walking alone. A warm hand brushed her palm and the jingle of bells breached the dreary silence. Jim Hawkins had fallen into step beside her.

She grimaced at his tweed jacket and knee-britches. "You're looking right smart. Where do you think you're going?"

He pointed to the open door where a faint drizzle caressed the lawn.

"Go with me? I don't think so!"

Jim took her knapsack of weapons and hoisted it about his shoulder.

"You really are a pest." She spotted an unruly tuft of hair poking beneath the brim of his cap. Licking her fingers, Cat smoothed it down. "If the serpent gobbles you up, I'd be rid of you at last."

Jim beamed at her, dimples deepening, but when he followed her, the bells heralded his every step.

Cat halted. "Take that bloody bracelet off!"

The lad shook his wrist and pointed. *This thing?*

"Aye. Bad enough I have this," she said, tapping her peg. "You might as well be ringing the supper bell and calling yourself the main course."

With a shrug, Jim plucked off every one of the tiny bells and flung them over his shoulder. He kept the copper band on and stroked it like it had great meaning for him.

One became two.

As they marched across the lawn, Cat glanced over her shoulder to the second-story window. The damask curtain fluttered and Vivian appeared. Guilt flooded Cat at the sight of the sling. She swiped the rain from her eyes, debating whether or not to limp back inside and make everything right. She'd already apologized a thousand times and to no avail. What was a thousand more?

Cat raised her hand in a pathetic attempt at a wave. Vivian's breath frosted the glass pane. With a swish of the curtain, her sister vanished, and misgiving settled upon Cat with the chill. Suppose this hunt did not turn out well and she never saw her sister again?

Leaving Vivian behind was for the best. While Cat worried about the doctor, she knew he wouldn't do anything to jeopardize his Dr. Jekyll persona with Rob around. Sad as it was to say, Vivian was probably safer in the hands of that rat than with her own sister.

"Bother her." Cat whirled around and continued her long walk toward the rutted road to Orkney. "I'll bring her something pretty and all will be well." Then she glanced down at her companion. His mouth was drawn into a solemn line.

"I hurt her bad, Jim."

He spat on her shoe. *I know.*

Cat nodded in defeat. She deserved that. "I'm giving it up," she whispered. "Starting now. No more Elixir. For Vivian's sake. And yours." But her resolution sounded hollow and empty.

Arching a skeptical brow, Jim held up a pinky finger. *Promise?*

"Promise." Cat hooked her pinky with his.

Just to make sure, Jim swiped a twig from the ground. He pointed at Cat, then snapped the twig in half.

Cat frowned. "If I break my promise…"

Jim took the larger half of the twig and snapped it again.

"You break me?"

To expound his point, he chucked all the fragments on the ground and jumped up and down on them.

"Now you're just being melodramatic," she said. "But aye, I get it. Woe to she who breaks a fae promise."

Jim slapped his hands together and gestured for them to hurry along.

When they passed the glasshouse, another set of footsteps fell into line. Whereas Jim seemed to glide above the ground, this presence slithered like a snake in the grass.

"Just like old times." Liam slung an arm around Cat. His fingers dug into her shoulder. "Nothing like a fresh kill to make the blood sing!"

"Piss off." Cat shrugged off his arm and caught a glimpse of his new face. Her eyes widened. "Christ, what in the name of sanity is that?"

"I'm back." Rocking on his heels, Liam tipped his bowler hat to show off his silver mask, which captured every perfect feature of his former face. "Do you find me pretty?"

"I find you as repulsive as always," Cat said. "Where'd you get a thing like that?"

Despite her loathing, Cat scooted closer. The mask was angelic and cold—just as Liam used to be before the burning.

"Rob. Made it just for me." Liam smoothed his brown hair back. "Jealous?"

"Why should I be jealous?" Cat marched on and yet the mask still loomed before her. Rob had memorized every detail of Liam's face, designed and forged the silver out of love.

"Remember the Isle of May?" Liam caught up with her. "You. Me. The smashing waves. All those lovely mermaid tits, the rocks slippery with blood. Almost as slippery as you that night at camp. Remember the nasty things you begged me to do to you? Or were you too high?"

Grinding to a halt, Cat covered Jim's ears and turned him around in case he read lips. "Nothing happened."

He stepped closer, tickling her chin with his forefinger. "I've seen every bit of you, Miss Mornay. The claw marks on your back, the mole on your inner thigh, right over a nice fat vein. Such creamy, unmarked skin. 'Stick it there,' you'd said, and the needle sunk in like butter. You wanted all the Elixir at once, but I gave it to you slowly. One drop at a time and oh how you mewed for more. Don't tell me you forgot?"

"I remember." Jim kicked at her shins; Cat held him tighter. "The needle was the only thing you managed to stick in me. Not that you need to know, but I'm still a virgin."

"It's a shame you were so high you couldn't even recall the best screwing of your miserable life." Liam shouldered her aside. "There isn't a virgin thing about you."

"I think I would know about the state of my down-unders." Releasing Jim, Cat hobbled after him. "I remember how you worked yourself into a frenzy…"

Cat saw his shoulder tense and smiled.

"Bollocks!" Liam picked up the pace.

"Good thing you'd smashed my face in the grass, because it sounded like you were trying to pick a lock with a wet herring.

281

And afterward, you collapsed on top of me, whispering his name into the back of my neck…" She didn't care if Jim heard. She wanted the wind to carry the truth for all to hear. "I didn't know who he was then. Now it's all so clear!"

When it came to Liam, Cat never had the upper hand. Now the hand was hers and she was going to use it to slap the shite out of him. "Charlie isn't really your brother, is he? Nor were the other boys. Blond hair, blue eyes, wispy things. Copies of an original. Now I know who your original is. I've even kissed him…"

"Shut up!" Liam whirled around, Culler at the ready. Cat whipped out her dagger.

A bark stopped them both dead.

Virgil sprinted toward them. The Border Collie trotted to Jim and poked the boy's hand with his snout.

Jim jogged after Virgil.

Cat and Liam glared at each other. A soft haze drifted over them, sizzling around their hate.

"The time will come," Liam said.

"Aye, the world is not big enough for both of us."

Liam tucked Culler inside his black coat and nodded toward the road. "Hobble along, peg-leg."

Virgil led them to the knee-high stone wall dividing the Balfour Estate from the wild crags of the north.

Seated under the canopy of a greenwood tree, Rob scribbled in a leather-bound journal, his boots tapping a beat on the lid of a steamer trunk.

The suitcase did not sit well with Cat. "Did you know he was coming along?"

Liam shrugged. "No one ever said anything to me."

Virgil pawed Rob's knee and Jim climbed on the wall to sit beside him. Cheeks flushed with cold, Rob continued to write until Jim poked him in the arm and broke his concentration.

Rob shut the journal and his face lit up. "The groom has readied three of my finest horses. Shall we?"

He was so wispy a gust of wind could blow him away, but Cat saw the sun in that smile. She turned to Liam and believed he did, too.

CHAPTER 18
CREATURES OF DARKNESS

They traveled north.

Across crumbling bridges and over treacherous crags.

They passed rune stones marked with Pictish symbols.

Forged across peat bogs and rode through emerald glens with not a soul in sight. The only sounds to greet their ears were the cry of a hawk and Virgil's bark.

Rob was on a great adventure.

His boots blistered his soles. His thighs ached and burned from riding all day.

For someone who'd lived his entire life cloistered behind stone walls and trapped inside his own mind, he'd never been happier.

Whenever he stumbled or stopped to catch his breath, his friends were right by his side.

Liam and Cat.

Even creepy Jim.

He called them his knights.

And so they traveled north, where even in summertime, the glens were grey with hoarfrost and the wind screeched like a flock of harpies.

Rob traveled on with no fear of death or danger from unnatural creatures. He existed in a heaven where a sickly whelp like him could walk in safety because he did not walk alone.

◆

By nightfall, they made camp along the banks of a loch.

"Is there anything I can do?" Rob wandered around the fire as Jim roasted hare on a spit. Jim shook his head and waved him away.

"Anything?" he called to Liam.

"Rest!" Liam was midway up a small hillock where the moss-covered ruins of a Roman chapel loomed.

Rob jogged after him. "Can I help you scout?"

"No! You may hurt yourself!"

"I'm not as fragile as all that," he muttered. He picked up a stone and skipped it into the loch. The stone sunk into dark water like so much dead weight. Too excited about tomorrow's hunt to sleep, Rob wandered the marshes in search of Cat.

He found her huddled on the left bank, hidden by shadowy reeds and curled on her side. Her face was dead white, her lips thinned and pleated by pain.

"Cat!" He raced to her side and brushed the hair from her face. Her skin was beaded with cold sweat. "What can I do?"

"P-p-please." Her teeth chattered with each violent spasm. "E-e-lixir. J-just one drop. Please!"

Rob held her shivering body. His eyes brimmed with tears, but he shook his head. It felt like the cruelest gesture, especially since he'd cut off her supply. "I don't have any serum."

Nor would he give her any if he did. He was not going to give in.

"Y-you do." Her fingernails sunk into his forearm. "You have it all. I know you do. Please spare just one v-vial. Mercy." With a cry, Cat clamped her hands over her ears. "Make them stop. Stop. Stop screaming!"

He spotted her peg lying against an algae-coated boulder. Her naked stump was red and raw. Rob lowered her to the ground and rose on unsteady feet. "I'll get you some water."

At the bank, Rob knelt in the pebbles. Water lapped around his knees, soaking his trousers. The serene loch contained an entire constellation. Then a scaly back breached the surface, scattering the stars. Startled, Rob backed away. Once his heart ceased racing, he squinted at the dark waters and saw only a ring of ripples.

He dipped a cautious hand in the icy loch and glanced back at Cat.

The huntress was a mystery to him. Her life consumed by perpetual darkness, her world ruled by monsters and evil men, but for Rob, the darkest hour always came before the dawn.

There was even light in Alec's death because it brought Cat to him. As for her hatred of Dr. Jekyll and Liam, that was something he could never understand. She'd called them monsters, but she didn't know them as he did. They were not perfect, but he believed—would go to his grave believing—they were truly good at heart.

So it seemed he and Cat lived in different spheres. Her world was an unfriendly hell, and Rob wished he could whisk her off to a place where there was no night. A destination, here on earth, where they could be together and walk under the sun.

When he returned, Cat had ceased moaning. She still shivered, but the spasms were less violent. He took her in his arms and drizzled water over her chapped lips.

"What's this place called again?" he asked.

"Loch Ness," she said.

"I thought I saw…" Gazing at the tranquil water, Rob shook his head. "Never mind."

"Vivian said someone talked her into taking my Elixir." Cat watched his reaction. "I had a chat with the doctor and he didn't know his face from his bunghole. She said 'He.' Is 'he' you? Did you take all my pretty green drugs?"

Rob held her closer. She was all skin and bones. "It was the only way."

"I ought to cut off your head and shite down your neck." She grasped his hand, twined her fingers around his, and buried her face against his soft wool sweater. "Why are you so cruel?"

He traced the seashell curve of her ears. Such small ears with hardly any lobe. Leaning in, he conferred a secret. "Because I love you."

Cat stared at him, a frown tugging at her brow. "Dreamer, you hardly know me. You can't fall in love over one stupid kiss—in only a few weeks. Besides, I'm too old for you."

"Only by two years." Rob hid his smile in her hair. "I like older women. They've much to teach me."

"I have one leg."

"I don't mind."

"I'd just threatened to cut off your head and shite down your neck."

"A physical impossibility." He tipped her chin up and forced her to look at him. "If you can find Manu Diaboli across space and time, why can't we find each other? I know my own heart. I know how to heed its call. My mind is made up. I love you, so don't argue with me or I may apply the same threat to you, though it is a rather ghastly thing to do to anyone's neck hole."

"You are, without a doubt, the stupidest boy I've ever met. You don't love me. You love the *idea* of me. I'm no..." Her lips twisted into a bitter smile and in her eyes, Rob saw all the

289

sadness of the world. "I'm no hero. Strip away the bloated tales and I'm nothing. There's nothing inside me *worth* loving."

"Stop it." He shook his head, never realizing Cat's self-loathing extended to such poisonous depths. "Stop saying that."

"When you leave your sheltered little nest, you'll quickly learn there are no heroes. Check with me in a year. Maybe ten. See if you'll love me then."

"I haven't got ten years," he said. "And you're wrong. Heroes exist, same as monsters. I'm surrounded by them."

"I'm surrounded by monsters. You live in a world of knights." She studied him with a wistful expression. "It seems we're at a crossroad."

"My world is better." Rob smiled. "Won't you join me?"

She raised her hand and tapped his cheek. It was meant to be a slap, but her fingers lingered against his jaw. "How young you are…"

Rob seized the opportunity to kiss her palm. Her shivers began anew and he held her tighter. Her left hand was closed over a pink and chalky object. "What's this?"

She opened her hand and dropped a piece of coral on her abdomen. It looked so out of place amongst the slate mountains and patches of ground frost. He'd only ever seen coral in an illustration. Never in real life. Never held it between his fingers.

Rob picked it up, twirled it around in the moonlight. "Where'd you get this?" he asked softly.

"Antigua."

"I was supposed to go there after my birthday." Rob closed his hand over the coral and swallowed the lump in his throat. No use crying over a stillborn dream. "I didn't know you'd been there."

"Da took us when we were little. Vivian stayed in the shade while I did cartwheels in the sand. We were supposed to sail there with your money. Heaven on earth, Rob... Heaven on earth is a tropical paradise, but I fear the gates are shut to me."

Another spasm zipped through her body. He crossed his legs and settled her more comfortably over his lap. "Nonsense."

"But I can see you there." A sad smile etched across her lips. "Strolling along the white sands, your skin browned by the sun. You belong there..." Her head sagged against his thigh. Her eyes were slits, her words slurred by encroaching sleep. "In the splendor and the glory...of Heaven."

After Cat drifted to sleep, Rob whispered a promise in her ear: "When this is over, we shall go there together."

◆

Cat woke to the gentle lapping of water.

For the first time in a long time, no jungle or monsters, rats or birds of prey infested her sleep. She closed her eyes, savoring the dream. She was in the West Indies, walking along the beach with Rob. They tracked footprints in the sand and this was how she knew it was a dream: two sets of prints, *four* feet, no peg.

Rob, too, was filtered through the lens of fantasy. He was taller, his face sun-kissed instead of ghostly white, his body lean and muscled. This Rob didn't look like he could float away with the slightest breeze.

She raised herself on her elbows. Rob's tweed blazer bunched around her. She drew it close and inhaled the scent of summer rain, but Rob was nowhere in sight.

Feeling lighter than air, she strapped on her peg and went in search of Rob. A crackling fire drew her to the opposite bank where Jim Hawkins sat atop a log, hunched over something on his lap.

A *clink clink* resounded through the quiet.

The head of a tiny copper hammer flashed in the firelight's glow. As Cat limped closer, she caught sight of Rob's steamer trunk. Her hand hovered over Jim's shoulder.

Before she could tap him, the lad's pointy ears twitched.

Jim dumped everything inside the trunk and slammed the lid. He whirled on her, eyes narrowed into suspicious slits.

"What are you building?" Cat peered at the trunk.

He hopped off the log, plopped himself on the trunk, and folded his arms. Black eyes gleamed with a defiant light.

"Rob will be cross if he finds you've gotten into his things," she said, reaching for the trunk's metal snaps. "I'd better have a look, make sure you didn't break—"

He snapped at her hand like a feral dog. Cat stumbled backward in shock. "Nasty pup, you tried to bite me!"

Jim bared his tiny teeth and snarled.

"You've the devil in you. I should've killed you when I had the chance." She surveyed the deserted bank. There was only this demon child and Virgil, gnawing on a rabbit bone. She drew Rob's blazer closer for warmth. "Where's Rob?"

He pointed up a rocky hill to the ghostly ruins of an old church.

"At least you're good for something!" she said and received an obscene hand gesture from Jim. Her eyes widened. "Bugger me, where'd you learn that?"

Legs dangling over the trunk, Jim leveled his hand in the air, his gesture for a person of small stature.

"Waverley?"

He beamed up at her.

Oh no. She knew what that smile meant; she'd seen it make a fool out of Rob more times than not. Puppy love. How revolting.

Cat squared her shoulders. "Aye, well, I want you to keep away from that lot. She's a bad influence." She limped off in a huff, then whirled around and wagged her finger. "And if you say you love her, I will strike you dead on general principle!"

Having performed her maternal duties, Cat climbed the hill. By the time she crested the top, she was cursing her blasted peg, her hell-spawn ward, and the entire universe, which she believed had gone stark raving mad. Couldn't she go on a bloody monster hunt without some starry-eyed boy declaring his undying love?

The chapel exterior was smothered in ivy, its walls crumbling to dust, which only confirmed to Cat that nothing in this world ever lasts. Leaning on her crutch, she tilted her eyes to the roof. There was no roof, only a sparse collection of trees silhouetted against the starry sky.

Rob said he loved her and he was just naïve enough to mean it.

Cat knew better. It wasn't possible or wise to fall in love.

Love made one weak and in these dangerous times, she could not afford to be weak.

Cat could not afford to fall in love.

Voices emanated within the nave. Rob. Cat grimaced. And The Hand of the Devil himself: Barclay.

Ducking into the shadows, Cat peeked through the window slit.

"So you want to be a monster hunter..." Liam circled Rob like a buzzard. His face reminded Cat of the gargoyles perched around old Tron Kirk. How could Rob stand the sight of him?

Rob was holding a broadsword in the most awkward way possible. Not only could he stand Liam's deformity, he didn't seem to notice or care. In fact, he looked upon the older boy with such blind idolization that it turned Cat's stomach.

"I want to help," Rob said. "Show me what to do."

Cat rolled her eyes. It was bad enough Liam let him tag along, but if he meant to let Rob join the hunt, she'd be forced to tie Rob up and kill Liam for stupidity and insubordination.

"Straighten up." Liam tapped Rob on the shoulder. He took another turn and nudged Rob's heel with the toe of his boot. "Feet apart. Elbows at an angle, like this..." A hand glided down the length of Rob's arm. "And for Christ's sake, this is your sword, not your cock. You want to slay the serpent, not piss in its face."

Rob's laughter rang through the nave. A grin etched across Liam's peeling lips. Cat wrinkled her nose. *He ought to have kept the mask on.*

Suddenly Liam's grin vanished. "The hunt's not for you." He plucked the sword away and propped it next to a moldy pew. "Taking down a monster is a nasty business and you're not the killing kind. Come morning, you watch from the beach. I'd rather you keep your hands clean."

When he was around Rob, Liam actually acted like a decent human being. She pressed her cheek into the ivy, recalling how Liam hauled Rob's cumbersome steamer trunk over hills and across ravines without complaint. Could it be that Hyde's Avenging Angel had a soul? Cat didn't want to believe it. Monsters had no soul.

"Ah, cheer up, mate. You may be shite at swordplay," Liam reached inside his breast pocket, "but I have something you might fancy even better…" He held a vial between thumb and forefinger.

Cat hitched in her breath. "Thieving piece of shit."

"What's that?" Rob studied the vial with a frown.

Liam rattled the silver pills. "The Chinese call it…"

"Dragon's Breath," Cat whispered, her fingers digging into the window ledge. *My Dragon's Breath.* She thought she'd lost it, but Liam had it all along.

"Watch." Liam uncorked the vial and placed a pill on the tip of his tongue. Locking eyes with Rob, Liam took a swig of his canteen, swishing the water from one scarred cheek to the next. He tilted his head and a ball of fire ignited the night.

Clapping in glee, Rob let out an ungentlemanly whoop. "That was brilliant! May I?" He was on the verge of bouncing up and down.

"Open your mouth. Stick out your tongue." Liam paused with the pill midway above Rob's mouth. "Be careful. Mind where you blow. Don't be lighting the trees on fire."

"Uh-huh." Rob nodded with his tongue still hanging out of his mouth.

Another reason not to fall in love with him: Rob was a *young* seventeen. If she wanted a boy, she might as well fall for Jim Hawkins, who, like her, was an old and tormented soul.

Liam drizzled water into Rob's mouth and turned him around. "Have at it."

Cat debated stepping in and putting a stop to this whole thing in case Rob set himself on fire, but his first blow resulted in a puny spark not fit for a baby dragon. Rob wandered beneath a ghostly plume of smoke, handsome face alight with pride. Cat couldn't help smiling.

It took so little to make him happy. If he thought Dragon's Breath extraordinary, she could show him the lost empire of Aventine or the Valley of the Kings at dusk. Why they could sail the world and... But what kind of thoughts were these? She was getting to be as hopeless as Rob.

"May I try again?" Rob asked. "I was a bit short of breath the first time."

"Dragon's Breath will be your undoing. As it was mine." Liam laughed. "You've still got water on your chin. Come here," he said, dabbing the excess droplets with the frayed sleeve of his coat, then swiped his thumb across Rob's bottom lip. Cat sensed a change in the atmosphere; Liam was no longer laughing. He seemed nervous, frightened even. "You're my undoing."

"Liam..." Rob shook his head.

"No, let me." Liam replaced his thumb with his lips. "Let me."

Cat shifted her eyes. It wasn't the first time she'd caught two boys kissing. There were nights aboard the *Hispaniola* when the grunts and groans below deck didn't imply kissing at all. As she waited for Rob to pull away and saw that he didn't, she wondered if he enjoyed kissing Liam more than her. Jealousy flooded her like poison. Of all the people to be jealous of! Not her beautiful sister, but *Liam?* She had to put a stop to this. Now. Before the two started buggering each other right before her eyes.

Rob pushed Liam away. "I'm not like you."

"You were kissing me back. You cannot pretend you didn't enjoy it." Liam ducked in for another go. "Don't say you were doing it to be polite. Don't say—"

Rob flushed from temple to neck. "It's a sin!"

Liam cringed. "My love for you is a sin?"

"I didn't mean it like that." A battle played across Rob's face.

"I've been in love with you for years." Liam's voice, never raised above a whisper, filled the church with longing. As he plopped down on the nearest pew, his entire body deflated as if the life had been wrangled out of him. With a sincerity that not even Cat could dispute, he croaked, "It's the only good thing about me."

Rob raked a hand through his hair, causing the blond strands to stand up in a chaotic tuft. "I'm afraid I can't love you the way you want me to. I'm so sorry, I—"

"It's late." Liam drew his legs up to his chest. The gigantic cross on the altar cast an oppressive shadow over him, making it appear like he was trapped behind the bars of a dungeon. "And we've a sea monster to kill."

Rob's hand hovered over Liam's shoulder.

Liam whirled around. "Leave me!"

Cat waited until Rob fled the chapel. He stumbled down the hill and she knew he wouldn't sleep a wink. Rob was so easy to read. But Liam? She'd thought she had him all figured out, but as she hobbled down the aisle, she saw his shoulders shaking in silent sobs and remembered Da's theory of monsters.

All creatures of darkness crave the light.

It held true with Manu Diaboli.

And where Rob was concerned, Liam was no exception. They had at least that much in common.

"Here to gloat?" Liam wiped his nose on his sleeve. "Or are you here to kill me at last? Lucky Kitty, I may let you."

"The time will come." Cat picked up the silver mask and handed it to him. "But not tonight."

CHAPTER 19
WHAT HAPPENS IN ORKNEY

Rob gathered his blazer closer, but the sea mist crept under his skin.

Into his bones.

Into his lungs.

They burned like the embers of last night's fire, which he'd curled next to, trying to sleep.

He didn't sleep a wink. Today, he was paying for it.

Rob was no longer on a great adventure.

Waves smashed against the rocks and crashed against the beach. He lost his footing on the slick pebbles, but a hand seized his elbow and righted him before he could crash on his bum.

Liam, silver mask filmy with condensation, glared down at him. Small patches of salt speckled the brim of his bowler hat.

Rob attempted a smile. "Thanks, mate."

Liam's eyes were as grey and unforgiving as the sea. Without a word, Liam dropped his arm and trekked on. Rob stared forlornly at Liam's back before the haze swallowed his friend.

Seagulls swarmed around the Old Man of Hoy, a red sandstone tower in the middle of the sea. Rob listened to the cawing of the flock with a heavy heart. After last night, he'd come to learn that love was a skill beyond his mastery. Love wore many masks and hid many faces, not all of them beautiful at first. He'd failed Liam and now his angel had flown.

Jim Hawkins sidled beside him with nary a sound. Sometime before the journey, the boy had made an improvement to his bracelet. Just as well. Heralding their arrival with a jingle of copper bells would defeat the purpose of sneaking up on *S. atlanticus*.

Cat limped by on her crutch and brushed her hand against his.

He flexed his fingers. Was it just a bump or did she mean to touch him? He turned to Jim for answers. The boy narrowed his eyes and jogged after his mistress. Rob watched Jim grab Cat's free hand, then peek at him over his shoulder with a triumphant smile. What the devil did that mean?

"We're going to the lighthouse." Cat pointed to the rocky path.

Liam was already midway up the cliff, marching with angry strides. The lighthouse, pockmarked with holes and disintegrating into rust, loomed on the highest bluff. If they all climbed to the lantern room, the entire structure might crumble beneath their feet. Rob swallowed his doubts and tried to be a good soldier. "How do we hunt the serpent from up there?"

"We don't. We're just stocking up on whale oil."

"Whale oil?"

"Liam's got a plan."

"Brilliant." Rob slapped his hands together. "What's the plan?"

Cat shrugged. "Better not to know."

"Do you know?"

"I have an idea." Shifting her eyes away, Cat tugged Jim along. "Stay here. Enjoy the scenery."

"Thank you for the invitation!" Rob called after her.

Cat held up a hand in welcome.

"Here I am," he sighed, gazing around the pebbled beach. "All alone."

A snout nudged the back of his knees. Virgil sank back on his hind legs, floppy tongue lolling out of his maw.

"I've neglected you, haven't I?" Between two overnight love confessions, he hadn't given Virgil much time.

Rob crouched down and scratched his dog behind the ear. He was rewarded with a lick on the cheek. Dog love was simple love. "There's a good boy. Wanna play catch? Let's play catch!"

Rob chucked a piece of driftwood and Virgil dashed after it, happy barking breaking the roar of the surf. The Border Collie leaped right over the driftwood and broke into a run.

"Virgil!" Rob cupped his hands around his mouth. "Virgil!"

The dog vanished behind an outcropping of rocks.

"Not again!" Rob chased after Virgil. As he drew closer to the waterline, waves sloshed over his boots and dread sunk like a stone to the pit of his stomach. Things did not bode well the last time he and Alec chased after Virgil. "You are the most disobedient…"

Rob stopped dead.

A bark echoed nearby, but he was too mesmerized to answer.

Virgil splashed over to him and dropped a bone at his feet. The bone was the size of a human femur, small in comparison to the others. The dog had led him into a graveyard of unnatural creatures.

Stripping off his cap, Rob stepped inside the ribcage of the adult *S. atlanticus*. He pressed his hand against the sun-bleached bone, marveling at the size and scope of the fossil. There were other relics scattered all over the cove. A serpentine skull plastered with a colony of green starfish. Kelpie skeletons spawning from the sand. And an undulating spine, a trademark characteristic of *S.atlanticus*.

Exiting the ribcage, Rob called to Virgil, except—no surprise—the dog was nowhere to be found.

"You are aptly named, mutt," he muttered, waddling into a tide pool. "Leading me into strange worlds and abandoning me when I need you most."

The water, once ankle deep, now rose to his knees. Silvery fish swam between his legs and ribbons of kelp floated in the crystal clear pool. His trousers were now officially soaked.

Spotting a purple sea anemone, Rob crouched to touch it. His fingers glided against jellylike tentacles before the anemone collapsed in upon itself, reminding Rob of Mrs. Nix's habit of pursing her lips when she disapproved of something— well, everything—Waverley did or said. He'd promised to bring Waverley and Mrs. Nix a present upon his return. Something pretty and unique.

He found an opal seashell snagged in a strand of seaweed so fine it could be mermaid's hair. Rolling up his sleeve, he dunked his hand in the water. The seaweed coiled around his fingers.

He gasped.

It *was* hair.

Once the initial shock wore off, Rob inched closer until he loomed upside down over the drowned girl. Her lips were tinged grey, her neck speckled with indigo scales. She was a beauty and not much older than himself.

He surveyed the boneyard.

No sign of Liam or Cat.

He was alone with the body and the desolate roar of the waves.

Help or no help, this girl deserved a proper burial and he might as well start the job. But when he tried to scoop the corpse out of the water, a stream of bubbles cascaded from her nostrils. Was he imagining things? He drew closer to make sure. The final bubble breached the surface.

The corpse's eyes snapped open.

Rob lost his footing on the slippery rocks and landed with a *splash.* He scuttled backward until he collided against the serpent's ribcage.

A tail, covered in iridescent cobalt scales, smacked the water's surface. The girl rose from the water.

A real mermaid.

Recalling the nasty things Liam had said about the murderous merfolk, Rob scampered out of the tide pool and huddled next to a rib bone in a shivering ball.

The mermaid stretched her arms, straining tiny webbed fingers to the sky. Green hair clung to her back in snarls. When she tipped her head from side to side, Rob spotted gills sprouting from her neck.

The mermaid peeked shyly over her shoulder. Pale blue eyes, fringed by green lashes, took in his damp hair and sodden tweeds. A smile etched across her blue lips. Her fin slapped the water and a peal of giggles broke the tension.

Rob smiled. This girl didn't seem like a monster. Nor did she seem interested in dragging him out to sea. "You're not so very frightening."

Her tail smacked the pool. *Splash.* The mermaid flipped around. One glance at her bare breasts and Rob blushed. The gentlemanly thing to do would be to look away, but his gaze lingered on her chest. He'd never been in the presence of a naked girl before and this first encounter was quite simply...magnificent.

"M-my name's Rob." He gulped. "What shall I call you? Do you have a name?"

She crawled toward him.

He backed away. The rib impeded his progress.

"Do you understand English?" His words came in an unpremeditated rush. "Of course you don't, what was I thinking? Are you all alone? Are you injured?"

She entered the ribcage and stopped inches away from him. With one webbed hand, she pried his knees apart and slipped between his legs.

"You are...you are..." He saw the deep blue sea reflected in her irises and felt the hypnotic tug of the waves. "Very beautiful..."

A kiss stopped his words.

This was wrong. Cat. He loved Cat.

He sputtered and tried to push her off, but the mermaid's tongue flicked inside his mouth and she guided his hand to her tail. And when Rob felt how silky and slick a mermaid could be, that fleeting window of guilt was gone for good.

It was the mermaid who broke the kiss. While Rob panted for breath, she cocked her head to the side, beckoning to someone in a language as foreign to him as Chinese. A reply echoed in the same strange tongue and another webbed hand caressed his cheek.

Rob jolted in alarm.

A second mermaid with raven locks and a fiery red tail watched him through the gaps of the ribcage. Summoned by her sister, she crawled inside and nestled her body against his. She stroked his face, wormed her hand inside his coat.

"What's going on? This is all rather untoward. I don't—" The red mermaid silenced him with a kiss. She was more aggressive than her sister, her lips mashed against his, drawing blood. It wasn't exactly a horrible sensation. As Rob kissed her back, the blue mermaid, not to be neglected, slid her hands up his thighs.

He broke the kiss, staring in a mixture of mortification and lust as the blue mermaid's fingers deftly unbuttoned his trousers. "Miss? Miss! Stop!"

Rob hitched in his breath. He couldn't believe what was happening.

The red mermaid wrapped her arms around him, preventing his escape. She seized his jaw and made him look at her. Unlike her sister, this one's irises were a ring of fire in black water.

"*Shhhh.* Does it not feel good?" This one spoke English, but her accent was so heavy Rob had to strain to hear over the blood pounding in his ears. She nuzzled his neck, nipped the underside of his jaw with sharp teeth. "Do you want her to stop?"

He writhed in the tide. His heart was going to explode. "N-no," he admitted.

"Then let us love you," she said, dragging him down.

Down.

Down.

"We shall love you *forever* if you come live with us in our kingdom under the sea. We'll treat you like a prince. We'll love you as a prince deserves to be loved. Say you'll come. Say you'll come…"

His lands.

His title.

His life and soul.

They could have it all.

His head sank beneath the surf. Bubbles issued from his nostrils. Rob shut his eyes and gave himself over to the red mermaid's promise of an underwater heaven.

To her sister's mouth.

His hips bucked beneath the blue mermaid and his hand went involuntarily to her head, fingers tangled in her green hair. "Oh God," he gurgled.

His eyes snapped open.

Coming to his senses, he struggled to surface, but the mermaids' hands detained him like shackles. His kicking stirred the tide into froth. Water flooded his nasal passages and trickled into his lungs.

Rob opened his mouth and screamed.

And the mermaids—

Released him.

The pool, once crystal clear, became opaque. Blood clouded the water like ink.

A hand looped under his arm and yanked him to the surface. Rob gasped his first greedy breath and immediately bowed over, choking water and spittle. Black dots swarmed across his vision. His ears still roared with screams. When he regained his senses, Rob looked up.

Liam loomed before him, a bloody sword in one hand, the blue mermaid's head in the other.

Liam's silver mask was splattered with blood. His gaze fell to Rob's lap. Despite his shock, Rob fumbled with his trousers and covered himself up.

The red mermaid let out an ear-shattering screech as Cat dragged her by the hair. Her tail smacked Rob in the face.

"This bitch is giving me a headache," Liam shouted above the screams. "Shut her up and let's be done with it."

Cat unsheathed her dragonbone dagger and pressed the blade to the mermaid's gills. The mermaid clawed and snarled at her assailant. She yanked the mermaid's hair harder; a drop of blood trickled down the girl's neck.

"Stop!" Rob crawled to his feet, but his soles slipped on the blood. "Don't hurt her!"

Cat paused and met his eye.

"Well?" Liam stabbed his broadsword in the muck and tossed the head in the pool. "What are you waiting for?"

"I can't." Her shoulders slumped. "I can't…"

"And you call yourself a monster hunter." He reached for Culler. "Hold her still."

"No!" Rob grabbed for Liam, but grasped only air.

Liam pounced, joining Cat and the mermaid in seconds. The mermaid's screams turned desperate. With a flick of his Bedouin blade, blood splayed the white-washed ribcage. The red mermaid collapsed, but her tail—this Rob would never forget—her tail still flapped long after her death.

Rob braced himself against the giant bone. Screams rang in his ear. He stared down at the red water lapping around his legs.

Liam handed Culler to Cat. "I trust you remember how to de-scale a sea hag?"

In a daze, Cat nodded. She was especially pale.

"De-scale and dismember," Liam ordered.

"Dismember?"

"Bait. We've got a bigger fish to catch." Liam cracked his neck muscles and adjusted his bowler hat. He wiped a streak of blood from his silver mask and marched back to Rob, halting on the other side of the cage. "Do you know what I call mermaids, Lord Robert?"

Rob pressed his forehead against the bone. He was going to be sick.

"Rats of the sea." Liam slipped between two ribs and caught him by the arm. "So my love's a sin," he whispered, "but a cock-sucking from a sea rat isn't?"

"Liam…"

With a sneer, Liam released Rob's arm and shouldered him aside.

Rob studied his hands. Mermaid blood was no different than human blood. He stumbled out of the fossil and began to run.

"Rob?" Cat called. "Rob!" His feet carried him to the water's edge, where he fell to his knees and retched in the surf.

CHAPTER 20
LOVE IN A TIME OF MONSTERS

Cat was up to her elbows in mermaid scales.

She worked fast and Liam's knife sped up her productivity.

The first time she and Liam went on a spree, they'd slaughtered an entire colony and had to set about harvesting their scales for Hyde's Elixir. She averaged six or seven an hour.

Two mermaids was child's play, yet her hands felt dirty all the same. Without Elixir coursing through her bloodstream, her mind was clearer, her dexterity unmatched. She daydreamed of her reunion with Vivian and how things would be right between them so long as she stayed clean. Fortunately, the first day of her rehabilitation was filled with many unusual distractions.

By evening, she'd collected a jar of iridescent scales and a pile of bloody meat.

After dousing the boneyard and tide pool in whale oil, Liam joined her and inspected the bait. He grunted in approval, grabbed a chunk of meat, and hurled it into the sea. It landed in the whitecapped waves with a *plop*.

"Go see to Rob." He picked up another cube.

She studied him with a frown. "I thought we were going to kill the serpent together."

"A one-legged hunter who can't even slit a sea bitch's throat?" He threw the next chunk with a grunt. "Twice as useless."

"Fine. I'll be happy to dig your grave." She turned to go.

"Kitty!"

"What?"

Liam gazed at the swell of the evening tide. "Why couldn't you kill it? Have you gone soft?"

Cat thought long and hard until she arrived at the true reason she couldn't kill *this* mermaid. "I didn't want to do it in front of Rob."

Liam snatched a cube, tossed it in the air, and caught it. "He pays you to kill monsters."

"He thinks I'm a knight."

He shook his head and tossed the last of the mermaid out to sea. "Soft."

She was about to say the same about him. Instead, she held her tongue and climbed the bluffs in search of Rob. She found him at the lighthouse, sitting in the weeds with Jim, that cumbersome steamer trunk open before them. They were in the middle of an argument with lots of wild hand gestures on Jim's part.

"Horrid!" Rob rubbed his brow. "My original design was much better."

Jim snatched a wrench from Rob's hand and began tinkering at something inside the trunk.

Rob rubbed his chin, considering. "Too complicated. It would never work. You overshoot yourself, lad."

The boy shook his head, then pointed at himself. *Anything you can do, I can do better.*

"Is that the way of it?" Rob slammed the lid. "Who asked for your help anyway?"

Jim pressed a finger to his lips. His eyes shifted to her.

Both Rob and Jim turned around. A swift flush stole over Rob; he ducked his head. He'd changed into a fresh shirt and trousers while she was still covered in blood.

Realizing too late that she might've cleaned herself up first, Cat cleared her throat. "So what is this mysterious contraption you're both working on?"

Rob gazed at the swiftly darkening sea. As before, Jim clambered up to the top of the trunk and crossed his arms. Cat rolled her eyes. They could keep their secrets. She was here to see about Rob.

Taking a deep breath, she snapped her fingers at Jim. "A moment of privacy?"

She expected Jim to protest, but he surprised her by hopping off the trunk.

317

With a final narrowing of his eyes, Jim grabbed a handle and dragged the trunk with him. He disappeared inside the lighthouse.

Cat made sure Jim was out of sight before she hobbled over to Rob. She would've liked to sit down next to him, but her peg made bending difficult. Not to mention awkward. So Cat stared down at Rob's white-blond head. Poor lad. First monster hunt and already molested by mermaids.

"It must've been horrible for you," she said. "How do you feel?"

Rob yanked a tuff of grass, his cheeks the color of a stewed tomato. "Mortified."

"Violated?"

"That too…I guess." He let the blades slip through his fingers. "Are you mad at me?"

"I suppose I forgive you." She sighed. "You're not the first to fall under the spell of a mermaid. Most hunters are especially susceptible to their charms."

He grimaced. "You're not."

Cat eased herself down. "Most *male* hunters and before you bring up Liam, well, he's immune to their charms for an entirely different reason. Now if they had been mer*men*…"

"You know about Liam?" Rob glanced over his shoulder. "Why didn't anyone tell me?"

"I figured it out," she said, chewing on her inner cheek. "Last night, I sort of saw you two...kiss."

Drawing his legs up to his chest, Rob buried his face between his knees. "Would that I could find a hole."

"Another one? Haven't you stuck your dirty thing into enough places today?"

He turned to her, aghast. "A hole I could crawl into and die!"

Flopping on his back, Rob rolled on his stomach and sort of squirmed around like a worm.

"For the record," she swatted him on the back, "I tried not to look at your thing, but what has been seen could not be unseen."

Taking the ostrich defense, Rob smushed his face firmly into the ground. "Please stop talking."

"Rather unfair, isn't it? That I should have one leg while you have three."

"Dear God."

Cat hid a smile. He was so easy to fluster. But there was a more pressing concern on her mind. "So did you enjoy it?"

Rob gazed up at her. Blades of grass clung to his cheek. "Enjoy what? The mermaids? Um..."

"Last night." It was her turn to blush. "What I mean to ask is: do you like snails or oysters...or both?"

319

"I don't understand." Rob brows knitted into a frown. "I've sampled both and like them all. I'm not a picky eater."

"*Oh no.*" Cat flopped on her back and clutched her head in her hands.

"I'm so confused!"

"You are!"

"I don't even really know what we're talking about or why we're shouting!" He draped an arm across his eyes. "Alec used to say I have no social skills and I fear he's right."

Cat stared at the sky and cursed the stars. Out of all the boys in the world, she had to fall for one who may or may not like other boys. She listened to Rob's quiet sobbing and felt like crying herself.

Love was the root of Rob's problems. He had too much of it. For everyone.

"Rob?" She nudged him with her foot.

He sniffled. "Uh-huh?"

"Climb on top."

"What?" He poked his head up.

"Climb on top of me," she said, spreading her arms wide. "Kiss me."

He wiped his nose on the back of his hand. Red-rimmed eyes scanned her bloody clothes. "But I just changed."

"Then prepare to get dirty."

Rob glanced at the lighthouse's lantern room. "I think Jim is watching."

"Maybe he'll learn something. Damn it, are you going to kiss me or not?"

He crawled over to her and hovered over her on all fours, his body a gentlemanly inch away from touching. She hooked her right leg around his waist and made full contact. After the mermaids, she expected him to be exhausted, but no, he felt alert.

His eyes were blue and intensely hopeful. "Does this mean you love me back?"

"I'm just trying," she grazed his lips with her own, "to make a case for oysters."

♦

"We can't do this."

"We can. Be quick." Cat dragged Rob back down when he tried to pull away. He kissed her lips raw. She fumbled with her own trousers. For the first time in her life, Cat wished she was wearing a skirt.

His hands were all over her. Under her shirt. On her stomach, inching lower and lower and yes, she wanted this. Him. All of it.

Suddenly Rob froze and rolled off of her. He curled into a ball with his back to her.

"I'm sorry," he said, in a mortified tone which told her he probably needed to change his pants again.

Cat tried to catch her breath. Her brow was fevered, her stomach hot to the touch. Her hand slipped inside her open trousers, fingers tapping a beat on her pelvic bone as she debated finishing the job herself.

"Uh, Cat?"

She heaved a sigh of frustration. "Yes?"

Rob tapped her on the shoulder. "I think you need to see this." He pointed to the ocean.

The sea sparkled like a blanket of stars under the moonlight.

A scaly back breached the waves. Cat fumbled with her clothes and searched the weeds for her crutch.

Rob helped her up. "What's going on?"

"A real monster hunt." Cat glanced down at the boneyard. Liam was perched atop a serpent's skull.

Cat whistled.

Liam tilted his head to the lighthouse.

She pointed to the water.

He nodded, but made no move to unsheathe his broadsword. His hand disappeared inside his coat; out came a canteen.

Directly before him, the dark waters bubbled and frothed. Summer nights, Rob told them during the journey, were when *S.atlanticus* came ashore to bask and feast on its natural prey: the merfolk. The creature's head broke the surface, following the trail of mer-meat. The rest of its body slithered ashore like an endless black ribbon.

Rob hitched in his breath. "Shouldn't we go down to help?"

"He doesn't need it." As she watched the serpent undulate around the fossils, the thrill of the kill stirred deep within her. She wished she was down there, but this was Liam's fight.

The serpent sunk into the tide pool and slipped inside the ribcage. Fearsome as it may be, the monster was slithering to certain doom.

"You're about to watch a true artist at work," she said. "Send a monster to slay a monster. If Jekyll were here, he'd appreciate the poetry in that."

"*Liam?*"

Taking her eyes off the hunt, Cat studied Rob. Was he being facetious? After all he'd witnessed? But Rob was in earnest. She'd heard about love being blind, but this was just too much.

"Liam beheads a mermaid right in front of you and you still can't believe he's a monster?"

"I've known him since I was eleven." He filled her in about his first year at Eton and the winter courtyard where his

323

attackers left him for dead. "He's my friend. My guardian angel."

"Don't call him that!" No wonder he was thrashed in school. She wanted to pummel him herself. "Hear this, dreamer. Your angel is a killer. Have you asked yourself what happened to your tormentors?"

"One left when his father took a post in India. The other boys shipped off…"

"So they disappeared? One by one." Cat turned back to the cove. Even as the serpent slithered toward him, Liam hadn't budged. He drew his cape closer and waited like a true bird of prey.

Rob fell into a long silence, broken only when the serpent lifted its massive head off the ground. "Why is he just sitting there?"

"He's got a plan." But from where she stood, it didn't look like much of a plan.

The serpent's feelers twitched, onyx body rising in the air. It recoiled like a cobra. A screech rent the night.

Rob gripped her arm, dug his fingers into her skin. "He needs a second."

Cat grabbed his arm before he could dash off.

"Let go!"

"You stupid, stupid boy! You're going down there? To rescue him? To die for him? You can't even hold a sword!" Cat steered Rob to the show at cliff's edge. "You can't help him by getting yourself killed," she said, her eyes fixed on Liam, who'd finally taken a swig of his canteen. He even took his time to screw the cap back on. "So watch. He knows what he's doing."

They waited.

The snake lingered in the air, frozen like the statue in Rob's garden. A forked tongue unfurled and the creature spewed a black tar-like substance at Liam. Leaping from his perch, he landed in a crouch. The spittle sprayed the skull; the bone fizzled and caved in.

Liam unsheathed his broadsword. His silver mask bobbed like a disembodied face on the dark beach. Sword at the ready, he swayed along with the serpent.

The serpent recoiled and struck. He dodged, dropped, and swished the water from cheek to cheek.

The monster spat and Liam blew at the same time.

Fire collided with acid and *S.atlanticus,* coated in whale oil, ignited like a fuse. A blast of heat struck Cat in the face. The ribcage and skull were aflame. The tide pool glimmered like slick oil puddles where starfish and anemones shriveled and died.

"Liam warned you monster hunting was a nasty business," Cat said.

The serpent shrieked in agony, twisting and writhing in the air.

She glanced back at Rob.

"Won't he kill it already?" Stumbling away, Rob collapsed against a rock and covered his ears. "Why won't he end it already?"

"Hyde's Avenging Angel likes to play with his victims." Mask illuminated by flames, Liam slashed the writhing serpent with his broadsword.

The creature's head slammed against the ground.

He raised the sword and brought it down with a *thwack.* Two strikes. Simple. Clean. Worthy of an artist.

And when the serpent was dead, Liam brought out Culler for the harvest.

"You should've hired Liam to kill Manu Diaboli." Cat watched Liam's deft hands at work. "He's the greatest hunter."

Leaving the serpent to roast, Liam climbed the hill and appeared before them with his mask splattered in blood and a burlap sack containing the serpent's salivary gland slung across his shoulder.

Stabbing his broadsword in the grass, Liam stripped off his bowler hat and mask. His face was surprisingly pink and vulnerable. His eyes went straight to Rob.

He tossed the sack to Cat without so much as a glance. Stumbling past her, he knelt in front of Rob and buried his face in the young laird's lap.

As Cat watched Rob stroke Liam's hair, she didn't know whether to pity or envy this boy who walked with angels and made killers into knights. In the end, she decided to envy him.

He lived in a world where she wished she belonged.

A world where it was so easy to fall in love.

A world without monsters.

♦

Cat climbed beneath the archway of the old Roman aqueduct.

It was a dry night, far removed from the downpour the last time she came home from a kill. She turned up her palms. They were saintly white, with not a sliver of blood. This time the kill had not been hers, and she was glad.

Drawing her coat closer, Cat blew into her hands and watched the sky flicker with a lovely green fluorescence. She shut her eyes. The screaming was still inside her head, but dimmed, like an echo at the back of a cave. She shivered, more from the cold and less from the absence of Elixir, which she hadn't even thought about on the journey home. She thought about Vivian instead, counted the days until their reunion.

Hanging her head, Cat recalled her sister's arm in a sling and moaned.

She *was* an abomination.

But if there was even the slightest chance of forgiveness, Cat was ready to move heaven and earth to atone for the wrongs she'd committed under the influence of Elixir.

Clunky footsteps approached from afar. Even with her eyes shut, Cat knew it was Rob. Whereas Jim glided and Liam slithered, Rob moved with all the grace of a bull in a china shop. The lad looked slight, walked heavy, as if he was determined to leave his footprints upon the earth.

"Jim said I'd find you here," Rob called.

"Jim *said*?" Cat opened her eyes and snorted at the ridiculous sight of Rob dragging his steamer trunk toward her.

"Mimed actually. You wandered off so suddenly, we didn't know what happened to you. Liam thought you might've tried to leap off a cliff."

"That would make things convenient for him, wouldn't it? Bah!" She threw her hands in the air. "I don't know why I bother with you. Since you confessed your undying love for me, you've kissed two mermaids and another man. You claimed to heed the call of your heart, but the only call you've heeded was the call of your cock."

Ignoring the quip, Rob called, "I know you've been melancholy!"

328

"Oh, I'm so honored you realize I exist again. Shouldn't you be with your best *mate*? Now that you've made up, I'm sure you'll be very happy together."

Rob swiped a strand of blond hair from his eyes. The apples of his cheeks were flushed with exertion, yet he glanced up and smiled, a hopeful and handsome silhouette against the Northern Lights. "I've something that will cheer you up." The trunk bounced over rough ground. Rob halted abruptly and glanced down at the steamer. "Oh dear."

Cat rolled her eyes and eased herself from the archway. She picked up her crutch and limped toward him.

Rob rubbed his chin. The trunk's corner was wedged between two rocks. "I daresay it's stuck."

"Future words from your future wife," she muttered.

Rob frowned in genuine confusion. "What the devil are you talking about?"

Did he really not know? Cat felt it her duty, as the older and slightly more experienced one, to illuminate him on gross anatomy. "While you were at Eton, haven't you ever taken a peek?"

"Peek at what?"

"You know…"

"Um." He shrugged. "No…"

"Compared yourself to the other lads?" She made a vague hand gesture.

"Compare what? My marks?"

She rubbed her brow. "Never mind."

He puffed up his chest. "I've always scored top marks."

"If this was something one could score," she said, "you win."

"Are we speaking of my trunk?"

Cat chewed her bottom lip. She'd seen Dr. Jekyll or whatever he was calling himself these days pat Rob on the head and wanted to do it herself. It took all her self-control, but she resisted.

"In any event," Rob unclasped the buckles, "since I can't move it, I'll just give it to you here. Would you prefer to have it sitting down or standing up?"

"I'd better sit down." Arching an eyebrow, Cat hobbled to a rock and watched Rob lift the lid.

"Close your eyes," he called over his shoulder.

"Is it going to hurt? Because I don't think I can handle whatever you're about to give me."

Rob loomed above her. "You trouble me, Miss Mornay." He placed an item of some weight, though not necessarily heavy, onto her lap. "Open your eyes."

Still laughing, Cat did as instructed and focused on her gift. All laughter ceased. Rob had kept his promise. "A leg," she said softly.

"I wish I could take all the credit. Jim got his sticky hands on it and made some improvements. It was a joint effort." He paused, waiting for her reaction. "Do you like it?"

Her hand hovered over the prosthetic limb. The knee, an intricate design of springs, allowed bending. The inside was a complicated network of mini-pulleys and supports. There was even a frightful steel foot with five toes. Even the toes had rudimentary joints.

A tear splattered the leg; Cat swiped it away with her thumb.

"It's just a crude prototype." Rob knelt in front of her. "I can do better."

Cat's voice was scratchy. "Help me put it on."

Once the new leg was strapped on and the hated peg discarded, Rob offered Cat his hand. Without the aid of her crutch, she took a couple of wobbly steps before finding her balance.

Tucking his hands in his pockets, Rob watched her circle around him. Her pace grew faster and surer with each step. "Try running."

Cat halted. "Running?"

"Aye." A sheepish grin. "It's designed to withstand a proper dash, but Jim altered it so you can leap and climb if that is your wish. The only thing you can't do is fly."

Cat dug her metal toes in the dirt. She was already flying.

"Go on." Rob nodded to the archway. "Give it a try."

Meeting his eye, Cat backed up and walked. Her walk turned into a jog. Cold wind plastered her hair to her face. The jog gathered momentum and then, the unbelievable happened.

Cat Mornay, the monster hunter with one leg, was running.

Sprinting.

Soaring.

She spotted the archway and leapt.

She landed with little grace and braced herself against the crumbling stones before she toppled over. Cat clutched her heart, trying to catch her breath.

Before her, the glen stretched to infinity, a blanket of darkness beneath a dazzling emerald sky. The world was as surreal as if Rob had imagined it especially for her. She was living inside his dream.

"Well, miss?" Climbing into the archway, Rob touched her on the shoulder. "Will it do?"

"It'll do." If she turned around, she'd surely crumble to pieces. Wiping the tears from her cheeks, Cat swallowed. "I didn't think any of this was possible."

"We're living in a time of monsters. All things are possible," he whispered in her ear. "Like Jim being a changeling prince in disguise, which is far easier to swallow than the lad besting me at everything."

Taking her hand, Rob turned her around to face him.

"Or that bastard Barclay having a soul." Cat stepped into the warm circle of his arms.

"And in a time of monsters," Rob said. "It was possible…"

Guileless eyes gazed into hers— the eyes of a dreamer— and Cat allowed herself to drown five fathoms deep. "To fall in love."

CHAPTER 21
THE ONES THEY LEFT BEHIND

"Take a walk with me." Cat's breath tickled the nape of his neck.

Rob's mouth turned to cotton. During the journey home, he hadn't a moment alone with her. Now the opportunity presented itself, he gripped the edges of his journal, crinkling the paper and smudging the words.

He glanced nervously around the camp. Two dim shapes dozed around the embers of last night's fire while Liam, who'd been in a snit ever since Cat revealed her new prosthetic, slept by himself inside a three-sided hunter's shed.

"W-where?"

Her hand slid over his knee and lingered on his inner thigh. Edging closer, Cat nipped his jaw. "I'll show you," she said, taking his journal off his lap and tossing it to the ground.

They tiptoed around slumbering Virgil and Jim and slipped past the horses lazily munching sweet grass. Above a sparse canopy of elms, a slash of pink streaked the sky. They were so close to home. Come midday, he would be laird of Balfour Manor again, but in this stolen hour before dawn, Rob was still on a great adventure.

She led him over a shallow stream. Neither speaking nor touching, they weaved through one moss-covered trunk after the next.

Rob stared at the elegant curve of her neck, longing to draw her into his arms, burrow his face in her messy tendrils, run his tongue against her salty skin and his hands over her body.

Just when the mere act of walking began to physically hurt, Cat brushed against him and surprised him with a kiss. A kiss which she broke too soon.

"We're here," she said in a breathless voice.

When he swooped in for another kiss, Cat ducked her head and pushed him away. Her laughter echoed across the forest cathedral, driving him into a kind of animal madness.

Rob scrubbed a hand over his face and groaned. "Why do you torture me?"

"Because I can." Cat nodded to a stone staircase covered in a blanket of lichens and studded with mushrooms. The stairs soared as high as the tallest sapling and verged off to empty air. "I'll meet you on the other side," she said, jogging up the steps.

"What are you up to?" he called after her.

"Do as you're told!" At the top step, Cat stripped off her wide-brim hat, flung it over the edge. Her cloak fluttered to the weeds below. Standing in a near-transparent linen blouse and tight trousers, Cat cast a sly smile over her shoulder before stepping into the void.

"Cat!"

Rob bolted around the ruin. Half-expecting to find her sprawled in a broken heap, he found her calmly spreading her cape on the grass. Her hat was propped atop a crumbling Roman column. More columns, some as tall as he, others knee-high stumps, surrounded them. A lichen-covered wall shielded them from prying eyes.

"Isn't it lovely here?" No longer laughing, Cat sat on her cape and patted the spot beside her. "We'll have the morning," she said, fumbling with the buttons of her blouse.

"Cat…" Kneeling in front of her, he caught her hands and realized that like him, she was trembling. "Are you sure?"

Cat slipped out of her blouse.

His breath hitched: she was wearing nothing underneath.

She grabbed the hem of his scarf and tugged him closer. "Your turn."

When their clothes lay in a neat pile beside them, Rob kissed the salty hollow of her neck.

"I'm through with Elixir," she whispered in his ear. "It's high time I put something good inside me. Can you help me with that?"

His hands roamed across the scars on her back, but her hands roamed lower and he was slowly losing the capacity for speech. "I'm up for it."

♦

Her mother passed away too soon. Her father had been too embarrassed to broach the subject. On the ship, he told her to cover her ears at night when the sailors were being friendly toward each other.

Nobody ever told Cat it was going to hurt and when she gasped in pain, Rob braced himself on his elbow. "I didn't know. I thought... Am I hurting you?"

She felt him pull out so she dug her fingers into his back. "Don't stop."

His eyes glossed over; it didn't look like he could stop even if she wanted him to.

Grateful for the go-ahead, Rob ducked in for another kiss. He kissed away her tears.

Cat focused on the canopy and soon the pain dulled into an ache. The sun wormed its way through the leaves and the ache gave way to a sensation much like Elixir shot right to the heart.

Just when she was starting to enjoy it, Cat caught a movement from above and tensed. Whatever pleasure she was beginning to feel vanished as a shadow blocked out the sun.

Liam stared down at her from the staircase's top step, his expression indecipherable behind the silver mask. Cat debated tapping Rob on the shoulder, but a painful realization dawned on her. Part of Rob's heart would always belong to another.

Staring right back at Liam, Cat clutched Rob closer. "Say you're mine."

Liam once called her greedy. And she was. She wasn't about to share Rob with anyone.

Rob buried his face in the crook of her neck. "I'm yours."

"Say you love me."

"I love you," he groaned in her ear.

She saw Liam strip off his mask, his naked face shifting from rage to heartache. *Let him watch. Watch me win.* "Only me."

"Only you."

"And you," he panted, "say you love me."

But she didn't say it and he stopped asking. Lolling her head against the grass, Cat shut her eyes. Even though she knew it would hurt her, she urged Rob to go faster. Her bare bottom bounced against the ground. A branch dug into her spine.

When she opened her eyes, Liam was gone and the sun glowed glorious and bright.

"I think I'm about to..." Rob pressed his forehead against hers. He grimaced like he was trying to hold back. "Are you?"

"Go ahead, go ahead," she said, giving him her full attention, "I'll catch the next one."

Rob collapsed on top of her in a shivering heap. A smile etched across his lips. "It's a new day."

She ruffled his sweaty hair. "It's a new world."

◆

Taking his horse by the reins, Rob squared his shoulders and walked a little taller. Across the glens, the ramparts of Balfour Manor greeted him above a swirl of fog. He puffed out his chest, his blood humming with anticipation.

He couldn't wait to see his family and household again. Would anyone notice the change in him? Mrs. Nix would, of course, wonder if his flushed cheeks were caused by fever, and Waverley would tell him to wipe that stupid grin off his face. No one would notice that he left home a boy and came back a man.

Stripping off his riding gloves, Rob smoothed down his mare's glossy mane. Another stupid grin appeared. Shortly after they'd made love, Cat had kissed the skin below his belly button and gazed up at him with a wicked glint in her eyes. "Fancy another go?" They were late breaking camp.

A nudge from Virgil brought him back to reality.

Kneeling to scratch his dog behind the ears, Rob shook the kinks from his body. Cat's addiction to Elixir had always been a mystery to him. Now he finally understood. Since this morning, his thoughts centered on two things: Cat and naked

Cat. Kissing her. Touching her. Having her. He couldn't get enough.

Virgil bumped his arm with a wet snout.

"All right, all right. What are you—" A hand tapped him on the shoulder. Whirling around, Rob didn't have quite the scare this time. He'd grown accustomed to Jim sneaking up on him. "What is it?"

The boy narrowed his eyes. Rob flushed under Jim's scrutiny, suddenly ashamed of his ungentlemanly fantasies about Cat. "Well, lad?"

Jim pointed to Rob's horse.

"Tired of walking? Do you want to ride?"

Jim stepped around him and unlatched the saddlebag. He grabbed Alec's rifle, which Rob packed for the journey but hadn't an opportunity to use. Jim shoved the rifle into Rob's hands. The boy's harried gesture sent the hackles rising on the back of his neck. He turned to the fae woods, which, from all outward appearances, was serenely blanketed in mist.

He glanced over his shoulder. Cat and Liam walked side by side. Leading their horses up a small hill, Liam whispered something in her ear. Cat stiffened and rubbed her bottom lip.

Between Jim frantically tapping him on the shoulder and the dog head-butting his thigh, Rob couldn't hear a word of their argument.

Liam said something else and Cat struck him across the face with a force that knocked his mask to the mud.

Rob leaped to his feet.

"Has the time come, you manky whore?" Picking up his mask, Liam wiped the mud away with his sleeve. His hand disappeared inside his coat pocket. "Has it?"

Cat unsheathed her dragonbone dagger. "I'll knock your bleeding block off!"

"Children!" Rob rubbed the spot between his eyes. "Can't we at least unpack before we start killing each other? This really is too much."

Sniffing the air, Virgil weaved between his legs. The dog *yip yipped.*

He swatted Virgil away. "Quiet, boy."

Virgil's barks transformed to snarls. Jim kicked Rob in the shin.

"Ouch!" Rob whirled around. The boy tipped his head back and howled.

"Christ. He's possessed." Liam pointed Culler at Cat. "You should put your pet down."

"Clear off, arsemonger." Shoving Liam aside, Cat raced toward Jim. The moment she touched the lad, Jim snapped and bared his teeth. She snatched her hand back, frowning. "What's come over you?"

Both dog and boy sniffed the air.

Rob shivered. The high-pitched baying sent an eruption of goose pimples across his skin. Something was wrong.

Virgil sped off.

Jim chased after the dog.

Cat ran after the boy. "Jim! Jim!"

A creeping dread paralyzed him to the spot. Rob glanced at Alec's rifle, recalling the morning of his birthday. Why had Jim forced the gun into his hands? Had the boy known he'd need it?

Much as he didn't want to, Rob had no choice but to follow.

◆

The panic, which had been mounting the moment that damned dog started barking, shrilled inside Cat. A cord of spittle clung to Virgil's muzzle as he clawed the greenhouse's outer walls.

Her steps faltered.

The glass was smeared with blood.

She bumped into Jim and gripped his scrawny shoulders. Her eyes swept across the shattered dome-roof and her hand snuck inside her cape. As her fingers tightened around the ivory handle of her pistol, a dazed Rob stumbled past her.

A droplet splattered her nose. Cat tipped her face to the sky. It had begun to rain.

Virgil whimpered.

A glass shard clung to the ceiling frame like an icicle, but when Rob pried the door open, the shard dropped and shattered.

The sound spurred her into action. "No!" She ran to stop Rob.

Liam shoved Rob aside and slammed the door shut. "Not a good idea, mate."

Rob's face was as white as a sheet. He turned back to the glasshouse. Rain sluiced down the walls, diluting the blood into pink water. "What happened?" His question echoed across the glen, a desperate, hollow sound. "What happened..."

Still clutching her pistol, Cat peered past the blood-splattered banana leaves and saw the jungle contained inside.

A man was slumped over the worktable, a scalpel still clutched in his hands. She couldn't identify the corpse's face, probably because he no longer had one. Or a bottom half. She spotted a severed leg nestled between an overturned pot of African violets and the hollow shell of a newly hatched egg.

Liam shuffled to her side. "Hyde," he whispered, more shocked than heartbroken over the massacre of his former employer.

Rob pushed past them and doubled over. Both Jim and Liam dashed to his side. Liam patted Rob on the back as he vomited in the grass.

If that sad piece of meat was indeed Mr. Hyde, then poetic justice had been served: he took her leg, the monster took his.

In no mood for rejoicing, Cat pressed her hand against the glass wall. All eight walls were intact. She studied the shattered dome again, certain she'd missed something. During the voyage on the *Hispaniola*, no one, not even Cat, suspected the egg was onboard or knew when it hatched. In a week, the spawn grew into the adult and by then it had been too late.

They hadn't been gone a week.

She tapped the sturdy glass. A four-day-old creature could not break through a wall this thick. It would take—

"Cat!" Wiping his mouth on his sleeve, Rob motioned her over and pointed at the talon prints in the mud.

Two sets of tracks.

One large, one small.

Mother and child.

Heading opposite the direction of the woods.

She saw the terror reflected in his eyes and knew the darkest hour was upon them. "They've gone to Balfour Manor."

♦

Cat and Liam darted from one window to the next, crisscrossing each other with a cold efficiency that separated monster hunters from ordinary people.

There was a bloody handprint on a first-story window. Small. Delicate. A woman's or child's hand.

Rob studied Cat's profile as she peered into the parlor where he'd played duets with Jim not long ago. What was the composition? The melody ignited inside Rob's head, a low drone escalating into a frenetic hive.

Cat backed away, her mouth hardening into a grim line.

"Anybody alive in there?" Liam mouthed.

She shook her head. How could she be so calm when the handprint might belong to her sister?

Rob's boots crunched broken glass. He wanted to see the tracks again, if only to make it real. The talon prints stopped several paces from the door and vanished into thin air. In the woods, he'd seen Manu Diaboli leap from tree to tree. Rob stared up at the rambling castle he called home. Balfour Manor looked deceptively serene, except for the shattered second-story window.

The melody played within his head. Rob glanced down at his hands. He was still clutching Alec's rifle. A cloud of bees blackened his vision and swarmed inside his lungs. A cough broke the silence like a shotgun blast.

"Shhh." Liam clamped a hand over his mouth, but the bees stung and pumped Rob's lungs with venom. Rob felt himself being dragged away from hearing distance of the monster. He collapsed in the grass, choking on sobs and spittle.

"Drink." Liam held a vial under his lips. Blue and red scales—what remained of his pretty mermaids—swirled in the cloudy water.

Rob coughed once more and the metallic tang of blood coated his tongue. He turned his head.

Strong hands flipped him over on his back. "Drink!"

"No!"

Liam seized Rob's jaw, pinched his nose, and poured.

He sputtered, tried to spit it out, but Liam clamped a hand over his mouth. The vile concoction seared a fiery path down his throat. His body spasmed, his legs rutted in the mud, and all the while, Liam held him until the serum doused the hive and Rob gulped one clear, unobstructed breath.

He gazed at the grey sky. It had stopped raining and a blessed quiet roared in his ear. He must've blacked out for a second; when he came to, his head was propped against Liam's thigh.

"Rob…" Liam gazed down at a handkerchief flecked with blood. "Why didn't you tell me it was this bad?"

"I bit my tongue." Sitting up, Rob bowed his head between his legs. He rubbed his chest, unable to separate the ache in his lungs from the pain in his heart. Cat, standing over his discarded rifle, stared at him, too. She tugged the brim of her hat over her eyes and picked his rifle up from the ground. Rob sensed Liam's eyes boring a hole in the back of his head. It struck him as funny that both hunters could be so stoic in the aftermath of a massacre, yet get so worked up over a few spots of blood.

"I bit my tongue," he repeated. The sadness in Liam's eyes was too much. In a fit of rage, he snatched the vial from Liam's hands and chucked it. "Never force me to drink your kills and for Christ's sake, stop staring at me! The lot of you!"

Virgil nudged his palm with a warm snout and licked his wrist.

A hand tugged his sleeve. Jim knelt beside him. The lad never looked at him with pity and that made all the difference. With a trembling hand, Rob reached inside his pocket. His fingers unfurled over an opal seashell. It had been meant for Waverley.

He pressed the shell into Jim's hands. "Waverley said you spoke to her. Can you speak to her now?"

Jim shook his head. *No.*

"Is she alive?"

No answer.

Rob's eyes brimmed with tears. He tried to take this as an indefinite response and pressed on.

"Finley?"

Another shake. *No.*

"Mrs. Nix?"

No.

"Oh God." Rob buried his face in his hands.

Cat crouched next to Jim. "Vivian?"

Jim blinked. Another indefinite answer. She seized him by the shoulder and shook him. "Did she get out?"

Sniffling, Rob asked, "Is there life inside the castle?"

A nod. *Yes.*

"Manu Diaboli? Mother and babe?"

Jim held up three fingers. A hush fell over the circle.

"Three?" Liam scooted closer. "Three what?"

"Three hatchlings." Cat peeled off her hat, her eyes wide with terror. "All her eggs have hatched."

Jim added another finger. *Four.* Four Manu Diabolii inside his home.

Rob found his voice. "And from your experience, Cat, how long do we have before the hatchlings grow into adults?"

"One week. Less, depending on when they hatched."

"Jesus." Liam, too, stripped off his bowler hat. Somehow, his reaction turned Cat's complexion white.

Rob looked to the fortress his ancestors built to stand a siege from Viking raiders, impenetrable to armies but not monsters. There was a new master of Balfour Manor now, and as they contemplated what an infestation meant to Scotland, the British Empire, and the fate of man, a girl's scream echoed from somewhere in the bowels of the castle, signaling the dawning of a new rule.

♦

They raced toward Balfour Manor. Rob's natural instinct took him to the front door. He'd barely had his hand on the knob before Liam grabbed him.

"What are you doing?"

Another screech drove Rob into a blind panic. Virgil barked.

Cat and Jim disappeared around the corner, chasing the origin of the screamer.

Rob tried to break free. "We have to help her!"

"By waltzing through the front door of a monster-infested property? What'd you think you're going to do inside? Kill all four creatures yourself?" Shaking his head, Liam hauled him by the collar and dragged him around a hedge. "The first rule of monster hunting: *never* risk your life to save another. Never stick your neck out for those who are already dead. That girl is fucked."

That girl.

That girl could be Waverley.

That girl was suffering.

If being a monster hunter required him to lose his humanity, he didn't want the title or the glory. He just wanted to save the girl.

They spotted Cat several paces away, her head tipped to the third story. Her hat toppled to the grass and when she turned to them, her face was streaked with tears. "It's Vivian!" She pointed to the floor-to-ceiling windows of his solarium. "Vivian."

Rob witnessed everything in muted detail: Vivian's purple dress in tatters, the sliver of blood on her temple, her left arm in a sling, and the horrific twist of her face as she smacked the glass with her good hand.

A shadow, shaped like a Devil's claw, yawned across the map-covered walls and vanished from sight. A second later, his automatons crashed to the floor.

Vivian whirled around.

A shriek from girl and monster transported Rob back to the fae woods.

To the morning of Alec's death.

To the stench of hiding beneath that sheep carcass and the maggots squirming under his collar.

No matter how fast they ran, they would never reach Vivian in time.

His attention swerved to Cat. Alec's rifle was nestled in the hollow of her shoulder, her head half-cocked along the barrel. He breathed a sigh of relief. She was an excellent markswoman. Didn't she shoot the hat right off her sister's head? Cat could shoot Manu Diaboli dead. If anybody could do it, Cat—

Then he noticed the tremors.

Her hands shook so violently she couldn't keep the rifle steady, much less aim.

"Cat!" Vivian slammed her good shoulder against the window. The shadow appeared and reappeared behind her. "Please help me. *Help me!*"

Cat pulled the trigger.

A spiderweb crack materialized inches beside Vivian's head. The bullet hit neither monster nor girl. "I can't..." The shaking rifle tracked Manu Diaboli. Cat cried in frustration. "I can't!"

Seeing that she was too distraught to hit her mark, Rob shoved Liam forward. "Help her!"

Liam snatched the rifle from her hands and propped it over his shoulder. He was a sculpture in clean, angular lines, his grip on the trigger steady and sure. Even so, he couldn't get a clean shot.

"Don't let it touch her," Cat said.

"I'm trying! She's moving too fast!"

Another crack blossomed over Vivian's head.

And then Cat did something Rob would never forget.

She guided the barrel and pointed it straight at Vivian's head—right between her sister's eyes.

Liam's finger paused on the trigger. His eyes flickered to her.

"One shot. Do it quickly." Her order boomed through the clearing. "She mustn't suffer."

With a nod, Liam aimed.

Cat turned her back on the solarium and closed her eyes.

But Rob saw it all, chronicled it all. The moment of desperation when Vivian rammed her injured arm into the window, the register of betrayal when she mouthed, "Cat…"

The rifle fired in a clean, sharp report.

Cat flinched and he watched the life drain from her face.

And the moment Vivian collapsed, Manu Diaboli pounced on the girl's lifeless body and had at her. A greedy braying echoed from the solarium, followed by the gnashing of teeth. Rob lowered his eyes.

"Is it done?" Cat's voice was small and meek, not one befitting a monster hunter.

"It's done, Cat," Liam said. It dawned on Rob that he'd only ever heard Liam call her "Miss Mornay" or "Kitty," but never "Cat."

Nodding, she stumbled away, only making it a few paces before sinking to her knees in the mud.

CHAPTER 22
THE SEASHELL CODE

After the shooting, there was nothing left to say.

The survivors huddled inside the hunter's shed on the outskirts of Rob's estate, cocooned in a silence broken periodically by Virgil's whimper.

Sniffling and shivering, Rob wiped his nose on his sleeve. He was all out of handkerchiefs. Rain dribbled through the pockmarked roof as he listened to the sky weep.

Across the shed, Cat stared through him with dead eyes. A drop of water clung to the tip of her nose. She hadn't spoken since giving the order to shoot her sister.

Jim was the only one who seemed impervious to the cold. The boy was lost in his own world, running his thumb over the spirals of Waverley's seashell like he was trying to decipher some secret code. Was he mourning Waverley, too? Rob recalled the last time he saw his sister. She'd been so full of life, declaring her undying love for this strange boy.

Who did she call in her final hour? Rob or Jim?

The possibilities, combined with Cat's horrific tales of the jungle, drove him mad. Did Waverley suffer, or did one brave soul grant her a quick and merciful death? He doubted it. What did the castle servants know of killing? Most likely his little Duck suffered and suffered greatly. Strange as it may seem, Vivian was the lucky one.

Hugging his legs to his chest, Rob gave in to the pain. It seemed impossible he should live and breathe when Waverley was no more.

Liam's icy hand grazed his forehead. "You're burning up."

Rob tried to muster a smile, but his facial muscles were frozen. Stripping off his coat, Liam threw it over Rob. The wool was drenched and did little to warm him up, so Liam scooted next to him and draped an arm around his shoulder.

Cat lolled her head against the shed and watched them through eyes ringed with black circles. Finally, to the surprise of all, she uttered her first words since their flight from Balfour Manor. "Did it feel good, Barclay?"

Liam sniffed. "Did what feel good?"

"Shooting my sister. It's what you threatened to do. Do you feel avenged? Is our score settled?"

"Avenged?" Rob turned to Liam in question. "Avenged for what?"

Liam removed his arm. "I followed your orders."

She snorted. "That's right. You follow orders. Cut off my ear." She yanked back her hair, displaying her crooked ear. "Cut off my leg. Retrieve the egg."

Rob cringed at her cruel words. "Cat, you're going through a lot right now, but Liam isn't to blame…"

"No, Dr. Jekyll or Mr. Hyde or whatever he calls himself is to blame. But he's dead. Just like our sisters and everyone in the bleeding castle because his Avenging Angel was so good at following orders."

Her outburst triggered a barking fit from Virgil. Cat stood up and marched over to Liam. She kicked his leg. "You killed my sister. The moment you brought back the egg, you killed her."

Rob sprang to his feet. "Out of mercy!" He tried to steer her to the corner, but she jerked out of his grasp. "Now is not the time to pick a fight. Let's try to get some sleep."

Liam remained seated, calmly rubbing his knee. He was not nearly as oblivious as Jim, who was still studying the seashell.

"Ungrateful Kitty," he said, never raising his voice above a whisper. "I did you a favor out of the goodness of my heart. You ought to suck me off in thanks. You did it for Elixir, yet not your sister. I guess we know what you care about more."

This time Rob had to throw himself at Cat to keep her from leaping on Liam. Once she stopped cursing in his ear, Liam's words sank in.

"Hold on, *what*?" Rob looked from one to the other.

Cat shifted her eyes away.

"Tell him about us, Mornay." Rising to his feet, Liam held his arms wide in challenge. "You want to air our past grievances. I can play dirty too. Tell him—"

"About your 'brothers.' Your Henry and Thomas and *Charlie*." She ticked off their names on her fingers. Virgil accompanied each name with a bark. "Your sick collection of pretty boys who coincidentally look exactly like him."

"Funny you should mention Charlie," Liam shouted over the dog's snarls. "Tell Rob how you murdered him in cold blood. At least I can say Vivian never suffered."

Between the fever and Virgil's incessant barking, Rob's head spun from these new revelations. He learned many unflattering things about Cat and Liam—things he didn't *want* to know, yet it all came pouring out. Sex. Drugs. Murder. Mutilation. Dr. Jekyll's double life as some sort of drug lord named Mr. Hyde. Now he knew Liam had followed them and watched them make love, which was not as disturbing as Cat *knowing* they had an audience yet encouraging him to…

"Shut up. Shut up. Stop telling me!" Right now, they were making it very hard for him to believe that people were good at heart. "This isn't a confessional. Instead of fighting each other, we should be working together to kill that thing."

"The only thing I'm going to kill is that piece o' shite over there." Cat stripped off her coat and rolled up her sleeves. "No pistols. No knives. Just you and me."

Tossing his hat to the ground, Liam tied his hair back and ripped off his mask. His black coat came next. Culler landed in the pile, next to the sack containing *S. atlanticus'* salivary gland. He gestured to the door-less entrance where the rain pounded the mud in sheets. "Ladies first."

"All the more reason I should follow you," Cat said.

"Fine!" Rob threw his hands in the air as they stalked past him. "Kill each other. I don't care!"

Tail wagging in anticipation of a fight, Virgil trotted after Liam.

Feeling sick to his stomach, Rob slunk down next to Jim.

Grunts and groans drifted in from the outside. A body thudded against the hut.

Rob scrubbed his hands over his scalp. Meticulous hair didn't seem so important now. "I'm surrounded by idiots." Then he remembered Jim. "Not you."

Lost in a trance over the seashell, Jim ignored him. Rob watched the boy's brows furrow with a heavy heart.

"I miss her, too," he said, listening to Cat threaten to cut off Liam's head and shit down his neck. Apparently she used one threat for all occasion.

"I was writing a story for her." He stared at his clasped hands. "About schooners, islands, and maroons. And her best friend Jim Hawkins." He swiped a tear away and nibbled on his bottom lip until he had control of his voice. "I guess she'll never read it now. Waverley…"

At the mention of her name, the seashell tumbled to the floor.

"Jim?"

Jim collapsed against Rob, his body spasming in the throes of a violent seizure.

"Jim!" Rob held the lad down and called outside. "Help. Help!" But Cat and Liam were too wrapped up in their stupid fight to hear. Jim's eyes rolled to the back of his head and foam seethed from his mouth.

The lad's flailing arm smacked Rob in the face, but he managed to pry Jim's jaw apart in case he bit off his own tongue. Afraid to leave Jim alone, Rob screamed for help until his voice grew hoarse.

As suddenly as it began, the seizure ceased. Jim slumped in his arms and stopped breathing. He felt as light and lifeless as a feather. Rob gazed down at the lad's blue face. "No…"

Jim's eyes snapped open. Back arching off the ground, he sucked in a *whoosh* of air. A cord of saliva dribbled from his chin. Jim opened his mouth and said, "I am. I am. I am…"

That voice.

While Rob had never heard Jim speak, his gut told him this voice didn't belong to the lad.

"I am laird. I must. I must. I must…"

"Waverley?" Rob clutched Jim's hand. The lad's eyes were still white. The connection was a tenuous one. If his life depended upon it, Rob would never let go. "Is that you? Waverley? Please speak to me. Please don't leave me."

And Waverley spoke through her best friend. "I must kill them all. Kill all the monsters. Kill. Kill. Kill…"

Jim shut his eyes. When he opened them again, his eyes were once again black, intelligent, and calm. The lad sat up and stretched as if rising from a deep sleep.

Rob grabbed Jim by the shoulders. "Is Waverley alive?"

Jim blinked. Rob held his breath. Hope was a dangerous thing; he didn't dare embrace it until now.

And then…

Jim nodded.

"Y-yes?"

A smile dimpled Jim's cheeks.

Yes. Yes. Yes.

◆

The last thing Cat remembered was a rock slamming into her temple. Then darkness. When she came to, her face was mashed in the mud, her arm half-draped over Liam. His chest rose and fell, which meant the maggot wasn't dead.

With a moan, she touched her temple and flinched. Her fingers were coated with blood. "What did you do to me?"

Sprawled on his back, Liam probed his swollen nose. "I'm too old for this."

"We're not done." Propping herself up on her elbow, Cat took a pathetic swipe at Liam, but only managed to smack him in the ribcage. Her elbow gave out and she landed back in the mud. "I can go all night."

The rain had ceased, but droplets from the canopy pelted them.

Groaning, Liam eased himself up. Blood dripped from his chin. "Might I suggest we continue in the morning?"

"We settle this now." The mud tasted foul. She couldn't seem to take her face out of it. In fact, she wished she could just sink into the earth.

"I'm hungry," he said. "Are you?"

"Why can't you just kill me already?" Cat began to cry because she hadn't eaten anything all day and to be perfectly honest, she was famished. But after Manu Diaboli ate her sister, admitting she still had an appetite made her feel like an ass.

Liam hooked his hands under her armpits. "Up. Up."

Too weak to protest, Cat draped an arm around Liam's neck and let him drag her into the shed. They collided with Rob at the entrance. His cheeks were flushed red and his eyes burned with fanatic glee. Oblivious to their battered and muddied state, he threw his arms around them and twirled them into a merry dance. "She's alive! Waverley's alive!"

♦

Rob paced the shed like a caged animal. "You don't believe me?"

"It's not that we don't believe you, mate." Flinching from his injuries, Liam extracted a small packet from his coat. It contained squares of rice paper and some dried leaves. His deft hands began rolling the leaves into a cigarette. "Sit down before you pass out."

"You both think I imagined it?"

Patting his coat for a match, Liam turned to Cat for help. She was sprawled to his right. Jim knelt beside her, dabbing at the cut on her temple with his sleeve.

"What's that?" she asked Liam.

"Cannabis. Ever tried it?" Sticking the cig between his lips, Liam struck the match, took a heavy drag and exhaled. He passed Cat the cig.

Cat darted a guilty glance at Rob, then shook her head.

"Come, come," Liam nudged, "your sister just died..."

Without meeting Rob's eye, Cat snatched the cig, took a puff, and handed it back to Liam. Sweet, sticky smoke filled the shed, making Rob's head swim.

Liam offered Jim the cig, but Rob intercepted. "Just say no, Jim."

The lad shook his head.

Propping a hand on his hip, Rob stared incredulously at the two hunters. "Waverley is trapped with those creatures and we're just sitting around. Get up! We need to move. Now!"

Cat took a second hit and picked stray leaves off the tip of her tongue. "Sometimes we want to believe something so badly…"

"Not you, too." It struck him as goddamn annoying that they'd been at each other's throats since the beginning, and the one time they saw eye to eye was to band against him. "She's alive. Ask Jim."

They all turned to the boy. It would've helped his seizure story if Jim didn't look so put-together.

"Tell them you spoke my sister's thoughts."

Jim gave him a thumbs-up.

"See?"

Cat scratched her bruised jaw and looked away. "Four Manu Diaboli…" Smoke issued from her nostrils. "You can't save your sister any more than I can save mine."

Liam pinched her in the arm. "What she meant to say, mate, is—"

"She's scared out of her wits," Rob paced, "isn't that right? Well, I am too and *I'm* going."

To add insult to injury, Liam added, "The only place you're going is to sleep."

Ignoring him, Rob raised his arm. "Who will join me?"

He was met with a depressing lack of enthusiasm. "All right, all right." Rob tucked his hands in his pockets. "You think we're outnumbered and outmatched. Manu Diaboli may be faster and stronger, but perhaps you've heard of a little-known tale about a lad named David. No? Allow me to educate you…"

Liam rolled his eyes and muttered, "Not the David and Goliath story again."

"Why?" Cat asked.

"Count yourself lucky he isn't comparing himself to Christ."

But Jim sat up, black eyes sparkling with interest. With at least one apt pupil, Rob spoke of honor, righteous crusades, and bravery in the face of certain death. It was a damn good speech, so good, in fact, that he wondered if a future in Parliament was his true calling. Having moved himself to tears, Rob was ready to race back out in the rain and take a battering ram to his castle. "This, my friends, is *war*. A war against terror. Manu Diaboli take over Scotland? Not in my lifetime! Now I'll ask again: *Who's with me?*"

Jim raised his hand. Cat grabbed his wrist and made him put it down.

Rob sighed. "Do you want to live as cowards or die as heroes?"

"I can't go back there," Cat said. "I-I can't."

Rob turned to Liam. His friend shrugged. "Sorry, mate. It's too much to risk on a hunch."

With a frustrated growl, Rob tried one last time, "You both kill out of hate. Why not for love?"

Cat stared at the ground. Liam's jaw twitched.

Their silence broke his heart. He knocked the cig from Liam's lips and mashed it under his boot. "You are not my knights!"

"Rob!" Liam pleaded.

He gave them the middle finger.

Liam turned to Cat. "Did he just...?"

"I did," Rob replied. "And it was jolly liberating!" He found a corner and curled into a shivering ball. For the first time in his life, Rob had never felt so alone.

♦

A swift kick to her prosthetic leg jolted Cat awake.

Liam loomed over her, Culler in hand, and for a moment, she thought he'd finally decided to slit her throat in her sleep. Good. She was about to let him.

He kicked her again. "Wake up, it's Rob."

Cat rubbed the sleep from her eyes and cleared the cannabis haze from her head. "What about Rob?"

Liam moved aside and Cat bolted upright. The corner spot where Rob slept was empty save for a crumpled woolen blanket.

"He's gone."

CHAPTER 23
THE GREATEST HUNTER

He never expected to live past infancy.

Weak lungs.

A paper-thin heart.

Rob figured he was going to die anyway. In a few weeks or months. A year at the most. If it didn't happen now, it would happen later. Given the blood he'd coughed up yesterday and the larger splotches this morning, it was a matter of waiting for the monster that had been with him since childhood to possess him completely.

He'd been waiting to die his entire life. Now he would do it on his own terms.

Rob watched Jim crawl into the priest hole. Waverley's "dark place" led to a network of tunnels and passageways beneath the castle. She was in there somewhere, the sole human heartbeat in a house of the dead.

He patted his pocket, making sure the vial of Dragon's Breath he'd lifted from Liam's coat was there. As Jim's foot vanished from sight, Rob knelt and scratched Virgil behind the ears. "I guess this is it. If something happens to me, it's up to you to make sure Jim and Waverley are safe."

The Border Collie whimpered.

Rob hugged Virgil. "I'm so afraid." He stroked Virgil's warm fur with a trembling hand. "God help me, but I'm so afraid…"

He received a lick on the cheek.

"I'll miss you, boy."

Slinging Alec's rifle over his shoulder, Rob took a deep breath and stared into the pitch blackness. "Kill something. Be a man."

This time he would not cower or hide.

He was laird. This was his home.

Rob was no longer afraid. A strange calm settled over him as he crawled inside. Death could be a very great adventure.

♦

Cutting through the statue garden was a rather roundabout way to reach Balfour Manor. Cat and Liam hiked up a steep hill, wasting precious time and energy when there was a quicker path past the conservatory. But Liam refused to go near the glasshouse.

Cat ducked under the arch of a serpent emerging from the ground. The garden was Rob's favorite place on earth. He once told her he used to pretend he was part of the strange collection of gods and monsters, immortalized for all time in stone.

Thinking about Rob made every step twice as long. Cat concentrated on the task at hand.

She massaged the stitch in her side and glared at Liam's straight back. He snaked around the Titan and a goddess with branches for arms. Cat watched her step. The fight last night had put a few dents in her new prosthetic. If she damaged her leg before they reached Rob, she'd be of no use to anyone. "Are you afraid to pass by Hyde?"

"Faster," Liam barked over his shoulder.

To her knowledge, Liam had been in Mr. Hyde's employ since he was a child. "Do you miss him at all?"

Liam's shoulders tensed.

Good thing her new prosthetic allowed her to keep up with his purposeful strides. "He was like a father to you, was he not?" Cat called. "One vile rat raising another…"

"Hyde plucked me from the gutter. He washed me, clothed me, fed and housed me. He even gave me a puppy—the runt of the litter—and bade me care for it." Liam jogged down the rocky hill. She trailed on his heels. "So I washed it, fed it, grew to love it. Then Hyde put a dagger in my hand and ordered me to kill it."

In the glen, Cat walked by Liam's side. It was the first time he'd ever mentioned anything about his life. Before this admission, she'd assumed he hatched from an egg.

She darted a curious glance at his face, but could see nothing behind the mask. "Why?"

"He was going to mold me into a great monster hunter, but first I needed to destroy my weaknesses. Love. Mercy. Compassion. A true hunter feels none of these things; a true hunter is no different than the monsters he slays. That's what makes him great… He showed me how to practice on my pup. How to draw out its suffering, how to bring a swift and merciful death." Liam flexed his fingers and curled them into a fist. "I was six years old."

When they reached the castle, Liam led them to the massive double door. Cat armed herself, ivory pistol in one hand, dagger in the other. Pressing himself against the wall, Liam extracted Culler and fell silent for a moment.

"Do I miss Hyde?" He studied his silver reflection in the crescent blade. For as much blood as it had shed, Culler looked surprisingly clean and pure under the morning sun. He snorted. "Am I not the greatest hunter?"

"No." When she believed him soulless for so long, this was the hardest truth to admit. He was here for Rob, and if being a great hunter meant being a monster… "You are not."

And neither was she.

Liam's lips thinned into a pensive line. With a grunt, he wrapped his fingers around the knob. "Ready?"

Nodding, Cat tightened her grip on the pistol and Liam yanked open the door.

♦

The tunnels beyond the priest hole were tall enough for Jim to stand, but Rob had to crouch or risk bumping his head.

His boots splashed against a puddle. Slimy water dribbled on his hair and soaked the shoulder of his blazer. He was grateful he couldn't see his hand in front of his face. When he struck a match, Jim knocked the book to the ground. He couldn't see Jim either, but sensed the lad frowning.

Rob bowed his head in shame. A spark—in the presence of a lurking monster— meant a swift and deadly end to their rescue mission. "Sorry, I wasn't thinking."

With a push to the small of his back, Jim nudged him on. Ten years imprisoned in a shed had transformed the boy into a mole, and with Jim as his guide, they navigated the darkness.

As they approached a fork in the tunnel, the powerful stench of thirty rotting corpses oozed from above.

"Urgh." Rob covered his nose with his arm. Feeling the tears come on fast, he glanced over his shoulder. Their last glimpse of daylight was constricted to a distant pinprick.

"There's no turning back." But he kept his eyes fixed on the entrance until a shadow blotted it out and a *Click* resounded through the darkness.

Rob froze.

Talons scraped along the wall and scuttled across the ceiling.

Taking a step backward, Rob raised his rifle and aimed. "Jim," he whispered, "are you there?"

He felt a tug on his sleeve.

The creature halted.

Click. Click. Click.

He wasn't sure if the monster was the adult or hatchling. Chances were if the Great Mother was involved, he wouldn't have time to wonder.

Sweat dribbled over his eyelid. "When you hear the shot, run. The tunnel on the left. I won't be far behind."

The creature moved.

His rifle shook, his finger slipped to the trigger. "On the count of three."

Click.

"One."

Click.

A rock plopped into the puddle. Lime dust rained on him. He coughed; the hatchling growled.

"Two."

Click.

His muscles were coiled into tight springs. "Three!"

As the monster pounced, Rob opened fire.

♦

Cat and Liam studied the pitiful remains of the hatchling.

The creature had been hacked into pieces and the only thing that remained was a squished face, pink and vulnerable, not yet covered by exoskeleton. One hatchling accounted for. Two at large. Plus the Mother. Things, while still dismal, were looking up already.

"It would appear," Liam poked the incision in the creature's chest cavity with the tip of his blade, "that we have an amateur hunter in our midst."

"I wouldn't say amateur." Would an amateur know to rip out Manu Diaboli's heart? "Perhaps Hyde isn't as dead as we think."

Cat straightened from her crouch and checked that the double doors were shut. The grand library was a chaos of smashed vases and books toppled from shelves. Other than a few ominous splatters of blood, the hatchling was the first dead thing to cross their path after slipping inside Balfour Manor.

The old nightmare was back in a different setting and a colder climate. She glanced down once more at the hatchling's face, and a killer rage seized her.

Vivian was dead.

Rob was likely dead, too.

All because of this creature, who looked so helpless and humanlike. Her boot came down on the face.

Squish. Stomp. *Squish.* Stomp.

Cat doubled over, gulping fetid air. The castle reeked of the jungle. Her fingers dug into her knees. One knee was flesh and bone, the other cold steel.

"Well," Liam tilted his head to the side, "there's a bloodstain that can't be removed." He swatted her awkwardly on the back. "Stop crying. I knew I should've never brought you along. You shame the profession."

"When this is over," Cat wiped her tears on her sleeve, "consider me retired."

"Giving up the life?" As if she'd uttered a blasphemy, Liam's eyes widened. "What will you do?"

She ground the heel of her boot into the Oriental rug to rid her sole of monster parts. "No idea, but this—" She waved a hand over the pulpy mess. "—isn't healthy for me."

He sighed. "Aw, well, no great loss. You're shite at what you do."

"Okay."

"I don't know why you get all the glory."

"Enough."

"You haven't had a proper kill since Africa, and even that was dumb luck. Seems like the only things you've murdered lately…are people."

"I don't know how much of this cheering up I can take," she muttered.

Liam opened his mouth for another go when the BOOM of a gunshot saved her self-esteem.

Cat jolted upright. Liam turned around and glanced downward. The ground shook beneath them.

Three shots.

Fired in rapid succession.

The shots echoed beneath the first floor. There was a rumble close by, followed by a loud crash—the sound of the earth caving in.

Cat locked eyes with Liam. "Shit," they mouthed in unison and bolted to the door.

◆

Once the dust cleared, Rob coughed and peeked over his shoulder. A solid wall of debris replaced the pinprick of daylight. He still had his arms wrapped around Jim, whom he shielded from the collapse.

He brushed the dust from the lad's hair, checking for injuries.

"Are you all right?"

Jim nodded.

Alec's rifle was gone, dropped in his haste to outrun the monster and the cave-in. He'd only his vial of Dragon's Breath and his wits at his disposal now.

But the hatchling was crushed underneath layers of stone. So too was their one chance of a stealthy escape.

"Onward?"

Jim took his hand. From this moment forward, they were going to leave by the front door or not at all.

♦

The servants' quarters, including the room she shared with her sister, were no more. Four to five rooms lost to a cave-in.

Cat stood over a rubble-filled pit and her optimism of ever finding Rob alive collapsed with the floor. She and Liam shared a moment of ominous silence. "Suppose he's under—"

"Shut up." Liam whirled around and weaved back the way they came.

Minding her footing, Cat followed on his heels.

His steps were jerky and uncoordinated shambles. "He's not dead."

"How do you know?"

Liam picked up the pace. "It's a bloody feeling, okay?"

Or denial. Out of the corner of her eye, she caught the bob of his Adam's apple.

"Rob is wicked smart," she said instead. "And he's got a demon boy to look out for him. He'll be all right."

But as they rounded a corner and entered a narrow hallway splattered with the remains of three housemaids, her tenuous grasp of Rob or any of them being "all right" slipped through her fingers.

Cat hitched in a breath.

A draft whistled through a cracked window, stirring the hair on one unfortunate maid's temple. This one had lost her cap— and the rest of her body below the neck. Cat spotted the body minus head sprawled in the corner, and had the sick impulse to unite the two.

A drop of blood plopped on the back of her hand. Cat glanced up and a chunk of someone's unidentifiable body part dropped to the floor.

She gasped and jumped back. Her foot slipped on something slimy.

Liam grabbed her by the elbow before she could fall. Hunching her shoulders, Cat focused on a clean spot on the floor. A few minutes inside the castle should've desensitized her to these pockets of carnage. But Cat could never get used to it. All the more reason to retire.

"C-can we just get out of here? Come on," she said, tugging on Liam's sleeve. He refused to budge. He wasn't even looking at her or the mess around him. His eyes were wide and unblinking within the holes of his silver mask.

Cat turned in the direction of his gaze.

A claw-shaped shadow spilled across the floor and ceiling like ink, too large, too all-encompassing to belong to a hatchling.

Over the hammering of her heart, she heard the tap of talons on hardwood and the first *Click.*

Liam dragged her into a tiny alcove. Her back slammed against the wall. He wrapped his arms around her waist, held her so tight a piece of paper couldn't slip between their bodies.

His mask chilled her cheek. "Don't even *think* about breathing," he whispered in her ear before the air pressure changed.

A *thud* boomed from behind him.

The Great Mother, landing at exactly the same spot they'd been standing, lifted her massive head and sniffed the air.

Click.

Cat squeezed her eyes shut and bit down on Liam's shoulder, filling her mouth with the taste of wool.

Click.

Liam's fingers dug into the small of her back.

Click.

They both flinched when Manu Diaboli screeched and sprinted toward the cave-in. Paralyzed to the spot, they waited and Cat counted each of Liam's rapid heartbeats.

"Is she coming back?"

Cat cracked open an eye. Only the dead eyes of the maid stared back at her. She shook her head.

"Follow me," he said, taking her by the hand. They slipped out of the alcove and snuck down the rest of the hall without a sound. At the bend, Cat had a chance to test out the running capabilities of her new leg. They sprinted down another corridor, putting as much distance between them and the monster as they could. Liam yanked her into a linen closet.

As soon as the door slammed behind them, he grasped her by the arms to keep her upright. "Hey, hey," he said over her hysterical whimpers. "Where are you? Stay with me. Stay with me."

Cat shook her head. She was in the jungle, sinking fast into insanity.

"No, no, no." His hands clamped around her temples, nails digging crescents into her scalp. "Listen to me, Mornay. If you can't get your mind right and Rob dies, I swear to you right now—" He tightened his grip and her skull creaked. "I will make you wish you were back in the jungle. Do you hear me? For Rob, bury the past."

Her breathing slowed. Her heart ceased racing. Finally, she nodded. "For Rob."

"Good." He let out a breath. "Good." Then he slapped her across the face.

"Ow!" Glaring at him, Cat rubbed her sore cheek. If he was trying to snap her out of it, this was one hell of a delayed reaction. "I don't think that was necessary."

"I know," he said, a bit sheepishly. "I just couldn't help myself."

♦

Waverley.

He must find Waverley.

Rob crawled through the shrinking tunnel and nudged the trap door open. Just as his sister mentioned, it led to the kitchens. Hoisting himself out of the floor grate, Rob turned to help Jim. They crouched between the great stove and the wall, listening for signs of human or monster. All he could see was a section of the oak island. The kitchens, always so rancorous, were silent as—dare he say it—a tomb.

Determining it was safe to come out, Rob stood up. His new surroundings made him want to crawl back into the hole.

Rob wandered around the corpse-strewn floor in a daze.

He knew them all by name.

James, the footman who served him his last supper with Dr. Jekyll.

Polly, the new scullery maid.

Finley and Mrs. Nix.

Oh God.

He slipped on a puddle of blood and landed right beside his housekeeper. Unlike Polly, Mrs. Nix escaped dismemberment, or in the case of poor Finley…being disemboweled. He spotted a fracture behind her ear and prayed her death was instantaneous. Perhaps she was even the first to go, mercifully spared the unimaginable horror of watching the others slaughtered and waiting her turn.

Rob drew her into his arms. She felt as soft as dough, and as he'd done many times as a boy, Rob rested his head against her massive bosom and wept.

He cried until there was nothing left. When he recovered, Rob passed his hand over Mrs. Nix's dead-staring eyes and laid her back on the floor. He folded her arms over her chest and kissed her chubby cheek. He crawled to Finley and kissed him on the forehead.

Rising to his feet, Rob squared his shoulders and walked straight to the pantry.

During his absence, the shelves had been restocked with Dr. Jekyll's serum; he knew it would be as surely as he knew Mrs. Nix loved him. He wiped the snot from his nose and the tears from his eyes.

Rob grabbed three vials, a larger orb-shaped glass bottle, and took his supplies to the sink.

Unscrewing the stopper, he poured the vials into the larger bottle, dropped a ball of Dragon's Breath inside, and watched the green serum bubble and boil.

"Life is not a matter of holding the good cards," he said to Jim, "but playing a poor hand well."

With steady hands, he replaced the stopper and slipped on Jim's hydra-skin gloves. The glass only felt warm, but if he'd been wearing riding gloves instead of hydra-skin, the heat would've burned through the leather.

"Snap to, Jim," he ordered with all the authority of laird. He cradled the bottle like a babe and crossed the kitchen on eggshells. If he slipped or dropped the concoction, they were both dead.

He was done hiding in tunnels.

Done being a boy.

And like Liam, he too had a plan.

◆

Following Jim's lead, Rob carried the bottle up to the third floor. The serum was a green supernova, illuminating the darkness like the kerosene-less lamp in Cat's dreams.

As he ascended the spiral staircase, a sheen of sweat coated his brow and dripped down his temple. His face was flushed with heat. On their short trek through the castle, they encountered no monsters, and he could almost believe that the green glow shielded them from danger.

At the moment, Rob was more afraid of the volatile concoction than Manu Diaboli. With every step, he imagined the Dragon's Breath fusing with the serum and the molecules vibrating faster and faster.

Jim weaved through the darkness by feelers, his head turning left to right, up and down. Waverley was here somewhere. Rob had full confidence that Jim would lead him to her. The lad hopped up the final step, glided across the landing, and jogged silently ahead.

Rob set foot on the landing. He stepped forward and heard the *snap* of a wire.

A battle-ax swung down and someone rammed him from the side.

Holding the bottle above his head, Rob crashed to his ground. "Oof!"

The ax cleaved the entryway like a pendulum and lodged in the floor with a shower of splinters.

Disoriented and certain he'd just peed himself, Rob inspected the bottle and heaved the deepest sigh of his life. He sat up and found himself face to face with his sister.

"Waverley?"

Her clothes and cheeks were streaked with soot and blood. There were still residual plumes of feathers in her hair.

"My God." Mindful not to jilt the bottle, Rob beckoned her closer. "Waverley…"

Her eyes darted left and right, savage and suspicious. She hesitated for a moment, then uttered a guttural sob and crashed into his arms.

"They came while we were sleeping. It happened so fast!" She buried her face in his chest. "Mrs. Nix. Finley. Everybody. I kept Vivian safe for a while, but she refused to stay in the tunnels with me. She was afraid of the dark and so bloody stubborn. On the fourth day, she went up. I tried, Rob! I tried to save her!"

"I know. I know." Rob held her tighter and stroked her tangled hair.

As Waverley descended into an onslaught of tears, Jim scooted closer and patted her on the head. Face still nuzzled against Rob's chest, Waverley grasped Jim's finger and their hands found each other.

"But I got them, Rob."

"Got them?"

386

Wiping her nose, Waverley stripped off her knapsack. Her tear-streaked face creased into a smile as she reached inside. "A laird protects her castle," she said, unfurling her hand. Two pink hearts, each about the size of a robin's egg, fitted neatly in her palm. "Dr. Jekyll said these will only buy you time until I harvest their mother."

Did he hear her right? His eight-year-old sister planned to kill the Great Mother?

Waverley pushed the hearts toward his mouth. "Eat them." The hatchling hearts made a squishy sound and smelled like raw liver. Blood dribbled through her fingers. An eerie spark ignited in her eyes, and Rob wondered if everything she'd been through had tipped her into madness. "Eat."

Rob's stomach roiled. Standing up, he waved away the offer. "Maybe later."

"But the Mother!" Waverley hopped to her feet and dragged Jim along. The lad busied himself plucking feathers from her hair.

"Let's focus on getting out of here," Rob said, balancing the Elixir orb.

"I've set up all the traps. It's only a matter of waiting, but Rob, the mother's clever..." Waverley lowered her voice to a whisper and gazed into the dark stairwell. "I almost got her down at the parlor. Rigged a shotgun to go off when she opens the door. The bullet nicked her on the shoulder and she never went inside the parlor again. She learns, Rob... She learns."

After touring a massacre and nearly being cleaved in two, Rob didn't think he could be any more unsettled. He was wrong. He felt like he was digging a grave again, deeper and deeper until he couldn't get out.

"All the more reason to *move*."

Over her protests, he nudged Waverley toward the stairs. Jim hooked his arm through his girl's elbow. Bottle carefully clutched, Rob took the lead. He peered down the stairwell and heard the thunderous clap of shoes upon stone.

Gasps.

Pants.

Frantic footsteps climbing, running, building...

Into a shot in the dark.

BOOM!

Cat burst onto the landing, her face white with terror. "She's right behind us!"

Two more shots.

Liam appeared on her heels, firing a blank into the void. "I didn't sign up for this shit!" He chucked his pistol at the monster.

A screech spiraled up the stairwell.

Without sparing a greeting, Cat seized Rob by the elbow. "Run!"

Rob and the children scrambled, running elbows to knees in a desperate attempt to put as much distance between them and the monster as they could.

Midway down the hall, Waverley whirled around and ran the opposite way. "My hearts!"

"Leave them!" Rob tried to grab her collar.

Upon his orders, Liam scooped up Waverley and tossed her over his shoulder like a cursing and kicking sack of potatoes.

The pack careened to a dead end.

Cat kicked open the door to the solarium. Easily the slowest, Rob rounded off the tail. He peeked over his shoulder. The atmosphere shifted and stirred like an oxygen-sucking vortex and then...

The monster leaped onto the landing.

Rob caught a flash of the creature's sleek black armor. He paused at the doorway. Standing on her hind legs, Manu Diaboli cocked her triangular head, mouth-pincers *click click clicking.*

Her onyx talons tapped the hardwood.

Click. Tap. Click. Tap.

Seven green dots reflected in her prism eye. Rob glanced at the bubbling orb in his hands, recalling Hugh Mornay's theory.

All creatures of darkness.

He held up the orb, swung it from side to side. Manu Diaboli stepped forward, hypnotized by the artificial sun.

Click. Tap. Click. Tap.

The creature dropped on all fours and when she pounced, Rob hurled the bottle at the monster.

CHAPTER 24
SOLARIUM

Cat lay in a pool of broken glass.

Ears still ringing, she twisted her head. Sunlight spilled from the shattered floor-to-ceiling windows. Acrid smoke and waves of heat streamed beneath the double doors. There was an inferno in the hallway and if Rob hadn't had the foresight to shut the doors on the explosion, they would've roasted in agony.

Raising herself on her elbows, Cat surveyed the rubble. Liam and Rob were sprawled next to her, the former shielding the latter from the blast with his body. She couldn't find the short people. Panic trickled in.

"Jim? Waverley?"

"Here!" They were huddled in the corner.

"Are you hurt?"

Waverley held up her hand. "I cut my finger!" The wound was as minor as a paper cut.

"Suck on it," she croaked. "What about Jim?"

The lad gave her a thumbs-up.

Grimacing, Cat sat up. Unbelievable. Had Rob succeeded where she and Liam failed? Had he killed Manu Diaboli?

"Mornay, take note," Liam said. "That's how you kill a monster." Picking up her train of thought, Liam stared at Rob in awe. "Christ, mate. What was that?"

Rob poked his head up. Despite the nick on his forehead, he was otherwise unharmed. "The reaction of two volatile substances." His lips curled into a grin. "Simple chemistry."

"Idiot!" Waverley crawled to her brother and helped him sit up. "You burnt my hearts."

"Little girl, show some respect." Liam thumped Rob on the back. "You're in the presence of a true hunter."

Rob clasped Liam's arm. While the two embraced, Cat motioned to Jim. He scooted closer and she inspected him for injuries. Jim didn't have a cut or bruise on him, proving he was more indestructible than she could ever be. She tried to examine the lump on Waverley's scalp, but the girl jerked away. "Don't stroke my head."

In the interim, Rob extracted himself from Liam's arms. "Well, miss?" His cheeks were sooty from the blast and his hair stuck up in tufts. Blue eyes glinted with pride. "I believe we've captured the castle."

"*You've* captured." She inched toward him and smoothed down the tufts. "I'd say you've put me out of a job." Dispensing with dignity, she crashed into him and peppered his face with kisses. "I thought I lost you."

Rob's lips sought hers. Cat kissed him long and hard and deep.

Jim made a gagging sound.

"Nasty," Waverley said.

"Now you know what I have to put up with, little girl." Liam cleared his throat and smacked Cat between the shoulder blades. "Enough. There are children here."

Now that she'd found Rob again, she'd never let him go. With great reluctance, Cat pulled away and whispered all the filthy things she planned to do to him when they get out.

A flush swept across his cheeks. Rob gulped. "Whatever you say, miss," he said, "I'm ready to go."

Liam shook his head. "And I think I'm going to vomit on both of you."

Rob smiled and Cat was just about to smile back when there came...

From outside...

A *rap* on the door.

Cat froze, watching Rob's expression twist into a combination of horror and disbelief. He shook his head. "Impossible!"

And yet.

Rap. Click. Rap. Click.

Cat peeked over her shoulder.

The knob turned.

She and Liam scrambled to their feet. A braying blared through the crackling flames. Liam slammed his shoulder against the door just as a very *alive* Manu Diaboli poked her head through the crack.

He slashed her face with his knife; the creature retreated and he shut the door, locked it. *"Why won't this thing die?"*

The Great Mother crashed against the other side.

Thump

The door splintered at the center.

Thump

Liam's heels dug into the floor.

Thump

He couldn't hold the door by himself.

Cat dashed toward Rob's worktable. "Help me!"

Joined by Rob and the children, they pushed the desk in front of the door. Freed from his station, Liam ran to the bookshelf and heaved; the shelf collided with the desk.

When the thumping ceased, they stood back. A heavy silence descended upon the solarium. They had built a passable barricade against the monster—and a prison for themselves.

◆

Cat wound up the birdman and stuck her hand outside. The automaton soared through the air, its golden wings catching the sun. Now would be a good time to learn to fly.

"We could climb down," Waverley suggested. Crouched beside her brother, she rubbed calming circles on Rob's back and urged him to breathe in the crisp air. She kept a sturdy grip on his elbow in case he plummeted to the ground. Sometime during the night, the bullet-hole-ridden window had shattered. As if to add insult to injury, Vivian's desecrated remains had slipped through the cracks.

The birdman landed on the bloody grass. Cat stepped closer to the edge. Her sister's body—if you could still call it a body—was sprawled facedown in a circle of broken glass. Vivian was free and freedom was a step and a three-story drop away. Cat's eyes watered from the smoke. She surveyed the slick wall beneath and the great gaps between window ledges. Without ropes, a climb would be difficult, though not impossible.

"I'll go first," Waverley went on. "It'll be easy."

Easy for Liam. Easy for Jim and Waverley, who were as nimble as apes. Cat could fend for herself. But Rob?

Rob wasn't doing so well.

Liam ceased pacing and joined her at the window. They knelt, one on each side of Rob, and listened to his labored breathing.

"I'm holding you back," Rob said. "Leave me."

"Nonsense," Liam said. "How could you even suggest that?"

"We're not going anywhere without you." Cat lowered her head, ashamed for thinking him a dead weight. "We live and die together."

"I'd rather you live," Rob said.

Liam took Rob's hand. "In a world without you?"

She and Liam were finally on the same page. Where would they be without Rob? Just two killers crawling and fighting in the Edinburgh cage. He raised them high and taught them how to be human. No, there was no world without Rob.

"We belong here." She propped her chin on Rob's shoulder and wrapped her arms around him. "By your side."

"Now who's speaking nonsense? You two are—*wheeze*—without a doubt—*wheeze*—the stupidest people I've ever met." Rob gazed down at the green void, but a weak smile flickered across his lips. "My knights… " He fired a dirty cough and Cat held him until the fit subsided. He felt so light in her arms.

She pressed her lips to his hair and met Liam's eye over the top of Rob's head.

Liam peered over his shoulder at the barricade, fingers tapping against his thigh. When he turned around, his pale eyes seemed to have lost some of their coldness.

Liam stood up. "Mornay? A word with you?"

396

Turning Rob over to Waverley's care, Cat joined Liam by the barricade. "What is it?"

"I have a plan," he said. "Help me move the desk."

"Care to tell me what that plan is?"

"I'll go out first," he lowered his voice to a whisper, "keep the monster off your back. While I'm slashing her up, you take Rob—and I suppose the children—and run. Don't be afraid to throw the children to the monster. I don't really care if they make it out alive. Just promise me you'll keep Rob safe. " As an afterthought, he pressed Culler into her palm. "Just in case I don't make it out," he added with an embarrassed shrug, "a killer needs a proper knife."

Cat studied the Bedouin blade in shock. A square of paper accompanied the knife. She stared at him in surprise. "What's this?"

He touched the back of her hand, stopping her from unfolding the square. "Read it after you're out," he mouthed.

Frowning, Cat tucked the note in her pocket. "What are you going to use?"

"I tamed the serpent, didn't I?" He slung a broadsword across his back.

"This is hardly a time to brag about your sexual conquests," she said. "Manu Diaboli is no serpent. This is a fight you can't win."

"You killed a Manu Diaboli." He grinned and backed away. "If a shite hunter like you could do it…" Swaggering up to the barricade, Liam rolled up his sleeves. "A little help?"

"What's going on?" Rob got to his feet. He glanced between the two of them, a frown rippling his forehead. At a time like this, Cat was grateful he was slow on the uptake. "What are you doing?"

"Not to worry," Liam said. "I have a plan."

Despite his false bravado, Cat detected a tinge of fear in his voice and she hated him a little less. She realized, with regret, that under different circumstances, they could've been friends.

Liam mouthed, "Ready?"

Cat nodded. "Rob. Short people—"

"We're only short because we're children," Waverley interrupted. Jim folded his arms and tapped his foot.

"Whatever." She tried to sound confident and optimistic as Liam shoved the bookshelf aside. "Barclay has volunteered to keep the monster off our back. When he opens the door, you run and don't stop—"

At long last, Rob got it. His eyes widened and he turned to Liam. "N-n-noo."

Liam clutched Rob's shoulder. "Now, mate…"

"I won't allow it!"

"I'll be right behind you. Here," Liam said, peeling off his mask and handing it to Rob. His scars were tender and pink, but not all that grotesque anymore. "Maybe my face will turn the monster to stone."

At his words, Rob burst into tears. "Ah, don't cry, mate." Liam wiped Rob's wet cheeks with his sleeve. "You've got a new angel to look out for you now."

"Don't leave me." Rob clasped Liam's face in his hands. "Don't leave me…" Wrapping his arms around Liam, Rob kissed him. On the lips. For a very long time.

Cat grimaced and averted her eyes. With a burning castle and the literal *mother* of all monster problems outside the door, now was not the time for jealousy. Yet the boys were still at it. "Snails," she muttered. "Bloody snails."

Beside her, Waverley said, "I knew it!"

Jim shook his head.

"Shut up," Cat snapped. "You too, Jim."

Jim held his palms up. *What?*

"I know what you're thinking."

Liam broke off the kiss. He pressed his forehead against Rob's and made a sound between a laugh and a sob.

"Ready?" Cat asked.

The boys continued to cling to each other.

Contemplating prying them apart, Cat raised her voice. "If you're quite finished!"

Liam broke the embrace. "Right." Eyes never leaving Rob's, he snapped a finger at her. "Kitty, assistance please."

Cat helped him move the barricade and Liam unsheathed his sword. Yanking the door open, he gave Rob one last, long look before slipping into a wall of flames.

Cat poked her head outside. She could see Liam, sword at the ready, tiptoeing down one end of the hall. A landmine of holes and debris stood between them and the stairs. She took the lead. "Move."

Waverley and Jim weaved past the debris and the patches of flames, racing down the stairs.

Rob lagged behind, his eyes fixed on Liam's back.

"Don't look back." Cat grasped him by elbow and tugged him along. Even she couldn't follow her own advice.

The Great Mother dropped from the ceiling and landed in front of Liam.

He raised his sword. An arch of cold steel struck black exoskeleton. The monster let out an ear-shattering shriek and Liam leapt back, raised his broadsword to strike again.

He just might pull it off. He'll kill Manu Diaboli like he killed the serpent. Cat dragged Rob down the stairs and into a fiery hell. Heat blasted her in the face. A wooden beam crashed in a shower of sparks. Cat ducked and shielded Rob's head with her arms. Eyes watering from the smoke, she saw only the dim shapes of Waverley and Jim zooming toward the front door and from somewhere above…

A roar: the same victory cry she once heard in the jungle and the fae woods. Manu Diaboli was always smarter, always one step ahead. As she pushed Rob into the fresh air, she was certain of two things: the monster had won and the greatest hunter was no more.

PART III
PARADISO

CHAPTER 25
LOVERS IN WINTER

Edinburgh, three months later.

Cat studied the note one more time. The message, scrawled in haste with soot from the fire and in Liam's crude, almost childish hand, was smeared beyond legibility.

Tron Kirk.

She lifted her eyes from the note.

The cathedral, covered in a fine dusting of snow, loomed before her. Cat stepped under an arch. The stony gaze of the saints pierced the top of her head. She passed a fountain overflowing with grey slush. The spot where Charlie had bled to death was covered with a slick sheet of ice. Cat hurried through the courtyard, fighting the urge to turn back and leave the bloody past behind.

It had taken her three months to summon up the courage to come here.

Since their flight from the castle, they'd returned to Edinburgh and to the promise of a happy ending which hadn't quite been fulfilled.

Her family town house belonged to the bank, but Cat never lacked for a pillow to rest her head. The door to Rob's town house on 17 Heriot Row was always open. Jim resided there now, preferring posh lodgings and proximity to his snot-nosed girl to wandering the dark city with Cat. The little sod was better off with Rob, though even Cat must admit, she missed Jim's company. Without him, it was as if she'd lost her shadow.

Slipping inside the iron doors, Cat entered a nave alight with candles. She passed row after row of sarcophagi, each one carved in a likeness of the deceased's face. Rob would have a tomb as grand as this, when it was his time to go...

She picked up the pace. Her boots pounded stone as memories of a blood-spotted pillow chased her up a dank stairwell. More and more these days, she'd prolonged her stay with Rob, holding him as he coughed throughout the night. Even though Rob was optimistic about his treatments with a new physician, she could feel him slipping out of her grasp. How could she love a boy who could fade by spring? Or give all of herself to him when his death seemed imminent?

Cat couldn't handle another death. So she protected herself the only way she knew how: she shut down her heart.

The days darkened faster these winter months. Her retirement was plagued with sadness.

She saw Vivian die a hundred times over. She reconstructed the many ways the monster deconstructed Liam. In her dreams, she'd see Manu Diaboli haunting the halls of Balfour Manor, moaning for her lost hatchlings and calling for Cat to come back and keep her company.

She wanted to go back.

To her old life.

Her old ways.

She didn't fit into Rob's world, but she was too afraid to face Manu Diaboli again. She wanted peace and hands clean of blood, but longed for the thrill of the hunt. Perhaps Liam was right and her killer instinct couldn't be suppressed. She was a monster hunter in civilian clothes, and maybe she could never be happy until she and Manu Diaboli met again.

Snowflakes rained through the window slits, spiraling in the air and melting into her skin. She climbed the serpentine stairs, shivering from the draft trapped within the cold stones. Tendrils of hair tickled the nape of her neck. Cat stripped off her hat and unfolded the note.

To the top.

In a long ago harpy hunt, Liam mentioned he was afraid of heights, and now he was leading her up to the cathedral's tallest spire.

Where the staircase ended, Cat ducked into a decrepit hovel buttressed by wooden beams. A straw pallet with a wool blanket was shoved at the farthest corner. There was no pillow. A pang tugged at her heart as she crossed to the window. Swiping a sleeve across the grimy stained glass, Cat peered below. The Royal Mile and all her tightly packed, peaked-roof buildings glimmered in a blanket of white.

"Dodgy lodgings, mate," she said, gazing around a room too monkish for the likes of Edinburgh's greatest hunter.

Suddenly her attention lighted on a loose stone over the head of the pallet. Kneeling down, Cat pried the stone free and stuck her hand inside. Expecting a loot of coins and weapons, she found a bundle of letters.

Cat unfolded the first letter, holding the fragile paper up to the light. The whorls and loops of her mentor's fingerprints mingled with the ink, a faint yet bold proclamation: "The greatest hunter was here."

Now the only things left of an extraordinary life were fingerprints and a sad collection of worldly goods.

And words.

Dear Friend,

I'm writing in the broom closet. The chaps have been especially cruel and the headmaster...

Rob's elaborate script materialized like wisps of smoke, transporting her to Eton's winter courtyard and into the mind of a lonely boy in need of a friend.

She came upon a second set of letters. Unlike the first bundle, these were crumpled, torn, half-finished. She studied Liam's unpracticed hand, trying so hard to form a reply worthy of Rob and never getting past the first misspelled paragraph.

Cat curled on her side. The straw scratched her cheeks. A tear slid down her nose bridge and clung to her chin.

"The wrong hunter died," she whispered, clutching the letter to her chest. "He belongs to you…"

Between those childish lines of scrawl, she saw Liam's heart, and everything she'd ever believed about what made a man into a monster fell by the wayside. And perhaps this was Liam's way of showing her that while lovers may wither and turn to dust, love never died.

Love was right here.

In a sad little room.

A lonely bed.

In letters too often read and replies never sent.

♦

Rob watched the snow drift outside his physician's window, counting the days until spring.

When the docks thawed, he was finally sailing for Antigua. But in the meantime, he just had to last the winter. The snow swirled in a flurry. He imagined Cat drifting with the snowflakes and flitting from lamppost to lamppost. He knew her transition to civilian life would not be easy. Nor was it easy for him to love a monster hunter.

Seated at the edge of a steel operation table, Rob eyed the framed maps of the human anatomy. The mysteries of life and death were on display from etchings of striated muscle to the twenty-seven bones of the hand. His attention rested on a map of the heart, every chamber, vein, and artery cataloged and labeled. Did love reside in that puny organ? As far as Cat was concerned, did love for him reside in her heart at all?

A week ago to the date, she'd waltzed into his town house from God knew where, stripped off all her clothes, and joined him in bed. She'd disappeared the next morning and hadn't returned since. Rob had no idea where she was now. She could be dead in a gutter for all he knew. And while he tried so hard to make her happy, she seemed determine to let her despair consume her.

Bowing his head, Rob recalled Cat's response when he'd confessed his love for her on the banks of Loch Ness.

"Will you love me in a year?"

"Will you love me in ten?"

Three months ago, Rob would've said yes with absolute certainty. Now he was still certain, though perhaps not absolutely…

The door opened and his new physician, Dr. Menton, waddled in. "How fares our young lordship today?" he asked, scribbling notes on a clipboard. His plump belly, jowls, and sideburns reminded Rob of a walrus.

"Miserable," Rob said. "And happy. Miserably happy."

The doctor frowned beneath grizzled brows, and Rob found himself missing Dr. Jekyll more than ever. "Drink this," he said, shoving a teacup in Rob's hand.

He sniffed the cup. The liquid gave off a sticky-sweet fume. "What's this?"

"Tincture of opium." The doctor checked his pocket watch. "To dull the pain."

Rob poked his head up. "Pain?" He gazed at the copper tubing leading to the operation table, which was powered by three levers. Five glass orbs lined the control station. "Is it going to hurt?"

"Not if you take your medicine like a good boy."

Rob took a sip and made a face. Hearing yet another man call him "boy" brought a foul taste to his mouth. After all he'd been through, it seemed nothing had changed.

"I haven't all day, Lord Robert. Drink up." Under the older man's stern glare, Rob guzzled the opium and wiped his mouth on the back of his hand.

Nodding, the doctor strolled toward the controls. "Take off your shirt."

Rob tackled his buttons with clumsy fingers. Grimacing, he studied his sunken chest and conspicuously visible ribcage. He turned to the mirror behind him. The human spine was comprised of thirty-three vertebrate, twenty-four that one could actually see. Rob counted twenty-four bones. His shoulders slumped. At this point, the only thing differentiating him from the skeleton pinned to the corner was the very mutable fact that he was alive. For now.

"I've lost a bit of weight." He attempted a smile, but his lips felt numb from the opium. "Maybe that's why my girl can't stay with me for long," he said, as the doctor attached two electrode pads to his chest. "She can't stand the sight of me…"

The doctor handed him a brown leather strap.

Rob frowned. "What's this for?"

"The jolt might make you bite your tongue in half."

"Oh." Studying the teeth marks on the strap, Rob tried to make light of it. "We wouldn't want that, would we?

"Try not to talk," the doctor said, helping Rob lie down and yanking a transparent dome over him.

Alone under the dome, Rob longed for his childhood doctor once more. Jekyll would've asked him about the girl. A draft whizzed through the laboratory, sending him into an episode of intense shivering. Biting down on the strap to stop his teeth from chattering, Rob watched Menton's rotund silhouette reach for the first lever. He shut his eyes and curled his hands into fists. If he listened hard enough, Jekyll's voice echoed in his head, conjuring up old feelings of warmth and love. "Think happy thoughts…"

As Dr. Menton pulled the lever, Rob was in Antigua with Cat by his side. He was at least ten years older, a healthy man instead of a skeleton. And when his hunter asked if he still loved her, even after all this time, Rob replied with certainty.

Yes.

With *absolute* certainty.

Yes.

♦

One afternoon, while on one of her aimless strolls through the city, Cat passed a hansom. The horse had just dropped a steaming pile and the stench struck her hard. She bumped into a nanny pushing a pram and dove in an alley beside a solicitor's office and retched.

Wiping her mouth on her sleeve, Cat leaned against the brick wall until her nausea subsided. A native of Edinburgh all her life, Cat lived and breathed horse shit and it never bothered her before. She shut her eyes, wondering if she'd caught a midwinter's stomach bug. Somewhat recovered, Cat checked her skirt for vomit before re-entering the crowd. Just as she was about to slip out of the alley, the doorbell over the office dinged and a slender gentleman in a top hat exited.

Cat froze and slunk back into the alley before he spotted her. He was fiddling with his gloves and carried a walking stick. His elegant profile was unmistakable. A long time ago, she'd mistaken him for her father.

"Mr. Hyde." She broke into a cold sweat.

The doctor was alive.

Alive and well while her sister was dead and gone.

The doctor whirled on his polished shoes and merged into the crowd. Cat stumbled into the daylight, blinking up at the sign over the office. *Mr. Utterson, Solicitor.*

Before she knew what was happening, she began to follow her former employer.

♦

Rob cracked his knuckles.

The sheet before him was an ink-blotted mess, but in between the lines he saw the deep blue sea and felt the sand between his toes. Swimming out of the hole he'd carved from the page, he was met with a drafty study and a burning pressure inside his chest. There was still daylight when he began writing; now it was night. A kerosene lamp cast a golden halo around his desk. There was also an untouched tray and a bottle of medicine, though he couldn't remember his new housekeeper ever entering his study.

Weak and sleep-deprived, Rob yanked open his desk drawer. He took out Liam's silver mask, his thumb brushing the hollow cheeks and caressing the regal nose.

He let out a heavy sigh.

His friend, once alive, was no more, but where was that thing that made Liam laugh and cry, hate and love? Where was the thing that made Liam move?

It had to be somewhere.

Liam promised to always be with him, but Rob felt no sign of his friend anywhere. A mask and a knife were all that were left of Liam Barclay. What would be left of Rob when it was his time to leave the world? Some money, a monster-infested manor, a little grave, and words...

Words lived while flesh faded to dust.

Setting the mask down, Rob picked up his fountain pen. He wrote of what he knew, what he dreamt of, and the people he loved. Cat and Liam. Jim and Waverley. Filtered through the lens of his imagination and committed to paper. In a frenzy to finish, his pen blazed across the page. He was so close to the end and so focused that he didn't hear the click of crutches being set against his desk.

Kissing him on the cheek, Cat plopped down on his lap and snatched the page from his blotter. "He had taken me aside one day," she read, "and promised me a silver fourpenny on the first of every month—"

Blushing, he grabbed for the sheet. "Give that back!"

Cat held the page at arm's length. "If I would only keep my weather-eye open for a seafaring man with one leg." A grin spread across her face as she reached for another sheet. "Writing about me, are we? Can I read more?"

"Not till I'm finished." Rob gathered his manuscript into a tidy stack and shoved it into the desk drawer. Her smile was good to see. He knew she'd been melancholy, then, quite out of the blue, she returned from one of her afternoon walks with flushed cheeks and eyes burning with purpose. "Then I promise you'll be the first to read it."

Rob tried, unsuccessfully, to tuck Liam's mask in with the manuscript without her noticing.

"I see you have your muse." Cat shifted and her leg stump poked out from the hem of her robe. She took the mask from him and frowned. Droplets from her damp hair rained on Liam and streaked his silver cheeks like tears. "Should I be concerned?"

"Never."

"Do you..." She shrugged and the green satin slipped from her shoulder. Her skin was still damp and flushed pink from her bath. "Ever secretly want me to..."

"To what?" Rob kissed her shoulder blades. He wrapped his arms around her waist. The robe parted and his hand slipped inside.

"You know."

"What do I know?" His voice was a growl. She was wearing nothing underneath. For the first time that night, Rob didn't think about his novel. "Is it my imagination," he asked, "or have these gotten bigger?" He didn't want to say it, but she didn't exactly have breasts before. Now he could throw her into the river and she would be very buoyant indeed.

"Wear it?" Cat peeked over her shoulder.

He paused, hand on her naked hipbone. There were curves where before none existed. "God, Cat!"

Cat twisted around and straddled him. Her robe pooled about her waist. She set the mask down, turned Liam's face toward the window. "Do you?"

He sighed. "Liam was my friend. Nothing more."

"You kiss all your friends like that? Like this..." Licking his bottom lip, she rocked back and forth. Up and down. They

417

were both breathless when she broke the kiss. "I'll straighten you out yet, Lord Robert," she said, popping the buttons of his trousers.

"I think I'm pretty straight as it is." His hand traveled from her hip and dipped between her thighs. She felt like the mermaids on that long-ago beach.

"What are you doing to me?" Her breath quickened and she pressed her forehead against his. "What are you doing to me?"

Cat parted for him as easily as the robe, and he slipped inside.

Afterward, his hand roved over the talon marks on her back. Her breath rasped in his ear like she'd just finished a sprint. She was at her most vulnerable. This was a perfect time to get her.

Rob nuzzled her neck. "Marry me," he whispered.

Her answer was always the same. Cat peeled herself away from him. Her chest was slick with sweat and covered in inky fingerprints. "No."

"I'll ask again tomorrow." He'd already asked every single day for three months. He thought she was finally weakening. "And the day after tomorrow. And the day after next…"

"I'm not the marrying type."

"But don't you want to be with me?"

"I am with you." She wiggled her hips. "We're as close as close can be."

"We can have children."

"We already have short people." She planted a kiss on his nose. "Savage girl and demon boy. Besides, all my Elixir days have probably turned my womb into a hostile environment."

He was still inside her and it didn't feel very hostile to him. "If we marry, people will stop talking."

Her lips quirked at the corners. "Then I'll be Lord Robert's one-legged wife instead of your wicked mistress. People will talk anyway." Cat ducked in for a kiss, but he jerked his head away.

He tried to keep the hurt from his voice. "Is marrying me so repulsive to you?"

She scrubbed a hand over her face, groaning in frustration. "I'm a monster hunter."

"What does that even mean? You *were* a monster hunter," he reminded her. "You don't still want to kill?" He paused. "Do you?"

He saw a visible tremble in her throat.

"Maybe the world needs killers as much as it needs heroes," she said, scrambling off his lap and snatching up her crutch.

"Cat, wait." He tried to throw the robe over her but she'd already flung the doors open, earning a horrified gasp from his new housekeeper.

She poked her head inside his study. Shrewd grey eyes took in Rob's disheveled collar and the silk robe puddling across his lap.

419

"Is everything all right, Lord Robert?"

He turned around to adjust himself. "See that Ms. Mornay has another bath." He flushed, remembering the fingerprints he left all over her body. His housekeeper probably thought he was some sort of deviant.

She nodded. "Right away." Her voice was stoic, but disapproval pinched her face. He found himself missing Mrs. Nix more than ever—as if Mrs. Nix would've approved.

Hearing the door click shut, Rob hunched over his desk and raked his hands through his hair. He picked up Liam's mask and muttered, "Women."

He imagined Liam saying, "Told you, mate."

Rob yanked open his drawer and took out his manuscript. At least this was something he understood. Cracking his knuckles, he snatched up his fountain pen and picked up where he left off.

"Jim," said Silver when we were alone, "if I saved your life, you saved mine; and I'll not forget it."

CHAPTER 26
THE STRANGE CASE OF DR. JEKYLL
AND MR. HYDE

Ducking behind a snow-covered rosebush, Cat peeked through the window of Dr. Jekyll's redbrick town house.

The doctor and his family had just sat down for supper. Tonight they were feasting on goose. Last night: haggis. The night before: roasted pigeon. Cat leaned into the frosty glass and watched Jekyll carve the largest piece for his youngest daughter. He had two daughters. One eight, the other six. The youngest one just lost her front tooth and liked to stick her tongue through the gap. The eldest was fiercely independent and given to tantrums. Jekyll reprimanded her the most, but oftentimes, Cat would catch them reading aloud in the parlor, her head resting on his shoulder, his hand stroking her raven hair.

Cat didn't know their names, but she secretly called the younger Vivian. The eldest she named Kitty and prayed her father never gifted her any puppies.

His wife, a homely woman with kind brown eyes, whisked past him carrying a piping hot pie between her chubby hands. The greasy aroma of baked eel spawned a fresh wave of nausea. Cat bit her tongue. She used to love eel pie, but she still hadn't recovered from her stomach bug. Or perhaps it was the sight of Jekyll's rat-fink face that made her violently ill. Ever since she discovered Jekyll still lived, she'd been throwing up every day for a week.

Drawing her cloak closer, Cat waited for the nausea to subside. Snowflakes tickled her cheeks, caught in her lashes, and melted into her tears. She wanted to linger a while longer and stare into the window of the past.

This used to be her life.

She had a father, mother, and sister.

For Jekyll to have survived the massacre and returned to hearth, home, and family was the ultimate insult.

Cat readied Culler. It seemed fitting to kill him with Liam's weapon. *Poetic.* First she was going to slice off his ears and make the man whimper like the puppies he made Liam slaughter. Since Jekyll created Liam, she felt it her duty to avenge his death too, and so…

No more hiding.

Cat stepped up to the window and let the firelight bounce off Culler's curved blade.

The effect was exactly as she'd hoped for. Jekyll's carving knife paused midair and the blood drained from his face. He looked like he was going to piss himself, and there was a second in which she could hear the cogs in his mind turning.

She slinked out of sight to wait.

Cat drew her new hat—a bowler—down over her eyes and flipped her cloak aside. Her prosthetic leg sank in the snow. Under the winter starlight, Culler gleamed like a blue crescent moon.

Cat had found her purpose. She was a monster hunter no more.

But tonight, there was a new Avenging Angel in Edinburgh.

◆

The door swung open and Jekyll's youngest daughter jogged down the steps.

"Pretty lady! Pretty lady!" Her stubby legs sloshed through the snow.

Cursing beneath her breath, Cat tucked Culler back beneath her cloak.

"I'm Maura." The cherub beamed up at her with flushed apple cheeks. "Da says you should come inside and sup with us."

Cat's attention swerved to the slender silhouette on the doorstep with his arm slung around his eldest daughter's shoulder. Maura seized her hand and dragged Cat up the stairs.

The other daughter introduced herself as Sabine. Cat raised an eyebrow. "From the Aventine ballads?"

Sabine beamed. "Da says I'll grow up to be a true warrior like Cat Mornay."

"Has your Da ever met Cat Mornay?"

"No, miss. He says Cat Mornay doesn't exist."

She brushed against Jekyll at the stoop. "Well played," she whispered.

The doctor's shrewd eyes swept over her bowler hat and trousers. "My dear, you are cold," he said, pressing a hand to the small of her back. "Come warm yourself by the fire."

And so Cat found herself inside Jekyll's parlor with his children swarming over her like lice. His wife asked no questions of where she came from or who she was, which made her conclude that they were used to taking in poor unfortunate souls off the street. Henry Jekyll: respected physician, loving father, doting husband, good Samaritan. He probably told his family she was a prostitute.

She was never going to kill him now. Failure made her sick and when his wife set her supper before her, Cat took one look at the jellied eel and turned veritably green. She stood up, dumping the children to the floor. "I'm sorry, but I-I have to go."

Jekyll barked for his daughters to go to their rooms. "Isobel," he ordered his wife above the scatter of feet, "a bowl, quick!"

So Cat vomited in a porcelain bowl held by the missus while the doctor held her hair and swatted her on the back. Her night could not possibly get any worse. She was dry heaving when she overheard his wife whisper over her head, "Poor thing, just a child herself and already in trouble."

"Isobel." Jekyll's voice was stern. "I would like a word with Miss—"

"Hyde." Cat wiped her mouth on her sleeve. "Are you familiar with the name, ma'am?"

His wife turned to him in question.

Jekyll's lips twitched. "Shut the door."

When they were alone, Jekyll poured two glasses of sherry. He drained one and handed her the other. Cat refused the drink.

"Kitty, kitty, kitty." He shook his head. "You've been very bad."

"If you're insinuating that I'm up the pole," Cat said, "I assure you I am not. I have the flu."

"How long has it been since you've bled?"

December had been a dry month, though nothing to be alarmed about. Cat's menstruation had always been irregular. In the days of forced fasting aboard the *Hispaniola*, she hadn't bled at all.

She plopped down in the cushy armchair and buried her face in her hands. "That is not an appropriate question."

425

"I am a physician." He paused. "Or was." His eyes roved over her body, taking in the tighter fit of her blouse and her new curves. "Shame on Rob. Surely you've done your best to corrupt my bright-eyed boy. The lad I knew would've asked you to marry him long ago." Propping his arm on the mantle, Jekyll traced a forefinger around the glass lip of his drink. "How is Rob?" he asked, frowning into his sherry. "Still blissfully ignorant, I hope. I trust you haven't told him?"

Cat stood up. Jekyll was making her lose confidence in the hostility of her womb. "I am not pregnant! As for Rob, he still mourns your death and speaks of you as a martyr. Maybe I should tell him not to waste his tears on a *coward.*" She snatched her hat from the cushions. "Who was the corpse in the glasshouse?"

"An old man who tended to the flowers." The sigh he uttered shook his shoulders. "I saw the Mother coming and I ran. I ran and I hid and that's why I'm alive."

"Clever you." Cat spat at his feet. "And later? When you knew the Manu Diabolii were heading toward the castle? Did you even try to warn the others?"

He drained her untouched glass. "Am I expected to outrun Manu Diaboli? I'm no monster hunter."

"Neither was Rob," she said. "But he went inside, didn't he?"

"He was never afraid of death." Jekyll turned around. "Did I ever tell you he was one of my first patients?"

Cat shook her head.

"I hadn't mastered the formula for Elixir then, but I knew I was close. So many sleepless nights, so many failed batches. I was missing a key ingredient, yet I couldn't put my finger on what. The search nearly drove me mad. Then a wee lad came along with *Mornay's Book of Unnatural Harvests and Remedies*, which he bade me read to him during his treatments, and I sent my apprentice to scout the coast for mermaid scales."

"Your apprentice was Liam."

"Aye," he said softly. "Would you believe Barclay aspired to be a doctor? He would've sold his soul to cure his friend. In another life, I believe he might've been a fine healer."

"But you turned him into a hunter."

"Empires are built on blood and greed." He swept a hand across his parlor's costly furnishings and expensive oil paintings. "The Golden Age of Monsters…" A sadness crumpled his face, pronouncing the sunburst of crow's-feet around his eyes and the lines on his forehead. "Is Rob's new physician treating him well?" He turned to her with a starved and desperate expression which reminded Cat of a stray begging for scraps. "How is his breathing? What kind of medicines is he taking?"

"You ask as if you cared." Cat waved him off and marched to the door. "Why don't you visit him yourself?"

"And trade his beloved Dr. Jekyll for a Mr. Hyde?" Opening the door for her, he shook his head with a sad smile. "I'd rather his world always be filled with heroes, fake as they are."

♦

Curled up in bed, Cat rubbed her flat stomach and tried to imagine a fetus growing inside.

She despised children.

They were dirty, whiny, needy ankle-biters who broke expensive vases and bit you when you tried to reprimand them. Just the thought of having another Waverley or Jim around made her break out in a cold sweat. Except she had nothing to worry about because she wasn't pregnant, and she wasn't stupid enough to play into Jekyll's mind games.

She was punching her pillow when the mattress shifted beneath Rob's weight. Slipping into bed behind her, he leaned over and dramatically dropped an enormous pile of loose papers in front of her face.

"I finished my book," he whispered, planting a kiss behind her ear. As exhausted as he sounded, his hand slid over her hips and tugged her nightgown over her bare backside. His lithe body spooned hers, lips grazing the slope of her neck. "I think a celebration is in order."

"Put that thing away." Cat swiftly tugged her nightgown back down.

"I'm trying to." He inched the hem up again. "Inside you."

What happened to the shy boy she met in the statue garden? This Rob was out of control, and she wondered if sleeping with him that first time was like opening up Pandora's Box.

"Haven't you done enough?" She scooted away.

"What did I do?" He scooted with her. "Why so sad, sea star?"

Cat buried half her face in the pillow and palmed the crinkled edges of the manuscript. Behind her, Rob shook with laughter. "You love me."

"I despise you."

"Do you really?" he asked, kissing the mole on her collarbone.

A bell jar on the nightstand crackled with blue sparks. Scorning candles and lanterns, Rob had outfitted the bedroom they shared with electric lights so her dreams may always be bright. Cat stared at the bell jar and shrugged. "I guess not."

When you gave the boy an inch, he expected a mile. His hand crept under her nightgown and he did heavenly things to her with his fingers until she forgot why she was mad at him.

Cat peeked over her shoulder. The tip of his nose pressed against her cheek. A wicked grin spread across his face, but his breathing was as short and quick as hers.

"Fine," she turned around and gathered his manuscript into her arms, "you do what you want, I don't care. I'm going to read."

His breath fanned hot circles on her spine. "If you think you can concentrate."

Her nightgown had mysteriously bunched across her waist, but she made no move to tug it back down. "Is that a challenge?"

He progressed to something else which jolted her forward and sent the title page fluttering to the floor. Cat squeaked like a mouse. She squinted down at Rob's spikey cursive.

"Read it aloud." Rob nipped the back of her neck. "I want to hear you."

"You're an even bigger egomaniac than I thought." The words blurred and bounced with the mattress. "Squire Trelawney, Dr. Livesey, and the rest of these gentle… gent…"

"'The rest of these' what?" Apparently, he knew his whole book by memory.

"Gentlemen." An entire chunk of manuscript scattered to the floor. She saved the first page, clutching it between her fingers with a handful of bedsheet. "Having asked me to write down the whole particulars about…about…about…"

Cat lost her challenge.

When they finished, Cat leaned over and picked up the cover page. Underneath the title, Rob had written his name four different times and scratched it out, settling on his full name. She saw R.L.S. amongst the choices and hid a smile, recalling the poem that kept her warm in the hunter's shed.

Crawling back into bed, she nestled in the warm crook of his shoulder and watched his ribcage rise and fall. His hair was damp with sweat and stuck up in a blond swirl. She patted it down and traced a line from his forehead down the bridge of his nose to his lips. *My prince. My love. My life.*

"*Treasure Island*," she read.

He turned his head and stifled a cough, but when he turned back, there was a sleepy smile on his lips.

"By Robert Louis Stevenson." Cat cleared her throat. "Squire Trelawney, Dr. Livesey, and the rest of these gentleman having asked me to write down the whole particulars about Treasure Island…"

Rob interrupted her only once, and that was to press a kiss to the back of her hand.

◆

In the parlor, Rob kissed the back of her hand and let the ring slide into her palm.

He'd been practicing the move with Jim and was happy that he didn't accidentally drop the ring. Cat withdrew her hand from his grasp and studied the sapphire with a frown. He'd recut the stone from his laird's ring and remounted it into a delicate gold band. It would look better on Cat anyway. The stone matched her eyes.

"Rob..." She glanced nervously to where Waverley and Jim were sprawled on their stomachs on the Turkish rug, a hand-drawn map spread before them. They were repositioning tin soldiers along a mountain pass. Waverley was even taking notes. It looked like serious business.

He turned away and sat on his piano bench before she had a chance to reject him. "I had it engraved."

Out of the corner of his eye, Rob saw Cat turn the band. "Across space and time," she read, her voice cracking. "Rob..."

He flexed his fingers and lifted the lid of his baby grand. "What would you have me play, miss?"

Her purple and black-striped silhouette lingered in his peripheral vision. She held the ring between thumb and forefinger and when she didn't offer a request, he played a few bars of Beethoven's Moonlight Sonata, which he knew by heart.

Cat turned around and the hem of her gown swished against the floor.

"Miss Mornay," he called, fingers still dancing over the keys.

She peeked around her shoulder. Lines of worry pleated her brow.

"I love you," he mouthed and had the satisfaction of seeing her brow smooth and a smile replace her frown.

"And I you," she mouthed above the music and sat on the settee.

Over Beethoven and Mozart, the short people convened their war council while Cat contemplated his proposal. Haunting, albeit nervous, music filled the parlor.

When he switched to *The Last Rose of Summer*, she slipped the ring onto her finger and Rob was struck with happiness so great it blazed through his body like a kiss of fire. There was pain, yes, a sword hacking his lungs into pieces, an ache so pure as to be divine. His spirit soared for one blissful moment before his fingers failed him altogether.

The notes which he'd played flawlessly all his life transformed into a discordant noise. Melody into cacophony. He stopped playing, fingers slipping on ivory keys sprayed with blood.

His blood.

Rob glanced up at a room muted of all earthly sound and the terrified faces staring back at him. Even Jim Hawkins, the picture of stoicism, seemed afraid. His eyes sought Cat's, and he wanted to assure her that this was only a minor hiccup in the scheme of their love.

Don't cry, miss.

I will find you across space and time.

Miss, don't cry.

One day we shall walk in the sun.

But for now he was so cold and when he opened his mouth, blood, not words, trickled over his chin. Rob collapsed upon his piano, still dreaming of palm fronds swaying on a distant shore.

CHAPTER 27
THE KNIGHTS OF BALFOUR

"Jekyll!" Cat pounded the door with her fists. "Doctor!"

She howled his name into the night.

Jekyll. Hyde. God. Devil.

It didn't matter anymore that she hated him or he hated her or that only a week ago she'd stood on that very stoop with the intent to kill him or that he amputated her leg. He could have her other leg. All her limbs. Her head. Her life. Rip the heart out of her chest. Just please, please open the door.

Cat glanced over her shoulder at the snow-covered townhouses and the smokestacks backlit against a winter's sky. A dark and unfriendly city crept in on her, made all the darker now the one light in her life was on the brink of fading.

In that moment, Cat did something she hadn't done since her return from Africa.

She prayed.

For God to stop arsing around with her.

For the Devil to take her soul and let her die in Rob's place.

For some otherworldly force to resurrect Liam from the dead so he could help her save the boy they both loved. Or at least share in some of the immeasurable heartache once Rob ceased to be. Out of all the people in this lonely world, Liam would understand.

And somewhere in the merging between heaven and hell, the red door clicked open and Dr. Jekyll stepped onto the frozen stoop in a striped nightshirt and red cap.

"Kitty?" The doctor cupped a candle against the wind. "What in blazes are you doing here again?"

Cat took one look at the shrewd little man who brought her life such misery, and fell on her knees. Knees. Plural. If it hadn't been for Rob, she wouldn't have knees to fall upon.

All her prayers answered, Cat Mornay ceased to hate.

♦

Getting Jekyll to come to 17 Heriot Row was easy.

All she had to do was say "Rob" and a fuse ignited in the doctor.

Kissing his dazed wife, Jekyll dashed upstairs for a change of clothes and his medicine bag. "Take me to him," he said, donning his top hat and jogging down the steps, black cape flapping beneath the gas lamps.

Cat paced the hallway, peeking through the bedroom door. In the hour Jekyll attended to Rob, he spent a minute injecting Rob with Elixir and the other fifty-nine unburdening his sordid double life. Mr. Hyde. Liam. His cowardly flight from Balfour Manor. It all came pouring out.

Falling to his knees, Jekyll said, "I was slowly losing hold of my original and better self—" His forehead lolled on the mattress next to Rob's limp hand. "—and becoming my second and worse. I am the chief of sinners, I am the chief of sufferers, too. Say something, lad. Please say something...."

Rob's breathing, doused by Elixir, returned to some resemblance of normalcy when before, every inhale and exhale rasped likes a hive of wasps. He touched Jekyll's head. "I forgive you," he whispered, without a second's hesitation.

Maybe it was the drug talking?

Jekyll echoed her doubt. "D-do you mean it?"

"Whatever you've done... " Rob's voice was weak, but the meaning resonated strength and certainty. "You will always be my true friend."

His words, just like his heart, were stronger than his body. Upon hearing them, the doctor wept.

Cat twisted her engagement ring. Her pale face stared back at her through the sapphire's prisms. To credit Elixir for Rob's actions was unfair.

Rob had befriended her when she was a loathsome mercenary and junkie.

He'd found something to love in a psychopath like Liam.

Rob was a rare species of human; one purely good at heart. As she listened to the doctor's soft sobbing, she realized what an honor it had been to know Rob and be his friend.

Cat shuffled through the dark hallway, bracing herself against the wall should she slink to the floor and never get up. She felt like there was nothing left of her and didn't know how she could stand, much less make it to the parlor. But somehow she managed to find the short people.

Huddled in a window seat, Jim held Waverley as she sobbed into the crook of his shoulder. Seeing Cat, Waverley dashed to her and latched onto her waist like a leech. Jim, mimicking his girl, hooked onto her bustle and buried his face in her skirt. Cat blinked down at the short people with red-rimmed eyes.

"Rob's dying, isn't he?" Waverley asked.

"Nonsense. Rob's quite comfortable. I have it on good authority that the doctor is curing him right now. Jekyll—"

Her eyes swept the blood-splattered piano. *The Last Rose of Summer* ought to be banned from being played or sung; the melody was cursed.

"Jekyll what?" Waverley pressed. "What's the doctor doing to save him?"

Crying. Never a good prognosis. Actually, it seemed Rob was doing more for Jekyll at the moment. "What doctors...do."

"What in bloody hell does that mean?"

438

Cat forced a smile and patted the girl on the head. To ensure symmetry, she patted Jim on the head, too. But that didn't seem like enough reassurance for Waverley. Cat's petticoat grew damp with the girl's tears. She hoped the girl didn't expect her to act like their surrogate mother and breast-feed them, or whatever mothers are supposed to do. She glanced down at Jim and it seemed like he was reading her mind. This biter wasn't coming anywhere near her breasts.

Once Waverley calmed down, she tugged on Cat's skirt. "Jim has a plan. I could do it myself, except Jim picked you. I've already killed two, which is far more than you can say, but Jim says hatchlings don't count so will you do it?"

Cat knelt down to their level. She felt very short and kind of mental. "Do what?"

"Kill Manu Diaboli," Waverley rolled her eyes, "obviously."

♦

Jim, using Waverley as his loud and obnoxious mouthpiece, revealed his plan to Cat. He drew a diagram on three separate sheets of stationary.

Cat propped her hand on her cheek, squinting at the sketches. Did he just draw this? Or had he been planning it all along?

439

She surveyed the map-covered walls of Jim's room. The maps were of a geographic terrain she'd never seen before, and there were pins and multicolored yarn connecting each target. Instead of a bed, Jim had somehow managed to sneak in a long conference table, which he now presided over like Napoleon.

Four crackling bell jars cast the war room in a ghostly blue glow. Her head swirled and her hair stuck up from static electricity. She felt like she'd been inducted into a Lilliputian military council, one in which she was the lowest ranking, albeit tallest, member.

"Is this what you two do all day? Does your governess know about this?" She gestured to the maps, the conference table, then paused to consider. "Do you even *have* a governess?"

"Of course we have a governess." Waverley was wearing a navy sailor dress with a big ink stain on the collar and her hair was braided on one side, tangled at the other. "You say hello to her every morning. Miss, you've grown dumb these past three months. Did my brother diddle the brains right out of you?"

Cat stood up. "I will not sit here and be insulted!"

"See?" Waverley smacked Jim on the arm. "I told you she was going to be difficult. Best send me instead. She's retired and has such *fancy airs!*"

Jim's tiny fist slammed against the table, bouncing the plans and almost knocking over an inkpot. Waverley clammed up. Cat caught Jim's stern black eyes. He pointed at her chair and she sat down in a huff.

Jim tapped his finger on the table.

Waverley folded her arms and glared at Jim. "I don't want to."

The lad reprimanded her with a narrowing of his eyes. Waverley turned to Cat. "I'm sorry," she said between clenched teeth. "Jim wanted me to assure you that we don't really know you're sleeping with my brother." She wrinkled her nose. "Even though we hear you two every night. You sound like monkeys."

Jim clapped his hands together and Waverley amended, "Seals. Jim says seals."

Cat's hand slid up her face and over the back of her head. "God." After the initial embarrassment passed, she squared her shoulders. "I apologize for not paying attention to you for the past...two months."

Jim tapped his finger three times.

Waverley said, "Three months."

Cat's eyes widened. "Has it been that long?"

They nodded.

Between plotting to gut Dr. Jekyll and making monkey sounds with Rob, she'd completely forgotten the short people existed. Come to think of it, between writing his magnum opus, mourning his immortal beloved man-friend, and *dying*, Rob hadn't spent much time with the short people either.

"I will try to look down more. And Rob too, if he lives." Cat sniffled and rubbed her runny nose. "Is the dog still alive?" A bark in the west wing assured her that Virgil was still around. Dogs were even shorter than children, making them harder to see.

"Here." Back to business, Waverley slid another sheet across the table. "An inventory of the weapons you'll need. If we leave now, we'll reach the hill in time for solstice."

"Solstice?" Cat turned to her ward. "Jim? You're leaving...you're leaving me?"

After months of watching him mime the tear between the worlds, she knew the day would come, but she thought Jim liked being her mate. She always assumed he'd stay.

The lad's eyes were big and sad.

"He has to go home," Waverley said. She turned to Jim, speaking for everybody at the table. "But can't you stay?"

Jim patted her on the head.

The girl's shoulders slumped.

"What did he say?" Cat asked.

"There won't be a window for another ten years," Waverley said. "It's now or never."

Cat struggled to find her voice. "I don't know what to say. I'm going to miss you...demon boy."

Hopping off his chair, Jim scurried up to her and pecked her on the cheek. Then he motioned Waverley to continue.

"Jim asks for full disclosure if we're to hire you as our monster hunter," the girl said. "We need you to tell us about Africa and how you killed the adult Manu Diaboli."

Cat arched an eyebrow. The short people were *hiring* her? "I don't…" She'd only told Rob about Africa. It was a story she didn't care to recount again, but Jim placed a reassuring hand over hers. Waverley, not to be outdone, touched her other hand. Their touch reminded her she might be pregnant, so she shook them off and tucked both her hands in her armpits and pressed her forehead against the cherrywood table. She was so tired. "My father was going to bring Manu Diaboli back to Scotland and it was going to be a wonder…"

By the time she wrapped up her tale, Cat was morbidly depressed, but Jim, who'd been jotting down notes, made some improvements on his plan and flipped the sheet around to show them.

Waverley whistled. "Brilliant."

But Cat chewed on her inner cheek and frowned. "Oh Jim, that's *cold.* He won't do it."

"Maybe not willingly," Waverley said. "But under gunpoint…"

"I don't want to put Jekyll under gunpoint." She didn't mention the stalking and attempted knifing part. Cat was tired

443

of killing, especially killing people. "Maybe we can just ask him?"

"Ask me what?"

Three heads whirled toward the door. Scrubbing the stubble on his jaw, Jekyll stumbled into the war council. He was all husk, no man. Bloodshot eyes scanned their faces. "Ask me what?"

"We want to ask you," Waverley began.

"To help us kill the Great Mother and cut out her heart." Cat studied the master list. "Jim has assigned us each a role. I'm the hunter. Jim's quartermaster. She's..."

Waverley slunk back in her chair. "The one left behind."

"You keep an eye on Rob, which is the most important job of all," Cat reminded her. "And Doctor, if you decide to join us, you're... Well, there's no good way to put this..."

She handed him the paper.

He read the sheet, let out of a whoop, and doubled over in hyena-like laughter. "It's all a game to you children! This is my *life* you're playing with." He crumpled the plans and chucked them at Jim. "Bait? You want me to be bait? Do you know who I am? Does the name Mr. Hyde mean nothing to you? Do you know what I can do to you?"

"Told you," Cat said to Jim.

But to the surprise of one and all, Jekyll pulled up a chair and sat down. He let out an ominous sigh. "He's hemorrhaged in his lungs." A solemn silence descended upon the council. He snatched up the ball of paper and dragged his hands over the crinkles. "What do I have to do?"

◆

While Jekyll went home to say goodbye to his wife and children, Cat crawled into bed beside Rob.

She pressed her head lightly on his chest and listened to the weak flutter of his heart.

Cold iron probed her hand.

Pulling back the blood-speckled goose down, Cat froze. For a moment, she contemplated prying Liam's silver mask out of Rob's grasp, but he clung to it like a cross and it seemed to bring him comfort in his final hour. Sighing in defeat, Cat kissed his lips. They were chapped and peeling, already tinged blue like a corpse's.

"If Liam had survived the massacre," she asked his sleeping profile, "would you sneak him into bed with us?"

Fingers lacing through hers, Rob traced her sapphire engagement ring. "You mean we can't take him to the West Indies with us?" A teasing smile. "Our bed will be big enough for three. You can have the middle."

"I think Liam would prefer you in the middle." Leaning on her elbow, Cat gazed at Rob, committing his features to memory. The straight nose, just a tad too long. The faint splattering of freckles under his eyes. Blond lashes framing a face that looked younger on the brink of death. She kissed his eyelids. "If you promise to get better, I'll probably make an exception."

She traced his jaw. It was baby smooth, without the slightest trace of stubble, and she recalled a long-ago dream of Rob strolling on the white sands, his skin browned by the sun. That Rob had been older. This Rob may never live to see eighteen.

Cat buried her face in his shoulder and wept.

"Tell me..." His emaciated chest rose and fell with every labored breath. Rob draped a limp arm around her and she nuzzled against him. His hand never let go of hers. "Tell me about Antigua."

Wiping her tears on the pillow, Cat peeked at his face. "It's always summer there and the flowers bloom year round."

"Go on." His lips curled into a dreamy smile. "I feel warmer already."

She kissed all five of his fingertips and shut her eyes. "The air is so sweet and syrupy you can taste it on your tongue like toffee. The sea is so translucent you feel as if you're sailing on glass. My father called it Heaven on Earth."

Rob had drifted off to sleep. "You will go there someday," she whispered, tucking Liam's letters in the crook of his arm. "I promise." She kissed him for the last time and snuck out of bed, knowing she might never see her prince again.

CHAPTER 28
THE SPLENDOR AND THE SUN

They worked through the day, breaking the frozen soil of the statue garden with picks and shovels.

Whipping off her hat, Cat wiped the sweat from her brow. Across the frost-covered glens, snowdrifts fell atop the smoky ruins of Balfour Manor. To her left, the briars of the fae woods resembled leafless spears dipped in ice. From her hilltop perch, Cat listened to the wind howl through the space between the trees and wondered if Manu Diaboli, transplanted from her native Africa, was prepared for an unforgiving Scottish winter.

Short days.

Dark days.

A season of eternal night.

Did the Great Mother miss her goddess the sun?

They were counting on it.

A swift darkness descended upon the garden of gods and monsters. Cat and Jim, assisted by Dr. Jekyll, worked swiftly, weaving from titan to serpent, digging holes in the snow and planting glass orbs in the dirt. When they finished, the frost had melted into slush. Cat stood back, basking in the heat of fifteen boiling orbs of Elixir, each one dissolving a pill of Dragon's

Breath and transforming the hill into a sun bright enough to draw the ultimate creature of darkness.

For the first time since she lost her mind in Africa and her soul to Mr. Hyde, Cat Mornay, monster hunter, felt like a knight.

♦

Rob never saw the sun again.

The morning he rolled over to an empty bed and Cat's sapphire ring on the nightstand, Rob could hear his heart break. It shattered like the glass of water he swiped to the floor in a fit of animal rage.

Waverley found him crawling on bare hands and feet atop the glass shards, searching for the ring.

"Rob!" With a cry, she dashed to his side and dropped to her knees. Little hands grasped his elbow.

"I dropped the ring. I dropped the ring." Rob shielded his eyes from a shaft of sunlight. Blood dribbled through his fingers and slid down his wrist. He'd shredded his hands to ribbons, but the pains of the flesh were nothing compared to the pain of being abandoned by the girl he loved. "Where is it, Duck?" he asked as if by finding the ring, he could locate Cat. "Where is *she?*"

Waverley shut the blinds, dousing his bedroom in darkness. She hesitated, brown eyes brimming with tears. "She's left the city. And Jim with her. They're gone to save…"

Her mouth moved, but he heard no sound after "gone."

Gone.

His love.

Gone.

His soul.

Gone.

His reason to live.

Rob bowed over, falling apart all over again, until his wails segued into coughs, the coughs into blood. He didn't protest when Waverley led him back to bed and injected a double dose of Elixir into his veins.

◆

The salivary gland of *S. atlanticus* was a soft black sac in the glow of the Elixir sun.

Cat handed her dagger to Jim and watched him dip the blade inside a slit he made in the gland. Venom fizzled against rare dragonbone. When he extracted the blade, it was coated in what looked like tar. He held the dagger in the air, waiting for the venom to dry, then handed it back to her with all due caution.

She passed the dragonbone back to Jekyll. He hesitated, scrubbing the icicles off his three-day beard.

"We can't send you inside unarmed," she urged. "Take it."

Jekyll wrapped his hands around the hilt. The irony must not have been lost on him. "Returning my gift, Kitty?" His voice was hoarse with fear. She didn't blame him. She was terrified. "What will you use?"

Cat opened her palm and her quartermaster handed her Culler, anointed by serpent venom. She slashed the night, drawing upon the psychopathic spirit of her old mentor for strength. She could kill now and make it look like a dance. "For the harvest."

Jekyll nodded and gestured for them to gather before him. He held out his hand and Cat took it. Jim laced his fingers through hers, completing the circle. They lowered their heads and the doctor, his breath coiling around him like smoke, looked to Cat and said, "There is no hate in a time of monsters. For he who sheds his blood with me, shall be my friend…"

♦

Rob swam from the green darkness and called for his sister. "Pen. Paper…"

Waverley, curled up in an armchair with sheets of his manuscript spread across her lap, poked her head up. "Rob?"

"In my study. My fountain pen. Paper." Groggy from sleep and drugs, Rob sat up and leaned against his headboard.

"You need to rest," she said, coming over to retrieve the goose down he flung to the floor.

"I need to write."

"But you've already written. I've just been reading your book. Why is Jim Hawkins the main character? Why does Jim get all the glory?"

"Another story. I have one more in me and I need it out." As the Elixir haze faded, he saw Cat. Their first meeting in the statue garden. Their first kiss. The first time they made love. Her lips, her moans, her legs spread for him, her naked body writhing beneath his.

All flashed before him.

All gone.

Happy memories seemed like an insult in this world without his other self. A world without Cat was a world *filled* with monsters.

"Out!" He began to bang his head against the headboard. "Out!"

"Stop it!" Waverley cupped her hands over his mouth. "Stop!"

"One more before I go." If he didn't exorcise his heartache, he was certain he would never die in peace. He might come back as a ghost and haunt his study until the words were down on paper. Words were his only comfort. Words kept this madness called Love at bay.

When Waverley filled a syringe with Elixir, Rob screamed, "For once in your life do as you're told!"

She jumped, eyes wide with fear.

"Pen. Paper..." Rob dragged a raspy breath. "Please, Duck, would you deny your brother his dying wish?"

Racing from the bedroom, Waverley returned with an armful of papers and a pen. She dumped them into his lap and fled the room in tears.

Left alone, Rob cracked his knuckles and began to write.

He wrote in a frenzy.

He wrote away the pain in his body and the pain in his heart.

In letters, he was a titan; a king confined to a pointy line of scrawl.

He wrote the manuscript in three days. Upon jotting down the last line, he raced out of bed in a fever, clutching *The Strange Case of Dr. Jekyll and Mr. Hyde.*

At the landing, the statue garden flashed before him like a green beacon in the winter's night. In the vision, he saw Cat standing in a circle with Jim and Dr. Jekyll, their hands clasped, their heads bent in prayer. His fingers curled in the air, trying to reach Cat. He could sense that she was afraid. They were all terrified and he wanted to tell them that there was nothing to fear.

For death could be a big adventure.

"I'm finished," he croaked. "Finished."

Rob collapsed and the pages flew from his hands, fluttering over his body like snow.

♦

The snow fluttered around Dr. Jekyll as Jim tucked three mini orbs of Elixir inside the doctor's black coat.

He wore hydra-skin to protect his torso from burns. Covering his entire body would've been preferable, but due to the scarcity of hydra-skin on the black market, they had to make do with a waistcoat.

Beads of sweat trickled down Jekyll's temple and puddled above his upper lip. He was so pale, Cat was afraid he'd collapse before he could slip inside The Gates of Hell.

"Mind your step." She handed Jekyll his top hat. "We can't have you tripping before you get inside."

"At a time like this, makes me wish I hadn't squandered all Rob's beetles on harpies." His eyes darted from her to Jim like a frightened hare. "Remind me why I'm doing this again?"

"Because Rob's life is worth ten of ours," she said. Jim passed Cat a handkerchief and she wiped the sweat from Jekyll's temple. "For love…"

"Aye, love," Jekyll said. "Bugger me."

In Africa, Cat got close enough to Manu Diaboli because the creature had feasted on fourteen men. When she went after Cat, the Great Mother, fat and gorged with blood, was vulnerable and weak.

They couldn't very well send fourteen souls to their deaths, but they still needed bait. Bait, according to Jim's Book of Ruthless Military Strategy, involved turning the doctor into the first line of offense: a human explosive.

Cold did not even begin to describe Jim's mind. When they asked Jekyll to volunteer his services, they were asking for his life. After eavesdropping on his confession, Cat knew the doctor couldn't live with himself after the massacre. Jekyll sought redemption; Jim offered it.

Cat clasped Jekyll's trembling hand, recalling Rob's words at the shed: it was better to die a hero than live a coward. "Thank you, Doctor."

Jim bowed his head. *Thank you, Doctor.*

Jekyll licked his wind-chapped lips. "No going back now, is there?"

She shook her head in regret.

Jim hoisted his rifle for emphasis. On the rifle, he'd outfitted a mini-spyglass for long-range targets. They'd come this far; there was no mercy for deserters. In the event Jekyll decided to run, Jim would shoot him dead. She glanced down at her ward and suddenly felt sorry for the usurpers of his fae throne; his return to power would be a bloodbath.

"My wife?" Jekyll asked. "My daughters?"

"They'll want for nothing. We promise."

The doctor let out a shaky breath. "So we bring the unhappy life of Henry Jekyll to an end." Propping his top hat on his head, he descended the hill and began a slow and careful trek into the woods.

♦

Though Waverley would later claim that she and their housekeeper carried him back to bed, Rob was certain it had been his angel.

For the next few days, Rob drifted in and out of consciousness. In his dreams, he was huddled beside his best mate in Eton's courtyard. Snow drifted around them, dusting Liam's brown hair like powdered sugar. Liam's face, restored to its former beauty, was a balm to his troubled soul. While Rob shivered with cold, Liam's kisses covered his cheeks, lips, jaw, neck, with a silvery heat.

He gazed around the shapes looming in the dormitory windows. What did he care if the Philip Cowens of the world watched and judged? If love felt this pure and this right, how could it possibly be a sin?

"Is this Heaven?" Rob asked, kissing Liam back with an abandon he could never summon up in life. "If this is Heaven...Where is Cat? Where is Cat?"

Rob woke up with his sheets soaking wet, clutching Liam's mask in his hands. His eyes swerved to the bell jar on the nightstand. During his illness, it had been removed so he could sleep—and die—in the dark, but now it was back and crackling with electric blue currents. Someone had replaced all five bell jars, transforming his room into an artificial thundercloud.

As Rob reoriented himself to the brightness, a slim shade stepped forward and stood over his bed.

"Jim?" Rob held out his hand.

The lad's tanned fingers wrapped around his ink-stained ones. His skin appeared pale by contrast, his fingers mere bones. This was how he knew he still lived. In Heaven, he wouldn't have such corpse hands.

"Is it really you?"

Nodding, Jim set a silver box on the nightstand and opened the lid.

"If you've come back to me, where is Cat?" Rob tried to sit up, but he hadn't the strength. His head sunk into the sweat-drenched pillow like a lead weight.

Jim turned to him with a solemn tilt of his head.

"Is she here? Please… Where did she go? Where is she?"

In reply, the lad passed a hand over the last bell jar and the copper wires ignited into a small explosion.

♦

An explosion mushroomed in the forest, backlighting the interior in a wash of flames.

Through her spyglass, Cat watched a giant claw-shaped creature careen from tree to tree. She felt like she was watching the devil dance behind the Gates of Hell.

A screech scratched the darkness and the devil vanished.

Reappeared.

Behind a trunk. In front.

In the gaps between the trees.

There. Gone.

On. Off.

The creature's prism eye materialized in her sight. She saw the statue garden, diminished into seven green dots, reflected back in the creature's lens. If she searched hard enough, she even spotted her own reflection.

Cat lowered her spyglass. Manu Diaboli lurched outside the fae woods and stood in the glen like a cancerous spot on the pristine snow.

Cat whirled around. "Now!"

At her command, Jim sprinted past the first planted orb. The glass erupted and a ball of green flames ballooned by his hip. The ground, covered in pitch, caught fire. He darted past the second orb.

One by one, the fifteen orbs shattered until the entire statue garden burned.

Backing into the circle of fire, Cat kept her eyes on the monster. A darkness, which could only be described as a shadow, zoomed across the glen.

"Get ready!"

Jim slid under the undulating arch of the serpent, tucking himself away from sight.

The garden simmered in wave after wave of intense heat. Her head swam with fumes of the extinct dragon and the dead mermaids.

Diving through the wall of flames, Cat pounced on the Titan's thigh and scurried up the statue's torso. She found a spot on the shoulder and surveyed the fiery sea.

Cat clutched Culler with clammy palms.

She wished she could say she faced death without a tremor of fear.

460

She wished she was as brave as Rob when he snuck inside the castle to save his sister.

She only had to face this creature once, but Rob fought a never-ending battle with the monster inside his body every day. The thought brought her strength and readied her for war.

The green flames shifted and frothed like the ocean in a gale.

Something was stirring.

Gathering momentum.

Running. Leaping. Flying.

A *whoosh* sucked all the oxygen from the air. An enormous shadow eclipsed the sky.

Cat held her breath.

The time had come.

The monster landed in the heart of the sun, onyx exoskeleton gleaming like a knight's black armor. She was here. All eight glorious feet of her.

Click.

Her triangular head twisted left and right.

Click.

Dr. Jekyll's blood dribbled off her scissor-pincers.

Click.

Cat noticed her jerky gait. One of the creature's prism eyes had been ruptured by the blast and her left arm dangled from her shoulder on a hinge. Cat shut her eyes and thanked the doctor for evening the playing field. At least Jekyll had not given his life in vain.

Cat stood from her crouch and The Great Mother halted.

The monster tilted her head. For the space of a second, hunter and monster measured each other. The creature's pincers resumed that infernal clicking. *I remember you.*

"I remember you, too." With a flick of Culler, Cat leapt into the air and collided with Manu Diaboli.

♦

Jim lifted the contents out of the box.

At the sight of the heart, everything clicked.

Why Cat left him.

Where she'd gone.

The enormity of her sacrifice.

Her life for his.

Rather than soothe him, the revelation broke Rob all over again. "Where's Cat?"

Jim pushed a sliver of the heart under Rob's nose.

Rob shook his head, refusing the offer. "Is she alive? Please tell me she's alive…"

The heart, glowing like a ruby bathed in blood, bumped against his bottom lip.

With a swipe of his arm, Rob knocked the heart to the floor. Jim glanced down and his black eyes blazed with fury.

The next sliver was not an offer.

Before Rob refused again, Jim shoved the foul rubbery thing inside his mouth. Tiny hands clamped over his jaw, preventing him from gagging, forcing him to chew.

As the disgusting piece of organ slid down his throat, he saw Cat.

Inside a circle of green fire.

Hacking and slashing.

Locked in an eternal battle with Manu Diaboli.

♦

Cat lunged.

The monster dodged.

The Great Mother pounced and the huntress slashed. Culler's venom coat disintegrated exoskeleton, lobbing the creature's injured arm clean off. An ear-splitting roar exploded from the monster.

Manu Diaboli swiped with her remaining arm and knocked Cat to the ground.

Her head struck rock. The monster seized her by the leg. A vengeful shriek rent the night. Talons crushed the steel supports and demolished the springs in her knee joint. Manu Diaboli tore

Cat's leg away from her stump. Her prosthetic slammed against the stone serpent and fell in a dented heap. As Cat crawled away, the acrid stench of burning metal singed her nostrils.

Reeling from the fumes and the knock to the head, Cat dove into her dream of Rob, now a man, walking under the sun.

The vision brought her peace and Cat ceased to be afraid.

She hoisted herself up on the Titan's thigh, turning around as Manu Diaboli descended upon her.

Cat buried her knife inside the monster's chest, but Manu Diaboli, always faster, always one step ahead, swung her good arm and...

"Oof."

The sound came from Cat.

She glanced down—

At the talon impaled through her stomach. Her foot left the ground and her back slammed against the Titan's thigh. Pinned to the statue like a butterfly in one of her father's collections, Cat raised her head and saw her stunned reflection inside the creature's prism eyes. Blood oozed from her mouth and dribbled down her chin. She waited for the pain to come, but there was only a wash of relief that the war was finally over.

And when she gazed into the face of the monster, she saw the relief was mutual.

Cat rested her head on Manu Diaboli's shoulders and the Great Mother embraced her like a lost hatchling. With her last ounce of strength, Cat twisted the blade and took them both into the splendor and the glory of the sun.

EPILOGUE
ANTIGUA

Ten years later

That blasted pup was at it again.

Sniffing the white sands.

Snarling at the mango-scented air.

Howling loud enough to wake the dead.

"Dante!" Rob sprinted after his Border Collie and dove into the surf. Dante was as rambunctious as his grandsire, Virgil, who'd died of old age five summers ago.

Matching Dante's speed, Rob tackled the pup beneath the waves and laughed as Dante resurfaced and paddled toward his master. Rob gathered the dog in his arms and received a sloppy lick to the face. "Come on, boy. Let's head back to shore."

Rob had been running along the water's edge all morning, and he felt strong enough to continue running to the end of the world. But Dante had other plans, and he chased the dog up the beach where a young lady was doing cartwheels on the sand. She was tall and reedy, her hair a tangled bird's nest, her bare legs baked brown from the tropic sun.

Waverley began a headstand.

"Really, Duck…" Propping his hand on his hip, Rob scowled at his upside-down sister. His ugly duckling had blossomed into a beautiful, albeit obnoxious, swan with no shortage of suitors. "Lieutenant Turner is coming for tea in an hour. He's likely to have a fit if he sees you in your bloomers."

"Bother Philip!" Her sand-encrusted toes wiggled in his face. "He's a blubbering fool and he can propose as many times as he likes. He and the other simple-minded suitors you've cast my way. I won't marry any of them and well you know it. I love Jim Hawkins."

Rob smacked her calloused heel. "Stop that. You'll get a headache. " He dashed off, jogging up the veranda of their ocean villa before Waverley could see how the mention of Jim Hawkins unsettled him.

She spoke of the lad as if he hadn't been gone from their lives for the past ten years.

The last Rob saw of Jim was at his bedside in that old townhouse on Heriot Row. He'd woken up that morning gulping air into healthy lungs and nursing a broken heart. When news of Dr. Jekyll's death reached Edinburgh and the papers proclaimed that a retired physician single-handedly slew Manu Diaboli, Rob journeyed back to Balfour Manor. He found the charred remains of Liam's body in the castle ruins and the identifiable parts of Dr. Jekyll in the fae woods. He buried them in the kirkyard, along with what was left of Mrs. Nix, Vivian, Finley and the rest of his doomed servants.

But at the statue garden, he found only Culler lying forgotten on the scorched earth. Monster and hunter were gone, their bodies vanished from the garden and disintegrated into stardust. It was as if Cat, his Cat, never existed at all.

After making sure Jekyll's widow and daughters were provided for, Rob accepted his commission with the Royal Geographical Society. In the spring of 1868, he and Waverley sailed out of Scotland, never to set foot on their native soil again.

They sailed the seven seas and to world's end.

To the Gobi Desert, where they saw sandworms that spanned the length of the Royal Mile.

To the criminal colonies in New South Wales, where they trekked across the red sands in search of the lost empire of Aventine. They'd found the fossil of an Ave in the Seven Hills and Rob regaled Waverley with the story of the first monster. En route to the Americas, he taught her how to navigate by the stars so she could always find her way home.

The loss of Cat, Liam, and Dr. Jekyll—all the knights who gave their lives so he could live—was intense at first, and the eve of his eighteenth birthday had been very black indeed. Over the years, his wounds did heal and the scar, while never forgotten, ceased to sting.

His life was happy and full, filled with new friends and experiences.

With the publication of *Treasure Island* and *The Strange Case of Dr. Jekyll and Mr. Hyde*, Rob liked to think he left a mark on the world. He had no cause to brood, but when he spotted the coconut cake and the card Waverley left for him on the veranda, the old wound reopened.

"Happy birthday!" Coming in from the beach, Waverley poured herself a glass of iced tea, plopped down in a chair, and propped her sandy feet on the table. "You're officially old. Maybe it's time I find *you* a wife and see how you like it."

"I'm not so very ancient." Rob took a seat opposite his sister. He used to think Alec was positively primeval, but Alec had been only twenty-three. He was now older than Alec, and while still slimmer than his brother, he'd developed muscles from his time at sea. Nobody dared call him "boy" anymore. "Besides, I quite enjoy the bachelor's life."

"You're a nasty rake." Waverley snatched Rob's Panama hat off his head. "I regret ever complaining about your monkey noises with Cat. Now I hear a whole giggling monkey colony from your bedroom." She covered her face with his hat and leaned her head against the wicker chair. "I miss Cat."

She drifted off to sleep, never knowing how much her words cut him.

"I do too," he said softly.

Dante weaved under the table and the seashells on the wind chime *clinked* a melancholy song. Rob stared off into the aquamarine sea, recalling a promise whispered in his ear when he was seventeen and dying. The tropical air was every bit as sweet as she'd described.

Rob swiped a finger across the cake and licked the icing. Cat's kisses had tasted like peppermint humbugs and Turkish Delights. *Confectionery kisses,* he thought, and a pang pierced his heart. He hunched in his chair and tried to remind himself that while Cat was dead, his love for her would never die. And when it was his turn to leave the world, his soul would find her, as he promised long ago, through space and time.

Dante's bark put a stop to his mourning.

The pup's snout rammed Rob in the shin.

Rob poked his head up and the dog dashed under his chair, barking at a presence behind him.

Standing up, he nearly clocked a young man in the chest.

"I'm sorry. I didn't hear you, lad. You shouldn't sneak up on..."

The stealthy visitor was the same height as Rob and wore a bright red military jacket with shiny brass buttons. Sensing a regal air about him, Rob peered into the stranger's face. Despite big black eyes that never seemed to blink, the young man looked every inch a prince.

Rob took a step back. Obviously, this chap didn't believe in personal space. "Say, do I know you?"

The young man inclined his head to the left, revealing pointy ears, and smiled. *Yes. You do.*

"Jim?" His tongue stuck to the roof of his mouth like he swallowed a spoonful of molasses. "It is Jim, isn't it?"

The young man nodded and held out his hand. Blinking away his tears, Rob grasped Jim by the elbow and gave the lad (he would always think of Jim as a lad) a loving swat on the shoulder. "You've grown up."

A chair crashed against the porch planks.

Waverley, sprawled on the ground, scrambled to her feet. *"Jim?"*

Jim Hawkins, full grown but no less creepy and mute, nodded, and with a cry Waverley crashed into his arms. She wrapped her legs around his waist and smothered his face in kisses. Their lips met in a long tongue-thrusting kiss.

Rob's eyes widened. "Waverley! Dear God, Waverley, control yourself! This is hardly ladylike behavior." Dante circled the young lovers and barked.

"If you don't unwrap your legs from around the lad this instant, I shall be forced to dump this entire pitcher of iced tea on you!"

Waverley and Jim were at it like a couple of cats in heat. Rob shook his head in disapproval. Had he and Cat been this self-absorbed, not to mention disgusting, when they were that age?

Lost in the commotion, Rob almost didn't hear the scraping of wood on the planks. It sounded like someone was dragging a chair across the veranda, and he recalled his description of Long John Silver: how his peg scraped the ship deck with a *scuff scuff scuff.*

Despite the humidity, the hairs on his arms stood on end. He stiffened, certain he'd gone mad until a gravelly voice said:

"I've sailed to every port from Brisbane to the Isle of Tortuga...in search of a dreamer who can build me a new leg."

She sounded so much like...

"You, Lord Robert, are a hard man to track down." When he said nothing, she pressed, "What say you, dreamer?"

"I say..." Not trusting his voice, Rob chose his words carefully. "This is a dream. A beautiful dream and I'm afraid to wake up."

There came the sound of a stick tapping on wood. "If this be a dream, why do I have this blasted peg?"

Laughing through his tears, Rob watched Jim carry Waverley, legs still wrapped around his waist, off to the beach. Dante chased after them, yipping at Jim's feet. At least they had a strict chaperone. Rob dug his fingers into the rattan chair back, trying to ground himself to reality. "I saw you impaled. I thought you were dead."

"Two halves of a heart," she said. "Jim made sure I swallowed every foul bite."

"Jim," he nodded, finally understanding, "W-w-where have you been all these years?"

The answer came easily to her. "In the space between the trees. But I didn't return to have a conversation with your back. Come on, let's have a look at you."

Slowly, Rob turned around and came face to face with Cat Mornay.

"You've grown up," she said, her eyes obscured by the shadow of her hat. "I have it on good authority, Lord Robert, that it's your birthday. How old are you now?"

"Twenty-seven."

"Twenty-seven." She nodded, and Rob could see a lump form in her throat. "A ripe old age."

"And you look like you haven't changed at all." If it was possible, she appeared younger. Then again, he'd been seventeen when she left him and he remembered her as the older woman. She still wore trousers like a man.

"Time passes slowly in the fae world, and I entered with a bite of life everlasting. I tried to get out. To find you… " Cat stripped off her hat. Her eyes still held the promise of the deep blue sea, but there were sorrow lines around her mouth that weren't there before. "But the gates closed and I was—"

"Trapped." Rob nodded, recalling a long-ago conversation about a ten-year window between the worlds.

"After healing me, His Majesty Jim kept me right busy as his Minister of War. He says it's the least I could do seeing as he saved my life…and the hatchling's."

Rob frowned. "The hatchling?" He caught something fidgeting behind her. A boy with his white-blond hair and her pointy chin tugged on her trousers.

"Hugh." Cat nudged the lad forward. "Why don't you run off and keep an eye on Uncle Jim. Make sure he doesn't ruin that girl before their wedding."

Hugh saluted her like a stoic little general. "Right-o, Mother."

As he passed by Rob, Hugh's blond brows knitted in curiosity. He tipped his head to the right, just like Rob. "Who's this?"

"I'll tell you later," Cat said. "It's a long story."

Rob's eyes followed the boy as he marched across the beach. The tropic heat never bothered him before; now he felt like he was on the brink of a stroke. He sensed Cat approach him.

"M-mother?" he asked.

"He is quite short, isn't he?" Cat whispered in his ear. "Aye, well, short people have their uses. If I tire, I can rest my elbow on his head."

Rob swallowed. "How old is he?"

"Ten," she said, then added, "See if I ever engage in a reading session with you again."

When his knees knocked together, Cat caught him by the elbow and made him sit down. She drew him into her arms and held him tight.

"You've come back…" Rob dug his fingers into her waist and buried his face into her stomach, inhaling the salty-sea scent of her clothes. "You've come back to me."

Pulling away, she placed her hand over his heart. "Here lies where she longs to be."

"Home is the sailor." Rob caressed her face, tucked the hair behind her crooked ear, and reveled in the absolute realness of Cat Mornay. "Home from the sea."

"And the hunter…" She brushed her lips against his and the world glowed glorious and bright: the dawning of a new day. "Home from the hill."

ABOUT THE AUTHOR

Born and raised in sunny Southern California, Teresa Yea prefers the shade because that's how she rolls. She is a UCLA graduate, a science geek by degree, bookworm at heart. *The Witch of Blackbird Pond* is her favorite novel and her crush on Nat Eaton is challenged only by her love for Jamie Fraser. A major movie buff, she has no qualms quoting *Pulp Fiction* and annoying you to no end. She can usually be found singing *Phantom of the Opera* in the car with dramatic hand gestures. Do not underestimate her petite stature for she is a feisty girl who is not afraid to head-butt people in the face. She is also very silly, but her secret evil is revealed only in her novels. Talking about herself in the third person is weird.

Sign up for my newsletter (http://eepurl.com/bftvYP) for VIP access to exclusive excerpts, the latest scoop on new releases, giveaways, and cover reveals.

Hang with me at http://teresayea.com

Chat with me on Twitter. Musicals and movies are all ice-breaking topics. Better yet, if you tweet me the lyrics to *Phantom*, we're already BFFs: @teresayea.

Follow my Facebook. Warning, I do 'Like' back with a vengence: http://facebook.com/teresayeawriter.

Follow my foodie, fashion, and nail polish-hoarding shenanigans on Instagram: @teresayea.

Check out what I'm reading on Goodreads: http://www.goodreads.com/author/show/13547246.Teresa_Yea

View my inspiration boards for upcoming novels on Pinterest: @litcon.

ACKNOWLEDGEMENTS

A million thanks and endless gratitude to the following people, without whom this book could never be written:

My husband, Eric, who had enough faith in me to suggest I take the leap into writing and supported me through a decade of artistic highs and lows. You are my love, my rock, my everything.

My parents, Steve and Connie, for supporting my career switch from doctor to writer and not kicking me out of the house.

My brother, Oscar, for putting up with my extremely loud typing.

My in-laws, Joy and Craig, for their unshakeable belief, enthusiasm, and support.

All these wonderful writers who have left their expert footprints on this manuscript: Sarah Glenn Marsh (you were the first Liam fangirl!), Ami Allen Vath, Heidi Lang, Kristina Perez, and Hilary Harwell.

Christa Heschke for championing my writing to the end.

Elizabeth Briggs, my pitch-wars mentor and indie publishing spirit guide.

My eagle-eyed copy editor, Stephanie Parent.

My cover artist extraordinaire, Jenny Zemanek, who totally got my "make it green" concept and took the design to unimaginable levels of awesomeness.

And all my readers. Thank you.

THANK YOU

If you've enjoyed LOVE IN A TIME OF MONSTERS, please consider leaving a review. Reviews help bring others to my work and I'd really appreciate your opinion, even if all you say is "a good book to read while pooping" because, seriously, people have to find *something* to read when nature calls and with your help that book could be this one.

Need something twisted to tide you over before the next GOLDEN AGE OF MONSTERS adventure? Turn the page to read the first chapter of BLACK HEART, RED RUBY…

An excerpt from
BLACK HEART, RED RUBY

Ava Nolan grew up in the shadow of her father's obsession with macabre artifacts. An elixir brewed from witches' blood. A cabinet of mummified cats. And Arabella's Curse, the missing prize in his collection: a ruby with the power to resurrect the dead. With a father who resents her existence, a dead-end job, and her expulsion from school to live down, Ava sets out to recover the ruby and reclaim her self-respect. Luckily for Ava, local legend says the ruby is buried in a crumbling mansion by the sea, not far from her new home.

But life as an amateur relic hunter is not without its share of emergency room visits. Or cutthroat competitors. And nearly plummeting to her death doesn't terrify Ava half as much as her uncle, a gentleman grave robber with a vendetta against her father and sinister plans for the ruby.

Entangled in a web of family treachery, Ava finds solace with a lonely boy who fills her nights with stolen kisses and her head with ruby lore. But there's something strange about Ben Wolcott. He's a bit too cunning, a bit too preoccupied with keeping Ava out of his basement, and much too interested in Arabella's Curse.

Bloodstains are the hardest to remove.

I scrubbed the floor until my shoulders screamed with pain. Heat from the desk lamp fried my back like a white-hot sun. I studied the brown splatters over my bed and blew an inky strand of hair away from my face. "Eff my life."

After the floor, the wall was next. Not that I was a neat freak or anything, but this stain had to go. This was war: Ava Nolan versus the spot.

As I paused to dab my sweaty temple, it occurred to me I could be doing better things on a Saturday night. In Santa Monica, life was one drunken party after another. There were no parties in Eckhart. Unless you counted the pulse-pounding bingo tournament held every afternoon at the senior center. Most of the locals were in bed long before the ten o'clock evening news.

I had no friends in this fog-choked town. No homework. And thanks to my expulsion from school three months ago, no diploma or future. Scrubbing a sixty-year-old homicide off my bedroom floor was the highlight of my night.

I dunked the brush into the bucket, flinching as my raw knuckles made contact with a brew of bleach and lye. A ribbon of blood trickled down the back of my hand. I wiped the cut on my jeans, slapped the brush to the floor and got back to work. What's a little blood in times of war?

"Just one more."

One more scrub should do it.

A clean slate. We could be happy.

You can't start a new life in a new house with the former occupant still splattered everywhere. My dad bought the abandoned Hopkins' farm at a steal. Sometime during the '50s,

Old Man Hopkins slaughtered his entire family before training his shotgun on himself. I got eight-year-old Mary Hopkins' room and judging by the size of the stain, I'd say her short life came to a particularly gruesome end.

Despite the stigma of moving into a murder house, I was determined to make a fresh start. Sure my dad, brother, and I weren't living in the most sanitary surroundings, but here in Eckhart we were hundreds of miles north of Los Angeles and ten years away from memories of my mother.

At the thought of Mother, fear gnawed at my stomach like a persistent rat. I dropped the brush and stared at the bucket.

I saw a bathtub.

Filled to the brim with soapy water.

And Mother.

Washing my hair.

Scrubbing my skin pink.

I could never be clean enough, not even when the water turned bloody.

To stem the tide of an impending freak-out, I recited an old childhood chant, invented the day Mother disappeared.

She was dead. The dead couldn't hurt the living.

But as I listened to the wind whistle across the eaves and the incessant mewing of a tomcat, I wasn't so sure anymore.

"Ava." My mother's voice clawed across the black skin of night. *"Ava."*

Lifting my sweater, I pinched my abs until the skin underneath my belly button became red and angry. The pain reminded me of my mother's touch. According to her, I was born rotten and whenever I threw a tantrum, she would dig her nails into my stomach so my dad wouldn't notice the crescent-shaped marks she left behind.

Sometimes she did this when I was already calm—just to make me howl. I believed she was testing me. When I remained unruffled even as blood dribbled down my navel, terror swarmed my mother's face like a cloud of locusts. "You have a dirty soul, my lovely. A wicked heart," she said, dragging me to the bathtub where she'd wash me as white as snow.

I was eight years old when my mother tried to drown me.

Mary Hopkins and I had a lot in common.

I rose to my feet and shook the kinks from my body. Mother was gone; all my resentment over her trying to kill me had long since scabbed and crusted over. The funny thing was, as much as I feared her, I still loved her. Not even an attempted murder, committed in a moment of temporary insanity, could break the bond between mother and daughter. My love was buried deep inside the chambers of my wicked heart.

In need of a breather, I sidestepped a fortress of moving boxes to get to my dressing table. I picked up my iPhone and checked my messages, hoping for a text, an @reply, a Like or comment on my sexy new Instagram selfie.

486

There were none.

Sighing, I lifted my eyes to the photos clustered around the mirror. While I'd yet to tackle unpacking, I'd spent the better part of this afternoon Scotch-taping each picture with care. In my sophomore Sadie Hawkins portrait, I was perched atop a paper moon and wrapped in the arms of Drake Elliott, the hottest guy in school. My attention traveled to Winter Formal. Homecoming. Senior Prom. I was the star of every event.

Leaning over, I peered at my cell, expecting a text in the space of a second. I did get an email, but it was only the king of Nigeria trying to sell me a diamond mine. Apparently, my friends had forgotten all about me. Maybe my selfie wasn't as epic as my make-out snapshot with my friend Cindy. I needed to top that.

I unwrapped my homecoming crown and, being careful not to bleed on the silver sparkles, propped it on my head. Lounging next to the bloodstains, I stripped off my sweater and struck a pose to show off my lilac push-up bra. I snapped the picture and typed "A Royal Bloody Mess" before posting.

A minute later, my phone dinged. I had ten Likes and five comments.

"Sweet."

"Gross, whose blood?"

"I don't get the crown???"

"Take the bra off!"

"I'll tap that."

"Me too."

The Likes poured in. Giddy from the attention, I typed, *"I killed someone, bitchz!"*

Drake's comment popped up. *"Hot! Let's do it next to the bloodstain."*

Leave it to Drake to post a public booty call. I smiled and replied, *"I'm open."*

Cindy added to the thread, *"We know ur legs are. Narcissistic slut J/K. FYI, the crown is LAME!"*

My smile vanished, especially after her comment garnered more Likes than my picture and some agreement about my sluttiness. I shut off my phone, feeling more lonely and lame than hot and popular.

I flexed my fingers and studied the weeping cut on my hand. "A royal bloody mess," I whispered.

The cat ceased its mewing and hissed at something or someone unseen. Setting my crown gently atop a velvet cushion, I glanced over my shoulder. Something was stirring in the air, an electric ripple that filled me with misgiving. I ran a hand across my forearm and discovered all the hairs standing on end. The ivy rustled against the wrought-iron trellis and somewhere on the lawn...

Footsteps.

Turning around, I listened again. Yes. Footsteps.

488

Purposeful strides crunching on weeds and nettles.

I crossed to the window to investigate. Beyond the slanted outline of our rickety fence, rows of leafless trees stretched to infinity, remnants of the old apple orchard gone to seed. My breath frosted the single-pane glass like icing.

When the mist evaporated, I realized I had an audience.

A tall figure leaned against the fence post, squinting at the beacon of light from my window. He tucked his hands in his jacket pocket and turned his collar up against the cold. His breath coiled about him like cigarette smoke.

Shouldn't most pervs scurry or hide when caught? This lurker had balls. He never budged.

I pressed my body against cool glass, trying to get a better glimpse at his face. The shadows cloaked his features, smudging out his eyes. Even so, they burned with the fanatical intensity of a traveler on a black pilgrimage. Judging by the way he was staring at me, one would think he'd found his Holy Grail.

His staring problem sent the hackles rising on the back of my neck. What a creep. As I tugged on my sweater, an infusion of revulsion and rage coursed through my bloodstream.

He'd seen me.

Half naked and in a plastic crown, of all things.

He'd probably tell his friends about the new girl at the Hopkins' farm and they'd judge and laugh. When they were

489

done laughing, they'd return to their comfy homes and tidy lives, relieved in the fact that no matter how bad their problems were, at least they weren't as screwed-up as mine.

As if he could read my mind, the stranger raised his hand. Slender fingers curled in the air. If this bargain basement James Dean expected to intimidate or scare me, he had another thing coming. But as I dashed to my brother's room, the memory of those ghostly fingers lingered. Perhaps this stranger was not waving at all, but beckoning me to join him on a dark adventure.

◆

He was a scrawny guy about my age, seventeen, maybe nineteen at the most.

Propped against the barn, he looked as pathetic as a scarecrow. Somehow he'd seemed scarier standing outside my bedroom window, a dark prince cloaked in fog and shadow.

His name, we learned after my brother put him in a headlock, was Ben Wolcott.

"I don't get you, Ava." Cam scrubbed the sweat from his buzz cut. "You wanted me to talk to him and here I am"—he kicked Ben in the ribs. Ben groaned and hacked up a string of bloody spittle—"talking."

"Stop it!" I latched on to Cam's brawny forearm and dragged him away from Ben. My brother and I had different definitions when it came to "talking."

"He's had enough, you idiot!"

Cam never knew when to quit. My brother's head, as our dad always said, was filled with missiles instead of brains—and it only took a spark to launch WWIII. As his sister, only I knew how to work the controls, but I wondered if I ever had control in the first place.

Cam cursed under his breath and booted a rusty wheelbarrow instead.

Point made, I drew my corduroy jacket closer to keep my teeth from chattering. Back in Santa Monica, I lived in tank tops and shorts, wore my bikini to the mall. Moving to NorCal was like moving to the North Pole. I was having trouble acclimatizing to Eckhart. One week in this seaside wasteland and I'd not only lost my tan, but was seriously thinking about investing in a whale hunter's jacket.

Fog swirled around the orchard of twisted apple trees. Uphill from the barn, our clapboard farmhouse loomed against a violet sky, all windows dim except for my bedroom where a halogen lamp flickered like a bug zapper. Dad was still asleep. Good thing I had the foresight to use my indoor voice when alerting Cam. Dad would freak at the sight of all this blood, yet this was the same man who thought moving into an *In Cold*

Blood crime scene was a good idea. Fortunately, my brother was easier to figure out.

"*Beat him up*," Cam said, "*No, not too much*. What do you want from me?"

"I never ordered you to beat him up. Don't put words in my mouth."

Cam—probably still smarting over my "idiot" remark—muttered, "I was only doing it for you."

I stepped forward to apologize, but the sentiment knotted around my tongue and left me feeling awkward and embarrassed. Saying sorry usually involved lots of bumbling, and I ended up sounding sarcastic instead of sincere.

Taking Cam by the hand, I dragged him away from Ben. "Remember your police record," I whispered in his ear. "Does it need another assault and battery charge?"

With a grunt, Cam jammed his hands in his pockets.

"Control your temper. For me, okay?" I seized his chin and forced him to look into my eyes. "Don't be like Mom."

Thanks to our mother, violence flowed through his veins like a genetic disorder. While I tried to fight this flaw in our blood, my twenty-one-year-old brother had all the makings of a sociopath. Dad and I lived in perpetual terror that Cam would kill someone and get put away for life. Murder woes aside, us Nolans were just like every American family.

Cam lowered his head. "Whatever."

Taking this as a sign of agreement, I pecked him on the cheek. "I'm a jerk."

He mustered a grin. "I know."

I looked to the boy wheezing in the weeds and debated calling the police. Negative. Dad's fear of blood took a backseat only to his fear of cops. All the interrogations they put him through after our mother's disappearance really did a number on his nerves.

In the interest of saving Dad another breakdown, I decided to take matters into my own hands. "Did he say anything to you?"

"He says he got the wrong window," Cam said. "He's here to see Professor Nolan."

"Dad?" It was hard acting like a badass when you were having convulsions from the cold, but I was determined to rebuild my defenses. I pulled my tangled black hair into a messy ponytail. "What does he want with Dad?"

Curling his hands into fists, Cam started toward Ben. "I'll find out."

I pointed to the horse trough at the far end of the barn. "Go sit over there and let me do the talking."

The thought occurred to me that Ben may have a gun or knife. But instead of fear, a secret thrill shimmied up my spine. Ever since my mother tried to drown me, I'd been a little in love with death.

493

Lifting a gaudy bangle from Forever 21.

Downing Ecstasy with a shot of vodka.

Driving ninety in Drake Elliott's Ferrari and then pulling over to hump his brains out by the side of the road.

The rush.

The high.

My mother and I had one thing in common: we desired all the things which would destroy us in the end.

Kneeling in front of Ben, I listened to his labored breathing. He lolled his head against the barn and studied me through the puffy slit of a swollen eye. He'd had ample opportunity to run, yet here he remained, which made me wonder if he was a little in love with death, too.

"You can thank me now." I dabbed his nose with my sleeve. His blood stained the corduroy a brilliant shade of red, my favorite color.

"For what?"

"Saving your life."

On impulse, I traced the shattered bridge of his nose. Underneath the blood and bruises, he was all angles and sharp lines. A blade for a nose. Daggers for cheekbones. I could cut myself slapping him in the face. Naturally I was intrigued.

Ben jerked his head away, wanting no part of my nursing. "Humility. Ever heard of it?"

"Humility. What's that? An SAT word?"

He snorted, then winced in pain. "Are you for real?"

"I'm the good cop." I peeked over my shoulder to make sure Cam stayed put. Glowering at us, Cam splashed slimy trough water over his face and proceeded to clean the blood from his knuckles. He could be as mean as a pit bull when riled up, but he was always sweet and loyal to me.

Following my gaze, Ben said, "You should keep your brother on a leash."

Apt words. Little did he know, I was already keeping Cam on a leash. "For someone who's just been beaten into a bloody pulp, you sure have a mouth on you. Hold still..."

As I dabbed his nose again, my sleeve slid up my wrist. Three old scars, reminders of my tenth-grade cutting days, caught the moonlight.

"You like to play with knives?" he asked.

I tugged down my sleeve, feeling as guilty as if *I* were the one caught peeping. "None of your business."

I didn't take a razor blade to my arm because "the physical pain was the only way I could release my emotional pain" or some textbook shit like that. This was an experiment to see how fast I'd heal and the answer was: pretty damn fast. My skin melded back after an hour, a shame, too, since I thought the blood droplets mesmerizing, each one an isolated jewel. I once asked Cam if I could cut him too and he'd shrugged, "Sure, what the hell." Cam healed just as fast and his blood had been just as precious. My brother and I were single-handedly putting Band-Aids out of business while keeping psychiatrists fed.

Ben, probably delirious from his ass-kicking, muttered, "He said you would be…good with a knife. You're exactly who we've been searching for."

"Who the fuck is he?"

He blinked—or winked to be more specific since he only had one working eye. "What did I say?"

"You tell me."

Ben opted for silence. Long, *awkward* silence.

"You said you were here to see my dad," I asked before he got any weirder. "How do you know him?"

"I was in his Occult History class last year," he said, confirming my hunch. Dad taught at UCLA until he was fired for failing to show up for lectures or stumbling in drunk when he did.

That was over a year ago. Why would Ben try to contact Dad now? And during the middle of the night? This guy took stalking to a new level.

"I suppose you followed him all the way up here to talk about your term paper?" I plucked a stray dandelion from the weeds, marveling at the way the moonlight turned the bulb iridescent. "My dad isn't exactly holding office hours from home. You're a long way from LA, friend."

"Eckhart's my hometown." Ben grinned, baring straight teeth coated in blood. "I came to ask him one question. Maybe you can answer it, *Ava*."

Despite our mutual hostility, I liked the way he wrapped his lips around my name. So calm. So cool. No fear. No shame.

"Fine." With Cam watching my back, I didn't see any harm in flirting with danger. "I'll play along."

"Come closer..."

Discarding the dandelion stem, I crawled toward him.

"Closer."

"Don't push it, perv," I said, inching forward until I was practically straddling one of his thighs.

The same tomcat raced through the brambles and the caw of a blackbird echoed through the deserted orchard.

His clothes smelled of grass after the rain. The peppermint sting of his breath scraped my lungs and stirred the hairs on my temple. "Has he found Arabella's Curse yet?"

A chill crawled up my forearm. No longer in a joking mood, I pulled away. "The ruby?"

"You know of it?" Ben asked, black eyes dancing in amusement at the sudden change in my expression.

Of course I did. No self-respecting daughter of Professor Mortimer Nolan could escape childhood without hearing about Arabella's Curse, the ruby with the power to resurrect the dead.

Magic.

Immortality.

The power of God.

Dad used to tell the best bedtime stories. There was the one about an ancient set of scrolls that foretold the apocalypse. Or the fable about a sword forged with the venom of a sea serpent that could vanquish the undead.

As a kid I couldn't get enough of Dad's tales of good and evil. Or stop marveling at his collection of macabre artifacts. An elixir brewed from mermaids' scales. An executioner's ax from the days of Henry VIII. His morbid cabinet of mummified cats.

But I wasn't a kid anymore. There was no magic in the world, no prophecy in the stars. The dead stayed dead. My dad, who once loved me most of all, could no longer stand being in the same room with me. And much like Bigfoot or the Loch Ness Monster, Arabella's Curse couldn't possibly exist— especially not in a dump like Eckhart.

"Fairy tales," I said, unable to hide my bitterness. Dad would do better chasing windmills than searching for Arabella's Curse.

The porch light switched on, dousing the overgrown lawn in an eerie wash of green. The screen door slammed and Dad marched down the steps, navy bathrobe flapping like a cape behind him. "What the hell is going on here?"

Cam jogged up the hill, meeting Dad halfway. Their shouting—well, mostly Dad's shouting—cleaved through the whistle of the wind. "She put you up to this, didn't she?"

This was going to be bad.

A drop of blood splattered my forearm. With a strained smile, Ben wiped his nose and collapsed against me.

"Don't discount a good fairy tale," he croaked. "The best ones begin and end in blood."

Made in the USA
Charleston, SC
11 March 2015